THE
SAPPHIRE ELIXIR

F. VOUTSAKIS

THEDESNA PRESS

Library of Congress Cataloging in-Publication Data:

PAu003603681

Acknowledgements:

ISBN-10: 0615630278
EAN-13: 9780615630274

For Valerie

1

A blue-eyed she devil must have cast a damning glance at Lambros Lambrou, or so he thought. Believing he was awake in the pious stillness of his darkened room, his nape bristled. Time, usually dotting along like dripping water, contracted into the spur of its nimble cadence. Gasping for a mouthful of air, the scent of smoldering flesh filled his nostrils.

Ever since his seventh year, upon nauseously repetitive intervals, Lambros found himself standing beside his bed mat, a throat-rasping singe of pine needles and smoldering lamb's wool depriving him of the sanity of slumber, coercing frenetic midnight verdicts over what to save from within the burning walls of the house. His first impulse was to save the toy his father had made for him, a little wooden boat he liked setting in the water and throwing rocks at, trying to sink it by tipping its tattered linen sails. That choice lasted until he was twelve. Then for a time, he thought about saving the curio he had bartered from Costa Kalivas, a boyhood friend. A prized possession, the burlesque drawing was of a marble-breasted Aphrodite entertaining two distended satyrs, the image pasted on a thickly varnished oval of pine. Costa had discovered it buried among his brother's things. Themi, the brother, used it to entertain his pubescent friends.

"I don't know what you do with it once you've looked at it a few times," Costa had said.

"You hang it on the wall, of course," the equally callow Lambros suggested.

"I'll trade you the picture for the boat that refuses to sink," Costa offered. Besides the image, which apparently appealed to some of the girls Themi entertained as well, Lambros liked the smell of the varnish.

Lambro's psychogenic fires usually began in the cooking hearths of his dreams and licked their way up a ladder or an open staircase on a seemingly preordained path to sibling bedsides. Then the flames would walk, like fully combusted men, down an improbable corridor, an ecclesial gauntlet of arched doorways and partitions with flickering, glass-eyed spy holes somehow magnifying the torment of everything that was sanctuary within. As he grew into manhood, a woman appeared in the dreams. Contortions made her face illegible, as if scribbled on paper.

She would open one of the doors and stand there, mouth agape, head aflame, a pail in one hand, sometimes in the right, other times in the left, a distinction, when Lambros was awake and could remember dreaming, he found interesting but ultimately lacking significance. A luminous silver sea swirled in the pail, but when water spilled onto the flames, it too caught fire. The apparition stared vacuously toward a distant vista, motionless, in what should have been an anguished consumption. He marveled at how quickly fire could spread, seemingly igniting both air and water.

Before waking from the convulsion of his cacodemon and gazing back at the depression his body left on the bed mat, the black sails of his imagination would unfurl and endure in him the anguish of others, usually his parents struggling to locate their children, indelible cries tearing at his rapidly aging heart. As years passed and the vision no longer retained the smell and taste of his youthful nightmares, the voices and cries over the fate of children were still able to induce in him the perceptible tremor to his nocturnal stance, making the floorboards creak. Then his father would shout at him through the walls, completely unaware of his son's hallucinations.

"Go to sleep - may a fire consume you!"

The boiling blood of martyrs, he came to believe over decades of such fiery nightmares, was less the result of passionate conviction than an inspired trance, the dreamer's conundrum over divine indifference, the wicked roasting of innocent souls. He concluded that the devil, or whoever the designer of this amusement was, prefers laying waste to the guiltless and the pious, because sinners, he imagined, must be tedious morsels, already masticated and expelled as they are, having already succumbed to his wiles. Lambros thought in such categories when he was quite young, when he was one of a half dozen or so boys attending a school of sorts and reading books, so few of which were available except through his teacher. Thoughts that made his head ache by day and kept him awake at night, igniting his dreams. Back when the idea had crossed his mind that he might become a priest or a scholar.

Now he was a grown man, and was neither. He had lost the habit of reading because of his travels and because where he lived a book was neither coveted or a commodity worth its weight. By day, he was all worries and work, worries about his orchards and fields, his animals, his children and his wife's benign, unvoiced reign over him, and by night, plagued with the same damnable nightmare.

His own trance would recede. His parents were still living as far as he remembered. Perhaps he was rehashing the noxious while lying awake, or dreaming within his dream again, a perception as corruptible as the belief that such imaginings are fetial messengers of fate. He sat up on his bed, sweating, coaxing an uncensored scene from his youth, he and his brothers and sisters sitting pensively on the shaded veranda above the courtyard, waiting for their father to return home from his cloistered barrel shop, a brick and mortar hovel squatting along a lonely dirt road leading to the port. In the ebbing autumnal light of coastal Epirus, where the sea and mountains had spent their cooling breezes on the vagrant memories of summer, the unrelenting midday had just passed. The scent of roasting chicken and marjoram wafted about the house like an incensed blessing of culinary sacrifice. Harvests filled the *ambari*[1] and the leaven of formerly empty cupboards, and for the season, the village women had abandoned the routine of serving trodden, putrescent dandelion greens, drizzled with oil and the juice of tart green grapes, lemons being scarce in those days of privation.

In that dire hour, as they waited for their father's return, Olga Stoyanova emerged from her tinted, tailored house standing along the same angled rise of road above the mud-splattered stone that was the Lambrou home. Olga was the frail, umber maiden married to Petros Stoyanova, a glass-eyed Illyrian with a splatter of native blood thrown in from his mother's race. Whose good eye, he would say (for one was pale with blindness) was the Greek eye, matching his mother's oracular black hue. Olga's toddling son, Evangelos, was barely two years of age, the very image of her god treading upon the earth. Left unattended for but a moment while she cleaned incessantly for a husband barely able to see between his belt and his feet, the child walked into the bowels of her hearth and tripped, as little-legged feet often do, beneath her cauldron of boiling lye.

Olga ran through the village and then to the sea below the village heights, her breast, and hands and hair alight, her son's name shattering the bright Ionian ether, awakening Triton from his mythic eon of

---

1   αμπάρι - underground grain bins, like a ship's hold

forgetfulness, the name echoing to the heavens, to Christ Himself, flesh dripping from the bony tether of hands frantically grasping the last of her Evangelos, blazing unto bone and ash. Beyond the phoenix of her torment, her son neither grew to become a herald of men nor an invincible brute among idols, as she had promised him in her nursery songs.

The skew of memory arresting Lambro's sleep drew its air and corporeality from the sight and scent of Olga Stoyanova, her hands smoldering, the men preventing her from drowning herself, the timbre of her voice and its piercing crescendo. Now, in another place, far from the sea of his youth, suspended in a waxing third decade, with children of his own and a wife lying by his side in a humble bed of devotion, Lambros assigned the torrent of his anxiety upon them, his slumbering heartbeats, as he was apt to call them. He never blamed poor Olga for his fits of insomnia. Instead, as was his custom since the advent of manhood, by the sheer force of his habitually surreal will, he managed to awaken contempt for some furtive female whose evil eye he surmised had set a curse upon him, a witch that roused the aural horror and olfactory recurrence of his fetid nightmare. With a talent for provoking loathing in unseen rivals, he abreacted this boyhood trauma into the receding stage of the hallucination, first from the eyes, then the nostrils, and finally, especially for Lambros, from the resonance of another's agony.

While derelict sleep tolled the darkness, unscathed by noumenal flames, he rose to his feet to assure himself of his children's wellbeing. Only then, could he return to his bed and close his eyes again. Tomorrow he would interrogate the loose tongues of the village and expose the woman he imagined had anathematized him, since at that moment he could not think of who she might be. Then, deferring sleep for one final imposition, he welcomed the amalgam of some invariably ugly face, a wicked emissary lifting the hem of her skirt as she walked the world to avoid the dust of discarded bones, and imagined ritually spiting his response before her feet three times.

In his reasoned contrivance, despite the ruinous, repetitive legacy of carnage and torture perpetrated by men throughout history, it was women, capricious, mood-infested, sensuously conspicuous creatures, who were the nexus of misfortune and all manner of predestined danger and doom. Routinely failing in child rearing and the instruction of the maladjusted mongrels of their wombs, they raise demons, or at least the human counterpart, wean psychopaths and feeble introverts with deeply induced frailties, terrorisms and blood lusts, invading the peaceable world to the detriment of humanity. Gradually, wearily diverting his anxiety in this way, his breathing would resume its quiet vascular journey.

In this instance, Lambros was prepared to return to some less than sopor state of sleep, completely mistaken in the sex of which living soul, if any, occasioned the recurrence of his nightscapes, since something as innocuous as striking a match could set off his nocturnal sweats. Until he would return to the kafenio for his morning routine, sipping gritty coffee in the shivering mountain air - a pleasure savored outdoors by most of the men as late into the season as weather permitted - he would not connect the recent rendition of his nightmare to a particular pair of blue eyes, let alone those belonging to Avram Karangelos.

An emigrant from Cyprus by way of Smyrna and then Thessaloniki, Avram was a perplexing rival, whose speculative mingle of Mesopotamian and Cypriot blood surged with an ancient and unnatural malevolence. His disdain for Lambros was not deep. It had arisen recently, but was known to every male with lungs capable of inhaling the blue hypaethral between the diminutive village of Lathra and the less than bustling town of Arnissa, among the five inhabited panoramas straddling and dipping their civilized feet into the primeval waters of Lake Vegoritis.

―――◆―――

Perched upon a blunted and dust-swept plateau, amid barren peaks, gazing gracefully from over her shoulder upon the pelagic expanse that is Lake Vegoritis, Lathra was ever the lovely chambermaid to her lakeside neighbor Arnissa, the settlement to the northeast, the Slavic Ostrovo of old, masquerading as a small town, a debutant of Macedonian outposts. To the south and east of Lathra, in the wake of a sweeping valley, fertile, skillfully cultivated loam lay at her pebbled feet and beyond them, a dramatic rise of resolutely ascending highlands of porous rock, scrub pines and fir, eventually overwhelmed by hirsute forests of fisher, oak and beech. Gently strewn sagebrush meadows sprinkled with anemone, ipheion, narcissi, galanthus, wild marjoram and chamomile, whisper their scented prayers onto the distant summit of Mount Vermion and its buttress of lesser peaks, like cherubic little siblings with cascading chins, bellies and thighs merrily scampering from the more barren red plane and constricting fringe of the Pindus Mountains. Here, as it transpired in a thousand ancient hamlets and shy secret harbors, in serrated cliff-top moorings and discrete mountain hollows, Lathra, or Kazvam, as her Ottoman predecessors called her, hosted disparate Anatolian-Greek diasporas, reviving stalwart traditions of Hellenic Asia Minor, a finale to the Treaty of Lausanne and its audacious exchange of Balkan exiles.

In the miasmic recurrence that is history, remnants and shadows of Ionian lineage endured, despite such blood having mostly drained into the crusty soil of migration and the billowing murder of two millennia. Inexplicably this archaic miscellany survived like the language conceded to this day, coagulated and splattered here and there with the colloquial nonsense of incursions and conquerors. Like veins peering through the skin of her peninsular past, this specimen of Hellene also harkened the brushstrokes and resilient shadings of Byzantium. The women, exotic, redolent, the black portent eye of indulgence, draped in the layers of deep-dyed cloth and bangles depicted by Gyzis; the men, weatherworn, fleshless, flint-boned peasants in dust-sullied suits, white shirts and vests, posing for portraits with protruding chins and dense, flattened, work-worn fingers resting on their knees, as if they were assassins. Fathered by tradesmen, merchants or fishermen, born of alien maidens from either shore of the Dardanelles, most of the newcomers hailed from Apollonia on the Rhyndacus, a promontory in the lake Uluabat, or from Chanakale along the straits of the Dardanelles and a few provident villages along the Sea of Marmara. Many were exiles twice removed, ultimately from homelands as remote as Cyprus, Crete and Mani. They followed one another in their Odyssean wanderings to places mimicking the sheltered grassy Elysium of their birthplaces, along bodies of marbled water in the land of their primeval tongue, the true shibboleth for Greeks, or for any people.

When forced to leave, a handful moved north beyond the Bosporus to the waves of wheat and flax summoning toward the dark heart of the Black Sea. Others, like Lambros, returned to the west and inland to isolated locales far from the clatter of political turmoil and the incessant annihilation of souls, avoiding the sun-drenched allure of costal Aegean towns, offering little by way of livelihood. Lathra suited these reclusive itinerants, with its precipice, like bucolic church steps gently ascending from a spoor, lapping lake, with its meaty languid fish and the alluvial valley capable of sustaining life, and the endless mountains west of Vegoritis.

Lambros was neither a native of Anatolia or Macedonia but from mystifying Epirus, the insular mountain nation of ancient Lydiaric repose, sheltered in the rugged fold along the spine of the Pindus and loitering of late upon a sham Albanian frontier. Memory of his original emigration waned with every sinking day, but like many young men after any number of Balkan conflicts, provincial feuds or crudely instigated famines, he left Yergola, the hamlet of his birth, allegedly in search of vocation and fortune somewhere else in the Greek-speaking world. His mother and father, who had many mouths to feed, stayed behind with his siblings, none of them straying far from parental influence and support. Work was a pretense for Lambros. From a young age, he was chronically disobedient and felt he had worn out his welcome. He grew into a clever but argumentative young man who typically fought with his siblings over trifles and nearly came to blows with his godfather, Panos Miltiades, allegedly his mother's cousin a few degrees removed. The Argentine of Athens everyone called Panos, for the six years he had spent in Buenos Aires tutoring the children of a Greek merchant, and for his constant boasting about how everything was better in Argentina, which prompted the perennially obvious question: Then why did you leave? Panos, educated in Athens, was a government sponsored teacher, a bachelor in perpetuity, an atheist of sorts, and a troublemaker, continually chased from each post he earned for espousing nihilist doctrines or fondling someone's wife or offspring. Lambros suspected him of debauching a local girl of slow wits, who when asked would expose herself or spread her legs for a single fig or pomegranate. The last straw was his adopting the self-interest of a paternal tone at a time when Lambros was scarcely able to tolerate it of his father.

"Why does the longhair address me as if I care what he has to say?" Lambros complained to his mother. "To hell with him and his rotting poker." A reference to syphilis, whose symptoms Panos already began to suffer, and would eventually reduce him to a scathing lesion of a man.

"The Nietzsche of Yergola has passed on to the great debate in the underworld," Pater Sophocles eulogized of Panos, the itinerant priest knowing him well and extolling his vices in the kafenio, but only after canting the threnody for his soul in the church.

"May a fire consume you, speaking of your godfather that way," Lambro's mother scolded her son, also unaware of his nightly phobias. Lambro's mother lived inaudibly between fits of distemper over her youngest son's insolence, but was too exhausted after fifteen hours of daily labor to rouse from her sleep and notice that he was roaming the house trying to escape imaginary flames. The decision to leave Yergola was thus merciful in her son's mind, and at the time relatively painless for all involved. As the years sped by, Lambros would lose contact with most of his family, and when asked by his children, would essentially portray himself as an orphan.

Destinations among vagabonds like Lambros, seeking escape, varied with the caprice of ancestral ties and the choice of travel companions. Cities presented the greater prospect of work but they also prompted a lingering dread, the blank stare of men chronically surrounded by strangers. Urban dwelling offered its own form of idiocy for these manly crags of hide and bone, more akin to wild goats than to wayward princes of revelry. The palate favored a noble savagery, survival fare and a superstitious insight into men and their evils that left those who were unlike them speechless or fearful in the face of such barbaric eccentricity. Practically misanthropic compared to most chronically social Greeks, men like Lambros preferred the solitude of a large body of water or the mountains and at most, tolerated the ceremonial assembly of souls occasioned by weddings and baptisms, holy week and the burden of burial. The manner and idiom, even of the less sophisticated regional polis, betrayed the sense of security earned in hale self-sufficiency and mastery over land and sea. Homesickness affected a young man's sleep and might result in a swift return home, or further uproot those like Lambros, who felt he could not return home to Epirus with the empty hands of failure. He would not forget Epirus, but he would rarely put her into words. It was enough that she resurfaced in the ulcerated apparitions and nightmares that plagued him, Olga Stoyanova ablaze, blaspheming Christ and the Virgin alike, the object of mercy at first and then, less than a year later, the chime of village say-so muted into callous whispers, dawdling pity eroding into disinterest, ridicule, and finally, censure.

"Do you know what she saw when she finally came upon the poor child?" the gossips repeated. "His charred little feet! God protect us from such stupidity!" When permitted to idle upon the idea of home, only the facile, feminine Apollonia of Anatolia surged in Lambros with any emotion, his exile from her forced upon him in the nod of manhood, unlike his venture from Epirus, an impetuous calculation of youth.

2

For a year or so, the new arrivals inhabiting the plateau and hills presenting their decorous shoulders to Lake Vegoritis lived peacefully alongside the natives of sorts, the *endopee*,[2] many of whom were deracinates themselves, mongrels descended from Slavic or Ottoman vagabonds, or else Naodites. The latter was a hashish-contrived taxonomy for an allegedly primeval race arriving in the region from before the Visigoth invasions, from before anyone could remember. An arcane tribe of metallurgists and priesthood of the craft of smelting ores and casting bronze - what Homer considered a divine talent bestowed upon men by the exiled gods of Olympus - not a single reference to the Naodites appears in either history or literature. Believed by the Anatolian endopee of Kazvam to have roamed from Neolithic settlements along the banks of the Araxes, according to local legend, the Naodites were also proto winemakers and pear growers, the pear being a shape of some carnal significance. Worshipers of strange and unheard deities, keepers of rites and sacrileges dating from the offspring of Cain or the age of Noah, the Naodites lived for many hundreds of years the way others did for decades (possible exaggeration being acceptable when it came to them). Bearers of no truth and worshipers of no single god, rumors persisted of a militaristic past and their appalling reverence for bloodletting,

---

2   ντόπιοι – a native only in the sense of being there before us

venerated as a supernatural act. In their times, the endopee insisted
that the Naodites reverted to speaking a corrupted Greek, densely
laced with Southern Slavic and Turkish slang, lest the pertinent locals
hear or decipher their intentions. Marks of the Naodites were a top-
heavy, Neanderthal muscularity and stature, a tawny hue to the hair,
ample breasted, large limbed, phenomenally fertile women and when
questioned, never admitting what or who they were. Everyone spoke of
the Naodites, but no one knew one, except by hearsay.

The vestige of what was Kazvam originally received the earliest
Anatolian refugees into their settlement of less than sixty souls without
protest, not yet knowing that reciprocal compulsory relocation awaited
them. At first, the Turks and other Greek endopee who descended
upon the region extolled the virtue of reducing the need to cart such
quantity of their barter to other lakeside settlements, the soon to be renamed villages along or near Lake Vegoritis, and to the ancient town
of the cleansing torrents, Edessa. Lambros tried not to dwell on the
idea that these same endopee, even the one whose home he now occupied, nearly all assorted Anatolian or Balkan emigrants of the Ottoman
yore, had returned to the coast of the Marmara. Perhaps one of them
would occupy his own house in his beloved Apollonia. Tolerance dwelt
at a comfortable distance. The others who stayed behind and continued calling the village Kazvam grew to resent the increasing number
of refugees slowly arriving on a daily basis, perhaps because they were
Christians, but also because they saw them as contradictions, Hellenes by
geographic coincidence only, speaking a rustic, slang-infested Turkish
grafted to an oddly inflected, co-mingled alpha-beta. Some of the arrivals adorned their lanky frames with the vest, the sash and the knife,
but nearly all had forsaken the fez. They arrived with a decidedly
Eastern palate, spreading their *sofra*[3] with Byzantine and old Ottoman
fare. Cuisine, music, dance, clothing and the minutia of liturgical tradition all bore a distinctive Eastern flare, for they had lived in the long
shadow of history that was Constantinople. They abandoned few of
these Anatolian traits in favor of assimilation to a wider governance,
even after the Ottoman endopee finally expatriated and the harsh treatment at the hands of endopee and native Greeks who did not welcome

---

3   σόφρας - Turkish short dining tables

them as fellow citizens, but rather saw them as louts and harridans no better than the Turks that preceded them. The Greeks who died after their arrival in Macedonia did so believing that their bones would some day rest in their homeland, Anatolia.

———◆———

Lambros rose at the cusp of dawn having doused the flames of his recurring nightmare. He was confident that once afoot in the orb of a mercilessly prying populace, he would soon jettison his afflicting curse back into the black-hearted dowdy so unjustly casting her spell upon him. He would need to be cautious, to protect against the inadvertent maligning of an innocent woman, but felt certain that a pointed investigation would yield the iniquitous iris prey of the lake, the woman set adrift in his imagination as the likely culprit. Arising from his bed slowly, his nightmare having left him deficient in the sleep necessary to sustain him throughout the day, he knew he would need a second *tourkiko*[4] before the ritual of the afternoon recline after ingesting one of his wife's lavish midday meals. He walked to the latrine, forty paces behind the house, conveniently situated beneath the shade of two unusually large old trees whose species no one recognized until a pair of Mennonite missionaries from America, arriving years later, identified them by their heart shaped leaves and creamy delicate flowers as a pair of prodigiously fertilized lindens. A vaporous fog shrouded the square, the vicinal road and any habitation down to the lake, its visible shorelines vanishing as if Lathra were a phantasm. When he returned to the house to wash his hands and face, he felt peculiarly green-gilled, a thick-skinned object of his own acuity, excruciatingly sensitive to everything he did and touched. Detail became conspicuous. He noted the cold water pouring into an earthen vase, rimmed with animations of Attic commerce. The sensation of the soap, the color of his buttons, a tint of ashen gray like the sun-dried bones of animals, the droplets on the painted table, a miniature oasis for a fly buzzing by his ears and grazing an eyelash. Then, in the dim

———

4 τούρκικος -Turkish blended demitasse or Greek coffee

light of dawn, hurrying beyond shaving the hollows of his cheeks and his dimpled chin, he applied a dab of olive oil into his impenetrable forest of hair, entwined and stiffened from hours of restless recline. He scrubbed his teeth with his finger dipped into a gritty paste smelling of mastic and mint and quickly finished dressing. A white cotton shirt, dark creaseless trousers and boots of wrinkled Corsican leather, or so he repeatedly professed with pride.

It was also his custom, being conditionally graced with clear weather nearly every week of the growing season, that Saturdays were reserved in part for traveling to Arnissa or Edessa to consider the purchase of tools and incidentals for his daily labors, whether it be fishing or farming. He rarely lingered in Arnissa, even though he knew many men from the region. Instead, he would rush to return to Lathra for a late morning coffee at the kafenio and idle conversation with the *barbas,*[5] tolerating their stories, often repeated in a single breath. All of the old men were prone to such repetition, being under some impediment of memory, or tongue. A few sat about, mouths agape, wits dulled by age and boredom, regurgitating what others just said. Barba Yiorgo suffered from a cleft palate - no one understood anything he said, so to gain an audience he posed everything within the cadence of a question. Barba Ianouli and Barba Cosma sported more hair in their ears than most old men could grow upon their heads, and thus were generally unable to hear the common refrain, "Yes, Barba, we've heard this before. Go to the damn barber for a trim and give us some peace and quiet." Lathran men often crowed with their luck, surviving into old age with hair upon their heads, not a single one of their society ever laid in his grave as a bald man. This they believed to be a physiological benefit of the fishy waters of Vegoritis.

———————

Lambro's wife was already stirring but his four children lay inert in the waning darkness. Dressed and booted, he engaged in another ritual,

———————

5 μπάρμπαδες - old men, or in its worst sense, geezers

usually performed right after his children went to sleep: noting each quiescent expression and the shallow sigh of their breathing. He drew close to their faces, inhaled, drew back and then exhaled a muffled prayer, uniquely tailored to what he supposed would be each child's concerns for the next day. The prayer ended by entreating God that they all survive him in health, happiness and close proximity "to your good side, since, pardon me, but you seem to have a temper at times." Despite the Ottoman suppression of any Age of Reason or absence of formal education within his wider ancestry, Lambros, who as a child received some education, basked in his dualist penchants and a maze of philosophical uncertainties for which he occasionally felt the duty to unravel and neatly categorize in his mind. God was no exception to this bit of inductive reckoning. For Lambros, He was, hazily, a reasoning deity among other idols, whose solace was all of observable creation, except for humanity, a creature meant to signify something profound about the Creator, but instead who became no better than His dogs.

"He has a good and a bad side, and if I didn't know any better, I'd think there was a grumpy twin to the monarch of the universe, a dissenter, a true hater of mankind," he would proclaim in an attempt to provoke debate. Other times he insisted that discussions of religion just flew round fruitlessly like flies about ripening meat. Men were already like gods, authoritative, magnanimous yet enslaving each other, jealous and violent. God's real amusement is quietly watching them try to surmount that which they are, to just live and avoid letting blood as a pastime, something so remarkably difficult to achieve. "What arrogance to deny the obvious with our puny brains," he once told a student, while sitting in a kafenio in Thessaloniki, with whom he struck up a meandering debate. "To plainly see that nature offers her wares in twos, day and night, hot and cold, life and death, black and white, two antennas on an ant's head, two horns on a ram's, two sexes, two breasts on a woman, two eyes in your head to see them and a pair of hands to caress them. It's futile and prideful to deny that the world is crafted with this number in mind."

"It's a simple inference to deny it, sir," the student replied, swallowing the humor he saw in this modest provocation, "drawn from the notion of the perversity of perception. It is just the way we see things, the mind's eye may cast things in pairs, but reality is not necessarily that way," he said. "Both the empiricist and idealist reaction to such dualisms suggests . . . ."

"Is that so," Lambros interrupted, staring at him blankly.

"They're philosophers, sir. I studied them in Athens and Heidelberg," the student went on to explain, without excessive pride, retaining a combination of respect with youthful exuberance. As a youth, his mother taught Lambros that so-called intelligence was a window to deviousness, that only intellectuals dub common people peasants. Simple people ought to know how to read and write to avoid a swindling, but not study anything in books, and certainly not the Bible. This admonition was in contravention of her son's teacher, who cautioned against the tribulations of illiteracy. She knew he admired his teacher above any man. "It will just confuse you," she drummed into him. The studious are less prone to remaining good, she believed. For Lambros, his children were changing his mind about this. He took the moment to think, to pose and ponder the nebulous question himself, before replying, unsure of whether this young scholar was attempting to embarrass him or educate him, which, in his mind, could be the same thing.

"Perhaps I should slap you on each of your two cheeks," he finally said. "Let's see if that helps you."

"Hmm, so you've read Mr. Moore," the student said deferentially. "A very good argument, sir."

———————

Lambros walked impatiently toward Yianko's kafenio, his mood tempered by a mounting headache. Two villagers strolled in the same direction. Their unhurried gait annoyed him, as if they were mentally accumulating their tasks for the day in order to see which they could avoid. He rushed passed them with a perfunctory nod. Procrastination, he thought, was a denial of the drudgery of work and earthly routines. The only thing that makes work tolerable is competence, or mastery over others who actually do the work. In contrast, Lambro's brisk, insistent stride matched his elongated armature, likened by some to the knotted limbs of a pruned tree. He was vain about his height and these comments and boastfully announced that blackbirds and doves would perch upon him if he stood still for long enough. This ability to attract birds while motionless was a talent developed in his youth in Yergola, along with the useful skill of snaring doves with a long string tied in an unassuming noose and concealed in the gravel. He was famous for the arboreal peace he embodied to doves or even a wary crow. The doves would step into the circle of string for a nibble at seeds or gravel and gently offer their leg for capture. With six or more, his mother could make a mouth watering stew baked with tomatoes, okra and potatoes.

"This is their heavenly reward, to have a place at our table," he explained to his children years later, parroting his mother. Capturing six might take half a day's fortitude when he was a boy. Today he had little of such envied patience. Everything about him announced recognition of him from a great distance, even to the most casual acquaintance, the vigorous stride, his right arm swaying martially against his pant leg. A wave of brown hair furled about a head of narrow molding and across a forehead wrinkled with worry. He possessed the kind of sharpened, volatile visage and weathering about his potent eyes that pulled some in and made others anxious. Even when engaging in the most casual of conversations, the forceful gaze and deeply scored crescents above the summit of cheekbone possessed the cogent possibility of unyielding menace. He worked hard at feigning disinterest in conversations, to suppress appearing zealous precisely because of the involuntary intensity creasing his face, often mistaken for anger even when his black eyes changed expression and turned into the softer, narrower color of soot, or when his mind limped along with the day's fatigue.

He approached the kafenio, veiled in fog, slowly coming into view, in unerring strides, but still yawning, his cockcrow tourkiko awaiting him. Yianko's was a stone and plastered structure in need of new clay tiles for the roof, with a drab, unpainted terrace, unadorned by signs or any other indication that it was not simply someone's house. The interior gave the same impression of temporariness, like a cafeteria at a train station, and looked remarkably similar to the building that occasionally served as temporary quarters for Albanian migrants, except it sported a sallow shade of yellow paint about the windows and doors. It was the closer of two *ouzeri*[6] to his home and suited him over the airs of urban feasibilities put on at the other kafenio, owned by Pavlides, with its linen draped tables, matching cushioned seats and tacky gallery photos featuring Aegean scenery and modern, well-proportioned women cut from the pages of French magazines. An excavator of antiquities from Paris and his small entourage of students and staff had wandered the countryside and dug about Lathra in the hope of discovering the region's secrets, as if Lathra were another Vergina or Pella, but found nothing and soon left, leaving behind a female attendant's dated magazines.

"The ancients knew better than to live up here," the Frenchman concluded bitterly before leaving for Southeastern Turkey and other ancient billets. Lambros failed to understand why Pavlides bothered to open the doors to his kafenio in the morning. The younger men who were his patrons tended not to rise before the roosters, the way their fathers did. Those who did usually accompanied their fathers to Yianko's ragged hospice. All the old guard met at Yianko's, the original kafenio for the village, dating back to when it was the only edifice in the plaza. Pavlides' place, however, offered more than coffee and conversation, so the young men supported the venture when they eventually rose from bed or finished their morning duties. They remained loyal through the years because of its meager, better than nothing nightlife and also because Yianko often closed his doors at mid afternoon to go home and would often forget to come back, attending to his four daughters and his wife, a demanding woman rumored to have lost her mild temperament after the birth of the last daughter.

"The son is coming, the son is coming - we're saved!" she shouted at her husband, moments after the birth of their fifth daughter. "Stay away from me or I'll make it so you will never be able to pee standing up!"

Besides electric lighting and somewhat garish appointments, Pavlides offered table football, a bar or counter where transactions could occur and, best of all, an operating indoor lavatory with hand basin, a great luxury, albeit with occasionally odorous consequences. The structure, including the commode, also had windows facing in the direction of the lake, the pinnacle of extravagance. But when the window to the

---

6   ούζερι- ouzo bars - alternative for a *kafenio* or *taverna*

lavatory remained open, prevailing winds at the most inopportune moments of public sanitation would breeze through the door and waft between the tables like an unwashed waiter, resulting in a common outcry of disgust, "Pa, pa, pa - shut the door, jackass!" Yianko's kafenio, on the other hand, sported seven bare tables with an odd assortment of seating squeezed about them. Tacked to the walls was but one withered photo of his parents, who had purchased the establishment from the former mayor of the village just before Yianko's father died and willed it to his son. The former mayor was a memorable Turkish pasha, a real estate magnate of sorts married to a Bulgarian convert to Islam, a boyish blonde nicknamed *Strigla*[7], the name bestowed by the local men as much for her shrill temperament as for her noisy protests over the painful humiliations inflicted upon her in the service of the Turk's perversions. Pavlides' other attractions were its proximity and breathtaking vista of the lake, the allure of consistently robust tourkiko and an exquisite galatoboureko, rolled and custard-filled phillo, drenched in sticky, heated honey, releasing with each sumptuous bite the gentle scent of nutmeg or cinnamon, depending upon the baker. Patrons said of Pavlides, a bit on the heavy side himself, "He dreams of owning a place jammed with fat men spending their last drachma trying to fill their bellies." Yianko's wife was renowned for her kourabiethes, confection-sugarcoated almond cookies. Gallanos, the miller, known in Lathra and eventually in Perea for his exquisite, weevil-free flour and hearty breads, had his wife compete as well, selling her divine ravani (syrup and farina cake) to Pavlides and her galatoboureko, less generous in its custard heart, but for this reason preferred by the younger men.

As Lambros stepped up to Yianko's terrace, an unusual waft of perturbation mingled with the smell of the coffee. The doors were wide open; the lingering curtain of mist had begun to rise above their heads and reveal a pleasant and dry day. Being avid conversationalists of the mundane, a small indifferent group of men sat on the terrace chewing their displeasure over months of drought and meager harvests, complaining about the escapades of lazy sons and insolent daughters, or the onion peel of existence. Inside, Yianko boiled coffee over a portable coal burner, atop a shabbily painted table set and shipping crate strewn

---

7   στρίγγλα - a hag or a shrew

with spilled grounds, sugar and chicory, the coal burner spewing its exhaust through a makeshift stovepipe of tin and clay shingles. On a smaller table to the right of him was a stack of white demitasse china, chipped by daily use. The village barber, Macarios Timonakis, sat with his son, Apostolos, by the large casement facing Kythera, the skeletal rise of limestone and sparse clumps of exposed vegetation rising above Lathra to a gentle, almost feminine zenith. Drolly branded *O Peponis*[8] by the village men, a name never used to his face out of affection, if not respect, Macarios arrived in Lathra by way of Crete, a poor young man with an indulgent wife and infant daughter. They had purchased a plot of Lathran farmland from his wife's otherwise heirless uncle, who died within days of his arrival from Chanakale, the uncle having long ago ventured from a village named Notios, southeast of Knossos, a village obliterated by angry Turks during one of many Cretan uprisings. Years later, the uncle returned to Crete to garner a wife, married a woman of humble birth and few prospects and then, immediately moved back to Anatolia only to be driven from his home once again by Turks, to what became Lathra.

Macarios possessed a sincere, tranquil smile occasionally giving way to infectious laughter endearing him to nearly everyone and accompanied as it was with a willingness to try anything, no matter how harebrained. He was also known for his foolhardy courage in confronting antagonists, no matter how outnumbered he was or capable they were of crushing his manhood. Upon arrival in Lathra, he extolled to his neighbors the value of growing cantaloupes, learning of their juicy medicinal virtues from a talented Jew who had apparently cultivated them in Palestine.

"On a barren stretch of wasteland with only as much arable desert as to fill a wagon," he bragged of the Jew, as if he were a long lost brother. "He grew them to perfection, the little rascal, like a gardener from Eden. We popped slices in our mouths as if they were grapes. All the time," he assured his audience. Macarios, who had never grown anything intentionally except his hair, which he wore long because he did not trust others to cut it, wished to replicate the golden orbs of refreshment upon his own arable plot, now that he was a land baron.

---

8   Ο Πεπόνις - cantaloupe man

"It's too far north for a large crop of cantaloupes Macarios," the men said amused with his enthusiasm. "Plus the soil here isn't right. You need soil that drains well, a sandy variety, not rock and clay. Stick to cutting hair," his profession in Chanakale, "and talking us to death." Exhibiting little patience or prudence and his famous audacity when told he could not do something, the barber quickly grew weary of cutting the surfeit forest of his new neighbors' heads, at times hosting the most prolific lice colonies known to humanity. Privately, he also wished to abate the ridicule contrived by a few of his younger and more infrequent customers, who belittled his barbering technique as less than masculine.

"He runs his hands though your hair, like a woman, the silly queer!" Spiros Terzellos lampooned. Macarios purchased the cantaloupe seeds and growing instructions by mail, from an American seed catalogue loaned to him by Pavlides, whose nephew worked in a restaurant near the stockyards of Chicago and mailed him things he believed would impress his uncle. The seeds arrived late, having apparently sat through an entire planting season on the floor of an Athenian post office. Ruining his back and blistering his sensitive hands in the process, Macarios tilled the indifferent soil and planted row after row of the crop. Half the seeds rotted in the cruel scarlet of Lathran clay. The rest grew to half their intended vine length and yielded cantaloupes the size of a child's fist. Wayward goats ate the few fruit miraculously growing to half-size. The vines and peels were fed to a Doxiades' pigs and earned Macarios a monstrous thirty-five drachmas.

"The Naodites must have pissed on them at night," Macarios complained to his neighbors, grinning agreeably. Temporarily ruined, the barber recaptured his fate and returned to cutting hair without commentary from the men of the village except for *Barbra* Ianouli and his occasionally maligning glances.

"Peponis has got iron balls, but the judgment of a Billy goat," he said, and that was it, except the men always called him Peponis after that.

To the left, before the other grimy windows facing Kythera and the dirt lane meandering in the direction of isolated homesteads, sat Vasilios Lambrou, the artisan in wood, an erector of structures large and small, and his younger brother, Andreas. First cousins of Lambros, they had followed him to Apollonia from Epirus and again to Lathra, when in the middle of the night, rifle and scythe-wielding Turks insisted they vacate their Anatolian home. Each were employed at a small woodcarving factory in Edessa, manufacturing church pews, ecclesiastic lecterns and altarpieces ordered by bourgeoning parishes throughout Macedonia and Thessaly. Carving by hand, the vanishing craft was in the throes of succumbing to the competitive stress of deadlines and the mechanized woodworks generated in the industrialized West. The shop found itself chronically subjected to the vagaries of archdiocesan aesthetics and parishes otherwise entangled in allegiances to either Athens or Constantinople. When orders waned and work halted, the brothers Lambrou plied their malleable skills for hire for the rustic fancies of compatriots and other construction projects in the region. As it happened, at that moment they were in the employ of the able miller of Lathra, Gallanos.

Yianko welcomed Lambros with a desultory grunt. A moment later, he set a foaming *tourkiko* before him at the table with Vasili and Andreas. A brief discussion ensued over the previous week's labors, the probable price of apples in lieu of a blighted harvest and the brothers' availability for other work in lieu of Gallano's project. With each peripheral glance, Lambros confirmed that his arrival had instigated some type of ill will. Confused by the silent treatment he rose to his feet and spoke impulsively.

"What's the problem here, *palikaria?*"[9] Thick eyebrows of suspicion arched in unison. He bent forward and whispered to his cousins, "Whose loose-tongued wife tipped the tobacco cart today?"

"The water from the lake," Vasili whispered. "They've heard about the engineer from Thessaloniki you've invited. They don't like it." Lambros curled his lower lip. Annoyed, he rose again, perused the roomful of faces and then took his seat, changing his mind, only to stand once more. "What's he doing?" Andreas asked his brother.

"A pumping station means prosperity for all of us," Lambros proclaimed as if he asked a question. "We can send the water to our fields and orchards and grow whatever we want. No more running to the lake in the winter or in blistering heat, straddling stubborn mules with urns of water, half of which spills on the rocks. Hasn't the season's drought forced this conclusion upon us?" No one answered. "If Pavlides can

---

9 παλληκάρια - young bloods

have enough water flowing to his fancy place, so can the rest of us."
Still eliciting no response, he glanced at Vasili and Andreas, looking for
a suggestion. Vasili shrugged and pursed his lips. His cousin, whom he
admired, continued with the most fluent plea he could muster.

"It's stupidity to resist that which will propel us into the future.
Will we permit the know-it-alls in Arnissa to flourish and use the lake
while we Lathrans forego the opportunity? And how about the bumpkins in Xanthoyia? The whole damn village hasn't read a book between
them. Even they'll have water before us." He waited for a response
again, sat for a moment and then rose to his feet to add to his argument.

With this, Avram Karangelos stood from among the men seated on
the terrace and walked inside. Not particularly tall, his weight, fluctu-
ating dramatically with the change in seasons, Avram nevertheless let
off an air of potency and immovability, reinforced to those who knew
him. A broad mustache dominated his face, concealing unsightly plum
lips, draping arrows of bristle tumbling toward a sparsely bearded chin.
The style was reminiscent of a photo he had once seen of a Menshevik
just before his hanging, the photo intriguing him not for the death it
depicted, but because the victim sported a Chekhovian beard fashionable among the Russians and French. Otherwise, he grew the whiskers
because his lips mimicked the swarthy textured amethyst of a Moroccan
or Libyan.

"He's an ugly fellow. What a Carthaginian must've looked like,"
the village priest once told Lambros. "I say there's not a drop of Greek
blood in him." His sullied, dark brown hair was helmeted and splashed
from his youth with small gray streaks running from the temples like
mercurial bolts of spiked madness, a trait he said he had inherited from
his mother's father. His hands were large and thick-fingered, dispropor-
tionate to his limbs and torso, as were his feet. He dressed unusually,
as if he were a scholar or public official abiding his constituents, in a
tie and loosely fitting gray suit, interchanged for one of brownish hue
every other day and a black one reserved for funerals and Good Friday.
Broken by a bully in his youth, his nose was crooked, giving him a sinister scowl from the profile. He turned slowly, preening an awareness of
his audience and the moment of conflict before him.

"We're as interested in progress as you are, Lambros Lambrou, but
we'd rather rely on the springs beneath the bald head of Kythera than

on the lake. The cold isn't the only reason the Turks turned their back to her. Vegoritis is a spiteful bitch," he said. "Four years ago, when it hardly snowed in the mountains and the rainy season gave us nothing but a squeeze of the sponge, it was as if the Titans had tilted Vegoritis and taken a long drink. If her banks can recede and dry up like that once, it can happen again, and even worse."

In a nauseous, syneasthetic moment, Lambro's head and belly became one. The chronic throbbing in the hook of his cranium lodged itself in an unidentifiable cavern of his innards. Ingesting this impression, he regurgitated the fleeting intuition that Avram was his cerulean eye of malevolence and perceived in the criticism a singeing flicker of flames. As suddenly as this notion came to him the disjointed sensation passed and the usual throbbing from behind his eyes returned.

"You're not being asked to invent the wheel or make a rooster lay eggs, for Christ's sake! When someone's very ill, don't we prefer to take him to the doctor in Edessa rather than let the midwife here kill him with her barnyard treatments?" He prevented any answer. "The engineer I've invited," he said pointing at himself, "is an expert. He'll educate us before we dig and build anything." Avram ground his teeth as Lambros continued. He looked about the room, flush with expectation, noting the shades of discomfort and embarrassment in each man's face, a common reaction among Lathran men in response to any public oration. "The springs of Kythera push up through the crust one day and somewhere else the next, but the lake is immense. Vegoritis is a faithful matron," Lambros continued. "And what if there's a fire? We can have a dependable source of water to quell the nightmare. We can prevent losing our homes. What I propose is a simple pumping system, much like they have on the islands," he said in a businesslike manner. In a display of nerves, Avram slipped his tongue between his upper lip and teeth and then gritted a smile. He stepped forward as the anticipation of the men flickered in their gaping mouths, static droplets of silver and gold twinkling like stars in a moonless sky.

"Watch," Timonakis whispered to his son, "They're going to brain each other."

"You want us to consider a water pump? Driven by what, a windmill? I admit, Vegoritis mimics the sea at times, but she doesn't have the sustained winds to justify windmills. Or are you proposing a system driven by petrol engine, with its noise and fumes and constant maintenance and the need to deliver fuel down the steep descent to the lake?" He had raised his voice incrementally. The others craned their necks listening. "I'll not stake my life or livelihood on a machine any more than I would the man who made it, my *kafirs*,"[10] an Arabic slip of the tongue, "engineer or no engineer! And by the way, with what money will the village laggards pay for fuel?" Some of the men grumbled in agreement, hearing anything to do with payment. Lambros sat again and listened attentively, a quality of character admired by everyone, including Avram, the ability to make one feel that he was truly listening and not simply biding time until he could spew his own fantasies and rationalizations. "Whatever system you install we'll grow accustomed to, Lambros. And when it breaks down it will appear as if we must move mountains to go back to the old ways." Lambros moved to the edge of his seat ready to rise, as it appeared to be his turn to speak, but Avram continued. "In any event, I will not permit the laying of pipes beneath the roots of my fruit trees. Not when the springs on Kythera and gravity can avoid this cost and labor and we can build a common well out there," he said pointing to the village plaza. "If the others here want to dig up the rock they inhabit, it's their business."

Avram scanned the faces, gauging reactions, and swung around to offer one last insight as he walked through the open doorway. "Look around you, Lambros Lambrou. All of Greece is drying up. If we barter Vegoritis away today, for a few more apples this year, for water to our doorsteps, so the lazy won't have to walk a few meters when their mules do all the work anyhow, then between Arnissa and Lathra the lake will drain into a sickly fly puddle. In less than a generation we'll be tearing ourselves to pieces over the politics of thirst."

Lambros was dumbstruck for lack of a response. Unlike some men, who would have continued talking until some connection or well of ideas sprang up in a flood of verbosity, he fell silent and remained seated. Unanswered, Avram scanned the kafenio and walked out with the valorous dignity of having the last word. Lambros watched him proceed down the dirt road. His shoulders square and head erect with ambulant vanity. He wondered how the man could side against him.

---

10 καφίϱς - infidels

They had fought alongside each other, bearing cowl and axe against the bad humor of forest fires which Perean settlers inadvertently ignited while clearing a few plots of sagebrush and pines. The soaring conflagrations had decimated orchards, fires laboriously extinguished because of a lack of access to inland water systems. He endured with him the ground-parching struggle against drought and together on that choking, sky-blotted night, witnessed Perean homes burning along the crest of distant hills, shooting embers into the sky as if the unyielding celestial night was forging a new star. Faint, peculiar layers of phobic memory filled his nostrils, roasting flesh, the scent of Olga Stoyanova and her Evangelos. Lambros took his seat and looked at his hands, palms pressed down upon the table. They appeared like the hands of another man. Only when his friend Timonakis and his son stood to leave, coldly, without salutation, dropping coins on the table that rolled about in synchronous arcs of curious beauty, clinking against the same empty glass, did he look to his cousins for consolation.

"Don't despair, cousin," Vasili said. "You know how it goes. Gather a hundred Greeks and you're stuck with a thousand opinions."

3

Avram Karangelos was doomed to his namesake by virtue of his birth from the mordant womb of Irsia Karangelos. Irsia's infamy spread among young women like a contagion of fear, a postnatal psychosis blamed for her having cleaved a ferocious betrayal upon her husband within months of Avram's birth and the onset of the boy's unremitting wailing and chronic inability to sustain sleep for more than a few minutes in duration. The child suffered from colic, in part due to his mother's insistence upon so quickly returning to her absurdly Bedouin diet, including the pasty lentils she loved with cashews and onions, laced with heaping spoonfuls of cumin and turmeric, her favorite dish as the story went. She reverted to offering the infant Avram heated goat's milk when the mildly toxic colostrums of her strenuously generous breasts were determined to be the cause of the child's discomfort. Weaning him increased her suffering, and an acute case of mastitis followed.

Irsia's husband, Samson Karangelos, was the son of a murky complexioned woman of unfathomable origin and a Cypriot cleric, a man of noble kith, from the region southwest of the Troodos Mountains, English educated, descended, he boasted, from pilgrims served by the desert fathers of the early Church. Samson was a devout and obedient son until his betrothal by arrangement to a neighborhood girl twenty years his junior, a pact he mutely endured as tantamount to sanctioned rape. At her formal presentation, the girl still stunk of urine and her mother's milk. He was ashamed and humiliated by the experience, the congruous grins and kisses, the inflated promises made by each family, the girl's future comeliness and his ability to spawn sons.

Samson met his Irsia while on pilgrimage, having vaguely contemplated a monastic escape from the marriage arrangement awaiting him in Cyprus. He had proposed a life mimicking his ancestors in the deserts of Egypt, the call to God and renunciation of the flesh, an alternative his father would find difficult to condemn or forbid without hypocrisy. The desert is where men bury their sins or succumb to them, his father taught him.

Irsia had left Limassol, just east of where Samson grew up, under dubious circumstances, allegedly inconsolable over the death of her mother, her father having died when she was but eleven. Rumors over her unruliness and mournful madness abounded. Fluent in English, her father insisted on a formal Western education for all of his children. She found temporary work as a tour guide in the Valley of the Kings, and then as a docent in a museum in Cairo. Samson saw her and immediately endured a public erection, a feat no woman had ever achieved for him. His hat set strategically before him, he listened carefully, mesmerized, barely understanding her lecture but recognizing the Cypriot-Greek inflection to words, like 'world' ('whorled') and 'kingdom' ('keengathoom'). A year older than Samson, Irsia proclaimed her carnality with every sway of her seismically voluptuous frame. Provoked by such willing sensuality, he forgot the desert, and the arrangement awaiting him at home, and impregnated her upon the apex of a euphoric wedding night, an erotically charged month after they met and courted, far from the custodial purview of their families. Upon their return to Cyprus, Samson's father avoided a feud with the betrothed's father at great financial cost and revolted against his son's choice of bride, engaging in theatrics of clerical abjuration that embarrassed everyone. Samson's mother, on the other hand, seemed to understand well the attraction and kept silent. Matters became unbearable with his family. Samson and his lusty Irsia reluctantly left their beloved Cyprus for Thessaloniki, arrangements made for work with Irsia's uncle, who owned a private school and who had lived in London. The uncle had tutored Irsia in English and knew her tempestuous nature, as a young girl, but felt obliged to accept his orphaned niece and her youthful husband. Samson wanted only to escape his father's disappointment and aversion to the marriage. Within two months, they returned to Cyprus, Irsia rabidly homesick and morose, privacy in her uncle's home having become contentious. The couple moved into her parents' house in Limassol, now occupied by Irsia's brother and his family and her younger, unmarried sister.

A few years later, with the precipitous birth of his daughters, his "perfume petals," the affable Samson received the bliss he deserved. Still a young man with a wife who yearned for a son to name after her dead father, Samson lived out the balance of his time on earth warding off Irsia's incongruous perversions, her insatiable needs and all the while, her Medusoid resentment of his circumcision.

"I thought you were born of Helen when I married you, not a bastard of Delilah," she complained during an afternoon of coitus, poised for gluttony, having made close inspection of her other favorite dish whose dangling puce remained exposed, even while not erect. Irsia's resurgence of craving for her husband, in spite of her resentment, tormented her and grew into a conspicuous addictive malady. Each night became a parody of their nuptial passion, much to the entertainment of her young sister and the embarrassment of her brother, despite relegating the couple to the furthest reaches of the dwelling. Everyone felt shackled by Irsia's antics and commotions. Her sexual proclivities prolonged throughout her third pregnancy, even unto the day of Avram's birth, and reemerged only a week later. In her postpartum malaise, a demented spiral of anxiety seized her by her most vulnerable of manias. The happy father had adorned his newborn son with the surgical symbol of Semitic convention. He thought it consistent with his own, that his son should thus resemble him, and consistent as well as with his wife's eccentric legacy which he surmised was Persian, or perhaps some Aryan refrain, perhaps the consequence of Alexander's exploits. Irsia became enraged that Samson dare perform the ritual upon her son without her consent, but not enough to shun him or suppress her affinity for devouring "the hammering head of his crown of conception," salivating the words before consumption.

Adding to her distress, she grew perturbed with the natural augmentation to her hips and once pleasingly, unyielding thighs. Attendant to bearing the extra somatic pounds of the infant Avram, her thighs adopted a gentle fleshy swing. Anxiety over her appearance fed episodes of self-loathing, which distorted into an aversion to watching anyone chew food, which she desperately tried to deny herself, without success. Orphaned crumbs falling from Samson's mouth invoked a particularly staid repugnance. Avram's incessant crying irritated her to the point that she could not embrace the child to comfort him for fear of the mounting urge to dash his head against a rock. The problem had remained unidentified, plaguing her to a lesser extent with her daughters until they had each weaned from her breast. The chaotic cauldron of budding lunacy dispossessed her of all motherly instinct but offered no reprieve or satiation of her prodigious incontinence and increasingly fetishistic compulsions and impletions which apparently included cucumbers, squashes and the eggplant of her *imam bayildi*,[11] another of her culinary favorites. Coupled with sleeplessness, these vain and vulgar impulses conspired to entice her momentary loss of wits and cut deeply into what one suspected in hindsight was a congenitally depraved heart.

Three months after Avram's birth, Irsia witnessed her husband's left hand innocently graze her unmarried sister's youthful and equally inspirational thigh, clothed in a form revealing cotton dress, as he attempted to retrieve the howling Avram from her lap. Her sister reflexively emitted an impish, scarcely noticeable little squeal, to which Samson naively blushed. Irsia hastily withdrew to the kitchen and returned wielding a recently sharpened cleaver, proceeding to wedge a vengeful blow into her sister's quivering thigh, severing the femoral artery, extracting the instrument with horrific difficulty, requiring both hands, as if the blade had imbedded in oak. Then, in a single merciless motion, she swung a second blow severing

---

11   Ιμάμ μπαϊλντί - the imam fainted (the eggplant dish that made the imam faint)

Samson's palm from his wrist, her final swing relieving him of his offending eye. Irsia's sister bled like a butchered lamb. The infant Avram slid to the floor from atop the slippery torso of his mortally maimed and unconscious father. Her brother found the child laying in the coagulating ichors of ravened angels, holding his breath in an interminable, trembling cry, as infants deeply wounded often will.

Irsia wandered away in a trance, walking through the village and then into the church, where she awoke to her crime and confessed to the priest. Days later, on the road to Nicosia and her mittimus, a gang of raucous men, official ghosts it was alleged, raped and murdered her. The perpetrators remained concealed in the crags of failed recollection and were neither sought nor discovered by any public authority. The sordid bards of the tale spun upon the lurid axis of Irsia's rapturous grin as she gagged and bled, bestowing upon her a saintly ecstasy, concealing in her anguish the angelic poison arrow beneath a bodice of remorse, occasioned, as is told, by her enticing and then deliberately enraging her captors into their sadism.

When confronted with this noteworthy version of events, Avram quietly denied the tale. But its origin was credibly relayed in a duet of infuriation by his sisters, Magda and Lydia, who preceded Avram in birth by six and four years and were, when their mother wandered off in her gruesome daze toward the church, innocently playing beneath the sheltered arbor outside the Karangelos home. As young girls, Irsia's brother moved the girls to Thessaloniki. As young women, they paid annual visits to Avram after he settled in Lathra, only to have their suggested return, on their last visit, inculcated in rather blunt terms by Maria, Avram's bride. After a weeklong stay, Maria grew weary of serving the demands of her husband's haughty and disdainful sisters. Resentful over the confrontation that ensued, and what they considered a rude reception by his wife, whom Avram supported in the quarrel, the sisters, agitated and awaiting return passage to Thessaloniki, mindlessly spilled the tale of their mother's bloody demise to inquiring gossips. Months later, when summoned and welcomed back to attend to their brother, Magda repudiated her truncated version of the story, which since its initial telling had circulated the village grapevine like a parasite. Later, she insisted that her mother had died giving birth to Avram. Their father, Samson Karangelos, suffered the fate of many good men reduced by the sting of such mortification

- conveniently rarely mentioned. The one detail Magda remembered was what her uncle had recounted of him humorously, not in a disrespectful way, that it was easy for Irsia to ensnare Samson.

"He was a dreamer," Magda had gathered from her uncle, "running from his father yet wanting to please him at the same time, wanting to emulate the Desert Fathers. But the desert monks only learned what tribesmen had already known for centuries. They too had come to the desert and baked in its irony that there was nothing there to learn except that what is unbearably hot by day turns unbearably cold by night, much like married women. But quite unlike Irsia," he added. "For this, the monks endured chafing skin, swollen tongues, mirages and the fear of standing still, lest one sink in the sand."

4

Still seated at the table in Yianko's kafenio, Lambros studied his hands. He took a moment or two to repossess them as his own, silently mouthing a rehearsal of his rekindled argument. He looked up and opened his mouth to speak, but the rhetorician in him stuttered and the order of what he thought to say escaped him. He remembered the early days when Avram had arrived nearly a month after him, both with the weary bale of exile, eager to plant roots again and, like Lambros, preferring an unknown destination rather than returning home. There was a sense of kinship and participation in a great odyssey, in the antiquity and resilience of being Greek, each man's story flowing just beneath the skin. Together they staked claims and, with the priest's help, renamed the village Lathra. Lambros rose to his feet, cleared his throat. The words came back to him, breaching the calm of disinterest and the men's return to coffee and idle talk.

"The belly of Vegoritis, the lake beneath your feet, is as vast as the one you see intoxicating the sun," he said with a ceremonious wave of his arm, "or quenching the thirst of Avram's titans," tilting his head to gage the reaction of Vasili and Andreas. Heads turned and he continued.

"Kyrios Agnostakis, the learned engineer, will arrive on the twelfth of the month and explain everything to us. I'll pay for his travel and I'll put him up in my home, and I invite you to join in this undertaking, when the time comes." Avram's bravado, his opportune departure, had set tongues wagging. The men that lingered in Yianko's went on to confront Lambros with their doubts, questioning the difficulty in laying pipe over thousands of meters of rocky landscape and below the frost line of compacted clay, bemoaning the cost of erecting a windmill or any other type of generating station.

"Change is an ordeal better suffered alone than under the scrutiny of one's neighbors," the Turk, the man who sold Lambros his homestead, had said to him on the journey from Edessa to Kazvam. "A man's profit creates envy. Contracts are better made with strangers." Lambros surmised what slithered beneath the reaction of Lathran men, evident in Avram's antagonism. What he proposed to his neighbors, by necessity, would require building upon the land of one or two men at most. These land holdings, which happened to rest their otherwise worthless, knobby shins upon the shores of the lake, would bestow for those lucky few the title of landlord, to whom the entire village would then cater. Avram possessed the foresight of such envy and cleverly couched his obstinacies in the form of a preference for Kythera. Thus, mostly for this reason, he and most of the villagers preferred the mountain to be the font of their progress, regardless of its reticent springs, precisely because no man would profit.

"You have little support for your grand ideas, *raia*,"[12] Menelaus Terzellos, father of Spiros, said with ermine sarcasm. "Here comes the *malaka*,"[13] Lambros thought, "ready to kiss Avram's ass." Terzello's typical parroting of other men's points of view was too much for him, and his laugh, like a cranking engine with no spark, annoyed Lambros as well. He erupted.

"What's grand about it, blockhead," he bellowed uncharacteristically. "What don't you understand? There is plenty of water beneath our feet, and the engineer will prove it. What more do you have to know?"

---

12 ραγιάς - Ottoman subject

13 μαλάκας roughly – imbecile, dolt, jerk-off

"To hell with your engineer," Terzellos fumed in return. "Tell him not to come. We don't need him to tell us how to bring water to our mouths."

The first Anatolian to enter the village before the great exodus and to stake a claim in the valley and actually purchase fifty-six *stremata*[14] of under-cultivated farmland was none other than Lambros Lambrou. He acquired this and an abandoned old house, roughly in the shape of a horse's hoof, a stone's throw from the center of commerce, nothing more than the original tousled kafenio. Far from plumb, the abode had belonged to an aging farmer he met in Edessa, that picturesque Macedonian settlement along the ancient Egnatian Way. Lambros had wandered there along his arduous journey with his pregnant wife in tow, inquiring of available land by the lake, offering proximity to wafture and fishing. He had heard rumors. Armenian refugees had found themselves herded into ghettos, in the outskirts of cities. He wanted to avoid the reminder of such calamity and poverty for his wife's sake. He headed for Vegoritis because it was among the most clearly discernable features on a map he saw hanging on the wall of a saddle maker, an exiled Macedonian he met while passing through Maditos at the start of his Anatolian exodus. It reminded him of the Apollonia of his imagination, floating upon its own emerald lake.

The Turkish farmer happened to be promoting the sale of his duchy at the top of his lungs, standing squarely in the center of Edessa's piazza, adjacent to the footpaths leading to her noisy waterfalls, those eroding nubile overhangs along an otherwise trifling river, whose tributaries had roughly been Lambro's guide through the interior of Macedonia. The farmer clamored the mercantile details of his estate like a grocer hawking roasted chestnuts. Sitting atop an old cart pulled by a tired gray mule of enormous proportions, he consummated the sale within an hour of Lambro's inquiry.

---

14 στρέμματα - a measure of land, approximately three per acre

The farmer explained his motives for selling the land this way. He had raised three daughters and married them all off, as was his duty, but unfortunately, he believed, to husbands who misrepresented their intentions. The sons-in-law had all promised their devotion to the clan, their assistance on the farm, but suddenly, for reasons obvious to everyone but the farmer, they chose to return to Bursa and Imbros rather than convert and assimilate in Greece. He continued the unhappy tale of how he argued terribly with them over leaving him without daughters to care for him in his old age, a necessity for one survived by no other kin. The farmer's wife was the only daughter of a Turk. She had died of pneumonia two winters before. She, and now their daughters, abandoned him, he complained. His beloved Kazvam, which he allegedly named, had become a prison of convoluted family clashes and harsh memories. In fact, the Afghan, as the locals bade him, was disgusted with Kazvam, weary of every drink of water and morsel of victuals sustaining the memory of a hand-blistering life there. The farmer boasted that he could speak three languages Turkish, a bit of border Slavic and Greek, which he could read almost as well as Turkish, unlike his neighbors who read neither and failed to speak clearly in any language. Indeed, all of Kazvam possessed the annoying habit of mumbling under their breath, chewing words rather than annunciating, as if words somehow grafted to their teeth before release. With his anomalously fair complexion and hair, faintly the color of the average Naodite, the farmer had managed to obscure his Muslim past in a cloak of practical wisdom and literacy. He predicted to his old neighbors the very permission he would eventually glean to remain in the land of the Greeks, long after his Turkic compatriots would flee back to their homeland. He wished, at fifty-six, to see the world, which in his mind was Alexandria and Rhodes, the land of the Colossus, which he refused to believe was no longer evident in her limestone crust.

After confirming Lambro's general state of homelessness, and having extracted his wistful nostalgia for Apollonia, the old farmer went on to describe in adept and loving detail the arable land for sale, which he had not cultivated since his wife died. He fashioned a glowing pictorial of the house, long abandoned for the warmth of the kafenio, saving the impression of Shangri-La-like splendor for his portrayal of the cobalt tarn.

"As wild as any sea and teaming with fish!" he boasted. Kazvam offered an ease of livelihood, precisely because of such intelligent fish that understand well their providence, ready for anyone with the means to extract them, or, as he suggested, "for all but an imbecile with clubs for hands." In truth, the water of Vegoritis retained a mildly fishy odor, precisely from such overabundance, but was otherwise of crystalline purity. Her depths were neither silt, nor mud, nor moss, but a shaman's bed of ancient psephite, her shores lined with cliffs, anchored boulders and, in places, opaque vegetation - a veritable washboard against which violent windborne maelstroms and thrashings would cleanse the nectar further still. "The fish jump in your boat," he proclaimed with a two-handed simulation of the fish flying through the air and then the not so clear pantomime of their flopping about on the bottom of a boat. Hooked through the gills, the gullible Lambros heard this and immediately agreed to the purchase.

Influencing his seemingly incautious judgment was a mounting desperation in finding an adequate situation to accommodate his wife's bloated condition. The farmer praised Allah for his good fortune in selling the land so quickly, sight unseen, for eighteen gold liras, having aimed high for twenty-two but happily settling for less. This stately sum was nearly all of what Lambros had saved through the years and included five liras retained from his bequest prior to his prodigal flight from Epirus. Expecting a strenuous negotiation, the farmer was so thrilled he offered the barely habitable house, which he intended to include without consideration, if pressed, in exchange for a handmade backgammon set that caught his eye as he perused Lambro's neatly tied possessions. Crafted of olive wood, imported ebony and mother of pearl, the exotically crafted set, strapped upon Lambro's back between layers of clothing and linens, had been given to him by his wife's Uncle Fotis, who purchased it in Constantinople on one of his infamous soirées. Lambro's wife professed never to forgive him for this impulsive exchange.

A prayerful, almond-eye Anatolian, with a graceful vigilance to her features and a fluid, thinly curved smile, as if layered in tempera, Elissa was fatigued and irritable from the difficult journey but still shining with the silken blush of her first pregnancy. She had ripened into her twenties before relinquishing her father's name, Tiros. Her arrangement was a hasty connubial pact, prompted by alleged coquettish intrigues of late puberty for which the Turks of Apollonia affectionately called her *Arzu*.[15] Lambros noticed her in a local emporium, waiting patiently to purchase coffee and sugar, observed her discretely at first and then minutely until her eyes met his and flounced away to mask what she felt of her blushing. He left the store impaled by love's amorphous lightning, despite every inch of her having been swathed in black, in mourning of her grandmother's death, except for her eyes and her charitable forehead with auburn locks peeking below a black headscarf. He hastened the request to marry her, to the delight of her nervous father, a man of the sea and son of a long line of red-eyed sponge and octopus divers, with skin like salted meat and a brackish temperament to match.

Derided by neighbors and family alike for his nuptial choice, Lambros covertly investigated the slander of her otherwise chaste character and found the swirl of accusation lacking in credibility. He bartered for her hand and received seven gold lires, a tiny but lovely quince grove and two large inlaid dowry chests filled with the necessaries for a new household. He confirmed his investigative skills on their wedding night, when Elissa refused to permit her groom to touch her below the waist. Three days later, as if to corroborate his faith in her, in a profusion of emotion, perhaps over anticipated pain, the girlish spotting of coital secretion appeared on the divan where overcome with emotion for a man whom a month earlier she had not known at all, she made love for the first time. Once married, the endearing Miss Tiros, daughter of a man whose courage bordered on the foolhardy, exhibited none of the unqualified subservience of youthful brides, nor reticence to criticize a husband but a month her senior.

"Eighteen lires for a run down house - a ransom," she nagged Lambros on the protracted, rock and cratered passage to what eventually became the home where their children would be born. The journey culminated in the farmer tendering the land title to Lambros in handscrawled, informal Greek. Because the Turk could not make out his cursive, he asked Lambros to dip his finger into the coffee grounds of his tourkiko and affix his insignia, besides dotting the line with a double lambda.

---

15 αρζού wanton

"You are a fool and I am the greater fool for following you," Elissa chimed like a noonday bell. "And my uncle's backgammon set! You told him you'd never be able to thank him enough!"

"Not even for a roof above your head wife?" Lambros retorted with mounting apprehension of impending regret over a reckless purchase. "Or would you rather go back to Turkey where they're killing foreigners for sport?"

The first words to ramble from Lambro's mouth, directed to his new neighbors with a smile, might as well have been a renegade belch, uttered in a state of bemused euphoria within minutes of his arrival and grand entrance into the village kafenio, and just after a cursory inspection of his newly purchased landholdings, which excited him greatly.

"Who's the imbecile who planted the heart of the village with its back to the lake?"- borrowing the farmer's expression. Gleaming gold-tooth crowns twinkled in jowl-dipped amazement at so brazen an insult, from a stranger who enunciated with hints of *Epirotiko* [16] peppered Greek. An uneasy silence followed. Lambros assumed they had not understood him since they were Turks.

"Wait till he loses the whole village in the bitch's fog, blotting the sunrise," an old Turk said under his breath. His floccose head made him appear as if he was wearing a fez when he was not. The others groaned in agreement. Then an anonymous voice, hoarse from cigarettes and screaming at livestock, replied in careworn yet still coherent Turkish.

"The Turk you bought the house from was the imbecile. What does that make you, *giagouri*?"[17] Another lone voice issued an audible refrain.

"Just one winter here and you'll know why our backs are to the lake ... brick for brains!" Lambros knew little of the ancient pharmacology of airborne disease, of discerning the difference between a breeze and a draft. The latter, according to local diagnostic quackery, was equivalent to Satan's flatulence, his katabatic flow of infirmity through which sailors might catch their death even when stranded upon land. Indeed, his first winter in Kazvam turned out to be a trying affair, with moonlight shining bitterly over a crusted layer of ice and snow and lasting a

---

16   Ηπειρωτικό - from the region of Epirus

17   γκιαούρης - infidel

month, with vast stretches of the region never seeing a footprint of man or beast.

His delight turned to embarrassment, then creeping doubt, but it was too late to rescind the purchase. The farmer had already shaken the Lathran dust from his feet for the second time, never to return. Years later, stories circulated through a returning vacationer that the farmer never made it beyond Crete, the temptress of Phoenicians and Venetians. An immodest, gently aging divorcee, allegedly evading a papal edict and the heavy hand of her Sardinian husband, persuaded him that the Colossus of Rhodes was as good as a fairy tale. The farmer went on to realize a sizable purse of drachmas as a land speculator, along with his *donna poco pensiero*.[18] The two were especially successful in the precipitous municipality of Agia Galini, an elevated little jewel of a port town with steeply circuitous footpaths facing the windswept Sea of Libya, famous for its meltemi winds sweeping past it to the jagged calcium of Cretan mountains. Apparently, the farmer failed to prescribe to his Lathran neighbors' Etesian homeopathy, and in Crete built his villas facing the sea.

Everyone in Lathra was convinced that Lambros had wildly overpaid for his furrowed fields overrun by budding mulberry trees, rocks and old vines that seemed to sprout from the ground daily.

"He bought an old Naodites vineyard," they said of him. His eight dingy walls and leaky roof were, according to the grapevine, no bargain for a fine backgammon set, which the farmer showed off before departing. But not soon after, having cheaply purchased the sun-baked fields of two additional locals who failed to sire male heirs interested in farming, or succumbed to crop failure and the drought some proclaimed likely to last forever, Lambros added fifty-six stremata to his barony. He went on to cultivate a small grove of mulberries in elegantly trimmed tree lines rather than wrestle them from their destiny, and added cherry, pear, apple and peach trees rather than merely rely on the staples of wheat, corn, oats and tobacco. In this, he set a trend for the region.

Within months of the original purchase, in his fatigue and loneliness, his yearning for familiar faces and Elissa's desire to have someone assist her in birthing her child, he wrote home to relatives and favored

---

18 woman of little care

neighbors from his previously adopted Apollonia. His letters beckoned them to heed the signs of the times and the Turkish pogroms and to follow him again, to rest their soon-to-be wandering soles upon the unassuming doorstep of the village he called Lathra. Lambros, it seemed, predetermined by the marvelous logic of hindsight, made a very astute purchase, one day admitted even by Elissa, except for the backgammon set. The horseshoe-shaped house, while the bane of its mistress for the first year of labored repair and habitation, became the largest and best appointed home in the village, easily accommodating Lambro's family, growing by one every few years until four children assumed the run of the house. The home enjoyed proximity to the village plaza with its parliamentary kafenio (the mayor ran the establishment at the time of his purchase) as well as the remarkable, all-in-one gristmill, bakery and apothecary. From the veranda, in one direction, one could observe the moods of the sky above Kythera. In the other, the cloud confined repose of what would become a lovely, ornate chapel in honor of St. George the dragon slayer. A transformed Mosque, built on the footprint of an ancient church, construction began on St. George quickly and occupied the village heights above the square that made survival foreseeable to those with vision. This was especially true in winter, when cold, angry winds and occasional mountain borne squalls kept those further a step from civilization from venturing beyond the village square or risking encounters with the voracious tongues and spiteful glances party to such isolated habitation.

———◆———

Lambros presented himself to his neighbors with a far from concealing mask of passivity, as if he were a stoic, or a contemplative despising debate and never-ending discussion. He liked everyone thinking he was nearly oblivious to the daily dribble of chatterboxes. This took effort, of course, and gave way to incidents of amusing exception, explosions in temper far more noteworthy than any customary gesticulation.

"The tongue has no bones but can break bones," Elissa reminded him after each of his tirades or a particularly vicious reprisal, which he immediately regretted and which made him feel like he had set himself apart from others, the last thing he wanted. He worked very hard at appearing as if nothing much occurred to him beyond the spirals of tobacco smoke encircling his head, or the ever more frequent sips of ouzo anesthetizing the quiet murmur of his inter-cranial discourses. Curiously again, the entire village was plagued with this risible inclination, citizens who spoke at length to themselves in the absence of a living breathing, conversant accomplice. This was scarcely a noticeable practice among the locals, thin-skinned, as they tended to be. But in response to any visitor's amusement in detecting the habit, the natives would take offence. The result was an unrelenting shunning until, hindered by sheer social awkwardness, the visitor deserted the anomalous hostel with its peculiar, seemingly inhospitable agronomists and mountain men.

Yet public apathy was not what others saw in Lambros. He was as socially keen and judgmental as any man could tend to be, and knew it well. Nevertheless, it was also true, that in the billow of his happiness, he rarely sought more than a supine afternoon with his wife and children. The only other harmony aroused in him was the hazing blue and silver tincture of the lake, the reflective nectar in the shallows of what hid invisibly in his eyes. He loved the deep, rumbling reverberation of the dynamite beneath his feet, planted squarely along the spine of his boat as the eruption quavered, lifting the boat atop its waves, a technique of such familiarity to the fish that some leapt into the nets and rowboats to avoid sedation at the hands of deafened fishermen. The Turk had been right about the lake. It teamed with fish.

While he generally aspired to ignore the idle commentary of neighbors and gossips and admired the socially comatose response, believing it prevented his succumbing to the caustic hearsay of his reputation as quick to anger, this practiced stupor did not prevent him from developing adept and conversant social skills. On the contrary, Lambros was literate among his village peers and generally polite, and very nearly charming to women, for in spite of his theories regarding their chronically disgruntled natures and malevolent invectives, he prized the innate warmth of femininity, albeit in a less than understood manner, or, as some might suggest rather cynically, in a phallic way. Thus, when prompted to forget his suspicions and naive variant of Ovid's misogyny, he would go to great lengths to show women respect and take pleasure in his adoration of their manners.

———◆———

Magda Karangelos seemed to understand this of Lambros Lambrou, and perhaps due to this understanding, or so she imagined, delighted in him, although never expressing as much to anyone but her sister, Lydia. Nevertheless, to the more than casual observer of Lathran discourse, her delight was subtly discernible, but not taken seriously. It was as capricious as the psychosis that visited the women of Magda's family, a genetic and gendered curse of demonic possession, perhaps skipping a child but never sexes, nor sparing any generation. Rumor had it that a violent temperament was as demonstrative a family trait as the color of hair and eyes and that, as an example, Magda's mother Irsia, very much resembled her own aunt Matoula, a woman whose fissured mental state provoked the murderess in her as well. The aunt had killed an apparent rival, a local woman she believed to be setting traps for her husband's weak-willed constitution, an assumption that proved correct. Lydia Karangelos also admired Lambros, but for no particular reason, or perhaps precisely because her more precocious older sister openly favored him in their private conversations.

"What a shame this horse has a rider," Magda repeated in her sister's presence often enough to have kindled a competing interest.

Once, on a frolic through the village, as the young men took turns riding a borrowed mount, Lambros rode by the sisters with a staged audacity that made them notice. While the others attained their reckless speed without grace and style, Lambros rode by at a brisk trot, remaining flawlessly vertical atop the newly saddled feral Thessalian. He cupped the reins loosely between the thumb and fingers of his right hand hovering above the horn, his left hand dangling elegantly by his side, his heels at ease and a finger's breadth below a brass string stirrup, his hat tilted forward and shading his eyes. Magda openly proclaimed her admiration.

"Look at him," she said huskily. "The *kavalaris*,[19] better than all of them."

As time went by, the two of them would blush in his presence and once, having imbibed a carafe of strong wine, they laughed at the thought of sharing him carnally, the way Arab women must share their men, a fantasy inspired by love-deprived Lydia. This amusement, like most others in their cramped and dreary days, proved rare and died away at night in the unpleasant presentiment of loneliness and the empty hour.

Inconsistent with such partiality, Avram's aversion to Lambros was equally absurd, and like the inscrutably grafted scion of the irrational that spawned him. He had, until disagreeing with him over the use of the water from Vegoritis, counted Lambros as a good friend. He admired him for his unassailable devotion to wife and children, for his defiant individualism, his courage in risking all that was familiar to him, and his forethought to purchase land in Kazvam when none of his kind had set foot in the place for a century, and all well before the ink had blotted on the Treaty of Lausanne. They had fought together the raging fires in the hills, occasioned by drought and cruelly impotent lightning strikes spawned by Vegoritis' rainless tempests. Avram also retained an ardent interest in Elissa's young cousin, the exquisite Danäe Dranias, upon whom, as it happened, Lambros exerted a brotherly influence.

Ten years Lambro's junior, Danäe was the only daughter of a scholar, a Greek of sorts educated at Cambridge and eventually employed at the Istanbul Institute of Technology, and his cultured wife, Iona Tiros, an illustrious, dramatic beauty by the age of sixteen, and stepsister to Elissa's mother. Well-educated, a teacher by profession, few could unravel Iona's cultural miscegenation, with its dense sprinkles of Hungarian and Romanian subtexts deriving from her paternal lineage. Gregorios Dranias, Danäe's father, was a philologist by profession, and incidentally an aficionado of antiquities, an eccentric, brilliant and intense mongrel of equally unplumbed, and some would say, shrouded heredity, tall and fair complexioned, with a face dominated by animated eyes, a tension across the cheekbones, and a thin, dismissive mouth, thankfully not passed on to Danäe. Upon formal introductions to Iona,

---

19 καβαλάρης – caballero or horseman

he misrepresented himself as a native of England, so adroitly had he suppressed his Balkan accent, and followed her about Cambridge for a month, neglecting work and studies even after severe sanctioning by his employer and colleagues, until her scheduled return to Istanbul. Their parting was wonderfully emotional. A week passed in her absence and he fell into despair, weight loss, insomnia, incontinence, concluding it better to lose his life than to forgo the chance to grovel in her presence once again. On impulse, having failed to arrange with the proprietor of his flat or his employer, he followed her to the revolving gate of Asia Minor, the city of open markets, the human sewer and mistress of usurpers, the purveyor of cabalistic lies, Istanbul. There he proposed to her father, requiring no dowry of him and persuading her with his devotion and willingness to stay near her as she had already decided against ever returning to England. He married her in a lavish ceremony and earned a teaching post as part of the contractual consideration of keeping a daughter near her parents.

As lovely as any flower they had ever seen and as tall as many of the men in the village, Iona's daughter, Danäe, was the flaxen-curled blossom in a copse of melancholic black tresses, except in winter when her hair would darken dramatically to the color of wet sand. One could not avoid being enamored with the promise of her amusement in the way her mouth drew out its charming smile and the shy seascape of her eyes glanced gently in the direction of the one who might make her laugh. Graciously drawn in her proportions, with a wisp of waist crafted to punctuate alluring hips and the nascent fruit of her bosom, she appeared, even draped in black for the months of mourning her mother's death, an ethereally seductive creature, leaving men as bated for the purity of her saddened expression as lusting for her beckoning silhouette.

Lambros revealed the circumstances of her escort and arrival in Lathra to Vasili and Avram. Danäe herself revealed it only to Andreas, years later. Avram, like most others, was transfixed. She had summoned Lambros to her in Istanbul, recently indentured there as a housemaid in the house of a financier of significant means, her parents both being ill and in short supply of money upon which to survive. The banker, the corsair of another's money, educated in Germany, fancied his presage of dignity to that of an aristocrat, a baron in a land of brutes and peasants. But noble airs did little to control his bestial urges. Besides furthering her education with respectable tutors and a library long ignored by the banker's own children, he routinely subjected his female staff to the most lascivious propositions and illicit groping he could manage out of site of his docile and inconspicuous wife. Danäe understood nothing of his appetites and uninhibited demeanor, nor why she was suddenly the sole recipient of his attentions when the household relied upon a litter of part-time staff. All but the butler and cook were young women and girls. Innocently yet instinctively, she feared such conduct would lead to criminality, even before she heard and understood the meaning of household whispers, rife with tales of the last live-in chambermaid. A doll-like fräulein in pigtails, from Leinzig, the fräulein succumbed to her employer's illicit requests at first, but soon she was unable to walk without discomfort from the abrasions, bruises and bite marks suffered along those improbable trails of feminine terrain. Unable to service her employer with his preferences, the banker's son contemptuously escorted her from the city by the hair, her name never uttered again.

As she lay dying of cancer, Danäe's father having died six weeks earlier of cholera, Iona Dranias counseled her only child, advising her of Lambro's whereabouts and the compassion she suspected he would display if not of his own accord, for she had met him and been impressed, then for the sake of Elissa, her niece, whom she loved dearly. Danäe buried her mother and that same day wrote to Elissa and Lambros a tear-stained letter, begging her rescue from the misery of servitude, from her employer's crude overtures and fondling, and the danger of a lugubriously suicidal imagination.

Without announcement and at great risk, Lambros made the grueling overland journey alone, a revolver tucked beneath his belt, borrowed from Avram to whom he confided his mission. He arrived in the city at night, dazed, hungry and shivering, paid a hired driver to navigate a maze of streets leading to the banker's house and knocked on the door at an unfashionable hour. After cursory introductions, he announced his business in snappish, unintentionally dismissive Turkish, demanding the immediate presence of the young Danäe Dranias. The staff was amazed. He smelled and looked like a dockworker at the end of a day's work. The butler and cook attempted to escort him back to the cobbled street, but he refused. The ruckus caused by this, alarmed the rest of the house. A short but brutish Turk, the banker arrived in his smoking robe and slippers with the kind of scowl one attaches to a man accustomed to having his way. He stepped toward Lambros threateningly, with his hand out before him.

"Sir, I can offer you nothing but a beating that will send you into the dullards of old age before your time," he said, raising his voice for the fear it normally instilled. The formality of his speech did not impress Lambros. He found it incompatible with the threat of bodily eviction, and groped for his weapon. At that very moment, the banker's effeminate son entered the foyer from the labyrinth of rooms beyond a darkened hallway, Danäe in hand, followed by other strays of the staff, filling the room with the curious. Cooing and winking slyly at the evening's coarse guest, the son distracted his father and embarrassed him, giving Lambros time to brandish the revolver, thumb the hammer back and discharge its lead into the ceiling. The shock of the blast in such confined quarters startled them all. In the midst of the melee, while his dazed but unharmed hosts instinctively fell to the floor, Lambros seized Danäe by the lapel and made his exit to the street, escorting her by a waiting taxi. Remarkably, the taxi driver had not fled at the sound of gunfire, so needy was he of the fare. Making their way to the wharves much more quickly than the drive to the house, they hurriedly boarded an aged trawler of questionable seaworthiness, hired on the spot, and set sail for home in the night. Confused by the destination Lambros had described, the yawning crew, a pair of sailors and a young African boy, carried them by the narrow breadth of a hero's girdle across the Marmara to the familiar shores and haunts near Apollonia, surviving the journey in shifting seas with barely enough potable water, an unforgivable oversight considering Lambro's skills as a seaman.

From there, tongues swollen and nerves frayed by the harrows of the crossing, they retraced the journey Lambros made years earlier with his pregnant Elissa, hiring a variety of vehicles equally as troubled as the sea craft. The land and sea journey took two inordinate weeks and, with the expense of the taxi, the boat, its crew, and truck drivers, nearly bankrupted Lambros but permanently endeared him to Danäe, in a fraternal way.

Elissa, encouraging but also fretting from the outset the danger inherent in her husband's mission, assumed that either death or lust, also believed to be itinerant cousins, aroused an intentionally prolong absence, or hastened the travelers' end. When Lambros finally arrived with Danäe, Elissa felt the compulsion to slap his face. Instead, she embraced him, tentatively, while announcing the news of her recently determined fourth pregnancy.

"If you leave me in this condition for another voyage of mercy," she cautioned tearfully, "you'll wish you had died at sea instead of returning smelling like fish."

———◆———

By this juncture, Avram had already married his heart-rending Maria, a homely girl from the nearby town of Naousa. Nearly half his age, Maria's alleged infertility, indirectly occasioned his learning her name, by way of witnessing her public thrashing at the hands of her sadistic and easily angered brother, Thanasi Karpathiotis. The son of one of the few remaining Turks amid inhospitable Greeks, hailing from the Island of Karpathos, Thanasi followed his father's example, acclimating family and cipher to life amid the Orthodox, choosing given names of Christian origin, inventing a fanciful lore of noble breeding and concocting a surname. Unlike his father, who had genuinely converted to Christianity, and more like his maternal grandfather, who lived with them but refused upon the onset of a stubborn senility to adopt the altered surname, Thanasi never quite abandoned his Islamic palate. He believed firmly in its legacy of regressive remedies for the sins and shortcomings identified in others, especially in Maria's case, for infertile women. He proclaimed aloud the blunder his father committed in permitting Masal,[20] Maria's childhood name before the family's conversion, to survive her birth and attend a local school, Turkish epithets slipping past his lips as his rage fed itself.

"You useless sow," he shrieked, tearing her hair, pinning her and flogging her with the reins still tethered to his mule, "as cold and barren as a cave, with the face of a pigeon. Who will marry such a creature? No man would risk the birth of such misfits! Maria, Maria, purest vessel from on high. Ha! What a laugh! Even their Virgin is ashamed to share

---

20 Μασάλ - Turkish for marigold

her name with you," he barked contemptuously. Avram crossed the street at a brisk pace, rather than simply stand by and witness the assault, and intervened without thought to more than the girl's terror and the improper reference to the Virgin slithering from the mouth of a heathen. Thanasi delivered the kind of Turkish street slander of Christians he had heard as a boy in Smyrna. "Eh, son of a bow-legged Jew, even the Jews have no use for you!" and other inventions of unqualified malice. Avram shouted his unerring vowel and walked toward them, his arm half raised, his eyes filed with fire.

"You there... mule driver with the heavy hand! You gather courage from the screams of women, I see," he said, threatening with his open palm. Thanasi turned his head slowly. A cigarette was dangling from his mouth. He snorted through his nostrils like a bull, ash spraying across Maria's face, trying to calm the mule, the loose ends of its tether pulling taut the bit in its mouth. Ignoring him, he turned his back and resumed his tirade without contemplating whether a stranger of no particularly menacing size or appearance possessed the courage to defy him or was merely puffing for the small audience of onlookers. Avram traversed the remaining distance in assiduous strides just as the reins struck Maria across the shoulders once again. Exhibiting their strength and usefulness, Avram wrapped the thick fingers of his left hand about Thanasi's throat, pushing him into the side of the mule, squeezing until his eyes became enlarged beets and he choked a cry for his mother's healing. Maria instantly confused admiration for the power of such a left hand. For love, for a protector, gratitude for what she believed must be a kind and vulnerable heart, which she might rely upon in the future.

Somehow, having never revealed it to Avram, leaving that same day she gathered a small bag of things and followed her savior to Lathra, like a suckling, probably on foot. She arrived at his door the following day, trembling, in a sagging traveling ensemble, the best clothes she owned, better worn than carried, a sea blue dress atop a barely hued petticoat, the bodice with a wide mustard sash around what passed for hips. And a long burgundy apron with golden tassels scrapping up the dust of the road, her hair enclosed within a sequined scarf, its pearl-drop tassels caressing her brow. He took her in after it became evident that she would starve rather than return home to the humiliation and reprisal her brother would prepare.

Months passed in a paradise of budding affections. Avram arranged for Maria to live and work in the gray stone and corrugated shelter a dozen meters behind Yianko's kafenio. He attended to her daily needs and was pleased with the charitable response showed to her affable qualities by the village women, tolerant at first because she was no rival beauty but also since she presented no airs of high character or endowment and was receptive to the blooms of casual conversation.

In a moment absent of lucidity, beneath the diffuse glow of a crescent moon, upon the earlier occasion of a deepening sunset and the delivery of a certain gratuitous parcel of pomegranates to his home, Avram unexpectedly kissed Maria upon her parched, forsaken lips. The embrace that followed, upon the threshold of his house, was not a particularly good omen, according to a little known wives' tale, signifying true love but an otherwise ill-fated union. Between tuneful whispers of gratitude and the divining affection of a second kiss, they agreed and privately wed in Arnissa within a week, to the pleasant surprise and spiteful pains of village magpies.

"This will be an unlucky affair," the chatterboxes prophesized. Happiness set in like an Armenian visitor. While she indeed could not conceive children of her own, her womb having been surgically hacked out of her at a young age, Maria set free the admiration of villagers, assisting mothers and offspring alike with any number of skills, from tutoring young girls in needlework and teaching them to tend to their parents' demanding whims, to midwifery. In one noted instance, she saved the foot of a young village boy named Pavlos Lourithas, who while riding his horse bareback, had his right foot trampled when the mount reared at the sight of a snake, throwing its rider overhead, dangling him by the rope reins. Maria sewed the nearly severed toes well enough to the foot for the regeneration of feeling and a barely noticeable interruption of his gait. She gained modest and desirable weight, and finally appeared to Avram as the little doting wife, even pretty in his eyes. In addition to her nightly call to his bed, a satisfaction of body and mind each reveled in for the first time in their lives, Avram felt needed and content, including her in the otherwise dull steps of daily cloak and custom. She presented a quality of warmth for him hitherto reserved only for inanimate things like clean socks of combed wool on cold feet, his fallow fields in winter or the sheen upon his newly polished rifle.

"A fit made in heaven," he repeated with contentment to the priest, who cautioned him regarding a woman he barely knew becoming so utterly beholden to him.

"Listen, Pater," he responded. "To tell you the truth, I'm tired of being alone. So you manage your own household and stick to your kyrie eleison in there," Avram said, pointing to the chapel, a place where he rarely set foot. "I'll decide what fits in my castle."

The following spring Avram traveled to Naousa again to purchase grape vines. Maria's brother observed him at a safe distance, but remained filled with venom and lingering, hateful delusions, despite the fact that Avram had achieved for him his stated desire, ridding him of his sister. A week after spotting him, having long healed the damage done to his vision by Avram's iron grip, but not to his reputation or distorted impost, nor having satiated his desire for vengeance, Thanasi Karpathiotis descended upon Lathra from the East like a silent, circling raven, a scavenger hovering above the plenteous patch of contentment whilst the gardener takes his midday nap. Konya, the village *tsobano*,[21] grazing his sheep just beyond the grassy hills announcing the entrance to the village, unwittingly confirmed for Thanasi what he surmised of Maria's failure to return to Naousa. She was happy and married to the man who attempted to extrude his eyes from their sockets. Slipping between the serried hills and into the village in broad daylight, without confrontation or discussion, Thanasi Karpathiotis murdered his sister the moment his vindictive glance seized hers in terror, dashing her skull with a large rock. She lay behind Yianko's kafenio, where she had continued to work a few days each week while sharing Avram's bed and sofra, keeping his home and growing accustomed to bearing her husband's name with ever titivating pride.

On that encroaching, moonlit evening when Avram returned home from his orchards and did not find her preparing a meal for the two of them, he searched for her without vexation, without thought to what life might become without her, and came upon her lifeless, gaping lips, the repose of her right hand lying gently upon her chest. Her middle fingertip outlined the gold cross, which dangled from imperceptibly delicate links beneath the cloth of her dress. A wedding gift from

---

21 τσομπάνος - shepherd

Avram, she removed it each night, spreading it around an invisible surrogate throat at the bass of the oil lamp illuminating their bed. There, alone, he wiped her brow with his shirttail and held her close to him, her cheek next to his. His love consumed him. He carried her home, lifted her to his bed and lay next to her in the night, imagining that she had prayed as the pain and heat of her wound dispensed her blood and shortened her breath into an unaided desire for sleep, giving way to the cold of utter darkness.

5

The eternal apprehends itself as the divine precisely in its divergence from that which it occasions, the finite. The fixity, the finite is nothing more than the burning breath of indulgence, the pliant bondage of the sensual. Like the puerile gods of antiquity coveting the opaque curvatures of Olympus over the translucent nimbus of heaven, like Zeus, preferring the imperfections in the femininity of flesh to the marbled ideality of a goddess, all men gazing upon Danäe Dranias pondered in bewilderment the same question. How could any creator be so unmoved as to conceive of so nearly flawless a visage and not imprison her within his palace for his own delight? One day, having observed her often enough during the year following Maria's death, Avram watched from behind a tree as Danäe escorted a pair of renegade goats to Konya's corral. Her arms were bare and she had pulled up her loosely fitted cotton dress and knotted the hem below her hip to soothe the prickly heat of the day, baring a leg well above the knee. He had never seen such lithe, seemingly hairless, graceful limbs. The effect of this nakedness provoked something more than mere arousal. From that moment, reliving his nightly embraces with his wife, he embarked upon contriving a scenario for the assistance and rescue of Danäe, anything to mimic the bond with his lost Maria. His manhood already felled, he followed her around like a duckling, waiting for the opportunity to render help, which rarely came of its own accord. Danäe was notoriously self-sufficient and reclusive of most men.

When kismet failed and nothing innovative came to mind to achieve this end, he resorted to artificially increasing the number of fortuitous instances where she might require some small kindness. The imitation of fate quickly degenerated into the most contrived and awkward of benevolences.

Encountering a momentary difficulty in persuading her laden donkey to walk to the gristmill nearly one hundred and fifty meters away, Avram volunteered to alleviate the beast of its burden and delivered upon each squared shoulder the two large sacks of grain to the mill. He nursed his strained muscles for days afterwards. The donkey brayed with delight, running off like a frolicking fawn, released from its indenture for an afternoon of munching on dandelions and chamomile. The time and effort he saved her, she spent fourfold catching the donkey. Polite inquiries and discrete contributions to her wellbeing, while appreciated in the moment, went largely unnoticed, at least as inaugurations of any amorous gesture. Danäe was as scentless and neutered a blossom as any exquisite orchid in the garden of earthly delights. Neither fit, strapping young men nor demonstratively provocative young women would elicit in her a prurient thought or sensual impulse. Her heart savored the care of four-legged creatures and hapless, wing-damaged birds, not the impassioned ineptitude and erect exuberance of youthful Eros.

"Humanity is a misadventure of God, always seeking to become what it isn't," she answered when asked by Pater Alexi of her preference for animals. "Animals alone are content with their lot, the lioness representing the pinnacle of creation, content to sleep the day away until her cubs and she next hunger."

"As good as profanity," the priest responded under his breath, being one of the few men in the village she engaged in such elevated conversation. "It's a good thing these bumpkins don't understand a thing you say or I'd have a rebellion of idiots on my hands."

Unusual enough, Danäe's education instilled in her an intellectual preference for the abstract, the two-dimensional intrigues of language and representational art, the latter largely gleaned from books routinely perused as a young girl, gifts from her father containing colorless templates of great paintings, sculpture and architecture. The books were lost with her parent's confiscated estate, but remained housed in the curatory of her memories. Studying a reproduction of a painting in a book borrowed from another devotee, a book containing snippets of the Masters, she ceremoniously returned the volume to its owner with a note, invoking in him, her teacher of late, the pondering aesthetic questions spurring her curiosity.

"How is it that men create such lovely silhouettes, such shadows of the corporeal, capturing things in their most wraithlike moment and yet they are not content with honing such divine talent? Instead, they opt to dissect the cadaver of that which cast the shadow." For her teacher's entertainment, she affectionately derided anything philosophical, since she knew he was precisely interested in rhetoric and reasoning. She gave off haughty answers on his behalf. "I possess a baleful head for the history of men's elaborate edifice of erroneous inference." The interest in the discipline was more of a habit, she insisted, instilled in her by her father, lovingly transmitted over long walks in the exotic evening air of their great city, once the haven of scholars and mystics, ensconcing the Orient and Occident with an intricate masonry of both sacred and secular contemplation. She nurtured her interest, unusual for a young woman, like a child relishing sugared sweets and found the promise of some tasty confection of cogent reasoning or dark and ominous revelation too compelling to resist. Until, after consuming many mouthfuls, she came to feel self-consciously stained with the white powder of her indulgence, ailing with the elusive and easily forgotten insight that over ingestion causes its own special form of dyspepsia.

Her habits and curious interests lent compliment to the intrigue created in the keen observation of her by others. Unmasking her facade became the tantalizing Lathran pastime, finding the concealed honeycomb of her persona or pulling back what some assumed to be a veil of sadness. The other most conspicuous diversion of mercy, which confounded the notion that she suffered with innate unhappiness, was her facilitating the play of the handful of young children scurrying about the village and including them in her adventures in aid of the lost or sickly members of the animal kingdom. Her gift fomented genuine affection in the children, who were otherwise anomalous and adult-like in the secluded monotony of their limited roster of games and knaveries. An endearing naivety blossomed in the otherwise nearly cretin tediousness of their lot. The eccentricity of these children was in first measure due to their having so few peers to mimic or contrast with, despite the roughly equivalent childbearing age of their mothers. Most of the recent nursing mothers arrived with young children already in tow. In their poverty and furor to establish households, these young women ascribed to a more prudish routine, not always to their husband's chagrin, over-labored as they all were, or to a regiment of complete abstinence. The women often toiled all day and into the night, hours longer than the men did, leaving little time or energy for sensual musings. Adulteries in such insular settings were unheard of and sexual relations prior to marriage virtually a social death sentence for the woman and any resultant child.

As years waned, a second wave of childbearing swept the village, with children often seven or more years younger than their siblings. Of course, it was likely that the peculiarity of such children also arose out of those obtuse and superstitious incantations and inoculations practiced in the name of a customary upbringing. There was no conscious harkening to pagan origins. Parents simply focused on the child's survival over its edification. This was a feature of the times, the lack of competent medical care, a poverty of biblical proportions and quite simply an ancient legacy of children who must thrive at their own peril. Like a litter of runts, the unlucky, through no fault of their careworn mothers, might not find a place at the tit and so, draw few if any breaths. Disease, injury and the apotropaic eye floating upon the winds of envy cut little threads pitiably short, maddening mothers with unending terms of mourning. The precious surviving pixies were certainly innocent but, of necessity, also precocious in the worldly skills of procuring food, handling the implements and techniques of farming and fishing and abiding by the rudiments of superstition and faith, the Church being the granite of authoritative endurance.

Elisa routinely combed kerosene through her children's hair to protect them from the raging lice infesting the village during drought and privation, the smell subjecting them to relentless mockery. Others clothed their offspring seasonally, in the same and only vestments available, testing the children's patience with their own stink and then again with cold discomfort when the clothing, which ultimately required boiling before being scrubbed by hand, was dried in the sun.

Medicinal remedies remained as primitive as they had been for centuries, more often coupled with chants, cupping and the inverted coffee grounds of rituals to cast out the sneer of devils. This postponed other herbal applications or remedies appearing plainly upon the horizon of chance and men's broader experience. Children routinely ate after the men and women had their fill, or as the hierarchy of family auspices dictated. A voracious child could reduce the productivity and health of a working brother or provider. As such, gluttony was non-existent. And yet, no child went hungry. Never would a mother conceive of denying sufficient victuals to her children, under any circumstances, let alone punitively. A common expression for the improbably delicious dish was "one so tasty, a mother would lick the plate clean and deny her child." Nothing was too great to sacrifice to keep children from shivering through the night or wailing in hunger, among the greatest of disgraces to which parents could subject their reputation.

The noble model of motherhood in the village was Rena Papachristos, a fallow cobbler's wife who with justified and fearful impatience made the trek from Apollonia on foot to join her husband already in Lathra, their last letters to each other filled with love and hope for a new life but also no specific notice of their respective departures. Papachristos unknowingly passed his wife and children on the journey back to Apollonia to retrieve them. Rena so starved her body on the journey to ensure her children could walk to their salvation that she fell ill on the day of her arrival, dying the following morning. Owning no land to tie him to Lathra and to ease the daily remembrance of his wife's sacrifice, Papachristos gathered his children and fled south looking for work in the cotton fields of Thessaly.

Besides rising early to assist in the labors of daily survival, the children attended church on Sundays and grammar school the rest of the week. They learned to read, to calculate the barter of commodity and currency and to cultivate an identity within the interchangeable history and myth of the Greeks. Their only other consistent activity was creating sobriquets of audacious barbarity for every member of society and their own households. At play, they would loiter about the two kafenia and the lake, or run wild with the goats and sheepdogs in the hills and atop Kythera. They used rolled balls of discarded green tobacco leaves for organized football games in the village square, created straw dolls wearing sackcloth garments and reenacted, or embellished, as some insisted, the daring of their ancestors' cunning and courage. Fetes and feast days marked their seasons of youthful impatience and when they might glean by reward or pilfer the sweets and abundance of delicacies from their parents' now envied Anatolian cuisine.

Quite unlike many Lathran fathers, Lambros enjoyed an unusual bond with each of his children. His delight in the unaffected merriment of their smiles, which filled him with an enviable contentment, he achieved without cosseting them. And the sound of their wailing, whether from a fall or Elissa's rare but infamous beatings with her sandals or broom stick, elicited an immediate panic followed by dejection and remorse at his not preventing their pain. Nothing surged the Acheron of his foreboding more than a look of terror in what to him was their susceptible, suggestive eyes, even when he instigated that terror. And when he did usher such fright in them, their fear revisited him with pangs of guilt floating through his insomnias and nightmares, in swarms of biting black flies, or puffs of malignant pollen burning him from pupil to vitreous. Or he would have dreams of losing them in an impenetrable fog, often rising and fumbling in the dark, striking invisible walls of utter desperation.

He fretted as well over his children's congenital predilection for nightmarish hallucinations. Sophia possessed a commiserate fear of fire. Stratos had recurring visions of dark armored giants pursuing him with fierce, mechanized, never before envisioned weaponry. Evanthia's vague evocations were of losing grip of her mother's ever unraveling hem, and the most serious quandary arose when it came time to bathe Nikos, who from a young age was plagued with an inexplicable fear of drowning in as little as a glass of water. Forcing him to drink to keep from dehydration or constipation was an ongoing ordeal until the age when hair enveloped his manhood and he desperately desired to wash it off.

Sophia, his eldest daughter, could especially swell Lambro's pride and lay bare his most concealed emotion, filling him with the blithe fragrance of what others could only conclude was sheer devotion. He believed his daughter unfortunate in her cleverness, especially her skill in comprehending abstract ideas and her aptitude for computation. She would surpass her teacher at the age of twelve and assume teaching the other children the rudiments of geometry after digesting the teacher's pristine, unused hornbook of Euclidian proofs. Lambros feared that available suitors would fail to choose a girl who might outwit a prospective husband and perhaps embezzle his estate for the sake of her kin. For this reason, he resisted sending her away for a proper education, the thought of which troubled him deeply and caused him additional sleep-less nights. He neither possessed the resources to educate his children beyond an elementary level nor wanted them to stray far and especially feared in his girls any mimicry of what he perceived as the weightiness of time lurking in the ambuscade hearts of young women like Lydia or Magda. He envisioned such unmarried specimens of femininity as secretly desperate to avoid the solitude of spinsters, notwithstand-ing their airs of confidence and significant education and the apparent wherewithal to thrive in an urban climate.

"She may tire of waiting for a husband," he warned his wife, "and then who knows what she might do. Education will make her yearn for escape, to disappear into the wide world." He worried and bemoaned his dread to Elissa often, and behaved as if it was her fault that Sophia was clever and perpetually seeking to know more than she should. When Elissa grew irritated with the implication, he sought an alternative scape-goat and settled his resentment upon Danäe, for offering so stark and stringent a model of such new feminine tolerances and interests.

"Then we should send Sophia to Thessaloniki to become a seam-stress, if you're so worried," Elissa advised.

"What a wonderful idea, my dear Elissa," he answered cynically. "Yes, why don't we simply feed her to the wolves roaming Kythera? Then at least Konya's sheep will have a night's rest."

Sophia, for her part, was actually a willowy, more carefree version of Elissa rather than a protégé of Danäe, despite an ancestral affinity in complexion and coloring and Danäe's sisterly solicitude toward the young girl. When angered, though, Sophia possessed her father's fiery glance that could make a man's testicles shrink. She inherited his unfor-tunate inclination for nocturnal loquacity, which on occasions of a full moon kept her siblings from sleeping soundly, an interesting genetic replication of her father's benign lunacy, as far as Elissa was concerned.

Sophia loved her father's steadfastness in the face of calamity or fail-ure, his decisiveness, once settling upon an enterprise, and most of all his minute attentiveness to her and his family, something she noted as a young girl, something wholly absent in other fathers. In the winter, the family would all trudge to the lake together, with their donkeys, the animals braying and protesting the large clay pots spilling frigid water along thinly covered spines, except the ornery mount transporting the babushka bundled Evanthia, an intelligent beast who knew to bray at the mere sight of its owner. Before the procession home, Lambro would blow the mist of his balmy, mastic-laced breath across Sophia's freezing fingers, and then thaw them beneath his arms, singing her a cheery praise of spring, warming her thoughts, conjuring an image of luxuriant summer heat. She also prized his defense of her on those occasions of inevitable sibling rivalries and discipline, enticing her father's favoritism in the most subtle, whining supplication and behaving as if she somehow earned his partiality with theatrical talent. Stratos was a year older and a head taller and abused his sister with the pet name, Karpousara - big melon girl. This was a twofold taunt, based on her love of the juicy summer fruit, which she enjoyed with feta and her mother's thick, porous bread, and of her pubescent breasts. By her thirteenth year, it was necessary to purchase a brassier and to dress her in what remained of her mother's youthful costumes from the old country. Nikos mimicked his older brother's ridicule and on one occasion stuck his hands beneath his shirt, poking his fists out into knobs. Her wardrobe and her brothers' teasing prompted additional ridicule by leering peers. Finally, it culminated in an episode of her mortification as a young girl, an illicit public fondling at the hands of the traveling tinker's overanxious son. Lambros would sufficiently chastise Stratos to tears of laughter or abject fear, depending upon his mood, in an effort to end the banter. Then he would secretly console Sophia with a coin pressed into the palm of her hand, which she immediately bartered at the *bakaliko*[22] for a handful of salted almonds or cubes of jellied fruit confections, taunting her brother, announcing her victory with each bite, flaunting her crunching, sugarcoated teeth.

Once, on a solemn Holy Thursday, Sophia dared to ignore her brother's direction to assist him with some chore, and instead stealing away beneath the steps of the veranda to paint her lips with a palm full of red dye reserved for Easter eggs. Stratos pulled her from her hiding place, drug her into the courtyard when he noticed the rouge extending beyond the corners of her mouth and without a thought to consequences, beat her with savage slaps across the legs and face with whatever his hands could reach, abusing her for the whorish path she might behold. Lambros heard the commotion and bounded out of the house,

---

22 μπακάλικο – a general store or grocery

intervening with identical, atoning violence, throwing Stratos across the courtyard like a ball.

"Christ is crucified on this day[23] ... don't temp me, ruffian!"

And with Evanthia as well. Her smiling eyes bathing brown in the shade would appear hazel in the sunlight and melt her father instantly. Anything she requested, short of frivolity, she received. Nikos, who resented this favoritism, compensated with all manner of creative sabotage of the girls' games. When the torments began or he feigned to slap his sisters in discipline or retribution, a single menacing glance from his father reminded him of Stratos and the infamous Holy Thursday.

Lambros equally loved his sons, Stratos and the younger Nikos, but not with the quality of mercy or heart-aching ardor evoked by his Sophia and his toddling Evanthia. With the boys, he was often impatient, but also spent far more time with them, both in the fields and in his travels. When they were young, he regularly accused them of being slothful and skilled only in avoiding work.

"My sons will grow up to be lazy bums if I don't boil their asses a bit," he often told Elissa, who thought he was too hard on them, concocting jobs to improve their work ethic and, as the boys confided in each other, "because he thinks we're mules like him." Once he made them remove rocks and small boulders from the fields to places so unnecessarily distant as to occupy them for an entire week. Then, a month later, made them retrieve the same rocks to shore up a falling wall or corral around the family compound. Toward the end of each day, the goats, mules and cows would return from a day of grazing on the hills flirting with Kythera for milking and for their oats or corn. The hired men released them into the square resulting in a comedy of chaos, a throng of four-legged beasts wandering around in circles or wreaking havoc before finding their way to their respective stalls with the help of a cacophony of bleats and whistles howled and hollered by their masters. Lambros insisted that his protesting sons have the stalls cleaned and assist in the task of attracting the correct animals. He complained angrily when a young goat or calf, thought to be tagging along, went astray or showed a dirty coat from lying in its own manure.

---

23 In the Orthodox tradition, the crucifixion is reenacted on Holy Thursday.

"Christ and the Virgin, why don't you give our neighbors the pick of the flock and just keep the scrawny ones for us?" he would say.

Lambros insisted that his sons help him prune trees through the winter, tend the fields by hand and irrigate in the growing season, pierce tobacco for drying and incise the art of the scythe for the harvest. He taught them how to swim, to fish the lake with short, polled nets and dynamite, but then would refuse to permit them to do more than light an occasional fuse. Mostly they rowed the boat and scooped up captured fish. As time and need conceded, he relied heavily upon Stratos, who managed to teach himself elemental Albanian so he could supervise migrant crews for the annual defrocking of Pomona's trees - cherry, pear and apple. Stratos was from a young age the type of boy who no amount of teasing or threat would grate or provoke; an anomaly among his quarrelsome peers. He ignored his playmates goading him into imbecilities or bravado, the way a sleeping lion ignores the flies about its face and the birds feeding off its twitching torso. When an Albanian youth humiliated and forced upon him a fistfight by striking first, Lambros turned his sniveling son around and forced him to reengage the bolder, barefoot son of a worker, instructing him on the way to raise his right hand before his face and strike with his left before felling his opponent by whatever means. Then Lambros walked away, because he could not bear to see his son take a punch. The bout ended in a notable stalemate with both boys bloodied and wrestling on the ground, where Stratos, the physically stronger and spryer, gained an advantage. Thus, with his standing in the village amended, he returned to his father to report: "I have vanquished my enemy and sent him back to the underworld!"

"Good," Lambros said. "Now go back and make him your friend, the way I hear the Americans do, even though he's a filthy heathen. You may need him someday."

Lambros jealously guarded his parental duties when it came to Nikos as well. He frowned upon the perfunctory responsibilities assumed by older siblings, when Nikos was too young to engage in the heavier labors of farm and home. His second son was a curiosity to him, so beautiful, as a small child, as to surpass his sisters and to make Lambros question whether he was the father. Nikos was inquisitive, superstitious and spastically spellbound by the vastness of the heavens. He often nagged his father to accompany him to the heights above Vegoritis or Kythera to gaze at the night sky and the halo of light to the north, to count stars and shudder in the soundless speckled night, marking the sacred drone of endless existence.

Lambros might quiver with rage whenever Stratos fought with his younger brother, usually over some innocuous advantage one perceived the other to have gained, but he was unable to bring himself to strike either of them without significant cause. Then, one day, Niko's innocence vanished, like a discarded tooth and Lambros realized that his younger son resembled him. The resemblance was obvious to others. The village men called Nikos, *Lambraki*,[24] whereas Stratos resembled Elissa and even more so her long dead brother, Marcos, who died at sea while still a youth, which endeared Elissa even more to her firstborn.

———◆———

Elissa was the sustenance and heartbeat of the Lambrou household and undoubtedly the most talented of the Anatolian women to have arrived in Kazvam, if by talent one meant domestically practiced. The fevered pitch of endless labor was especially remarkable from late August though November, when she toiled day and night preparing victuals for winter rations and, along with Danäe and at times Yianko's wife, an array of foodstuffs all requiring concentrated preparatory skills. *Trahana*,[25] for example, was among the most cumbersome, a staple of winter survival, tiring to prepare, but substantial and satisfying before the battery of cold, eaten for breakfast or at midday. Beginning with a cavernous vat filled with scrupulously pure milk, she added the heart of wheat, sometimes adding broth with the fat skimmed off of a half-dozen recently boiled fowl or chickens, and heaps of flour and salt. Then she would ruin her back blending the mixture into dough. Hours later, she would lay the concoction in a room of meticulous cleanliness, lined with pristine white sheets, and then dry, hand roll and crumble it into the atoms of a porridge

———

24 Λαμπράκη - little Lambros

25 τραχανάς - wheat heart and chicken broth porridge

boiled and eaten since the return of the Heracleidae. The trahana was then stored in large clay pots in cool places, filling bellies until April.

Elissa was also the mistress of *petmesi*, a delectable, edible preservative made from grape nectar and used in the process of jarring blanched vegetables and fruit for storage. She was among the only women in the region who had learned to cut and cure a delicious type of bacon, a skill taught to her by a Russian, an alleged tourist passing through the region, whose stay in Lathra ended abruptly with his being hunted into the mountains for his thefts from Lathran households. The Russian was handsome. He had tempted Elissa with his chiseled chin and painstaking flirtations, with flowers and the poetry of intimate glances, but she resisted, and apparently did so without difficulty, leaving for another his seductive words and the perverse pleasure he took in knifing raw meat.

"Slicing the loin is a sensuous art, like inserting one's sword in the ravenous sheath of a desired woman," he had said to her. Not quite offended by the image, she said nothing to Lambros.

"I'm not going to tell my husband you said such a thing to me, only to prevent him from slicing you into pieces."

She also knew how to reduce the slaughtered swine into cooking butter, and how best to stuff *kavourma* [26] into the beast's intestines for *loukaniko*.[27] While the men ate their fill of the charbroiled loin with intermittent sips of ouzo, she would layer the balance of the kavourma, swimming in fat and salt, into clay pots. She taught the other women the best technique for using and preserving *agourida*, raw grapes used in lieu of lemons. Selecting the finest of the freshly picked pears, she would wrap them individually, bury them in *sitari* [28] or *krithari*,[29] and store them in the ambari. (The rhyme sung to a popular folk tune while working.) Retrieved all winter, the fruit was a recollection of summer sweetness. She learned to hang nets and baskets full of ripened grapes from nails rapped into the rafters in the oldest and coldest part of the Turkish house, where, with the perfect temperature of its interior, they retained their freshness for months on end.

---

26 κάβουρμας - ground meat

27 λουκάνικο - lamb, pork and garlic sausages

28 σιτάρι - wheat

29 κριθάρι - barley

Of the two parents, Elissa stressed the necessity of the children's education more than Lambros did.

"A man is the same as a mule," she taught her sons, "until he can read and add the coins in his pocket to know if he is being cheated or slandered." This inclination was the consequence of literacy in both her parents. Unlike some Lathrans who could scarcely write their names. The most vocal illiterates resented the presence of any "blackbird in the midst of doves," segregating anything even remotely smelling of book learning from practical acumen.

"Listen to them, filling their children's heads with bird droppings, the shit of heathens and communists," the illiterate squawked, preferring instead to bask in crude ironies or asinine sarcasms, considering such habits of language the hallmarks of intelligence. As his children grew and exhibited a talent for their studies, the dissimilarity between Lambros and some of his neighbors seethed into another caldron of resentment.

Avram further instigated this, arguing at one point with Lambros over whether to increase the teacher's pay or to encourage the man to leave for an engagement elsewhere. He suggested replacing the teacher with one of the older children, like Sophia, who could already read and perform basic arithmetic. Lambros prevailed, being the mayor at the time, and retained the teacher, but the effort to marginalize the children's education reemerged every so often. As the years sped along, condemnations of book learning increased. Cast against provincial wisdom and an understanding of the land and its simple people, warnings of the evil intent lurking upon the pages of literature became more frequent. In time, the issue regurgitated along the lines of political or religious allegiances and so, the heated variance and dissent over water systems flowed roughly along these polluted courses of men's minds.

6

Lambros remained standing at his table having rebuffed the half-truths and dull-witted reservations of his mustachioed audience with what he deemed the inexorable logic of modern innovation. But he still felt his performance inadequate. His infamous temper surged through him like a fever combating the infection of irrationality, a debilitating business that made him dizzy.

"Nothing but a hole in the water," he mumbled to Vasili, regarding his efforts of persuasion. His skull ached above the eyes and atop his wits, but he resisted the temptation to defame Avram. The Cypriot had proven his skill at blending his neighbors' reticence with long-standing indignations. His intrigues had apparently garnered him a league of support. Suddenly, he was an adversary commanding respect. For the first time in many years, Lambros felt the irksome sense of being captive, imprisoned by an enemy whose frequent encounters he could neither avoid nor surmount, reminiscent of the aversion he endured in his last days in Apollonia, the chronic disgust he felt in the company of authoritative, blue-lipped Turks. Despised, back then, for his indifference to what he saw as a second-rate, parasitical culture, the Ottomans, as he preferred to call them, were in his rendition nothing but a patriarchy of power. Incestuous, bloodthirsty, prideful, with no accomplishments to speak of except laying waste to armies of peasants or what he imagined were fattened Hapsburgs prone to opulence and feminine luxuries. Any civilization the Ottomans possessed they bought, if at all, with blood, he believed, or else proverbial palms greased through the savvy of scheming Greek and Armenian spies. A bureaucracy clothed in the theology of militarism, crumbling from its immoral inception. A little insight can be a ruinous thing. He could not help this mind-cleansing resentment. When in Apollonia and its nearby villages, the blind conformity a Turk could educe was an authority before which he felt the embarrassing need to cower in an abundance of caution and self-preservation.

"Whatever good they gathered from the likes of Mohamed they abandoned a long time ago," he uttered under his breath to an Assyrian, a converted Christian and neighbor in Apollonia who hailed from Urmia, the land of his ancestors. The Urmian turned out to be a liar who betrayed Lambros, informing on his every word and deed to the Turkish authorities.

"What do you mean?" The Urmian had asked.

"Everything they possess is stolen from Byzantium or Persia or your ancestors," Lambros said, as if he knew anything about vanquished Assyrians or Ottoman legacies. The Urmian's response made him shiver.

"They knew enough to take the very best, though. You know, you can be sliced for kebob and fed to their street hounds for such blasphemy." Lambros understood already. "But I won't repeat what you've said, brother, so you needn't worry."

"All converts are to be mistrusted," Lambros told his cousins after the incident. The disingenuous use of the word brother had incited his early exodus from Apollonia.

Only a month ago, in hushed conversations, Avram had asked Lambros to intercede and help cure his obsession, the pathological urge to resurrect Maria in the foible of indifference that was Danäe. Lambros attempted to dissuade him, gently.

He had mistakenly assumed that Avram possessed no particular interest in Lake Vegoritis. Nor, did he believe, he had ever raised his voice in opposition to its use, when in fact, upon the initial suggestion of irrigation, Avram was overcome with a flood of intuition like a gypsy seer peering into what he perceived would be the bleak manmade landscape of a parched, waterless earth.

"Once you build a machine to make things easier, it will take a new machine to fix what it ruins," Avram warned. Foremost in his resentment, however, was that irrigation would prove far more beneficial for the grain and tobacco farmers in the valley than the fruit growers like him, perched upon the hills and ridges to the Northeast of the village. Of course, it would delight the village women, bequeathed the luxury of running water. This became another reason to resist it, Avram insisted, since it would marshal the habit of additional demands for luxury, luxuries incompatible with lives pulled from the hard clay and the lake. He was convinced of the inevitable desiccation of the region surrounding Vegoritis, and while he did not truly perceive it as a problem plaguing the entire earth, it would surely become a problem for their insular society. Having not uttered a word of discontent to Lambros, Avram had indeed engaged in a discreet and cautious instigation of allies denouncing the idea of the pumping station and promoting it as a clever vestige of hollow leftist promises, a position seemingly contrary to the very notion of progress, but one skillfully integrated and garnered nonetheless.

"What do you think will happen when Vegoritis goes dry," Avram had privately argued to Gallanos, "that the Russian proletariat will run to you with a canteen to quench your thirst? Don't be stupid," he told him. "Their lofty ideas are nothing but schemes. Everyone wants Greece to dry up like the Arabian Desert. Then they will use the Bulgarians and Albanians as mercenaries and claim her for themselves. Then someday, Achilles and Odysseus will be hailed as one of their ancestors and the legacy of their sloppy tongue." His anger was palpable when he spoke of such political implications. "The Bolsheviks are no different from the Turks. They could not care one iota for the rest of Greece. It's the sea they want, our miraculous, temperate sea and its depths, and the islands that they don't have. Maybe the Kaisers or the English or the other book-blushers swooning over the idea of Greece, who are in love with the ancients, will stop them, but maybe they won't."

Confuting his opposition and the flood of questions prompted by Avram's timely departure, Lambros sat down to his now foamless demitasse. Vasili leaned forward and looked him in the eyes to calm his apprehension.

"How much pipe and how many men will it take to make it all the way to the fields?"

"The engineer will calculate this for us when he looks things over next week."

"Andreas and I will help you then," Vasili assured him.

"Whose land were you thinking best suited for this, cousin?" Andreas said leaning forward to avoid the reaction the response might elicit from the men straining to listen in. Heads rotated. Lambros stifled his reply and spun a final glance about the room.

"Take your pick," he said. As quickly as that, the conversation vaporized like a puff of smoke. One could hear the *barbas* slurping their coffees, hurrying their words in crouching vocalizations, another belching an audible accompaniment to his digestive disorders and Yianko chewing on a sesame stick.

"Damn it, Yianko, give me another coffee or something, it's noisy in here," Lambros said, ready for provocation. Yianko ignored him.

A moment later, Lazaros Zervas pushed his outstretched digits onto the table, lifting himself up from his seat. During the heat of the debate, he had sat silently, savoring his thoughts, stroking his beard and jotting notes to himself on a small piece of paper, shifting his attention only to gaze through the window facing the naked perimeter of Kythera. He greeted Vasili and Andreas when they entered but did not change his vantage in order to sit with them. They seemed genuinely surprised to see him there. Now he strolled over to their table, carefully pulling the remaining chair out with both hands and sitting without utterance, appearing friendly, but with the guarded benevolence of a stranger.

"You may use the portion of my land that dips down to the lake, where it borders on Terzello's little spit of rock," he said in a rather odd, unhurried way, looking around the room after he spoke, making eye contact with the men at other tables not privy to the conversation. He looked at Vasili and then out the window toward Kythera again. "It's a bit further to have to dig and lay pipe, but I won't require compensation or rent. I only ask that you situate the whole wretched business as far from my domicile as possible, so the noise of the engine doesn't disturb my sleep." Lambros was dumbfounded. "You and your engineer will still need to persuade the others along the way, though," Lazaros continued. "As you can see, Avram has been busy, poisoning the well to the idea. He's been at it for months, you know. They're convinced that if our little enclave is fitted with plumbing, we'll be at the mercy of others. Foreigners and communists will descend upon us like a swarm of locusts or the Turks may want to come back." Lambros inquired with nothing but a glance. He studied his face as if he were an apparition preparing for an imminent vanishing, or waiting for a lunatic's reversal of temperament, the clam followed by an outburst of curses. Here was a man who barely uttered a sentence to him in the years he had known him and now was offering up his solitude like a plate of sweets. He noted the use of the word *us* in describing himself among the village of Greeks. This was a new perspective as well. Most of the villagers derided Lazaros as the *Americanaki*, the little American. They openly worried that America might decide to send Greece all her mentally disturbed.

"Is he talking to me?" Lambros whispered to his cousins with caution.

"I think so," they both said.

"I am," Lazaros said, flashing his teeth in a mad grin. "I have quite a bit of lakefront land between you and your fields."

———◆———

At that time, Vasili and Andreas were among the few in the village who enjoyed any rapport with Lazaros. The brothers had earned his respect and gratitude for the help they provided him in completing his abode, scratched and concealed amid the cliffs facing the lake. "A secret within a secret," Vasili called the place. The only other individual who knew him at all was Danäe, by virtue of the interest she shared in his books, then her countless questions about America and, finally, her ardent ear for highbrow western music, she preferring the intimate mood swings and chromatics of Chopin and German lieder and the manly splendor of Wagner, especially *Tannhäuser* and *Parsifal*. Her father had taken her to Bayreuth to experience both. Lazaros preferred the jeu de perlé and the high Renaissance, whose polyphonies he had inexplicably linked in his mind to turn of the century modernists.

"Embellished vibrato and bombast is the demise of music," he argued to Danäe, "and that assiduous staccato musicians have toe-tapped to ever since Scarlatti." Hyperbole for its own sake, she believed it to be.

The rest of the villagers possessing any curiosity, viewed Lazaros as a peculiarity at best, a foreigner who spoke what sounded like an exaggerated and oddly accented Greek, perhaps, as they speculated, because he was hiding from a speckled past and from those who knew him well enough. Austere, brown-bearded, a withered willow of a man, yet below the beard, still in his thirties, Lazaros looked like someone who had come to despise the most fundamental enterprises of the living - eating, sleeping and procreating. He inherited the estate of his uncle, an old man from America, Antonis Zervas, a beloved emigrant referred to by the locals as Ó *Neyorkesos*.[30] Old man Zervas lived in an old Turkish house erected upon a lonely tract of dried grass and gravel along the isolated tassel of cliffs east of the village, a tract of land he won in a card game.

The house was barely visible to passersby. At its highest point among the rocks, the parcel twisted at an abrupt, reptilian angle down to inaccessible jagged steeps and then out again toward the lake. Essentially, a worthless haven for ground wasps, snakes and rodents, the plot was as close as the wolves would venture to the haven of men. Too rocky even

---

30 the New Yorker

for fruit and olive trees to be cultivated, the land mimicked Kythera in places, virtually barren of vegetation except for a scraggly mountain sage whose elfin magenta blossoms flowered profusely throughout the aestival seasons, but whose stem and leaves were unfit for decent tea and so tough and unsavory that even goats would not eat them.

When he first arrived, Lazaros immediately preferred the most secluded vista and was generally unimpressed with the large, abandoned house, which the Neyorkeso had inhabited with his entourage of animals, both wild and domestic, and which faced in the direction of the dirt road and village commerce. Lazaros commissioned a builder from Edessa to build him a shelter facing the lake. The spot he selected was famous and named by locals and the fisherman of Farangi with the grammatically questionable "*Mavrotripa*."[31] Essentially a cave, it appeared at a distance as an unnatural blemish mottled upon the face of a formidable pitch of chard-blasted rock above the green-brushed shores of Vegoritis. Like the largest in a series of poking toe prints left by titans, Mavrotripa possessed a cavernous shaded core and a great unyielding boulder for a crown. The opening was twelve meters across and ten deep. In the early morning and late afternoon it cast somatic mirages from its interior walls out to any ambitious fishing boats, sun-baked illusions of men shaped liked beasts, ambling aquatics and large bull headed phantasms, reflecting sunrays off its stalactite-encrusted ceiling seven meters above its wind polished floor.

Halfway through his work, the builder, receiving his fee in full and having extracted much of the usable materials for the project from the old Zervas house, leaving the house uninhabitable, abandoned the job and ran off with a worker's daughter, absconding to an enchanting cliff top *Hora* [32] on the remnants of a sleepy Cycladic atoll. The girl's father vowed to behead the seducer, thrusting the tiny mountain village of Akration into an infamously gory feud. The builder had managed to outfit the interior of Mavrotripa for a hermit's survival. There was an opening between the boulder and the mountain supporting it, through which smoke could rise from a fire, and he had built a flue. And there

---

31 μαυρότρυπα - the black hole

32 χώρα - main town

was raw framing of oak and olive wood and reflective white stucco covering the cobwebbed stone to the rear of the cave. But he had not begun work on the more daunting project of the façade, upon which habitability was contingent.

Enthralled by Lazaro's architectonic inspiration, emboldened by the challenge of hauling stone and wood beams to the lofty heights of Mavrotripa, intrigued by the engineering intricacies required to meet Lazaro's ascetic specifications for the fascia and portico and his desire for concealment, Vasili volunteered to finish the project, without consulting his brother. The price was the cost of the materials, a reasonable allowance for a day's work, an occasional bottle of ouzo and an open invitation to visit their creation when the urge came.

"Have you lost your mind?" Andreas complained. "What this madman wants is not possible! And it's certainly not possible for the two of us to accomplish." It was common knowledge that the eloping builder had employed a crew of six from his home village to haul materials to the site.

Lazaros wanted his lair to disappear the way paint, applied thickly with a palate knife, becomes visible in its application upon too detailed an observation, but disappears upon viewing the work in its entirety and at the intended distance. In this case, he wanted invisibility from the only place the cave would be detectable, up from the surface of the lake. The result of the labor was an architectural marvel, a miniature monastic refuge visible only to those who ventured into the cove and preyed upon those deepest fathoms of the lake for sustenance, a very few men. The fascia underwent a remarkable transformation from a grotto surrounded by jagged rock, originally impeding ingress, into a contiguous surface with its environs. Painstakingly, Vasili and Andreas applied the thickest of stuccos in a painterly blend of crushed stone and the russet soil taken from the nearby footpaths. The application magically redacted the dark blemish of Mavrotripa from view, matching the granite hue of its precipitous terrain and becoming discernible only upon foreknowledge and close inspection. The rough, hand-hewn windows were in irregular shapes and sizes and added to the cloistered appearance of the dwelling. But it was the remarkably unobtrusive arch of its oak door, shadowed by a lintel of rock, which revealed the breadth of its maker's talent. A work of consummate arti-sanship, Vasili carved the door, a dancing bas-relief of nymphs and naiads, centaurs, gorgons and griffins, in the courtyard of his home, over the course of a preoccupied autumn, through to its completion in the heart of winter. He realized his work without a novice's trial and error. The gifts of a subtle aesthetic, a nimble hand and an eye for ana-tomical proportion all proclaimed their birth. Andreas had borrowed from Lazaros a slim volume of drawings depicting the whirlwind of legends and myth the American had so vividly sketched in words for the brothers. Vasili studied the book and made a paper drawing, a one-to-thirty scale preceding his work in wood. At one point, maniacally focusing upon the loaned volume, Lazaros repeatedly asked for its return, even contemplating rescission of the contract when a response was not forthcoming.

Upon completion, through a cloak of vaporous fog, on a Sunday morning when no one was milling about to observe or comment, Vasili and Andreas dragged the door by ox drawn cart. Then, without speak-ing, as the sun burned the fog into the sheerest of mists, they carried the door up the cliff. Lambros and Stratos helped them, and set it between a trilith of heavy beams framing the solitary cleft haunting the numi-nous undulations of the lake. Lazaros acknowledged the return of his book with great relief and entered his new dwelling. A fire was burn-ing on the remaining portion of stone floor with not a whiff of smoke to spoil the fresh air. Absorbing the stark symmetrical beauty of its interior, he inhaled the scent of the fir planks sloping above as a ceiling. He turned and gazed out upon the spectacle of Vegoritis and thanked the brothers, embracing them warmly, having grown weary of living in the remnants of the old house. Nervously seeking his patron's final approval, Vasili escorted him back through the grotto and onto the small stone landing facing the lake, shut the heavy door and revealed his carved masterwork. Lazaros had not seen the dwelling or the door's exterior until then. The artist forbad him to visit Mavrotripa altogether until his work was completed. Overcome with emotion, Lazaros dabbed his eyes and reached for the maker's hands, reverently touching his lips to the callused knuckles as if they had delivered the Eucharist or the curative of his soul.

Back in the kafenio, Lazaros stood from the table to leave, followed by the cousins Lambrou. Each man took his turn shaking his hand robustly, in the American fashion. This drew a wink from Yianko and the few stragglers and barbas remaining in the place. Lambros was pleased but still appeared anxious, swallowing the dry aftertaste of doubt settling in his throat. Lazaros risked the discontent of his neighbors who already barely tolerated his peculiarities and his pronouncements, ranked among the mumblings of a congenital idiot.

"Everything comes down to water for you, Lambros. You are Anaxi-something-or other reborn," Yianko laughed, "or one of those ancient windbags."

"Thales," Lazaros corrected him, "water is Thales. The nozzle of the bellows is Anaximander. He believed that there is something indestructible out there and that everything must return to the very thing that it came from. But both the static and the ephemeral pay reparations, don't they? Being is subjected to the decrepitude of time."

"Okay, *kserola*,"[33] Yianko mumbled.

"Throw out the corpses but save the dung," Lazaros replied. "Heraclites."

"Christ and the Virgin, I regret saying anything," Yianko complained. Lazaros turned away and spoke to Lambros.

"Work on persuading Terzellos and his sons," he whispered to the cousins. "They're apparently the wedding chest and daydream of every maiden in the village. Fathers are willing to give up a heavy dowry, an inheritance, to gain such son-in-laws. Don't ask me why. They're as ornery as donkeys. Speak with Kyriazis, too. He's been negotiating with Gallanos to purchase the high ground abutting Avram's little mound of fruit trees. You know, the ones rising uphill from the valley, just past the old Turkish wall. The trees are old and fruitless. That may be an ideal location to extend the pipe down to the valley. Gallanos wants to remove the trees and plant grapevines, for his son to manage. His son has big plans as well. I hear he wants to marry Timonakis' eldest daughter, the one they call Nomia. He wants to breed enough new little Lathrans to populate a whole village himself. She's a wide-hipped Naiad, so he may accomplish his goal. Once you

---

33 ξερολας - know-it-all

persuade Terzellos and Kyriazis of the value of a manmade spring, the others just might follow. Gallanos wants more mouths to chew his bread. You should taste the bread the French make," he digressed, "as tasty as his impermeable dough, but soft and yielding like a needy woman. That's another matter, I know," he said, admitting his distractedness. "Doxiades has also mentioned needing water to expand his barnyard, or whatever that awful place is, for his reeking pigs. They drink a lot of water, I suppose. I've heard him say as much with my own ears. Then there are the women of the village. Water for crops and livestock is fine, boys, but water and the soapy cleanser for every kitchen and washboard - that will persuade the real bosses around here! It is women, who control the bed and bellies of men, for more than two-thirds of their miserable lives. I suspect it's the same in this little crook of the world, or at least enough to change the minds of the husbands."

"How do you know all of this? I've never seen you speak to a single one of them with more than a hello," Vasili said.

"Yianko . . . he tells me everything, all the gossip. He's like an old woman that one, and I'm his pet goat. He talks to me to civilize me, to keep me from eating his flowers. It's funny because he thinks I'm not listening." Lazaros turned to leave but looked back toward Yianko and acknowledged him.

"Goodbye, Mister Billows. Are you going back to your cave?" Yianko asked with a hint of sarcasm. Lazaros grinned and waved goodbye with his palm pointing toward him.

"You're cursing me?" Yianko asked, knowing the answer.

"Good day, my friend," Lazaros said.

"Thank you, sir." Lambros said politely. The four of them shook hands again.

"I'll give you one last piece of advice, since I'm in so talkative a mood," Lazaros said as he prepared to leave. "Keep the priest out of the debate. Naturally, he will try not to take sides, but you know how he is, like a shepherd's dog, preferring to keep his flock close at hand and manageable. In the end, being a man of authority, he will side with those who abhor change." He turned to leave but then hesitated and stood for a moment with his mouth partially open as if deciding whether to go. "A priest will bless his whiskers first, won't he?"

7

The priest in question was Pater Alexis Goreckis. He did not reside among the hundred or so souls calling Lathra home, but he could, and did, exert as much influence as a patriarch over so precariously a marshaled clan. His flock esteemed him as their symbol of the tenancy of Christ, but they also wondered aloud if he belonged in a rural diocese. A common simile among locals indicating distress in a social setting was "like a priest, nauseous with the smell of incense." This maxim came to be after a specific scandalous episode in the surrounds of Apollonia, where the sexually tormented archimandrite cast aside his censer and robes and succumbed to the devious, swollen-lipped Hetaerae of a Turkish magistrate. An impious man-eating feline, her lewd expression, pierced nostril and indiscrete beauty mark distended the otherwise censored passions of the virile cleric.

"Look at her," the archimandrite told an underling on the eve of his demise, as she walked by, the pendulum of hips swinging hypnotically, her scent impaling him like a poison arrow, "she's built for sin and it's God who has sent her to torment me. I fear I will not survive her presence in this world." Once consummating her conscious seduction and desire had spun its taut cocoon about the archimandrite's wits, the Mistress of the East, as he called her, abandoned him for another specimen of authoritarian manhood, a caliph of sorts, an Arab with camel bags full of money, passing though Apollonia in search of his own demise. Thereafter, the shamed cleric, who came to despise the very smell of churches, disappeared. Legend had him extending his days in the impenetrable, menaced heart of East Africa, administering the liturgy in the open air of its desolate poverty, in the land of unsounded souls, preaching the gospels with the sky as his dome.

Villagers attended Alexi's liturgies if not for their religious significance then for the frequent theater and consistent attempt at edification of the simple and occasionally illiterate. His was one of the few avenues of entertainment, with the exception of traveling puppeteers and gypsies, whose annual stopovers of startling dramas and raucous comedies kept children sleepless for days and everyone reenacting the characters for months. Religion for Lathrans was like an old friend lulling you with confidences and promises of loyalty in the future. Conducted with genuine fervor, Alexi's liturgical canons were nonetheless sporadic, since he serviced three local congregations, of which Lathra was the smallest and most isolated. Generally, he graced each parish with a visit on alternate Sundays. When weather did not permit travel, he came even less frequently. During Holy Week, the citizens of the other two nearby villages traveled to whichever church was hosting. On other high days of prayer and fasting, like the Annunciation or the Epiphany, he tried duplicating within the same day, at the churches in Arnissa and Perea. The unpredictability of his schedule kept all three flocks guessing, his way of providing an inkling of the divine puzzle of God's will. But mostly the uncertainty depended upon whether a burial service was suddenly required, which trumped a marriage already scheduled, or whether an infant might enter into the mysteries of the faith. On more than a few occasions he left wedding and baptismal parties in the lurch, languishing without a blessing at the reception, an affront blistering beneath the breath of hosts.

In Lathra, he performed his idiosyncratic liturgies in the rustic stone chapel of Saint George, hovering between Eurus-swept heights overlooking both the village square and the sparkling reflections of Vegoritis, with its intricately carved yet potent altar and resonance of icons influenced by the aesthetic legacy of Fragos Katelanos. St. George was Alexi's favorite church. Congregants bore relatively attentive witness to his sermons, often with more gravity than they thought worthy, since most of them failed to understand much of what he was preaching. His stipend was meager, essentially paid only for services on high holy days but not Sunday liturgies. This meant that gifts from parishioners were his mainstay. A chicken, a basket of newly harvested fruit, some sweets for his children, a shank of mutton, a bottle of wine or cognac, or a few loaves of fresh bread, which he would wrap in his robes and carry home to his family. He supplemented his income by translating foreign documents into Greek, when village or familial business required, or simply writing letters for parishioners who would not admit to illiteracy.

Unbeknownst to Pater Alexi, or anyone else for that matter, in the last few years of his paschal duties, an anonymous hand had been providing him with the expressively prepared text of his sermons. Early on Sunday mornings, Lazaros would awake in the darkness and stumble his way to the Church, whose doors possessed no locks. He would light a candle before Orthros, leave a coin offering in the velvet-lined basket and quietly lay a carefully hand-printed text, rarely more than a page in length, on the ornate little table within the altar, the table upon which the holy bread received its ritually incision into sacred morsels of the Body of Christ. At first, Pater Alexi ignored the gifts, throwing the first few out without reading them. Eventually though, he held only a few back from the congregation, the ones whose theological inquiry echoed in too eccentric a voice, or those the author modeled after his readings of certain Latin exegetes. These the priest kept in a velvet pouch, at the foot of the narrow armoire holding a spare set of vestments. Meister Ekhart was a source Alexi recognized at once and rejected. He read them for himself, but offered no other soul a peak. Others were in the style of or a reaction to the fathers of the early Church, like the commentaries of Origen, which Lazaros enjoyed for their measured gnostic flavor. Some of the homilies were full of verve, sounding of the Reverend Harlan Johnson, whose voice echoed outside of the Tabernacle Baptist Church in Chester, Pennsylvania, sermons that Lazaros stopped on occasion to listen to as a teenager. Lazaros and his mother would walk by the Tabernacle whenever they attended church from time to time on their visits to his aunt, who lived in town with her daughter.

"Go on in," he would tell his mother. "I'll be in soon." He wanted to listen to Harlan Johnson, the displaced Alabaman, the warrior for Christ, preaching with a tongue of fire. A tall white steeple and cavernous hall with numerous pews, the Tabernacle sat directly across the street from an Orthodox Church, also named after Saint George. Situated on an elevated lot above the sidewalk, the Greek Church was a converted edifice with a grand wall of surrounding its half-acre of grass and trees, the wall with vaulted rock atop it, matching the church's stained glass clerestory. To Lazaros, as a boy, it may as well have been the Temple of Solomon.

In those instances when such indiscernible influences proved too confounding Alexi would hold the sermons back and substitute his own, or substitute a paraphrased version of the homilies of John Chrysostom, like the time Lazaro's thesis suggested the irrelevance of the distinction at the heart of the Nicene Creed, of Christ begotten not made, a heretical conception, Alexi concluded. Another was an abbreviated piece noting the way iconographers depicted the seraph in holy icons hovering above an earthly scene in their angelical bearing, or standing before an unobtrusive color of heaven, either blue or an unearthly green. In either case, the feet of the seraph seemed planted perfectly square. Yet when touching the corruption that is the earth, the feet of saints, martyrs, of God's angels or Christ Himself, the iconographers depicted as slightly askew.

"Who looks at their feet, for God's sake?" Alexi said aloud, standing before the icons, verifying the observation. "You're supposed to look into their eyes," he said, as if addressing the author of the sermon. A third was a firebrand sermon of how men naturally fall into corruption at the mere slight of hand of demons, and that the father of lies himself may seek redemption from the ingenerate God before men know to ask for it.

Alexi soon recognized the eccentricity of the sermons as compared to his own bland elucidation of the gospels and began studying and quickly memorizing as much of the text as he could for his own use. As time went by, he abandoned the pretext of memorization and simply read them slowly, deliberately, as if he were reciting a poem or announcing a noble invitation, or with a trembling voice, telling the parable of the prodigal son for the first time. The kergyma was usually mindful of that Sunday's gospel and rarely argumentative, more akin in style to the poetry of the psalms, and rarely contained a mere regurgitation of sanctioned theology or the gospel story itself. They conveyed the faith in the manner of a prayer, or like an icon, as a window to heaven, likened by Pater Alexi to the way the lake reflects the image of youth standing along its banks, always lanky, narrowly discernable, a floating impression of the light of Orthodoxy obscured by the ripples of human frailty.

Aside from this, Lazaros and the priest scarcely engaged each other for the first four years of their acquaintance since Lazaros rarely attended a liturgy. Pater Alexi could not remember when he surmised the homilies to be a gift from him or remotely from Danäe, for there were no others in the village who could mimic the psalmist so lyrically, but he never mentioned the suspicion to anyone. He read them aloud and let the parishioners think what they would. If the author was standing among the congregants, so be it. The author seemed to want to remain anonymous anyhow since never was a page of them signed.

"Unlike Christ Himself," he argued in the little mirror above the wooden pegs that held his vestments, "it's the message that presses upon the souls of men, not the messenger." Such was the sentiment when taken to task for the garbled meaning of what he read to his flock. For their part, the parishioners usually reacted with patience and a measure of tolerance of what they often deemed to be the simple-minded ramblings of an overindulging cleric.

"He's senile," the old women would whisper. "Tipping too much *tsipouraki* [34] if you ask me, when he should be sipping the bouquet of Christ," the cantors and old men squeaked like iron hinges. Alexi, who was generally bored by his third liturgy of the month, would read to himself at certain points of the Orthros and even during liturgy. He would stand before the holy table and read poetry or theological treatises while the cantors stretched their sonorous doxologies. The less familiar congregants mistook this as studiousness, necessary for liturgical purposes. Once, when a visiting cleric confronted him on the habit, he defended himself after the service, informing him that the reading selection was always of some religious significance.

"The maniac is lying about what he does at Christ's table," the visiting cleric told Alexi's deacon. Strictly speaking, Alexi was not lying. The poetry was religious, albeit Western, the hymns of the Breviary, the Carmelite poets, St. John of the Cross, Hildebrand. He indulged in entrancing the mind to a degree he thought minor and felt as if he was not betraying his office as a priest. But this was a rationalization only Alexi believed. His wife also thought less of him for it, but never told him so.

One would not say that the inhabitants of his diocese categorically obeyed Alexi, but by in large they respected his opinions with certain mutinous exceptions. He objected vehemently to parents who baptized their children with customary Christian names, and then would turn around and permit siblings or neighbors to call them by some ancient moniker or concoct a Turkish or pagan *paratsoukli*. [35] Thus, he disapproved, for example, of the name Danäe, for its mythical and seductive

---

34 τσιπουράκι - grape skin pomace brandy or distillate whose principle value is the swift inebriation it bestows

35 παρατσούκλι - pet name or moniker

associations. In her instance, of course, he overlooked it with nothing more than a passing comment, recalling for her the debate found in the *Dialogue with Trypho* and the *Discourse to the Greeks*, wherein Justin Martyr investigated the pagan origins of a virgin birth. Zeus and his adulterous rapes in the form of golden rain, as a bull or a satyr, contrasted with the birth of Christ, the very purpose of the Parthena Maria fully explained. Danäe understood what he was getting at, but avoided taking offense, dismissing his didactic, nearly scolding tone as a hazard of his vocation as a steward of souls, she would say.

Everyone had some brand or another of paratsoukli. The unofficial crowning was usually the result of a fellow villager or member of the victim's family noting some fidget or character trait or physical shortcoming, or a particularly scathing, amusing or embarrassing episode befalling the victim, an escapade or escape from harm. Hence, Timonakis' eldest daughter, who's Christian name was Nikoleta, was donned *Neronomia* or *Nomia* when she was yet a babbler. Her aunt noticed the child's propensity for playing with water, for dancing wildly, and peeing herself whenever her father bowed the tensile lyre of Crete or slurred a welcome variant to Anatolian renditions of Orphean revelry.

"She will marry a musician and live by the lake," her quixotic, devising aunt prophesied as the girl's graceless entrechats reduced control of her bladder. The oracle, if not fulfilled was at least buoyed by the prediction. As a girl, Nomia assumed a fascination with Vegoritis, taking every chance to play upon its less trodden shorelines and discover its hiding places, at times not returning home by nightfall and forcing her father to send out search parties. Kyriazis' son, whom she eventually married, grew to be an able amateur singer with a sensual voice described by the younger women as "the honeydew of submission."

"What heathen pea brain afflicted you with that name, daughter?" Pater Alexi protested bitterly, overhearing the other children shouting, "Neronomia the mermaid".

Danäe and Elissa commonly referred to Kyriazis' wife as "the Medusa". The bee keeper who lived beyond the valley southeast of Lathra, but counted himself a Lathran nonetheless, was called the *Petalouda*,[36] named by the men for no other reason than his being observed

---

36 πεταλούδα - butterfly

on a single occasion gesturing with an effeminate carriage, making the children howl with laughter. The Petalouda's three salacious daughters were "the Maenads," purportedly avoided by the young men of the village. At least one glaring exception was Terzello's otherwise gauche son, Spiros, whose paratsoukli was *O Ethopios*,[37] for his narcissism and stagy overreactions upon hearing his name in any capacity but praise. As a young man approaching twenty, seizing the opportunity to cure his erectile insatiability, he endeavored to wrestle the virginity of all three of the Maenads before each of them reached the age of eighteen.

Pelagia and Alexandra Gallanos, prudish, gangly, thin-haired, but carefree and endearing daughters of the miller, who appeared nothing like their morose father or inane and corpulent mother, were by their late teenage years invoked by the more vicious tongues among the young men as the *Papadies*,[38] predicted by all never to find husbands. Terzellos was *O Gavos*,[39] behind his back, of course. The origin of this cross was unknown but most likely a smear upon his profound illiteracy and slow-to-speech coarseness. Lambro's paratsoukli was *O Lalas*, a silly play on the echo of his given name and surname. Pater Alexi was, beneath the breath of the cautious, *O Minotavros* (the Minotaur). Merciless derision, a sforzando of every living soul known in one's lifetime, continued unabated and in many cases followed a person to their demise.

Alexi also protested the inveterate rituals of Lathran transplants, whether recently contrived or having their origin in some prehistoric race, scornfully berating ancient practices and superstitions such as sprinkling the snippets of children's locks onto the surface of Vegoritis after celebrating the child's first Christian name day.

"Petty little remnants of idolatry," he carped. "You people are hillbillies born of bears. No better than the Naodites you see hovering behind every tree."

"What's the difference Pater? The old people speak of the Naodites, you bore us with your long-dead saints and your Holy Ghost," Dimitri Baralís once responded.

---

37 ηθοποιός - the actor

38 παπαδιές - the priest's old ladies

39 γκαβός - the dim one

"God forgive him, for he's a young fool and has no idea what he's saying," Alexi said with the kind of condescension that often instigated argument. "Don't wager against God, Mister sperm-for-brains," alluding to Pascal's wager when no one listening would have ever heard of him.

"I don't need your prayers, Pater," the boy responded insolently.

"God will damn you then!" Alexi responded, losing his patience, "for denying Him like a common heathen. Christ will forget your name when it comes time to vouch for a big mouth like you. So you'd better recant!" When Dimitri Baralís died of a self-inflicted hunting wound, that very year, his family overheard rumors. Alexi had mumbled something disrespectful to his deacon: "God decided not to wait to kick his ass into hell." When he heard the comment, Dimitri's brother wanted to choke the life out of the priest at his brother's forty-day memorial and make a show of it. He waited until after the service and grabbed Alexi by his robes, twisting him to the ground before Lambros and the other men interceded. The scandal followed the priest on his rounds like a homesick goat until old man Baralís, unable to bear being near his son's grave, moved his entire clan to Evia, to a fate unknown. Others in the village blamed the hunting accident on the Naodites, their revenge for the youth disparaging them.

"There's a spy among us," they speculated. "The snitch squealed on the poor boy, and now look what happened, he shot himself."

Of particular outrage to Alexi was the raising of bonfires upon the equinox, wasting valuable wood resources that participants hauled to the summit of Kythera's naked scalp. This was allegedly a veneration of Phocas the Cyprian, a celebration of sorts instituted by Avram, but Alexi believed none of it. He insisted it was a regurgitation of island sun worship.

"The ignorant hoping to ward off the cold of the coming winter," he criticized openly. "Put a coat on, idiots!" Perhaps it was an unrealized Demeter rite transported through time for the sake of the harvest. No one could say exactly. "These are meaningless, pagan imbecilities," Alexi admonished, when he knew they were preparing for the rite. "God will ask what you were doing down here while your brethren were in need and your souls lay unredeemed. What are you going to tell Him? I was tending to the leisure of my idols and lesser gods, O Father of the Universe," he said in a slow, mumbling enunciation. Nevertheless, the stubborn custom from antiquity of creating new gods seemed to trump such ecclesial displeasure, and the flock largely ignored him when he was in such righteously combative moods.

———•———

Lazaros preferred keeping his vicarious attendance to the house of God undisclosed. On Sundays, in the throes of dawn, after delivering the untitled copy of his homily to Alexi's table, he would return home to embrace the remnant of his own faith. As the final canted strains of Orthros undulated across the breeze from the open doors of the church, he would throw open the great door to Mavrotripa and fill his lungs full of bracing morning air before ingesting his breakfast, broken pieces of Gallano's impenetrable bread soaked in a bowl of goat's milk with a heaping teaspoon of refined sugar. One of two meals a day, his milk and other food he kept chilled in clay urns sealed with a large cork, each crock cradled in a fishnet sling and submerged into the lake at the end of a long rope dangling from a stake wedged between a rock and the door. Then, in the open air of the landing, he would perch himself upon his only cushioned chair and read aloud, in English, a chapter or two from his King James, savoring the resonance of the language and the luxury of the cushion, commissioned by him of Yianko's wife, Persephone. No one lurking in the bushes or rocks would have understood what he was reading, except for the obvious phonetic ring to a biblical name or place. This routine then gave way to perusing the mail he received that week. Mail usually comprised of small boxes of books sent from Philadelphia, from his personal library, or recordings of the masterworks of Western music given him by his parents through the years, or those he had personally purchased from Wanamaker's, on monthly excursions with his mother.

On those occasions when church was in session, he would crank his Victrola also shipped from America, and read and notate to its scratchy strains, flexing the muscles of his natural melodiousness with his favorite exercises for the ear, the joyous mordents and cascade of scales of early Beethoven or Schubert, his favorites in the morning. Then, if time permitted, he might move on to a sampling of dulcet lyricism extolled by a Dvorak or Brahms or an occasional Russian and so on, finally closing the morning out with the piano. Debussy, Schumann, Chopin, warmed by the mnemonic embers of what he inferentially came to consider his idyllic youth.

Lazaro's mother, Irini Arvanakis Zervas, a connubial mouthful that failed to suit her discerning aesthetic, trained her son from an early age to appreciate the wonders of Western Europe's fine art and music. A confident, self-motivated woman of unusual learning, she arrived in Philadelphia from Alexandria accompanying certain artifacts extracted from an archeological expedition, the dust-caked bowels of a Ptolemaic tomb linking the inquisitive Miss Arvanakis to the land that her Cretan grandfather found himself drawn to as a scholar of Greco-Egyptian antiquities. She accompanied the artifacts to the University of Pennsylvania, not knowing, of course, that she was destined to remain with them. While she missed Alexandria, Irini found the old American city invigorating from the moment of her arrival. And from her drive in the downy ride of an otherwise cantankerous Buick, fell in love with the surrounding counties, the woodlands with their round, abiding hills and elfin folds of grassy meadow parted by limpid rivulets of measured volatility, swelling into great brown rivers parsing the city, channeling its grand commercial port. For years afterward, she enjoyed walking along the Schuylkill, watching rowers and passersby strolling along its banks. She marveled at the large-limbed specimens of oak, chestnut, maple and the occasional elm, or her favorite, the copper beech, trees she described to her family back in Egypt as great, twisting, primeval creatures stalking civilization within the city's limits. And while the city's zoological garden and museums provided diversions and pleasure to her, it was not until the winter and the happenstance of a short drive east into New Jersey, to the little barrier island of Brigantine, that Irini fell under the spell of the idea of staying in America. Named after a foundered two-mast ship; originally an Indian settlement, and then one for whalers and privateers, the bucolic little ribbon of sand presented itself to the majesty of the Atlantic like a sea nymph entwined with her frothy sailor. The romance of the island and its past intrigued her. She delved into its origins; the name being a variant of the French *brigandin*, the foundered vessel perhaps a model of a more famous French ship commandeered and renamed the *Good Fortune* by its illustrious captain Bartholomew Roberts.

In the early morning of that first lingering winter, she stood utterly alone, staring at the white-capped fury of the ocean, her wool coat buttoned to the chin, a scarf protecting her ears and mouth for as long as she could stand anything around her face. A colony of gulls and seafowl pecked at the sand. Others perched on a bulkhead against a well-worn gray sky, watching her watch them. One flew away for a distant morsel but came back with nothing in its beak. The birds reminded her of the thin, wasted men of Alexandria, waiting on the docks for work. Something in that illustrative moment made the decision for her.

"In all my life I never felt so alone," she wrote to her parents, "but yet I am never alone. The ceaseless roar of the ocean is my unfailing companion. And you, my dear family, are on the other side of its pacifying chord, unfading, never to adjourn. The sound fills me at once with a savage sadness and an inexpressible bliss. I will stay here until I am no longer so compelled." Until the end of her life, Irini remained drawn to the Atlantic and the barrier island with its tiny lighthouse. She returned every year, staying at the stately hotel on a stanch and grassless dune above the beach, reaffirming her seminal emotion, and because she despised the mosquitoes and shied away from the manners of summer bathers, nearly always in the winter.

Fluent in her native Greek but somewhat less in French, and in time to a conversational extent in English, she bestowed her voracious memory and natural inclination toward music, art and literature upon her son with the gentlest of mandates and predilections. Even as a boy, Lazaros took to the algorithmic intricacies of music as naturally as one could expect in a home without instruments. This was initially at the expense of the plodding impassivity of reading books from his parents' library. He studied piano from the age of six with a teacher whom he soon surpassed with Gieseking-like agility and memory of a score. The overpowering urge to play endured until he completed grammar school. Thereafter, insidiously one must conclude in hindsight, the insatiability of reading the next undiscovered dip of the quill came to share and slowly supplant absolute pitch and music as a career or primary interest.

Lazaros was born but a few hundred meters from the Greek Orthodox Church that sprung up in the center of the city a decade later.

His first exodus from the dark fissure of his mother's fluidity, his first breath was in a splendid suite at the Pennsylvania Hospital, where, as his mother remembered lovingly, "we were treated as if I were giving birth to a prince," merely for the fortuitous first nativity of the year, at precisely 12:03 am. Tutored first in highbrow and patristic Greek and only later in the grocer's elocution, Lazaros, of course, learned English in school, but also with a clever ear, picked up the interestingly blended concoction of his mother's academic inflection and his father's indiscernible brogue. He struggled in school as a young boy, unable to sustain focus upon dry instruction and rote memorization and suffered the humiliation of his father's fits of disappointment whenever Lazaros would fail to read his lessons promptly or properly, sullenly recalling the tersely pointed push of his head toward the open book sitting upon his desk.

"Read, read, read," his father growled impatiently. The young Lazaros, the embolus, the "*kefala*"[40] as he was sometimes derided for his large and embolic head, which he grew into as a young man, preferred playing outdoors with his friend Freddy Chycka, as he declared out of the corner of his mouth in a snide Edward G. Robinson retraction of the tongue. "My pal, Freddy Chycka," he loved repeating. Freddy was the neighborhood hooligan, the pied piper of aspiring delinquents, three years his senior and a rotten apple according to Lazaro's mother, fit only for saucing. Fortunately or not for Lazaros, he soon lost his friend, shortly after Freddy's influence had entered his blood stream like a drug. Freddy got himself arrested at the age of fourteen for abducting a witless but perky waitress named Roberta, a girl of eighteen. He had convinced her, permissibly at first, to be rope-tied to a tree in an isolated thicket of Fairmount Park. Then, with dissolving consent, stripped and molested her with exploratory tickles and kisses upon "her sour spot," Freddy having not yet arrived at the understanding that the lips might prove more romantic to a girl. This was all before discovery by the girl's brother, her customary driver to the Olympus Diner, where she worked. The malcontent brother left his sister tied to the tree to beat the hapless young seducer nearly senseless, all but leaving permanent handprints about his throat until Freddy knocked him on the head with

---

40 κεφάλας - big head

"whatever I could find, for Christ's sake!" She of the raven locks and black mulberries for eyes, the agreeably plump *kooklitsa*[41] of an old San Juan legacy, frequently observed at the Olympus by Freddy whenever his dad would treat him to hamburgers, was always smoothing and pulling at her uniform, running her hands down the synthetic fabric of her skirt desperately clinging to pleasantly rotund hips. She was also the same kooklitsa who acquiesced to molestation by the lecherous forty-year-old owner, Manos Mihalides, *O Glaros*,[42] his preferred name. Minister of the gnarled, knobby veined, lunar-worshiping cucumber, Manos boasted that one look at his serpentine distension and both whores and virgins alike would yield to the temptation to tame the dragon.

On one watershed occasion, before the episode in the woods, just as the ladies room door delayed in reclaiming the medicinal wintergreen cologne emanating from within, Roberta raised her skirt north of the upper thigh to adjust her slip and stockings, knowing that Freddy was watching. He grew faint. Great pools of saliva collected in his mouth, nearly gagging him. He couldn't help but return at closing to the scene of his education regarding that most arousing of devices, the garter snap. The lights to the restaurant were still on, but when he tried the door, it was locked. Cupping his eyes with his hands against the window, his brow pressed against the breath-sullied storefront, he could see ambulant soles of open-toed footwear pointing skyward from behind booth number eight, and the black hedge of the Glaros, the drooling mustachioed lip framing a set of gritting yellow teeth, giving Roberta, the eventual Mrs. Miguel Sanchez, "the once-over." Freddy learned quickly that the once-over was never really over.

"Damn it, you always want more in fifteen or twenty minutes," he once explained to Lazaros. Sanchez became the matrimonial surname to Roberta's reversal of fortune, once recalled to live in San Juan with her grandmother, the edict issued by her hysterical parents approximately three days after Freddy tied the young Consuela to the tree. Unforeseeably, Roberta's brother served a recidivist sentence for aggravated assault, a negotiated result stemming from his attempted murder

---

41 κουκλίτσα - doll

42 γλάρος - the seagull

of Freddy Chycka, which he naively admitted to while testifying at Freddy's juvenile hearing for debauching his sister.

"After I got him on the ground, I tried my best to strangle the sick bastard," he testified in suddenly fluent English, his wicked grin like a demented jester, "except the little prick hit me on the head with a rock." The translator blushed and fell silent. The judge nodded to the constables. Arrested as he stepped down off the witness stand, he shouted at Freddy: "You better hope they don't put me in the same cell with you."

With the departure of Freddy, Lazaro's preferences soon returned to listening to music with his mother, shopping at Wanamaker's or simply enjoying the impulsiveness and erratic digressions of a cosseted youth. By his fourteenth year, as a feature of his gloominess over losing his only friend and as much as he previously resented his father's commands to read, he slowly grew captivated by the solitary activity, its details easily erasable from the mind's inclinations, ever escalating unto the reclusive enthusiasm of his manhood. Initially, he propelled himself by reading the terse temerity of gun-slinging heroes in those plaudit mythologies of the American West. Wyatt Earp and Doc Holliday were his favorites, men with ungovernable tempers, quite unlike Lazaros. Then from a quick rendezvous with Poe, Crane, Defoe and Melville, in that order, not being so fond of Mister Clemens and southern writers in general, he moved effortlessly through a condensed version of *A Tale of Two Cities*. This choice, inaugurated like all of his early selections, by English teachers, instigated a brief career of reading the entire corpus of Dickens, accomplished roughly within twenty-nine months.

Lazaros became so protective of his paginated property that he would search for hours when a single volume was misplaced and spit his malicious contempt when someone failed to return a book he had loaned him. At times, he felt guilty in his addiction, especially when dwelling upon his mother's loneliness after his father temporarily fell on hard times and took to bouts of gambling and drinking as a profession, chumming around town with two former co-workers, Irishmen who were better at both. At the height of her son's fixation for the written word, Irini preferred watching him play or sleep in the grass beneath the great beech tree in the park near their home rather than grow pale beneath the cloistered lamp of protracted studies and the chronic ingestion of literature. For while Irini could read English she could not sustain the effort over the length of more demanding fiction to keep pace with her son, since reading them in French translation would have been slow going and Greek translations were unavailable. Thus, Lazaros being the respectful and appreciative son that he wanted to be, took pleasure in meticulously re-telling her the stories, or reading her an especially lyrical passage.

Lazaro's father, Alexandros Zervas, was the son of a merchant from Patras and a saintly woman named Ourania Amigladakis. Lazaros never met his grandmother, felled as she was before he was born, in the spark of her still youthful exuberance, by a rock meant for Alexandros, thrown by his youngest brother, whose name Lazaros never learned, striking the young mother in the temple. Maternal radiance sacrificed in an instant. Years later, catapulted into an early manhood and a dark fatalism, the younger brother drowned the guilt-ridden refrain droning in his head, jumping from a tree along the banks of a river and immobilizing his neck. "My mother," he said, before he jumped, longing for burial near her ipheion and iris covered grave, leaving, with this last woeful episode, an appreciably dark mark on his brother Alexandro's already sable soul.

The eldest of the three boys, Alexandros was educated in Athens to become a lawyer. Detesting the banality of the law, he abandoned his studies and went into business with a youthful partner, manufacturing and selling precisely those products that at that time earned his father a living - ceramic and marble replicas of Hellenic era pottery and other trinkets sold to the bourgeoning Athenian tourist trade. As he tired of allocating greater profits to his partner, who possessed the kiln and the skill to fire and paint the product, Alexandros sold him his share in the concern. The trifling sum he received he invested in a ticket to ride to Athens and a business suit that served to bolster his gift of persuasion sufficiently to land him employment with a small exporting company, necessitating travel to London and eventually America. There, under undisclosed circumstances rumored to have been at a dance venue in Spring City, Pennsylvania, he met Irini Arvanakis. He married her in an Episcopal Church in Royersford, graciously permitted to use that genial house of worship for a sacrament conducted by a visiting Orthodox priest. The couple settled nearby in Philadelphia, content to raise their only son, born nine months later.

Later, Alexandros earned a position of ownership in a small marble importing business along the city's Main Line. Fearful of traveling anywhere outside the United States and not being permitted to return to his adopted home, he never returned to Greece. Over the years, he lost all touch with his father and remaining brother, Antonis, the eventual donor of Lazaro's Lathran estate. His cultural estrangement, surmised by some to be due to a morose temperament, was actually an element of a deeply masked impecuniousness of spirit cloaked in the quirk and quandary of homesickness but related to the loss of his mother under the circumstance of a projectile meant for him. In response to such bemused and suppressed emotion, he gravitated to anything Greek to remind his son from whence the spring of Hellenism filled his well. He traveled farther than necessary to patronize fellow Greek merchants, spoke only Greek in the home, despite flamboyant fluency in both crude and discriminatory English, and articulated a marked elitist distaste for the marriage of Greeks with non-Greeks. These habits, which alienated his neighbors and at times his customers, nourished in Lazaros a son's vague resentment at first and then, as he matured, the very opposite - a mystifying and tortured desire to return to Greece in search of some indiscernible epiphany.

Once Lazaros graduated from the University of Pennsylvania, having studied piano, composition and art history, much to his father's dismay, since a modern Hellenistic legacy dominates none of these disciplines, he set out to reclaim the world as a work of art of his own.

"Art must approximate the intent and function of cave drawings to abide the title," he qualified in his youthful arrogance to a tetchy professor, provoking a famous debate ending in fisticuffs. He composed music that attracted some attention, but mostly in the form of invitations for further, albeit higher musicological study. His *String Trio* received a performance and earned an honorable mention at a composition competition in Stowe, Vermont, but he missed the performance for lack of traveling funds and because he misplaced the papers announcing the award, and its time and place. So he never heard the *String Trio* played except as it effervesced in his head.

The work presented difficulties for players, at times requiring them to choose when to bow certain fixed phrases in relation to the other players' parts. Entire passages he meant to have float in time and explained this feature as less his imitation of any fondness for improvisation but more his homage to the unrestrictive and imprecise notation of early polyphones and Byzantine chanting and as he added, "The idea of arresting time through a sequence of impulses in sound." Anticipating the ersatz and short musical attention spans of the future, his desire was to grant the same sense of frivolity and freedom within the confines of fixed notation, as jazz appeared to have.

"The notes are static, but everything else is in flux," he clarified. "You can change the how and when of things but not what you are," he told potential performers, regarding the directive in the score. The response was nearly always the same, polite rejection. One woman, a tall reed-like violinist with lazy eyes, a distinctive beauty mark just above her upper lip and a permanently cheerful set of pearled teeth with prominently pink gums, spent time examining the score.

"I especially like bars 19 through 31, if I could only play the violin part," she said, decrying her own limitation instead of the composer's ear, her verdict provided with a wistful bob of the head and shrug of the shoulders, making her unremitting smile appear simulated. Pity must have welled inside her because she took him by the hand, entered a soundproof closet and tried her hand at the violin part, at times failing, but occasionally, through labored fingering, summoning the urge of the music and then smiling iridescently with her consummation of the triple stop. Lazaro's heart swelled, his lips trembled and his eyes filled with the kind of heavy droplets of memory that cling to one's lashes for a lifetime.

"This is where you deliver something," the woman said after measure 19, "where the drama deserves a strict interpretation. The rest seems like you're trying to cram its entire universe into an instant."

"I am," he acknowledged shyly. Unfortunately, his directive to each player, for random playing of certain parts, proved misunderstood even by his hired scrivener, who charged Lazaros double because the original notation was so sloppy and obscured by little comments across the manuscript. Lazaros was so happy to see the manuscript penned so splendidly, with its deep black ink and italicized flair reminding him of Japanese calligraphy, that he said nothing. The scrivener had relegated the composer's directive of freedom to play a particular passage to the first few stanzas instead of the other heavily condensed parts of the work, those very moments originally intended for the players' interpretive gestures.

His *String Quartet* also received a thorough study by a local quartet of students called The Bigelow Quartet, after he posted an advertisement on the university bulletin board announcing the discovery of a manuscript, the music of an allegedly unknown Czech composer. The ad read in part:

> Wanted - More than adequate technical proficiency required to premier   a newly discovered and yet unpublished String Quartet by the 20th Century Czech composer, Jarmil Vrabec, a student of Leŏs Janáček: The work recently discovered in the archives of the Prague Conservatory remains unperformed to this day. Contact Lazaros Zervas, owner and publisher, etc. etc.

The students took the bait, inviting him to attend a sight-reading of the quartet. Only later did he reveal the ruse, explaining that few musicians would want to try their hand or waste their ear upon a composition by a neophyte, let alone one of Greek origin, Iannis Xenakis being a generally unknown post-Viennese school exception, not yet composing. (Witness the fate of the sonically staggering music of Roberto Gerhardt.) Rather than throw him out for perpetrating the hoax, the cellist, an ingratiating Australian woman, and her unusually sensitive husband, the first violinist, seemed intrigued by the lengths to which Lazaros went to hear his work performed, and befriended him, tolerating his peculiarity and his affinity for fanciful bylines. But even as this act of kindness blossomed, his music career was essentially over. His compositions, perhaps nine in all, sat idly ever after in a box in the basement of his father's house.

Some uncountable years later, upon a chance meeting, an eminent music scholar, Professor Jon Hunt, reviewed the pseudonymously composed *String Trio* and *Chamber Miniatures* and upon the authority of the good professor's official recommendation, the composer from Barcelona, Leonardo Balada, invited the reincarnated primitive of these very same musical intrigues to study composition under him at Carnegie Mellon. The parallel of this fictional plagiarist, the character who takes from the composer what he foolishly deprived himself, holder of the intangibles and manuscripts within his soul, declined the invitation. A fool cloisters his muse and neurosis follows.

STRING TRIO

Insomnia penned for Lazaros his erratically stylized dramas and his prose of dizzying variety. Profuse with characters and events of no particular interest to the pedantic tastes of his peers or publishers, he would finish one work and hastily draft the next on the opposite side of the same scribbled pages. He approached the vocation of art episodically, with little staying power and then suddenly, without much thought, gave it up. It was this way with literary pursuits as it had been with music, a short, prolific burst of creative vitality and then silence. In fact, he composed his prose along the same conceptual lines as his music, soon abandoning that formula for the structural genius of the great masters.

Then, as if disgusted with art, he began entering into numerous harebrained business ventures that no one else would have conceived as capable of sustaining earnings let alone generating profits, regardless of whether the idea ultimately proved correct. Among his most notable business undertakings, but by no means the only one, was entertaining a partnership with Manuel Greigel, a self proclaimed violinmaker living and working in the flaunt and affluence of Haverford, Pennsylvania. Greigel took Lazaros on, even though he was a pianist and quite unable to judge the quality or origins of any stringed instrument unless it was pointed out to him. Larry, as Greigel liked to call him, lost his sizable investment. Griegel, whose unknown talents abounded, according to him, was actually missing a vital aptitude required for the success of the business venture - the ability to make a violin. He had made a half dozen or so homemade guitars and a mandolin incapable of being tuned, but never a violin. When neither of his prototypes sold, since they could not be tuned and sounded like an expiring cat, he neglected to pay the rent on his work studio, for which Lazaros was held liable in court. Griegel went on to make his fortune selling hotdogs on city street corners.

Then Lazaros obtained a position at Theodore Presser's, in Bryn Mawr, as a proofreader and editor of music manuscripts. There he met a sultry young clerk by the assumed name of Rita Benson, who persuaded him with the devious promise of her smile and seductive wardrobe, to enter into a business venture with her older brother, a stockbroker for her father's company - B. Archibald Prendergast Investments. The senior Mister Prendergast, Esquire, already disbarred for charging thirty-five percent of the value of a decedent's estate as a legal fee for its probate, encouraged his son to bend the few rules of decency that existed between broker and client. He insisted on his son realizing comparable profits, to aid in the quest to remain a free and employed man. When the son could not achieve such lofty percentages, he compensated by investing at the local race track and with side bets at South Philadelphia boxing rings, taking on gullible associates and clients like Lazaros to fund his habit.

Ignobly fired from Presser's along with Rita, Lazaros next took a position as an American associate for Breitkof and Härtels of Leipzig attempting to interest small orchestras and music schools in their Musikverlag Studienpartituren series. Lazaros was an appallingly inept sales representative and received no remuneration for the one sale he did make to the Buffalo Chamber Music Society. His last gamble was betting his last few dollars on a mobile shoeshine vending business, a modified bicycle with a set of rear wheels and a magical box between them, a monstrosity nearly dragging the ground behind the pedals and the driver's seat, constructed by one Albert Maynard Bickings. Albert was a decently schooled man. He fancied himself an inventor, with a few unsold patents to his name. The gears, like the unaccented beat of the inventor's brain, once adjusted and calibrated by a series of cumbersome manual switches above both the box and engaging the bicycle chain, moved in tandem with the pedal power of its then stationary rider. The customer merely stuck his foot in the box, at the tail end of the bicycle (an image whose metaphorical potential was not lost on Lazaros) and voilá! The customer went on his spit-shined way, presumably content with his own dapper reflection in his polished shoes. Albert tested his invention on his own shoes many times over and it worked well.

At first, Albert tried borrowing the money from a local bank. He dressed in his Sunday best and put forth his stiffest, most grammatically colorless English in a candid mimicry of the Caucasian man about business. Every banker refused, the last one, upon Albert's second visit, addressing him as if he were a boy being explained why he could not have a paper route.

"We can't lend money to you," the banker told him.

"And why not, Mister Banker?" Albert asked. "I'm good for the money."

"Hmm." The banker hesitated and lowered his voice to a respectably private level, when previously quite outspoken. "Well, to be perfectly honest . . . it's mostly because you're a Negro, Mister Bickings, and we don't lend money for commercial ventures to Negroes. It's our policy, sir," he conferred with as much respect as he could muster, "but also because your idea is unlikely to succeed." Interestingly, Lazaros had also advised Albert that he thought the invention idiotic. In the end though, he went along with its sheer frivolity, the idea's impracticality dissolving like a headache, because of the unfairness of the banker's reasons and Albert's dejection, his liquid, downcast eyes. Lazaros acquiesced as an act of contrition for his prior imprudent investments and emptied his pockets, the burden of money having peeled away his soul. He lent Albert the last one hundred and sixty-three dollars he possessed for the prototype, the horsehair brushes, the polishes and the right to receive a second *Shine Mobile* of his own, as long as Lazaros agreed to a fully executed covenant not to compete, since these machines would "catch on like wildfire." Albert promised hard, anticipating selling one machine in every North American city. Unfortunately, his first customer had an unplanned for shoe size, not meant for a world inhabited by pygmies, Albert being the shortest grandson of a slave, sold as a gentleman's servant, or at least the smallest man Lazaros had ever met, save for the midget that sold vegetables at Christy's corner market. The customer's laces and then shoe tongue tore to shreds in less than the ten seconds that it took him to realize what was happening and to extract his mangled footwear from the contraption. Albert spent two days in bed recovering from the especially vicious slap across his forehead and for his brush burns, suffered from his being dragged along the sidewalk in front of old City Hall in downtown Chester, by his irate customer, who happened to be the very last of the bankers who refused Albert the loan for his investment. Albert was noble enough to return some of Lazaro's investment, twelve dollars of it, and vowed to repay him when he worked out the kinks in his design, minus a small fee for the damage to his original *Shine Mobile*, the entire pathetic affair marking the end of Lazaro's business enterprises.

Destitute and too proud to request assistance from his father, infatuated with the daughter of an Athenian born importer of fine coffees and teas who measured a man's prowess either by the breadth of his dick or his wallet, Lazaros finally succumbed to what was alleged of him - an inherited tic and malady of the spirit. He checked himself into Norristown State Mental Hospital driving himself to the "*Resort*", as those who knew him best would hum the ditty to a famous Depression era tune about sparing dimes. "Lazaros is a few nickels short in the old cash box," they said of him.

Doubtful of his self-analysis at first, the doctors at Norristown permitted him an extended holiday when during the perfunctory intake interview, Lazaros interrupted the questioning to deposit coins in a newly installed vending machine, pulled what he thought was the appropriate lever, but actually tore the door of the product chamber completely off its hinge. Then, taking advantage of this circumstance, sank to his knees, leaned back on his haunches and howled in a charade of exuberance, flailing his arms before the mouth of the machine, his fingers dancing in an exaggerated come-hither antic as if awaiting a cascade of coins instead of breath sanitizers.

Lazaros believed he'd find himself greatly entertained by lunatics. He spent a week or so trying to be entertained, debating a shackled and privately penned patient named Gary Munson. Gary and he talked about matters of hygiene, the insidious encroachment of the combustion engine, and the cause of tuberculosis, which Gary argued came to America through filthy immigrants, like Lazaro's father. The meaning of Veronica Lundy's involuntary reflexes also caught Lazaro's attention. Her grimace he found ecstatic, her humming, a melodious suspension in D minor in a turbulent 9/8 time signature, her rocking back and forth while thrusting her arms forward as if pushing an invisible man away from her, appeared to Lazaros like some type of strumming upon a primal instrument. Gary was soon sent back into the prison population from whence he arrived, which was good because Lazaros concluded that he was truly insane and, contrary to his initial assumption, quite boring. Poor, frail, fleshed like snow Veronica choked on a piece of gristle, presumably from the red meat the doctors insisted she eat, swallowing it without chewing, which eliminated for her the disgusting distress of masticating red meat, causing her to deny her vegetarian, diseased mind sufficient oxygen to survive another minute.

Actually, the stay did Lazaros little good. The lone exception was his friendship with Walter C. Wheeler, a commuter who, when he was there and conscious, claimed to be a great nephew of William A. Wheeler, the Vice President of the United States under Rutherford B. Hayes, another man who sacrificed his career to tend to his personal problems. Lazaros found him to be a brilliant conversationalist and thinker and hummed the Gary Owen march or Yankee Doodle every time he saw him. Walter beamed. He was a big man. Long arms, broad shoulders, thick-necked, with an ominous grin etched across his hairy face. He wore clip-on ties, never buttoned his oxford shirts, and pants too small in size that stayed up without suspenders or a belt but were difficult to take on and off with but a single hand, so he wore his clothes until someone complained or he could no longer stand the compost of his clammy joints and groin. He loved loud colors in his choice of clothing, matching his theoretical propensities and his rabid bite into disagreement over virtually any subject under the sun. Walter, who preferred his middle name, Conrad, was for a short time an associate professor of Philosophy at nearby Swarthmore College, was involuntarily committed at first for having purposefully severed his left arm because no matter where or how he laid the perfectly good arm at night it would stiffen up and interfere with his ability to sleep comfortably. To execute the procedure, he hired a Dr. Günter Schinderwolf of nearby Media, an infamous practitioner stripped of his medical license for his macabre interpretation of the Hippocratic Oath and his willingness to intercede on behalf of patients in any way implored, including euthanizing them. (Dr. Schinderwolf had apparently suggested the procedure selected by Wheeler as tranquilly as he might have suggested the option of a sedative for sleeplessness.) The good doctor eventually became a gleeful resident of another of the Belgian style cottages at the *Resort* and routinely practiced upon himself, his scalpel smuggled into the facility in his shoe, the result being untoward mutilation and involuntary commitment. Walter would come around to visit his Prussian pal.

"Sleep is like the peace found within true breathing," Walter would say, leaning left to compensate for the lack of balance to his torso. "It's the prerogative of genius and its highest accomplishment. *Either/or*, or was it *The Sickness Unto Death?* No, no, no, it was definitely the *Diapsalmata*! I forget things so easily while on holiday!" Walter possessed German translations of the angst-sweetened Dane and was among the first American scholars to be enthralled with his concept of dread, walking about carrying and quoting from whatever volume he was browsing at the time. "It's not any different than cutting off an ear for love of a whore, or infuriation over Gauguin," he retorted irritably when confronted with the madness of his masochism for the sake of a good night's sleep.

The only other good to come of Lazaro's stint in the *Resort* was the occasion to impregnate the bovine Niina Krohn, the peach-downed, round-faced inmate of Swedish descent - although her name bore an extra Finnish "i"- who looked like she should have a white sash with bold red letters obliquely adorning her ample chest, saying "dairy queen," not at all congruent with the scars crisscrossing her wrists like lizards. Listening carefully to his incessant reckoning on "the absurdity of what is called sanity," she kissed him tenderly and checked herself out of the hospital. Six months later she had her baby at Chester Hospital, paid for by Alexandros Zervas, whose legerdemain and financial endowment eventually cured her of her chronic despair, replacing the sun of her unscrewed psyche with the son she imagined she might raise, the treacle little bean that had grown within her. Niina named her newborn son Lasso Krohn, bastardization of the Nordic Lasse changing the "e" to an "o" to accommodate Lazaro in some small way and, as Lasso came to believe years later, because she liked cowboys who lassoed steers and in the golden north, reindeer. She returned to her homeland to raise her little "mortal of a Greek hermit," which she affectionately had advised Lazaros was his sole purpose in life, to be the misanthropic ascetic she believed he longed to become. Alexandros lavishly rewarded her decision.

The disgrace of this largely undisclosed and unpublished indiscretion and the inability to rise above the unremitting exhibition of his various neuroses, half of which he found to be enviable human traits absorbed like a psychic sponge from the hospital's various patients, precipitated Lazaro's decision to leave his parents. He was convinced they would remain a fixation of his woe. Upon this debased understanding of himself and the death of the *Neyorkeso*, his father's brother, Lazaros found himself the fortunate donee and heir to the Zervas homestead in Lathra, his father generously relinquishing his brother's testamentary gift and confiding in his friends.

"I gave it to him just to get rid of him, before he knocks up a nurse, for Christ's sake, and I run out of money. Maybe the mountain air and goat's milk will straighten his ass out."

———◆———

Lazaros set sail for Greece at his first opportunity, the cash portion of his prodigal inheritance stuffed in his wallet, money he requested and received freely, his ardent intent vocalized each day. Greece nevertheless eluded him for nearly two years. The journey itself became another purposeful testament to the desire to live outside oneself, to be unreported to any living soul. The voyage was uneventful. Beginning at Le Havre, after each day's walk or peddling, for he bought himself a bicycle, and after a brief spending spree in Paris, where he stayed in a tiny hotel across the river from Notre Dame splurging on local cuisine and wine, he would settle for extended periods at whatever distance his endurance and local fascinations deposited him. He tarried especially in the towns and villages along the Seine, preferring places with old libraries and good book vendors like those in Grenoble and Yvetot, where he remained long enough to improve his French. He also tasted the local *la fleur des pois* including, in Yvetot, the sisters Benot-Biche, delectable and ever lubricating of men's imaginations, who shared a pleasure in his curious accent, his ridiculously dulcet manners and his assiduous endurance, which apparently, for the first time in her life, produced an intense gratification in Lady Lucy. Lucy then clued in her sister, Lilly, who partook as well. Lilly mentioned as much to Madame Nemean, who feigned disapproval but summoned Lazaros to run an early morning errand and seduced him with apparently less thrilling an effect upon the etui of her carnal requirements. Her husband's displeasure, of course did not depend upon the success of the mating. Upon questioning, his wife revealed the affair. Monsieur Nemean punished her with a coarse and particularly lewd evening of retribution, for which they were infamous, and then offered Lazaros, the following morning, a pugilist's tutorial resulting in a bit of deafness to the left ear. The jealous husband's friend, Jan-Georges Canette, another partaker of Mme. Nemean, interrupted the beating, short of Nemean making Lazaros an invalid. Jan-Georges, a local figure of some nominal authority, encouraged Lazaro's immediate departure, fearing his mistress' lurid pillow talk might run its course and compromise his good name and health.

From intoxicating Yvetot, Lazaros escaped with his manhood intact and his remaining dollars and artifacts, except for inadvertently leaving behind two slim first editions of hyperbolic Baudelaire and parabolic Maupassant discovered on separate occasions in a box beneath the same vendor's table. He agonized for weeks over the financial and literary loss, for the local merchants had made an art of overcharging him. With affections for the French fading and the wounds of his unfortunate escapades having healed in the spas of Aix-les-Bains, he wandered away from France to roam the Alps of Italy and Austria with little in the way of desire, intrigue, or warm enough clothing. He spent a winter in Vienna eating sausages and drinking beer, gaining precipitous weight and meditating on the meaning of the baroque in language, usage, human emotion, in everything, taking copious notes for a writing project on the subject. Then, fortuitously, in his recollection, he lost his sense of direction and wandered on foot for several weeks, venturing into Hungary. As evening approached, walking along a backwash of a road to Kaposvár, it began to thunder and then rain heavily. He knocked on a door seeking shelter. A woman answered and invited him in. He stayed for uncounted months in the simple home of the pimply faced young widow who had answered. Since his months in France, he had not met anyone with whom he had had more than a cursory conversation. He noted in his profuse diary entries that the widow's body was as limber as a dancer's but her face blemished with pock marks and possessed a lumbering, horse-like quality that made him want to laugh when she grew serious or emotional. He barely exchanged a dozen words with her each day, but enjoyed her cooking and her soft bed in exchange for laboring in her garden.

The garden was very special to Lazaros. An amorphous wash of tranquility overcame him when he walked into its small sphere of influence. Two long rows of all the vegetables one might desire cordoned off by a fence of sorts, smoothly sanded tree branches oiled to a rich, wet, walnut hue and posts carved with figurines of cats and rabbits peering from behind flowers. The twists and turns of the hand lathe and carving knife, its dark knots, its dimpled calluses and figurative flora connected him to the hand-wringing detail of the gothic churches he had seen, and the portraiture in the Louvre and The Hague with their erotically carved frames, mitering the nameless immortalized souls, harbinger to his harmlessly inquisitive mind. Then two rows of laden grape vines, draping in lavish clusters of purple flesh, exposed to the full halo of pagan nourishment. And finally, along the perimeter, an array of gray benches of both wood and stone with intermittent fruit trees abuzz with bees and the nectar of ripening fruit. The widow's work was her replication of the heavenly labor.

That winter, she having made him a new wool coat with a high collar of rabbit fur, they traveled together by hired vehicle and made their way to Budapest, touring the city with the intention of returning to the widow's home after he had his fill of sophistication. Before departing, he stumbled upon and attended two performances of Bartok's *String Quartet No. 2*, a work he had not heard before. The experience, its lyric barbarity, awoke in him his original mission and the desire to settle in a quiet place and compose. As spring approached, the widow's tears flowing with yet another man's unexplained departure, he walked south, wallowing as he went for he felt he loved the widow in an inanimate way, the way a child loves a favored toy.

The trip took him another month despite hurrying through Bulgaria, except for a brief stay in Bucharest to recover from a stomach ailment that kept him close to the latrine of a Gypsy settlement. From there he moved on into Thrace, walking at a penniless pace to his destination, the corrupted fugue of this journey recalled in dissociated fragments, but with great satisfaction, the theme lost but then resounding in his memory. The sisters Benot-Biche, the bucolic beauty of French villages, the hearths of Swiss chalets after teeth-chattering treks through the woods and mountains, and the young widow, whose home was a pillow of comfort he would not experience again, the last woman he ever kissed and held close to him but whose name he soon forgot.

8

Lazaros rarely ventured among his Lathran neighbors but when he did, they consoled themselves in their stupefaction. He seemed to speak in riddles, incongruously, much as they occasionally alleged of Pater Alexi and Danäe. Among the men, Kyriazis remained particularly suspicious, accusing Lazaros of arrogance, suggesting that sheer intellectual vanity was at the bottom of his Americanisms and openly suggesting that he harbored a counterfeit desire to confound his fellows, offering them nonsense posed as pearls of wisdom with which to rob them later.

"Quiet envy in men arouses the preoccupation of the Maenads," Lazaros pronounced, to fuel a reaction.

"What kind of worthless dung is this?" Kyriazis bellowed, feeling thwarted, unable to discern the American's motive, since he behaved as if he cared nothing for the opinions of others. Lazaros usually took his time answering such outbursts, being careful to show his audience, whose ears would have perked up, that he was not offended, then, with a knowing smirk he replied, "The kind that men walk around." At least most would walk around. An exception was Gallanos. For over a year of effort, Gallanos saw only promise in Lazaros, the man who seemed to receive dollars from America on a weekly basis and never toiled to earn a living. "The mark of a truly learned man," he said on more than one occasion, and with the kind of enthusiasm reserved for few other people in his life.

"Another deluded one here," Kyriazis remarked, as if Gallanos were an old irritant. "Heap an extra handful of oats in front of your laziest mule because he can walk in circles, and then hope that he'll pull your plow in a straight line someday."

At the time, Gallanos was engaging in a rigorous pursuit of Lazaros, openly courting him to wed his oldest and homeliest daughter, Pelagia. His campaign encompassed a host of both traditional and outlandish solicitations. First, he arrived at Lazaro's dizzying cell pulling a prize goat that nearly dragged them both off the precipice and into the lake. In his hands were intimations of the dowry he thought would prove enticing to the American: one of his wife's aprons, tied full with her handmade confections and a dozen white figs. The figs were a great treat, plucked from one of two prodigious trees that few in the village even knew existed, hidden and nurtured in his court-yard, droplets of olive oil applied to each budding fruit to induce early harvests, symbols of the family estate he planned to offer the young American. Lazaros thanked him, ate a few figs, but rejected the goat and the confections and said nothing more. When this and a few other efforts proved ineffectual, Gallanos presented him with a tiny cloth purse containing gold coins and bearing the image of a monarch he believed to be the king of Belgium.

"Because rich Americans are really only interested in becoming more rich," he told his wife. He also offered him a kerchief Pelagia had been made to embroider with the words, "I loves America." Soon after, Lazaros, desperate to dissuade his frequent guest, mentioned that he would likely return home someday and that Gallanos might not see his daughter for many years.

"I'll miss her, but so be it," he answered, "if it's best for my daughter, then yank-nee yank-nee-doodalee-dani it will be." Finally, Gallanos resorted to a series of arguments. Since Pelagia showed intellectual promise in grade school, she would be a suitable bride for an intellectual like him. She did not eat much, which happened to be true. She liked Mavrotripa, when indeed she feared heights. She did not snore when she slept, like her "noisy, confounded sister." Actually, she habitually cried herself to sleep, especially upon hearing of her father's humiliating intercessions. Pelagia would provide him with tall, vigorous male offspring to preserve the Zervas name, when by that day's anatomical standards her hipless frame looked as if she could not pass an acorn let alone stalwart males. Lazaros politely resigned himself against this enticement or any other bearer of dowries. All the while, unknown to her father, Pelagia was secretly obsessed and bemused with her Óread,[43] the lovely Dimitra, the newly arrived sister of Yiorogs Doxiades, Pelagia's lesbian verity revealed to the object of her affection in the chaparral confusion of bodies crowding the Church during the feast day celebration for Saint George. Dimitra smiled sweetly with her suggestion, innocently puzzled at first and then with feminine, deprecating mercy replied:

"If I don't find a new husband soon, your kind offer to wait upon me hand and foot will be taken into consideration."

———◆———

Lazaros was the taciturn spectator to life in Lathra. To the learned few, erudition rarely encountered in so improbable a setting, he was capable of articulating his ideas interminably and with great provocation. An

---

43 mythological mountain nymph

encounter was always memorable and usually occurred after he had imbibed enough to quiet his nerves, his tongue swelling and letting loose famously slurred assertions on every subject under the Parmenidean sun. Thus, his spiritedness and rhetorical abilities varied greatly depending upon whether the debate or symposia accompanied food and drink. In fact, Danäe found him at his most edifying and entertaining when in such an unrehearsed state of didactic intoxication he would paraphrase the ancients in an attempt to bolster an already convoluted argument, whether or not his comment had anything to do with the quarrel or the long, lost line of reasoning.

"He's a fountain of ideas when he's had a few," she would say. No one really resented these infrequent, mandrake infusions and diversions but, on occasion, he did provoke, and in turn felt accosted by Pater Alexi's legendary temper, infuriating the priest with some inflated irony or deliberate fallacy. When Alexi opined that nothing great comes quickly, not even the gift of God's fig, Lazaros responded: "Freedom is the adherence to the proper way of thinking and doing things, not the mere contentment of our fickle wills," as if the metaphor had somehow grafted to his point. The priest's temper flared uncontrollably.

"What do you mean by that? It has nothing to do with what I said!"

"Why, Pater, I would think Epictetus' meaning is plain enough."

"This is inflammatory! An unrelated and moronic commentary," Alexi said on the verge of shouting, his face flushed. Two converging veins bulged like lighting bursts across his forehead. "The essence of freedom is subservience to the good, to God. Fine, fine, I agree ... yes." Lazaros always sucked his opponent into his conceptual framework, never the other way around. "St. Paul might have said as much, but the kind of freedom you insinuate, ha! It's nothing but a myth! A man can change his mind in the same way he changes his garments, but not much else. He is constrained by his sin. That is the extent of his freedom! Your damnable ancients and their abstractions," he bristled.

"Pater," he responded calmly, to annoy the cleric further, "you know that all wisdom, everything of any value that we have ever learned, was gleaned from before the birth of Socrates, before the advent of the inner eye. Our ancestors existed for many hundreds of millennia, but men have only possessed the inner eye for the last two or three."

"So Homer, the Pentateuch, Aeschylus were composed without the inner eye?

"Perhaps," Lazaros said.

"The ramblings of an absurd goat," Alexi spit back, looking around to the audience for confirmation of his right to be annoyed. But almost everyone in attendance had already dropped the thread of the debate and raised their glasses. "You're the devil's infuriation when you drink, damn you! May you have an unlucky year," the priest snapped uncontrollably. "Devil entwined man, driving me to such blasphemy," he muttered beneath his breath. An uneasy silence ensued. He walked away angry with himself. A moment later, when the torrent abated sufficiently for him to collect his thoughts, he walked back.

"I didn't mean to upset you, Alexi," Lazaros said and reached for the top of the priest's retracted hand, deferentially, trying to kiss his knuckles, missing his target and managing only to slaver upon his draping black sleeve.

"You know, my lathering American, when one of us clerics loses his faith, it's not like when it happens to another man. It's far worse, like losing a wager with God. A faithless priest loses his very identity. He is a caricature of his race, a dilution of the blood of the saints, a bastard to the noble language and craft. Nor does it matter by what means faith is lost, whether through some illicit reasoning picked up in a book, or subversive ideas passing from the pestilent lips of a friendly voice at the kafenio - that lazy man's lyceum - or from some Caucus or Black Sea buffoon who spouts revolution while he eats caviar from between a whore's breasts. Losing one's faith for us is the spiritual equivalent of losing a child." Lazaros was in awe of the depth of feeling extracted from the usually well-mannered Alexi, who, after composing his nerves, rambled on. "I was warned once, by a well-meaning prelate, who shortly after giving me his advice conceded to that state of blissful non-being where one awaits judgment from the grave. He whispered to me that even Jesus Christ could not bear the weight of so many words in his name. He knows better than anyone that words are as useful for concealing meaning as they are for revealing it, that's why he taught in parables and clothed his message in meager garb. Anyway," Alexi said, hurriedly making his point, "incessant doxology satisfies men, not God. So I will say not another word." Alexi had stepped into Lazaro's digression quite naturally. Lazaros could not help himself and spoke.

"And yet: The Word which I spoke will itself judge you,"[44] (offered without a hint of contradiction). The conversation ended effortlessly, softly, a fatigued mind resting upon an opponent's disowned pillow.

At one of his infrequent public forays, Lazaros interrupted a debate between Alexi, who refused to take sides on the issue of public water, and a castigating, resentful Lambros, who insisted that he should. The occasion was an autumnal wine festival held in Arnissa. Revelers were enjoying music, dancing, sampling *mezedes*,[45] sipping the wines made from biting, indigenous grapes purportedly sown centuries ago by the Naodites, a sore point of contention with Alexi, who insisted that the Naodites did not exist.

"You cannot remain indifferent to the future, Alexi," Lambros chastised, addressing him informally, something he might never have done without having polished off a carafe of wine himself. "Irrigation increases yields and profits. Basic sanitation will eradicate disease and ignorance. Life will be easier." Alexi laughed heartily.

"All that will come from a little fishy water?"

"Yes, all that," Lambros snapped back. There was an unusually droll tone to the priest's qualms on the subject. It irritated him. Now Lambro's flash of resentment fueled the priest's temper.

"I can deny it and I will ignore it, my nerve-racked friend," Alexi said. "How do you know that I don't agree with Avram, even though he's essentially a faithless cretin?"

"You agree with him?" Lambros asked losing his composure. "And here I thought he was as good as a Naodite, as far as you were concerned, with his bonfires and Cypriot spells."

---

44 John 12.48

45 μεζέδες – Hors d'oeuvres

"Avram's bad habits have nothing to do with this water you're obsessed with. How can bringing a man's outhouse beneath his roof, where he eats and sleeps, give meaning to his life? How can this be a mark of civilization? You're no better than the English and French who live with dogs in their parlors and boudoirs and believe it's a mark of distinction and class."

Lazaros chose that moment, in the ascension of each man's umbrage, to disrupt them and confide in both his inebriated deductions.

"I expect God to have succumbed to the routine of ruminating upon an unbearably glorious vista, Lazaros said. "Sprawled before some celestial kafenio."

"You're interrupting Lazaro," Lambros complained.

"No, no, no, let him tell us more." Alexi insisted. "Anything is better than arguing about water and finding the truth in the elements . . . like the scatterbrains of antiquity who knew no better." When inebriated, and thus invited to issue comment, Lazaro's explanations tended to encyclopedic proportions.

"If not," he interrupted, pleased that he was granted the stage, "He, God that is, is resting in an unearthly meadow. Having scattered a fragrant floral array of His own majesty, He chats with His higher order amidst lovely weeping trees, caressed by a gentle uranic breeze and the whispered ripple of tepid, delicately azure springs, all a short walk from the mansions of the righteous. For Him, every day is one long Sabbath, now that He has finished making the universe, now that men can finally see themselves in His image and, in a fit of creativity, have even come so close to figuring out how He designed a few things. Why, with mass and energy being kinetic kissing cousins and time slowing so elegantly into its own curvature." Alexi's mouth gapped wide. He was as dry as a desert and needed a drink. He interrupted intent as he was upon avoiding the dunes of further anger.

"Christ and the Virgin Mary," Alexi said, crossing himself, "what's this have to do with what we were just discussing?"

"I told you," Lambros confirmed, sitting back in his chair. But Lazaros went on.

"I imagine that He takes long sips from a gem-encrusted chalice filled with nectar and listens to the strains of old seraphic madrigals echoing in the expanse of heaven, music more inebriating than the harmonies of Palestrina, or the Byzantine hymn to the Virgin. And His eyes fill with tears, the melodies evoking the memory of His primordial labors and love for the lesser creatures of His imagination." The priest's face contracted into a bewildered frown, but he beseeched him.

"Continue with the poetry of your error."

"His mind having long ago grown numb with the suffering of innocents," Lazaros explained, "He is inclined to forget what comes next, for if He is perfect, He must be denied nothing, short of pure error, and so must be permitted the luxury of tears and forgetfulness. Consequently, He forgets, too, somewhat in the vein of how men, when they are engrossed in some other exertion or endeavor of art, innocently forget to tend to their animals or their wives and children."

"So judgment will not come for men?" Lambros jumped ahead to the perceived triviality of a conclusion, gulping the last of his wine. Suddenly he appreciated the digression from his discussion with the priest. His face was a turbulent gulf of curiosity.

"Of course it will. Judgment will come on the day when God notices the smoldering of the once perfectly blue little sphere above which His feet still dangle, the place He conceived as Eden, where men were to romp about in His image, now having become a den of vipers and a bed of thorns, a hell, burning with the fires of avarice. Then His anger will reawaken and, being reminded that His temper had reached its limits once before, in one terrible swift moment of wrath He will extinguish the Earth in a single curse of divine restitution."

"Hmm," Lambros agreed, shaking his head as if he understood what Lazaros meant.

"In the final inference of our arrogance," Lazaros went on, "God's *lyssa*[46] will appear to us as if the sun was extinguishing according to some excruciatingly protracted operation of the laws of physics. For how are the vagaries of seemingly incalculable power any different than the disgruntled belches of the Earth, with its volcanoes, typhoons, and quaking capable of swallowing the whole of humanity?"

"Fascinating," the priest interrupted. "You have strayed into the stratum of lunacy and sheer imbecility, and coincidentally, so far from the teachings of the Church as to surpass the Muslims or the atheists in their

---

46 λύσσα - rabidity

idiocies." Lazaros smiled, his teeth gleaming without a shimmer of gold in the order of his amusement.

"Then you've misunderstood me, Pater, but educate me, please," Lazaros said. The priest stretched his neck. He pinched the skin above his Adam's apple, preparing himself for the labor of responding to Lazaros in highbrow Greek. He wanted to show his audience that he could match any intellectual pomposity the American could muster.

"Faith has always been a remarkable, enigmatic thing," he said, breathing deeply, "the lack of it, as ordinary and mundane as anything men do daily. God neither ruminates nor hesitates in His memory of men's lack of faith. The indifferent, He minds far less than the dim-witted proselytizing of atheists, or the silly ovism of modern monists. But don't fool yourself, my Americanaki, the faithless live in fear even while they claim to shun divine favor. And if they manage an insight, or surmount the idea of life as a barbaric spectacle, it doesn't help. The fear still creeps in. So keep thinking it through, my Lazaro. Just refrain from telling others what's going on in that brain of yours, so they don't mistake your meditations for outright apostasy. Otherwise, they'll lock you up for the madness you're feigning. Then I'll have to sprinkle you with holy myrrh to return you to the fold of the baptized."

"Madness is a kind of possession, isn't it Pater." Lazaros inquired. "And these possessed, the madmen, the innately perverse, the irrational, they speak to God, don't they?" Pater Alexi hesitated. "Wasn't it to Christ that the legion of devils directed their words after they possessed a man?" quoting Gregory the Dialogist from *The Third Dialogue*. Alexi sensed that he had used authority against him, a tactic of his, encountered before. Use scripture or the fathers of the Church, even if it only supports a minor point in the argument, and it appears he knows the business of religion better than the cleric. Alexi knew the passage from the Gospel of Matthew regarding the two Gergesene demoniacs, a unique episode exhibiting the power of Christ to offer damnation before the last judgment. Was this Lazaro's whole point? He wondered. His mind raced. He was citing a church father interpreting the passage in scripture. Of this, he was certain. But which one? He decided to change the subject.

"You have God hanging about an azimuth palace, as if there is such a thing as divine corporeality. Dangling His feet, sipping nectar, whatever other nonsense pops into your head. These all limit His nature."

"Wasn't it Christ whom Adam and Eve heard afoot in the Garden of Eden?" Lazaros responded to the digression. "Like a lord walking about his estate."

"Heaven and the garden are a place like that, a place we can walk through and appear in, but only for those who'll never enter," said Alexi.

"Is it more like a Buddhist's illusion than a cathedral for the soul? So the kingdom of heaven only echoes within the one it inhabits?" Lazaros said, intoning the answer to his own question. Discussions with Lazaros made Alexi feel like his laundry was hanging out for all to see, his mind fluttering in the wind. He had to settle himself and escape a potentially endless interrogation, but could think of nothing in response.

"Yes, well, I have to ride my hobbling invalid of a horse to Arnissa. I'll see you in two weeks and we'll resume our little talk." Lazaros bit his lip and raised his eyebrows but was obviously disappointed. Lambros rose as the priest walked away. It was the second or third of those few, infamous public symposiums between the cleric and the ever searching recluse, the man striving for a clarity of thought that eluded him.

"What do you think, Lambros Lambrou?" Lazaros said, contemplating the priest's reaction.

"It seems to me that educated men talk a lot about things for which there's really very little to say," Lambros responded. "Would you like another glass of wine?"

"Yes, thank you," Lazaros said, pleased with the observation. "I'll help myself, my friend." Lambros felt compelled to continue the discussion at some level. Otherwise, he thought, Lazaros might retreat into Mavrotripa and converse with the lake for a few months before resurfacing.

"I for one think heaven must be a place where no one needs to be persuaded of anything," Lambros said fluidly, the inspiration spinning effortlessly from his thoughts into words. Lazaros was pleasantly surprised.

"I like that idea myself," he said. "To their health, the Naodites who made the wine."

"To their health," Lambros replied.

———◆———

Within a year of settling in Mavrotripa, Lazaros began hosting a pair of aural phantasms, as a recluse will often suffer. While not constant, they occurred often enough to have driven another man insane, to self-destructiveness or the chronic anesthetization of his senses. The first of these revenants was an ethereal arpeggio, probably from the *Valse Romantique*, a piece Lazaros had played as a youth. He failed to recognize the serration of harmony as being from that particular purveyance. Instead of F Minor, the chord resonated in an acoustical apparition of B flat major, evoking a quivering surge of giddiness, quite the opposite effect of the original pluck of notes. Later, he ended the just as maddening inquisition over whether the arpeggio was from the pen of Debussy by willfully concluding that it was. It was not the entire gem or declaration of the theme, just the essential denouement of its color, a faint grace of notes gently but clearly strummed over the washboard of the senses. Its modesty would unremittingly carry itself atop the waves of his breathing until he forcibly interrupted it by antidote, usually focusing his mind upon some other distracting sound or music: the gentle waves lapping below his lake front perch, the dingle of buntings on the rocks above, or the excruciating creak of the ropes beneath his mattress might suffice. But at times, especially when preoccupied with some other busying work of the warren, only the most inspiring orchestral bombast worked to cease the recital within his skull.

The other incessant ricochet in the caverns of his cranium was what might only be described as an oratorical contest between Henry the Fifth, straddling his steed before the walls of Harfleur, demanding capitulation of the French lest his men defile their "shrill-shrieking daughters," and a competing, less than concise paraphrase of Sganarelle's shameless boast.

"A physician in the teeth of my protests," his inner voice declared, "I have resolved to remain in my profession, since blunders are always the fault of the dying patient, who courteously never complains to the negligent in spite of himself."

This cacophonous oratory invariably raged when he was most idle, especially on long walks when his mind would go blank observing a flittering bird, a fish near the shore or the imperceptible movement of air visible in the highest limbs of the trees. It might abate with self-prompted discussions over finer points of philosophical significance but then reappear while reflecting over trivial matters of hygiene or diet and the like.

"My nails need trimming. The pears are not ripe enough for the digestion." After a third or fourth observation of this nature, Sganarelle would reappear and douse Lazaro's narcosis, or the piano imbedded in him, strum like a harp's vibration the faintly colored trembling of song.

When the recurring debate grew especially tiresome, Lazaros retreated to his lair for long stretches of isolation, adamantly cranking his Victrola, subjecting a few rare recordings to repeated performance, recordings he purchased in Paris and gingerly carted with him in his travels. A reliable antidote was studying and scribbling notes on the wonders he discovered in the isorhythmic motets of Guillaume Dufay or the *Missa Pange Lingua* of Josquin des Prés, among the rarest recordings he owned. When all else failed, walks to Yianko's kafenio and an hour or so, of sipping ouzo or cognac would drown his surreptitious orators into capitulation. Weeks later, with Harfleur captured and Sganarelle sedate and counting coins from an imaginary purse, Lazaros might reach some plane of peace.

During one particularly lengthy period of suffering he spent a month transcribing by ear what he discerned from his recordings of Dufay's *Ecclesie militantis* his *Nuper rosarum flores,* and the *Salve flos Tusce gentis,* beginning a scholarly treatise he envisioned on the music. A month and a half later, the debate ended with the melodic tapestry of the motets replacing the rumbling voices, casting him into a trance. He found himself repeatedly singing the words, "and his heart was moved by his divinity." When left unfettered, the debate between Shakespeare and Moliere could flower into what appeared as open madness. Lazaros would recall strands of recent arguments he concocted on behalf of the Henry of Agincourt fame and level them in opposition at the insipient arrogance of Sganarelle.

"Come now, my surveyor of bones and fleshy tissue. You are a worshiper of method, are you not? You contrast yourself favorably with a peasant's faith, or with the failings of the clergy. Shall I condemn your method each time one of your colleagues deducts fallaciously or, worse yet, secretes the motive for a false conclusion? Then why behave as if your method is above reproach, that in succumbing to the charms of error, one properly woos the truth." This occasionally incomprehensible but mostly consistent chitchat appeared to an onlooker like the echolalia of a lunatic.

The musical apparition also strummed along when he overslept, or when he had not encountered a cognizable voice for long stretches of time. Ambling along, he tried to ignore the malady and then suddenly it would vanish with the equally incognizant application of antidotes. Incessant thinking or repletion of the mind was perhaps the cause, self-induced forgetfulness the antidote. He spoke openly of these ailments to no one. Although Danäe had observed a concurrent facial tick and contraction of muscles like a puppeteer's pulling at the mouth and fore-head, making Lazaros appear as if he were attempting to think some obstinate discomfort out of existence. Only on that one occasion did he offer a vague description of the malady to her, describing it as the unwanted strums of an imp's harp echoing within him. For the most part though, he chose not to conceive of these notes and voices as an affliction. He rationalized that Argive mercenaries spoke to themselves as well, "and aloud at that, as often as they managed to speak at all," at least according to Homer. "Come to think of it," he said to her, "so did the sons of Priam. The ancients," he said, "confused the minor meta-phor of talking to oneself with the act of conversing with the gods, the very same divinities who routinely inspired the strum of Apollo's lyre in them."

9

A long arid week of tension and avoidance transpired between the instigation of conflict between Avram and Lambros and the unheralded arrival of Stavros Agnostakis, the engineer summoned from Thessaloniki. Avram contented himself with denying Lambros any opportunity to hone his argument in public. All week he avoided the kafenio or anywhere that accident and coincidence might provide a forum. Instead, he took the opportunity to travel to Naousa to meet with the authorities investigating Maria's murder, from who he received a summons in response to his letter of a month earlier. The notice stated the blunt, authoritative intention of the lead inspector to follow through with an investigation of Thanasis Karpathiotis and in the second sentence requested Avram's presence. In the mean time, Lambros bolstered his resolve to appear as unaffected as possible by the embarrassing dispute with Avram. He laid his faith in Lazaro's cooperation and the findings of the engineer and what he believed, or perhaps deceived himself into believing, would be a decisive campaign to convert Terzellos, Gallanos and Kyriazis to the merits of public water and a sanitation system beyond the household hole in the ground.

Agnostakis was an administrator at the reformed University in Thessaloniki, an associate professor of civil engineering trained in Germany, proficient enough in the hydroelectric technology of the day for Lambros to engage him as a consultant. He possessed none of the aspirations of typical young men - unloosing the latticed corsets and garters of city women or making his fortune. His dream was of erecting high-scaled suspension bridges and trellised towers of steel over the many great precipices and canyons strewn across Greece. Because projects in steel were a rare commodity in so stifled and pre-industrial an economy, the engineer supplemented his income and reputation with the occasional irrigation project, the rage among Peloponnesian and Cretan vegetable growers and now Macedonian tobacco and grain growers. Well traveled, the engineer came to Lambros, solicited through an in-law in Thessaloniki, Danäe's uncle, Mihalis Sefilianos. Mihalis was a policeman and through the family grapevine became aware of Lambro's ambitions for Lathra. He relayed as much of the project as he knew, to appease his wife, who was Elissa's cousin and the daughter of her Uncle Foti of the relinquished backgammon set. Mihali cared little for any member of his wife's family but especially Lambros and the throng of men like him whom he thought disgraceful for abandoning their parents to forge a living elsewhere. Mihali insisted that his parents reside with him much to his wife's consternation, a fact and circumstance perpetually in need of justification to her.

"Men like that never become wealthy," Mihali complained to his wife. "How can they? They never stay in one place long enough to learn where the money is hidden. Usually in another man's pocket!"

Introductions to the engineer took place at a wedding performed at the Cathedral of St. Dimitrios. Stavros Agnostakis was a friend of the groom's family and knew Mihali well enough to garner an invitation. He saw the Lathran project as a worthwhile detour along the way to earning the extra money he needed to return to Crete, his birthplace. He dreamt of a supervisory post in the government's public works department, rifling and blasting roads through the island's spiny topography.

The men sat beneath a fragrant arbor of bougainvillea. Barba Ianouli, a relative of the bride's family, was also invited. The spot was far enough away from the ruckus of the reception to hear each other speak but also to hear the bride and groom zealously consummating their union behind the closed shutters of her bedroom, the arbor inclining against the shutters like an eavesdropping old woman. The lovemaking was audible above the din of clarinet and bouzouki, the whirling, throbbing, hooting guests, the dancing and marauding children. Optimistic for the same heated spoils from his wife, Mihali fulfilled his duty with the artifice of enthusiasm, openly suggesting that the engineer supervise the Lathran venture. Lambros was a bit tongue-tied, uncomfortable with the ecstatic couple's vocal complement to his thought process, but delighted at the prospect of an academician's guidance over his project, convinced that the peasants of Lathra would shrink in awe of the engineer's sophistication and technical prowess.

"Listen to him go, he's like your water pump, Lambro, pumping away at your little vixen of a lake. How long do you think he can give it to her like that?" Mihali said rising to his feet, trying to peek through the slats of the shutters. Ianouli gave a maligning glance, like lizards darting from his eyeballs - the bride was a niece to his cousin. Ianouli possessed the annoying habit of laughing at jokes too soon and to those who knew him, of forecasting the demise of love or of men's dreams before they knew it themselves.

"The groom is an impudent rabbit! He grumbled. "He ought to be taught a lesson."

"You're just jealous barba Ianouli," Mihali said, "jealous you're not young and your parts are not stiff with cast iron anymore!"

Lambros invited the engineer to meet him at his home, providing him with little more than a vague description of his bearings beyond the retiring village square. Unfortunately, for both of them, Stavros Agnostakis arrived early and could not resist stopping in Yianko's kafenio to quench his thirst. He perused the patrons and their battle with boredom before ordering a beer. The beer arrived tepid and without carbonation.

"You know once you have refrigeration you won't have to drink warm beer," he said cheerfully. "The Americans drink their beer ice cold. It's very refreshing that way." His presence naturally aroused suspicions and more than a few guttural remarks regarding Lambros and his presumptuous invitation. When asked his business, he introduced himself. A sip later, he mentioned his impending inspection of the land and the lake.

"I'm here to test and estimate the cost of an irrigation system to the valley of fields I passed," pointing behind him, "approaching your charming little village. A Kyrios Zervas, an American, I'm told," having retrieved from his shirt pocket and checked a piece of paper with the name written on it. "I'm eager to meet him. I like Americans. I want to ask him about the Brooklyn Bridge."

Finishing his drink, he left and proceeded to Lambro's house carrying bags and equipment under each arm. Together with his host, he immediately carried on to the forlorn shoreline of Vegoritis just below Lazaro's nymphæum. The engineer's presence initiated a kind of spiteful resentment that within an hour spread its sarcoma throughout the village. Previously advised by Lambros of the appointment, Lazaros emerged on high in front of his abode, sun bronzed, looking as if he were a threadbare tsobano who had spent a day in the wild searching for a lost lamb. His appearance startled the engineer.

"Who's the unhappy looking fellow up there?" he asked, watching him navigate the steep descent.

"Kyrios Zervas, the American. He's harmless, nothing to worry about," Lambros reassured him. "He's an intellectual like you but a bit burdened in the mind, if you know what I mean. A recluse of sorts, but a good man nonetheless."

"Burdened by what?"

"Who knows? Once in a long while he talks about things with my cousin Danäe, things that concern him but make no sense to anyone else around here. Danäe says that he came to Lathra to disappear from the minds and mouths of others and, like most foreigners, because he is in love with the idea of Greece. She says that he believes a man exists only in other people's words. Here in Lathra, the earth, the sky and the lake are real, but he," Lambros chuckled, "here he says, men are invisible, so invisible that he doesn't even appear to himself when he looks into the lake." Lambros sighed.

"You don't say?" Agnostakis responded, cautiously intrigued. Then as an afterthought, Lambros continued. "He's peculiar, it's true. Like a cowboy, but instead of a gun and a ten-gallon hat, he carries books and his thoughts atop his head."

Lazaros descended slowly. The engineer discussed the logistics of the terrain with both men, and offered a cursory calculation of what would be required for laying the pipe and the other related costs of construction. The engineer tested his ambulatory English on the American. Without a response, he abruptly decided to make a list of the tests he planned to run the following day, before concluding their conversation. In his burning proclivity for solitude, Lazaros, who at the time just so happened to be suffering from his previously mentioned aural recapitulation, grew wary of lengthy discussions with strangers. As a result, when such conversations were anticipated or made inevitable, as this one had been, he subtly, nearly indiscernibly, counted the words palavered in his direction. At a specific count of lexical immoderation, depending on the nature of the conversation and his tolerance for the conversant, he begged the person's indulgence to permit his retiring to his home to consider the import of the subject proposed thus far. The engineer stood bewildered and squinting, decoding the kinesics of the lunatic foretold to him.

"He was counting to himself!" The engineer said, using a handkerchief to wipe the sweat from behind his neck.

"I didn't notice any counting," Lambros replied.

"He counted my words, I tell you!"

"That's not possible. He asked you all the questions one would expect. How could he count and speak at once or listen to what you were saying at the same time?"

"I don't know." A few moments passed and the engineer said, "Perhaps the same way someone simultaneously accomplishes any other two things at once, Kyrie Lambrou. We can all work and talk at once, so why not count while listening? But my question is why count my words?" Lambros was unconvinced. No one in the village had ever noticed the quirk, because Lazaros rarely engaged or entertained any stranger with more than a few grunted utterances. Most villagers, Alexi, Danäe and Yianko being the glaring exceptions, simply never had the occasion to watch him speak let alone count to himself silently, and of course, Lazaros found the first two interested in his pontifications. Lambros respectfully commented that perhaps it was the discourteous habit of setting one's eyes upon a speaker's mouth, or something far off in the distance, which permitted such an impression.

"Instead of what?" the engineer asked him. "Staring into a person's eyes? If you ask me, that's as good as disrobing the soul," the engineer said, doubting himself. "As strange a man as I've ever met," he said.

"Hmm, he hardly said a word and you gathered all that?" Lambros said. "Right. Well, you know the old adage, if we take people with their faults, they may forgive us ours. If a man is wealthy, his faults are acceptable; if he is poor, he's just crazy and they lock him up."

The sunlight muted to dusk when Lambros escorted Stavros the engineer to the veranda where Elissa served them an evening meal. The men ate, drank and discussed everything from the corroboration of Lambro's ideas on water for the village to the availability of Danäe, who awakened the guest from his recent indifference to the feminine aesthetic. Brushing past them before they had reached the veranda, the wild vines of her hair pulled back and draping over her sweaty nape, her dress covering a thirst-quenching nakedness beneath wafting cotton sticking to the aperture and shoulders, the hush of her timidity throbbed like a hummingbird. She had asked Lambros to borrow a rope halter so she might shepherd a boy and his donkey to their stable before nightfall. She retrieved what she had come for and went off.

"She's quite something to see," the engineer whispered as she walked away.

"She's my cousin and I can tell you, she's uninterested," Lambros replied pensively, "and I suspect as cobwebbed down there as a cave in the desert." The engineer was disappointed and offended by the comment. He did not laugh as expected.

"An improper thing to say of such a lovely creature, let alone your cousin," he said. The first woman to so completely turn his attention and she apparently suffered from the malady of chronic juvenility or as he surmised from her cousin's suggestion, an underactive libido in a land of the venerated phallus. (The ancient custom of decorating or flaunting a statute of inspired satyrs on one's house or in one's yard was still a custom.)

"You're right. I apologize. It was an undignified thing to say. She's a good girl. Just not interested in the handiwork of Eros and his rigid arrows," he said pointing a finger skyward.

The following morning Lambros and his engineer walked the sunlit gauntlet of gently leaning homes with thickly mortared walls of stone and gardens wilting in the relentless August heat. Even the shade trees retracted earthward in a prayer to the great god of moisture, the heavens having abandoned them for months. They arrived at Lazaro's enclave and the shore of the lake carrying surveying instruments and a pick and shovel to test the depth of the land's resistance to laying pipe below the frost line. Within minutes, four young men greeted them, led by Terzello's excitable son, Spiros, and his friends, including Apostolos Timonakis, Pavlos Lourithas and Tassos Kyriazis. Lambros welcomed them.

"Spiro . . . boys . . . how are you? Come and meet Kyrie Agnostakis. He's the engineer, come to help us with. . . ."

"I know who he is and why he's here," Spiros interrupted, turning to the engineer, "and he can go back to where he came from." The others, faces tensed with nerves, heaped on derision and curses: bullshit maggot, niggling mule, mama's boy, the pasha's pussycat and what not.

"Watch your mouths!" Lambros said, surprised at the disrespect shown to a stranger.

"There'll be no irrigation to the fields without each land owner approving it. That includes us," Tassos replied with inflated dignity beyond his years. "I have a parcel of my own, you know."

"Yes, Kyrie Lalas, who appointed you governor?" Pavlos Lourithas said, raising his voice to a manlier decibel where it cracked in its falsetto.

"You're joking, right, Church mouse? Where have you heard such nonsense?" He snapped back.

"The whole village rejects your grand ideas," Pavlos replied. Lambros turned toward Spiros.

"We've changed the mind of the Americanaki, anyway," Spiros retorted. Lambros knew this was not true. Spiros and his friends had never ventured up to Mavrotripa to discuss anything with Lazaros. Fear of the unknown made the man and his haven unapproachable.

"We'll see about that," Lambros insisted and walked toward the footpath snaking its way up the cliffs to Lazaro's dovecote. The engineer tried to follow, but Apostolos and Pavlos stepped before them, blocking the path. Lambros reacted at once, his voice menaced with the same mortification he had tamed during his exchange with Avram.

"What are you three ding-dongs doing, taking orders from the likes of him?" Sensing danger, the engineer appeared to shrink in demeanor, the heat of malice gathering in the spade of his back. He stepped forward, his gesture conciliatory, his shoulders slumped, his gaze dipping toward the lake, wanting to disarm whatever bad blood he had walked into.

"Let me explain the benefits of the system to you boys."

"Boys," Spiros objected. "Listen to grandpa."

"No, No...." the engineer said to reassure him. Then, a rock struck the engineer in the face, driving him to his knees. Lambros yelled out the indistinct vowels of shock and anger and sank beside the engineer. Then in one fluid motion rose from his side and spun toward Spiros, striking him across the mouth with an open hand. Spiros spun to his left and stumbled with the force of the slap, stunned. Standing nearest to him, Lambros then turned and grabbed Apostolos by the shirt with both hands, his feet fixed wide apart as if prepared for a blow, and then pushing him until Apostolos fell upon his haunches. Wielding to his right, he punched Pavlo squarely in the breastplate, rendering him breathless. Tasso was immobile, as if the violence surprised him. Pavlo and Spiros threw stones and dirt by the fistful, driving Lambros back. Apostolos joined them. Finally, even Tasso raised a large stone and threw it at the engineer, who had risen to his feet. The missile struck him in the small of his back, felling him again. He sat on his knees for a moment, holding his face wound. Immediately appalled with himself, Tasso appeared ready to come to the stranger's aid. As suddenly as the clash erupted, it ended with the preordained arrival of Vasili and

Andreas, scurrying up the sloping path from the road. Both had agreed to meet Lambros and assist the engineer with laying sight lines.

"What's going on here?" Vasili bellowed with his bottomless growl. The youths dispersed at the sight of the brothers, known for their potency and reckless abandon in a fight, their reputation arising from a single well-publicized incident that took place in Edessa, the brothers holding off three times as many aggressors defending a friend against a charge of cheating in a card game.

Andreas gathered the theodolite and charts. Vasili escorted the bloodied engineer to Lambro's house, where after ambulatory recuperation, but against Elissa's insistence that eating yet another meal would somehow help, he embarked for Thessaloniki, bandaged and scornful of the very air Lathrans exhaled.

"Christ and the Virgin Mary, we invite the poor man to help us and these clowns want to stone him to death." Vasili said to Lambros. "They hate your ideas about the water pump more than I thought, cousin."

"The engineer forgot his book of charts," Andreas announced.

"I'll get him to come back," Lambros said. Vasili chuckled incredulously.

"Don't waste your time, cousin. He's not a moron. He won't come back."

Then Andreas spoke. "Some of us are meant to be thrashed and others to do the thrashing."

———◆———

Avram Karangelos was not in the village that day, but Lambros still believed him to be the instigator of the intimidation of the engineer. He had underestimated him once again. Somehow, he thought, the Cypriot had undermined his neighbors' ability to reason, inciting them into animosity and fear, as if they needed help. Distrust, entrenched in men easily led by the nose, like Terzellos and Kyriazis, resonated in the hollow heads of their sons. But Lambros was wrong in this instance. The antagonism of the sons had surfaced for selfish reasons. Spiros Terzellos was desperate to possess the cosmopolitan daughter of a schoolteacher, a girl he met while in Thessaloniki. He told no one about her. Then suddenly, he wanted nothing more to do with the soil that spawned the chestnuts of his father's argil imagination. Being a man who nurtured a deep desire to keep his sons near him for everyone's protection and sense of security, Terzellos wanted to marry them off to village maidens with land grants for dowries, preferably adjacent to his own fields and orchards, to have sons and land grants over which he could continue to exert control. Irrigation and running water might defeat Spiro's excuse for wanting to leave Lathra. And so, lust and love spurred Spiros into enlisting his daft cohorts from the village, who would follow him into the most foolhardy of enterprises simply for the right of counting themselves among his inner circle. Tasso Kyriazis also wanted what Lambros could not have known, to leave Lathra, to become anyone but what he perceived himself to be, a hayseed, a merchant of his own seclusion and boredom. The unhurried change of seasons perturbed him, especially after visits to Edessa and cosmopolitan Thessaloniki. Like many youth, he viewed the Lathran brand of isolation as an absurdity, the plodding routine of its life unbearable. His dream was to live in the Athens of his imagination.

Lambros returned to Elissa's table, with his children seated to either side of him. Most of the village dined at a sofra, low to the ground, like the Turks and Arabs still did, but Lambros found the elevated Western table to be a mark of a civilized people and had Vasili build him one, with benches and a pair of chairs for himself and Elissa, when his cousins first arrived from Apollonia. The two kafenia both had tables, but many of his neighbors found Lambro's table to be a sign of his arrogance.

"A man's feet should be planted on the ground when he eats," he told visitors who commented or laughed at him. The afternoon's fish stew sent its hulking steam up into his face. He felt defeated, his thoughts sullied with a racing contemplation of wider implications to the encounter between villagers and his engineer. Elissa stared across the table, obviously dissatisfied.

"What a disgrace to send the poor man packing like that," she whispered.

"I've made enemies of my neighbors," Lambros bemoaned in response. "This is the price for progress, for the water. A price I failed to calculate."

"When have you ever calculated anything accurately?" Elissa snapped without thinking. The insult stung like a hive full of aggravated bees. His features clenched like hardened plaster. In a burst, he rose to his feet and stared at her with a ferocity she had never seen before.

"Never repeat your displeasure with me in my children's presence," he said, looking down at her and then toward the children, the words grinding between his teeth. Elissa rose from the table, resentful of his nerves and moved toward a large bowl of yogurt lying on the floor in the coolest part of the room. She had prepared it earlier and it was nearly ready to eat. She removed the cloth cover, lifted and propped the bowl against her hip, and dared to answer.

"Have you been drinking again?" she quipped carelessly. Lambros turned and strode toward her, his jaw contracting further, his eyebrows arching up into his boiling brains, fully engulfed, and his eyes menacing as a sickle swipe. The children trembled at the sight of him. In a few sharp strides, he reached her. His eyes turned to coal. Extracting the bowl from her grasp, he poured the yogurt over her head. The bowl hit the floor with an unsettling thud. Elissa yelped in disbelief and held her breath, then stood silently, trembling, her arms to her side, the yogurt dripping in thick, disgusting splats from her face and hair to her shoulders and bosom, then onto the floor. The girls began sobbing. The boys moved away, afraid their father might strike out at them. Lambros stared at her for a moment nervously biting his lips but exhibiting no other emotion. He left the room, sat on the veranda for a count of thirty and then walked away from his home with a brisk, martial stride that did not slow until having exhausted his emotion he reached the clarity of insight that was the time spent in his cherry orchard, along the versant slopes beyond the valley. Sitting beneath the trees, he pondered the details of the pumping station, bemoaning to passing insects and lizards how it might never come to fruition. Lathra, and what was left of the day, lay behind him when he finally decided to turn back and meander home. He faced his village in the downy haze of dusk. Vegoritis shimmered. A jade glint of his envy reflected the southern cleft of Kythera, arresting the usually pale blue reflection of a cloudless horizon. He strolled by Pavlides' and saw the lights and activity of the kafenio, but decided not to go inside. By the time he arrived home, it was dark. His family had already gone to sleep. Elissa alone lay awake, still waiting for him, still vacillating on whether to greet him with the iciness of unresponsiveness or the warmth of a muted apology. Ultimately, she regretted her criticism, as she had all of her uncensored comments of late. She told her daughters that she disliked quarreling with their father. His nerves had gotten the better of him because of what happened to the engineer and here she was accusing him of taking the time to douse his worries in ouzo, an accusation she knew to be an exaggeration, if not false. Lambros walked gingerly across the creaking floors. He bit into a piece of dry bread leaning alongside his bowl of uneaten stew, which he could smell but barely make out atop the dark tabletop, a table Vasili had years ago joined for him from the scraps of a blighted cherry tree. He chewed quickly, drank the wine swirling in his tin cup just beyond his plate and went directly to bed, still hungry but wordlessly fatigued.

"She poured me a cup of wine," he thought. "She mustn't be too angry." Despite her best efforts to rinse the yogurt from her hair, a faint smell of it came to him as he lay next to her. A moment passed before he felt cold strands of her wet hair touching his neck. She embraced him from behind and kissed the back of his head. Her breathing and the purse of her lips against his skin elicited his guilt and mercies, mingling in a low, guttural growl, perceptible only to her trained ear. Then she moved away and he heard the rustle of her discarded nightgown.

10

On that same precipitate afternoon, a forlorn and sedate Avram Karangelos entered Naousa for the first time since Maria had come and gone from his presence. From the moment he looked down at her corpse, frozen in her fright of departing, he suspected the murderer to be an agent of her brother, a hired assassin embodying Karpathioti's sinister logic or some inane convention of Islamic honor. Which of the two applied was irrelevant. As far as he was concerned, both were currencies of the same malevolence. Confirmation of his suspicion came upon a chance encounter with Konya, the seldom-heard tsobano, who had been hiking with his sheepdog in the hills above Avram's peach orchard. Avram noticed the sheepdog running off suddenly, down through the orchard. Then he saw Konya, like a straw man, weatherworn, standing beside a sage bush, strumming the blunted tip of his walking stick through a pile of wool and bones. Strands of tissue stuck to the end of the stick - all that remained of a lamb devoured by wolves. Avram approached with reverence but with sufficient commotion to announce his presence. He said nothing until Konya spoke. It was common knowledge that Konya took the death of his wards and other four-legged creatures as personally as Danäe did. Only wolves, and men like wolves, raised his ire. The two of them stood together, staring at the aftermath of gnashing ingestion and several mounds of freshly deposited dross, the odor swirling with the foul, blood-drenched digestion of wolves.

"I'm going to beat Draco for losing the scent of this little one." Draco was Konya's prized sheep hound. "She wandered off at dusk. Now look at her; nothing but wolf scat and tatters of hide."

"I'm sorry, Konya," Avram said. Konya raised his head and removed his hat. The wind blew his hair back off his forehead and revealed the line of blemished skin the sun had not braised. The weight of emotion lingered on his face from the frantic search through the night. His clothes, burdened with dew and perspiration, weighed him down. He looked at Avram in a disquieting way, as if he might drain his troubles into the other man's eyes.

"And I'm sorry for your loss as well, Kyrie Karangelos. At least you have but one man to hunt and avenge. I must track an entire pack and kill them all." The sinister way he intoned the words "but one" and "kill them all" piqued Avram's interest.

"What do you mean - but one? How do you know it was one? Do you know something of how my Maria died?"

"Kyrie Yianko told me."

"Told you what?"

"That she had been slain by a man."

"Yes, but by who?"

"On the day before she was found, I met a stranger walking toward the village. He was over there," he said pointing toward the hillside south of the dirt road leading into Lathra. "A ragged fellow he was, his eyes glazed and shallow like a dead fish. He was a man bearing a grudge to be truthful, thinking back on him."

"He asked me about her. He inquired which house in the village was hers. I told him that I knew nothing about her except that she was your wife, Kyrie Karangelos. Whether he found her, I have no idea." Avram's pulse quickened. "The following week I heard from Kyrie Yianko that she was dead, killed by a coward," he continued. "That's all."

"Why didn't you say something to me, Konya?" Avram said impatiently.

"I am telling you now, Kyrie Karangelos."

"Did he say who he was? Describe him to me!" Konya's face creased into a grimace. Avram stepped toward him.

"I mentioned it to Kyrie Yianko a week later, but no one else asked me anything. I didn't want to burden you in your grief, sir, and honestly, at the time," his voice sank with the truth, "I made nothing of it. I didn't connect the man to her death."

"Burden me? What did he look like this wolf who asked for her?" Konya stepped back from the lost lamb and turned toward his camp. Calling their master, the bleats of sheep and his dog's howl spanned the distance of the valley. The light of the morning sky was absorbing the ruby clay into its airy corpuscles. Even the shadows appeared earthen. Tints of amber gleamed on the tips of tall grasses beneath the trees. Konya sighed, prepared to move on, and then looked at Avram before speaking.

"He resembled your wife," he said. Konya looked him squarely in the eye for the first time in their encounter then walked away.

Avram had little to say to the authorities, who originally traveled to Lathra from Thessaloniki to investigate Maria's murder. He had accused Thanasi Karpathiotis with little more than inference drawn from the incident that brought Maria to Lathra. Now, to bolster his case, he could present to them the testimony of Konya. He believed this would make a difference.

Thanasi, for his part, lived in a cloud of remorseless aggrandizement and hallucination, an obscene replication of his lethal obsession with his only sister, whom he had repeatedly abused as a young girl. Voices echoed behind the imbecility of dull, indolent eyes. His private mantra grew into justification, a mandate of divine vengeance. Known in

Naousa as an easily angered brute, a man to avoid, he loathed the very existence of women, who were no more valuable than the rags used to wipe oneself he would say with a few drinks in him. Women, in turn, obliged him, generally shunning his presence. The exception was his sickly mother, who found no fault in her son and his pathetically perplexed and obese wife, Calliope, an orphan sold into indenture from the alley of her origin in Corinth. A poor, doe-faced creature, privately praying to Jesus for deliverance, her youthful comeliness had been replaced by the birth of her first child, when she began suppressing her fear of Thanasi Karpathiotis with gluttonous consumption of sweets and dried fruit by the fistfuls.

"You should have married a baker, you worthless barrel of lard," he spat at her, slapping the swaying cellulose beneath her arms. "Go pig, go tend to the children and forget about stuffing your mouth with honeyed tarts."

Arranging for a meeting in advance, Avram entered the mayor's office in Naousa and met with the Police Investigator, Eleftheris Marios, a chain-smoking bureaucrat from Samos, who had left his sleepy island for work and chasing women in Thessaloniki. Not the original official that interviewed Avram after Maria's death, Marios was cooperative at first, more empathetic, almost cordial until he learned that Maria was born a Turk, the chief witness against Karpathiotis was a tsobano and a Vlach to boot, and the encounter with the alleged perpetrator was prior to and nowhere near the scene of the victim's demise. Avram tried diverting Marios from his adverse conclusions and told a story he believed to be true regarding the pedigree of Maria's father.

"Their father was a Greek from Smyrna, I tell you, a Greek posing as a Turk, then, wherever he went in the free world, a Turk posing as a Greek. He was always hedging his bets. One could never tell what his clan was. He wanted to avoid the worst when the Turks regained control. He left Smyrna for Chios. Somehow, he ended up in Karpathos. I guess they figured him out for the snake that he was and threw him and his donkey off the island. I knew his extended family from Smyrna, I tell you! The family name back then was Akhisar. He took the name of a Turkish town back then, too, not the stupid Karpathiotis his son calls himself now!"

"No kidding," Marios said, yawning. "A lot of trouble to go to."

"What's the difference anyhow? My Maria was a Christian when I married her. She was a good woman, generous and kind to people." Marios disengaged his official interest and looked toward his vehicle.

"Please, please do not ignore this point," Avram said.

"Look, friend," Marios interrupted, "I can tell you that you won't find much interest at headquarters when a Turk kills one of his own. They're a sickening bunch. They don't tolerate their daughters and sisters praying to Christ when their prophet is pining for more sultanas to join the harem in the sky." Marios permitted his attention to wander away from the conversation. Avram showed his impatience.

"You're joking, aren't you?"

"I'll speak with this Karpathiotis, but unless he confesses, don't expect much else to come of the investigation, especially since your tsobano will probably be unwilling to leave his girlfriends to testify against the Turk. Tsobani are like the monks on Oros, preferring the company of the mute, but always seeing things they shouldn't. May Allah gouge their eyes out," he said laughing at what he thought was a clever parallel.

"You can come and speak with Konya in Lathra," Avram pleaded. "He's there every Tuesday afternoon. He lingers in the kafenio that sits beneath the two large trees on the village square. He eats a hot meal, has a few drinks and talks to an occasional human being. I tell you, he's not a ewe brained lunatic like some tsobani!" Marios looked at him with counterfeit pity, but said nothing and then looked away again.

"I thought as much. What did I expect from a bureaucrat, a pencil pusher, nothing more," Avram grumbled. Far from offended by the slur, Marios nevertheless intended to extract punishment for the comment.

"A bureaucrat is it? Where are you from anyway, Smyrnioti?" Avram did not answer immediately.

"I was born in Cyprus," he said.

"Your name is Turkish, Kyrie *mavrangelos*,"[47] the Greek adaptation of his name. Avram's face flushed with anger. Listen to this ass wipe, he thought, and turned up the palms of his hands in a gesture of inquiry.

"What good are you then, Kyrie Policeman, if you can't spend the time to interrogate a man who slits the veins of fratricide? If he confesses, then you will have him, ha! You take me for a clodhopper! What

---

47 μαυράγγελος - black angel

benefit is there for the liar to suddenly tell you the truth? Am I Christ himself to make a man spit the truth that is choking him?"

Marios stood impassively, observing a man with his young son seated on a cart filled with satchels of apples. To his right a young woman walked across the dusty square. Her head was covered, but she was otherwise smartly dressed in light blue with a white laced floral pattern to her traditional dress and a sash of indigo outlining her hips. She carried herself in a deliberate manner, her eyes ever watchful, darting at inconceivable angles to catch a glimpse of who might notice her. He lit a match for yet another pre-rolled cigarette retrieved from the small pocket in his vest, purged the smoke from his nostrils and then spit a piece of tobacco extracted from between his teeth in the direction of Avram.

"I'll speak with him and let you know, Kyrie Karangelos." Marios walked away, the cigarette drooping from his mouth. He headed back toward the main square, following the young woman whom he soon overtook in conversation. Go to hell, Avram grumbled as he watched him. I came all this way for this prick. May the plague consume your flesh!

Avram walked toward the station where he intended to secure a ride for hire back to Lathra. He sat idly on a crate by the door of the kafenio next to the departure station in the main square of town. He slumped forward, his hands covering his face, resting his eyes. Everything appeared red to him. Racing specters hovered in the pallid light of recollection, moving him toward Maria's death as if it were still to come. A dull, useless throb announced itself to his previously insensate mind. He waited for any activity to distract his attention from the apparitions of a glowering heart. His thoughts meandered to the day he met Maria and nearly squeezed the life out of Thanasi Karpathiotis. He wished he had simply squeezed a bit harder, a bit longer. It never entered his thoughts that had he kept to himself he would not be in Naousa at that moment and that Maria would not be the Eos of his loneliness. He remembered weeping into his hands as she lay within her timbered cloak of darkness, her face not at peace but inert in her fear, as if before admittance through heaven's gate she had tread upon the molten bones of the underworld. He recalled the cantor's cadence, a voice that normally pleased him, but that day had made him wince. The threnody for her eternal memory sounded alien to him, a tone apart from the priest's usual rendition. Maria's was an unrequited life of sighs, he thought. He wished to ease the panic from her face with a kiss, but had not done it and regretted this, too. The casket, covered with earth, had captured her terror intact, for all eternity.

"Vengeance is a divine attribute," he reasoned aloud. "Hera, Zeus, the God of Moses and even the murderous Turks, all of them are vengeful. Who am I, a worm in the scheme of things, to resist the most divine of sins?"

The opportunity to leave Naousa and return to his life in Lathra passed before him in an instant, without a tear or batted eyelid. Neither did he consider his battle with Lambros, his fruit and chestnut trees, his sisters, or Danäe, the elusive, purest form in which the idea of beauty floated through his thoughts. His original plan to ask for her hand had spoiled on the vine by arguing with Lambros. Now he believed he had done this purposely because he could not forget Maria. He rose from his seat before the transport arrived and began wandering through the town. Its quiet, meandering dirt streets ebbed gently into shallow drainage gullies, streets with isolated shops and kafenia and the brownstone schoolyard in its midst. He purchased *kefalotiri*,[48] some bread and olives, drank a few glasses of local wine, and walked again. The wine was like love itself, not like the swill served in Lathra that tasted like the thick-skinned grapes reserved for crafting *Retzeli*, a labored mixture of boiled quince and pumpkin squash in limewater, blended with crushed grapes into an intense, concocted sweetness. This is all that men are good for, he thought, to labor and grow things that are good to eat and drink. For all the rest they try to accomplish, they are useless and unworthy of existing. By the last sip, Naousa became a foreign land to him. He imagined Maria to have hated her every breath there, dreaming of rescue from a subjugating creed and incestuous desideratum.

As the heat of the day burned the wisp of any breeze off the surface of the leaves, Avram began a somber, unconscious search for Thanasi Karpathiotis, roaming through a maze of redundant homesteads and adumbrated alleys. When eventually he stumbled upon him in the courtyard of his father's old home, tending to his animals, Avram's shirt had stained with sweat and his mind become deadened with his coarse

---

48 κεφαλοτύρι - a hard cheese

design, an anvil upon which he incused intention into shape. Thanasi's mother sat in the shade upon a thickly cushioned, deep-seated chair, waiting for the assistance she required to extract herself. She faced the entrance while Thanasi's children ran through the courtyard chasing a scrawny spotted goat. Calliope had begun kneading dough at a nearby table, preparing for her next indulgence, when Avram called out.

"Karpathiotis!"

"What!" "Who's there?" Thanasi shouted from behind the wall. Avram remained concealed. "Who has the gall to disturb me, *tzoglani?*"[49]

"*A arkadas-dan mazi,*"[50] Avram replied grimly.

"I have no friends," Thanasi replied in Greek. He twisted the torso of the goat away from him. The goat bleated, hobbling away past the house and the wall. Avram stood motionlessly, one hand against the cold stone, waiting for a sign of life at the edge of the courtyard, his thoughts mislaid in each shallow breath. There was no question but also no resolve, nor did he feel any concern that the Karpathioti's children might suffer as witnesses. They were invisible to him. Shrewd in discerning paternal displeasure, the children immediately scattered upon hearing their father's familiar growl. One of the boys, the older, turned his head as he walked by and looked at Avram's face, expressionless like a bird's but filled with fatality. He looked through him as if the boy was not there. Thanasi's mother raised her sluggish eyes to the entrance. Calliope twisted her neck behind her, to discern the commotion.

"Death is come calling and here is his messenger!" Avram said. Thanasi bent down and brandished a knife pulled from his booted leg. He stepped forward, inching his way close to the interior of the wall. Within three steps, he reached the narrow opening of the courtyard, hesitated for a moment and heard nothing except what he believed were the footsteps of someone walking away. He stepped into the opening and turned sharply toward the exterior wall. Before he could raise his hand or thrust a blow, Avram took hold of his throat with a fulgurous right hand and twisted the wrist of his bladed left hand, pushing him into the courtyard. The recollection of Avram's grip returned to the Turk in a panic, the struggle eye-to-eye and brief. Thanasi summoned

---

49 τσογλάνι - Turkish transliteration for young smart ass

50 In Turkish: "a friend from the past"

all his might to free himself but Avram thrust him into the wall. The blow to his head sapped him of the strength that may have saved a last sputtering mouthful of air. His blackening eyes darted toward Calliope but she missed them, casting hers about the yard, frantically searching for her children. Struggling without success to arise from her chair, the old woman mouthed a persistent scream with a strange masculine quality to it, ululating fear like an animal trapped in its own state of panic. Avram squeezed, as he never knew he could, robbing Thanasi of the earth beneath his feet, a choking squeal muted into a crimson death throe. Retinal vessels burst into trodden mulberries. Calliope, having risen to her feet, hurried in a graceless waddle to the opening in the wall just as her husband fell back against it and onto the ground, his expression lifeless, the brown bruising flooding beneath his skin. Blood trickled from his nose and mouth, like venom. Calliope stepped back. Avram wiped his hands on leaves he tore from the arbor above his head. He turned back into the yard and bent to lift the knife lying at his feet. His grip fused his calloused flesh with the handle. The old woman's shout fizzled as she choked on her phlegm. Calliope returned to her table trembling, unable to speak. The memory of her parents came to her. She heard voices in the distance.

"My children," she said hesitating at first and then turning to her mother-in-law, "I must take them away from here." But she did not move. Avram approached the old woman, pulled her by the hair and in one unhesitant motion slit her throat. She watched him. A gurgled puff of air spurted up at him. He blinked and turned his head but droplets of her blood caught him on his chin and the sweat soaked collar of his shirt.

"Tell his sons that Maria is avenged," he ordered in sterile Greek. The old woman feigned defiance for a moment, silently spitting a curse. Then blankness filled her eyes, and soft oblivion across her face as her head fell back unnaturally. Calliope began weeping only when she realized that Avram had spared her. He passed a woman - a neighbor - at the mouth of the courtyard. The woman avoided looking at him and walked into the courtyard briskly. A few steps later, he heard her scream.

"Murderer! Murderer of mothers and sons!" she shouted twice.

Avram retraced his steps and returned to his spot on the crate, converting a few coins into a ride on an open wagon out of Naousa just before the commotion over the Turk's death converged upon the square.

Marios was preoccupied with the young woman in the light blue dress, so no one could find him. He had followed her on her way home near the outskirts of town, suggesting a picnic for the two of them. When the young woman's protective mother caught sight of her daughter laughing nervously at everything the strange suitor had to say, she chased him away with her broom.

The neighbor who had spotted Avram described him without a mustache, and as a large and unkempt ogre. Calliope, still pale and transfixed with barbaric images of her husband and mother-in-law, seemed overcome with the sudden realization of their demise, and her freedom. She found no words to assist the authorities, ignored the rapid succession of their questions, and looked past them as if she were in a trance or awaiting someone's arrival. A physical description left wanting, one of the children essentially supplied the remaining portrait of the assailant.

"He was a monster with a repulsive face," one of the girls cried out, "with a nose like a hay hook." As a result, the civilian searchers walked by Avram's crate in haste and without pause, despite the blood about his collar.

Because of certain lurid conjectures regarding her past, comments made in her presence by people she knew despised her as the oafish consort of a miscreant Turk, Calliope felt certain that an allegation of complicity was imminent and ran for her life, her children with her. Indeed, the locals had already begun accusing her of having serviced the assassin carnally in exchange for her husband's murder. Marios found the suggestion laughable and contemptible. Is there a more brainless race of hayseeds, as dry between the ears as the manure they feed their fields, he thought.

"No," his mind went through its steps as he spoke to a local authority, "why did he spare the fat wife but kill the mother and leave her head hanging by a spindle of spine? Hatred and vengeance inspired this killing."

Hunted for a month in the barren wilds of the Macedonian frontier before her apprehension on the border, Calliope wasted back into the fawn of her youth, like Rena, feeding her children before herself with whatever she garnered from strangers, gypsies and the unyielding landscape. Roused from their general state of shock by her capture, Calliope's children wept inconsolably as the authorities escorted their mother into a waiting mobile prison. Then, before the vehicle pulled away, levitating their terror to pitiable heights, Calliope hammered her hands and head against the window of the vehicle shouting their names, breaking her nose in the process, smearing the window with her blood and tears. As the engine of the vehicle turned over and rumbled, the authorities dragged the emaciated little lambs across the yard of the outpost into border housing and the temporary care of ill-tempered guards. From that moment, Calliope prayed for death.

A few days later, the children became wards of the government's inanity. The police escorted them to Volos and from there to an orphanage in Athens. A year later, the boys arrived in Smyrna to live with their father's distant relatives. The girls as much as disappeared as if they had never existed. Calliope knew that a reunion with her children would not occur except in her anguished dreams. The locals presumed her destined for execution or at least life long imprisonment after trial, a spectacle summarily scheduled in Thessaloniki. The evidentiary basis for the capital charges leveled against her was nothing more than a few disgruntled busybodies and the affidavit of the arresting officer, the singular protestant being Eleftheris Marios, who at her initial inquest, confided to an associate that he regretted ignoring Avram Karangelos. The need to convict her proved unnecessary. While awaiting trial, separated from her children, imprisoned in the nadir of her sorrow, in utter silence and without hope, dwelling on her increasingly constrained breathing, Calliope refused nourishment, water, and finally medical attention. Three nights passed until her fluid-filled lungs could wield her breath no longer.

Avram had long since returned to Lathra and without explanation, gathered a satchel of his belongings, including a photo of his parents and sisters taken before he was born, and left everything he had worked for to his sisters, preparing in his own hand a document tendering his land and home. Lydia and Magda, for their part made no genuine inquiry beyond the first.

"Why are you doing this?" He gave no response. Magda assisted him in silence, cooked for him and stuffed provisions into his satchel. Lydia sat at the kitchen table in a stupor, watching her brother move about the house as if it were a shrine, gathering items preordained in his memory, observing his sorrow at each discovery in a drawer or a container, like incisions of an infernal past made upon his soul. And as she had done since moving to Lathra to care for her widowed brother, Lydia obliged him with an obsequious compassion, which only a sister could, kissed him tenderly upon the brow and wept in aching spasms as he walked out the door.

11

Inspector Marios and a young, wheat-whiskered assistant from the police barracks in Thessaloniki arrived in Lathra in an official capacity to investigate and conclude a report on the whereabouts of Avram Karangelos.

"Where is the infamous tsobano?" he asked.

"Up there," a youth said pointing toward the sun-blistered summit of Kythera, shading his eyes with his other hand.

"To hell with him - I'm not trekking on rocks in this thin air to find a stinking sheepherder. Go tell him I'm here and request an official audience with him at once." The youth sat squarely on the wall of Yianko's terrace, unmoved. "Hmm," Marios said with an air of parental failure, and lit a cigarette. "I thought as much; a village of uncooperative mules. That's what they said about you all in Arnissa and Perea."

Speaking to the sisters Karangelos, Marios exuded confidence in his ability to apprehend his man, posturing more for his assistant than for his audience, at least at first. Marios was prepared to offer not a shred of genuine exertion over what he finally and privately believed to be a justified act of vengeance served upon undesirables responsible for the murder of Avram's wife. Nevertheless, he followed protocol and interviewed the family, and a few known associates. He engaged in his usual prurient banter with women whom he perceived to be in need of an attentive gesture or word and quickly surmised that both Magda and Lydia might be susceptible to the extravagant pearls of suggestion from a man offering such attention. He ordered his assistant to move on and conduct interviews in the kafenio, but first requested that he retrieve his notebook from the official vehicle, accomplished like a dog recovering a thrown stick. Authority, like the idea of a big dick or a wad of money, is an aphrodisiac, he believed. But only for the types of women he preferred - the type the sewer of modern progress seemed to spawn. He lived by this crude maxim and repeated it enough times to have created a useful reputation.

Marios discerned that Lydia had observed her sister's preening in his presence and sensed in Magda an attraction to his worldly, urban comportment and authority. Theory verified reflexively. The connivance of seduction germinated soon after drawing his second conclusion: all unmarried sisters so close in age and approaching, as he again correctly surmised, the middle of their second decade were, when in the presence of an available man, as competitive as rival border nations. He moved ever so minutely toward Lydia, whose darker eyes and thinner carriage he preferred less, but whose subtle, envious glances toward her sister he deduced as the less complicated prospect between the two women. He pulled on his thin black tie and stroked a wrinkle from his white shirt. Lydia observed him, his finely combed hair pulled back behind his ears and, as he looked back up, the forceful brow staging his official business. While Magda retreated to the kitchen to retrieve a plate of candied quince and cold water for their guest, Marios evoked in Lydia the idea of her irresistibility. He leaned toward her, nearly whispering into her ear, his mastic-laced breath caressing her neck as it curved away from him like the lissome stem of fragrant lily.

"What a pity to waste such charm on this loveless landscape," he slavered, resting his gaze and the foam of his craving upon her lips then aiming the arrow of concentration up into her eyes. Lydia construed his languid eyelids, the reddened tint of his complexion and its musky secretion as elements of longing. He succeeded and set ablaze in her a blush of prolonged intensity, a long-neglected sheath of sensation and awareness of her femininity.

"Lydia," he said again, tremulously, a comical allusion of artificial emotion for anyone listening, except her.

"What?" She flushed with a kind of sweetened shame, the question melting down her throat.

"Meet me behind the wall of the courtyard before I leave today. I want to ask you something in private." She tried to ignore the suggestion.

Normally, it might have prompted a melodramatic protest, but all she could muster was ingesting the glaze of her name upon his lips. Her face softened. She looked up at him. Shy acquiescence, as he would remember it. Magda returned with a spoonful of candied cherries, centered on a tiny plate of latticed porcelain with floral design, the presentation as delectable as a bride laid bare for her groom and an accompanying glass of water set next to it, like a stern chaperone.

"I hope cherries are acceptable instead of the quince," she apologized.

"Oh, Miss Magda, the cherries are delicious, I'm sure," he replied, his baritone descending in half octaves. "My favorite, how did you know?" He tasted the cherries and drank the water until he emptied the glass. She watched his mouth, the incising calisthenics of mandibles and the dart of tongue that wiped his lower lip. "Delicious water, too. It has a faint aftertaste of something. I can't make it out."

"It's the taste of the fish from Lake Vegoritis," Magda informed him and smiled, revealing a subtle disorder to her teeth. Mindful of this, she tightened her lips as if to swallow her teeth and smiled again, as if forcing her smile from behind a grimace, making her appear annoyed rather than pleased. This had no effect on Marios. He had already studied the exotic allure to her mouth and had, as she turned toward the left, showing what she thought was her more refined profile, moved on to her curvaceous posture. Lydia noticed little if any of this. Momentary indecision consumed her thoughts and made sterile her senses. She glanced at him and suddenly excused herself, proceeding directly to the courtyard, where she fidgeted unobserved, obscured by a large, heathery thorn bush and the high wall of stone standing at right angles to the house.

The sisters had held their tongues throughout the interview. Their focus had been on the cordialities and minutiae of the encounter with the handsome inquisitor. Oblivious to the recent tempest between Lambros and their brother, Magda and Lydia referred Marios to Lambros, whom she believed knew more about her brother than they did. Lydia had also mentioned Yianko in a benevolent manner.

"Yianko is a kind man," she said. "He gave Maria a cabana of sorts behind the kafenio when she first arrived in Lathra." Marios, however, had already interviewed Yianko.

"I like the Cypriot," Yianko had said to him, "but I'm not surprised he's under suspicion, considering his gruesome heredity. His mother was a murderess, you know." Throughout the village, the implication that Avram may have murdered a man and his mother met with recondite stoicism, heightening the investigator's belief in his culpability. The interview with Terzellos was yet more terse and ended with his warning Marios to leave Lathra well before nightfall.

"The mountain road leading to this place is not so forgiving on the way out. It's been known to swallow whole little taxis like the one you're driving."

Magda apologized for Lydia's unusual rudeness and bade the inspector goodbye, offering him a limp handshake, the discrete consolation of balmy flesh she permitted herself with men. He stood uncomfortably close to her, but she liked the smell of him, the conspicuous lothario of epic aptitude. She sensed why women might not care if men like that were untrue. "Impaling any woman with a raised tail", she told Lydia when she returned from wherever it was she had run off to.

"Goodbye, Miss Karangelos," he said, "I hope to have the charming prospect of speaking with you again." Marios left for the village square, walking in simple direct strides. He lit a cigarette as he walked. Then, doubling back past the Karangelos residence, he encountered his assistant for a moment and sent him in the opposite direction to find and begin the interview with Lambros. He walked a bit farther and discovered that Lydia was indeed enticed by his suggestion. She stood by the wall, waiting with bated indecision over what she might permit to transpire, breasts heaving, the tip of her tongue moistening her lips with the embryo of desire. She appeared more attractive than her sister did, if only by virtue of such tension and obvious willingness. He hoped for nothing in particular but the enjoyment of his influence over a woman deprived of adoration. For Marios, one measured women - young or old, large or small, married, widowed, abandoned or unclaimed - solely by what they might educe of his carnal imagination and, even more, by the weight of their perceptible proclivity for such indulgence. A willing adulteress, even of meager appeal, was invariably more valuable and pursuable than the youthful narcissus of disinterested beauty. Lydia encapsulated the best of both worlds. She was lovelier than he first gave her credit in the dimly lit clutter of the Karangelos home, and needed only the prick of a thorn, the blade of his seductive aptitude, to uncover her need, her desperation for a man's embrace. She saw him and stepped forward into his final stride, looking up at him, waiting for the furtive incantation of her name once again. At the very most, she hoped to discern in him an apprehension in taking her into his confidence, the timid courteousness of revealing more than he wished of his desire for her.

"Lydia." He said. "Like a gem of Sardis," his only utterance.

She lowered her face for a moment and then gently moved between his arms as he pulled her toward him, her lips parted and drenched with curiosity. Neither thorn of rose nor the pungent mire of corruption could have forestalled the flowering lotus of her quiescent passion. When finally they were to part, he embraced her one last time, her head upon his shoulder, her contentment a figment of his theatrical imagination.

"My brother is gone, leave him be . . . but come back for me," she whispered. Marios kissed her again and left. She ran back to the house and lied to her sister, telling her that she went for a walk to the church to light a candle for Avram. Later, in her prayers, she begged God for forgiveness for the lie; that it not attach to Avram's destiny.

Nearly an hour had passed before Marios located his assistant and took over the interview of Lambros. Again, Marios found himself the inquired, and fully admitted to the dismissive response he offered Avram regarding the murder of his wife and the likely offender.

"Who knows where he is, sir," Lambros said gravely. "I wouldn't tell you even if I knew. I, for one, hope you never find him."

"An innocent woman, the dead man's wife, is accused of the crime. She is condemned because of my error," Marios responded.

"That may be, Kyrie Policeman, but I don't know her. I've known Avram for many years and although he has turned into an adversary and led a rebellion of sorts against my idea of an irrigation system, I cannot work for his demise or imprisonment."

"Your what?" Marios asked impatiently.

"A water pump to deliver water to the fields and the homes in the village."

"Tchk," the investigator said, clicking his tongue against his teeth with officious disinterest and then a sideshow of mannerism, a subtle arch of the eyebrows, a creasing brow, the mouth clamped, his head bobbing up once - an inimitable genre of the negative.

The day vested freely, unoccupied with more than the sounds of scurrying children and mothers' labors. Marios slapped the Lathran dust from his pant legs and tapped his shoes on the step up to his seat in the vehicle, and threw his still-burning cigarette out his window. For the first time since he had been with Lydia, he had not accounted for her in his thoughts. The negation became an affirmation. He knew her for but an hour and she had beguiled him away from his official distractions. This realization did not concern him. On the drive home, he became conscious of his feeble attempts to dismiss her from his thoughts. He dispensed with his usual post-coital remorse quickly and wondered superficially if he had pleased her, an idea that rarely entered his mind. Believing in nothing but his own prowess, he drew and savored from his mulling image, the scent of her rising from beneath his collar like a faint and fragrant ode, and from the heated honey of wildflower smothering her proffered confections, the scents swathing gracefully upon his hands and wrists and about his face. He had run his hands through her hair, tracing waves of supple kisses upon her neck. The assistant interrupted his thoughts with a theory regarding Avram and Calliope, the victim's wife.

"Perhaps Karangelos did know the Turk's wife after all," the associate quickly reasoned. "He did tell you that he knew them from Smyrna."

"Nonsense," Marios mumbled back. "Avram Karangelos loved his wife, profoundly I suspect, like a fool. He avenged her death. It's as simple as that. Some have it in them. Some do not. He did." Marios thanked the associate scornfully for his amateurish speculation. Silence again consumed the long journey back to Thessaloniki. Lydia's dark, incarnadine complexion reappeared to him in the gray of the road speeding by his window, her blue-black hair, a painted mare's mane, the snap of his belt, her skirt and petticoat riding above sequent thighs the sun had never seen.

12

Avram walked south through the valley of Lathran cropland descending and then climbing again to a mercifully gentle elevation of parched grass unprocurable for fodder. His hurried departure left a dark depression of the felled lea. Vultures hovered over his gradually vanishing exodus and wolves would follow and sniff for signs of lesion, exhaustion or the demise of prey. Through rocky passes and dusty cart-ways, seemingly abandoned by time and men's commerce or any marks of modernity, he walked at a steady pace for uncounted days, losing his way a few times, finding his path again by shadowing the river Aliakmon. Then he headed toward the coast, seeking passage through the Cambunian Mountains, resting by nightfall and beginning again each dawn. Passing within sight of Olympus, he climbed for a half a day through the black pine forests, on what he believed was the base of its northwestern slope, but then relented and turned back toward the visage of men. There, he stumbled upon a tiny settlement and encountered an old woman some thirty meters outside a circle of five Kurgan-like abodes, long, squat, narrow and unadorned. She wore the color black and looked like the morbid rind of rotting fruit, standing alone by a large rock, surrounded by yet another ring of smaller rocks, like a planet and its moons, the music of the spheres, both rocks and dwellings, evident to anyone who might stumble upon the scene. She wore a straw hat and walked with a cane made of indigenous black timber, carved with a crude depiction of a horse on the head of the long handle at right angles to the stick. She spoke with a strange accent, Vlachiko he thought at first, but not. She referred to the village as Xóros and invited him into one of the lodgings. Avram followed her into a room devoid of furnishings except for a table and a single chair. She asked him to wait there, he presumed for service of a meal, and disappeared into another room. When she returned a few minutes later, she was standing outside the house and the open door waiting for him to come out. Her hands were empty, apart from the branch of a conifer whose tips appeared glazed with sprinkles of silver, shimmering in the sunlight. She struck the branches on the ground in the shape of a triangle and then a circle.

"Grow accustomed to your poverty," she told him, then turned and disappeared into the forest. Later Avram asked a few peasants riding atop an empty cart, near the village of Elásson, men who appeared to know something more than the average plodder did, whether they had an explanation for the tiny size and isolation of the spherical village Xóros and the old woman's inhospitable behavior. The men proved equally uncongenial.

"I've never heard if it," the younger one said.

"There's no village Xóros, stranger," the other man said. "You had the bad luck of encountering a priestess.

"A priestess!" Avram said skeptically. "What kind of priestess?"

"A descendant of the centaurs, what the ancients in these parts called the Kurganyi, since they never set foot upon the earth except to die, sitting always upon a horse. Or maybe she was Dhrakhmanian. Who the hell knows?" The old man explained that at some point long ago, perhaps in the six hundred and sixty fifth summer after the birth of our Lord, the heirs of the Kurganyi being recent converts, apparently fell victim to an apocalyptic frenzy and believed that a battle between Christ and Satan would ensue over the souls of the living and the dead. In their collective panic over what might come next, they abandoned their homes, sold or let loose all of their horses and livestock and stockpiled provisions to subsist in a cave, thinking they might outwit the judge of us all and survive the next year without sowing or gazing upon the sun or the moon.

"They disappeared," the old man said. "And were all judged anyhow, I suppose."

"That's what you get for wandering in the forest," the younger one said. "She's cursed you now, so keep moving, you're not welcome here." The two turned their heads mechanically. "He's doomed, the poor beggar," the young one said as the cart creaked on its away. Avram was alone again. The hair on his arms stood on end. He felt someone watching him, the surveillance running along the spine. He walked on and wondered what type of curse might be fitting for a man with his litany of sins. Perhaps I'll drown in a lake or the sea, he thought to himself, gasping for air like Karpathiotis and his old brood hound of a mother.

Crossing numerous streams and the river Pinios, he reached Larissa in Thessaly by nightfall. He couldn't remember how many nights had passed since he left the old woman and Elásson. In Larissa, he rested for a few uneventful days, sleeping for long hours beneath a cluster of pines on a bed of wilting needles, just outside the town. Foraging for anything he could sink his teeth into, he settled for a wild pear near the top of a tree, dried by the sun but at least not riddled with worms, a handful of mushrooms, upon which he gambled poisoning, and a string of sunflower husks discarded on the footpath near his bedding. Someone had walked by but not disturbed him. Those days dissolved after he left the place, as if he had never been there. Perhaps an aftereffect of his encounter with the two strangers and the village Xóros, he thought. His empty stomach made him forget the old woman and her curse for the time being.

Proceeding strictly along the main road, speckled with the occasional village and outpost, he ventured southeast onto the mottled port city of Volos, where his shoes had finally frayed to threadbare strips of cracking leather causing him to stop and nurse his blistered feet. The city was sea-swept in its gaiety and frivolity, all color and light and the aroma of strange botanicals and for this reason did not fit his mood. He remained there for four days at a widow's storied boarding house with rooms to let for an unending parade of sailors and foreigners frequenting the establishment. He ate well for the price. The room was clean and the house quiet during the day, as its mistress insisted it would be, but at night, it was lively with women's laughter, music and creaking bedsprings. He spoke to no one. He stayed until a local cobbler found the time to repair his shoes, for he feared purchasing a new pair and blistering his feet further, since he had no idea how far he might walk.

His shoes repaired, and otherwise having retained enough interest in his continued existence to not consider staying longer in Volos, he chartered a seat upon a vessel whose destination was unknown to him until he sat along the stern, bathing in the cool spray of the Aegean and inquired of the captain's nephew, a wild-eyed youth of fifteen.

"Skiathos," the youth said, smiling as if love and wealth awaited him there. They sailed directly to the island of nestled beaches, the haven of boat builders and fishermen of the north Aegean, men who fished and built boats, not because it was lucrative, but in the grip of a hardy delusion, observing the bravado of antiquity, of a manhood derived solely from the sea. The island's blond inhabitants intrigued Avram. From a distance, they appeared like Nordic pallbearers in their black caps and jackets. Save for the occasional short one, or extended length and obeisance of the nose they failed to appear indigenous, until two days later when he became accustomed to their blank stares and muteness. Then he noticed the imposing nearly lupine hairlines, the subservient, mildly heightened cheekbones whose subtle configuration asserted a presence, second after the beak. Their features fooled everyone at first and confused him, at first, but now, clearly, they appeared Dorian, a race indissoluble.

Avram squatted on Skiathos for twelve days in an abandoned stone structure that offered little but a good clay roof and a nearby well with pure water drawn from a mountain spring. The water, unlike that of Vegoritis was light, bodiless, like filtered sea foam; you drink and drink and your thirst remains unquenched. He had purchased a handful of provisions from a grocer while in the main town and inquired of a quiet place where he could rest undisturbed. Alone, a half kilometer above the port, he nursed his feet and the ache in his temples and took inventory of the shallow depressions between his ribs. Remorse was not a dietary hereditament peculiar to the Karangelos clan, but his appetite had waned with days of trampling contemplation of his recent crime. He wondered if he should have slit the wife's throat as well, but then concluded that he was glad to have not left her children orphans. He did not remember Calliope's name, for Maria had not spoken of her, nor did he know of her fate.

While having Magda sew into his pant leg three gold liras, previously stored in a box buried five paces to the right of the thriving flora of his Lathran courtyard, and departing Lathra with pockets spewing increasingly devalued drachmas, Avram still worried about his impending pennilessness, fearing a type of indigence he had never known before. He had long ago devoured the victuals prepared by his sisters for his journey. Settling into his ascetic, neglected manger, he devoured his purchased provisions at a faster pace than had he been walking, and was still hungry. He decided to visit Skiathos town the next day for a hot meal, to rekindle the fire of locomotion. He tramped into a disheveled kafenio, with its dirty transom facing the world, and sat at a table with a viable view of the port. He ate a meal of herring with onions swimming in oil and lemon juice, two thick slices of dry porous bread, black olives and stingingly unrehearsed *retsina*, whose piney, pithy density seemed unusual for the normally stringent tang of the wine. A light rain began to fall. The graying spirals of clouds commenced the overreaching evening chill of whatever season it was. He couldn't remember. The island's fragrance filled his nostrils, *Nihtolouloudo*, the fabled foot flower releasing its perfume only at night and disappearing by day, mingling with the nymph of the sea, with her olive wicker hair like the tentacles of squid and her breasts lying upon his eyelids in a harem's dream.

He meditated over his meal, imagining he would like to return to Smyrna, where he had eaten the best fish he ever tasted, and then visit his father's cousin Thalia, who raised him and his sisters for fourteen years. It was her culinary talent that resurfaced in his memory as home cooking, a reminder each time he became displeased with the art of sustenance served to him. Smyrna also served as a mnemonic synonym for the vicious machinations of Turks and Greeks, and his exodus from Anatolia. Thea (Aunt) Thalia as he called her was the wife of Christos Calphapanaiotis, a distributor of Smyrna carpets, silks and other fine cloths and gossamers. Christos successfully traded in replicas of the fabled Ottoman carpets manufactured in Uzak, in a hand mill owned and operated by a forgettable Armenian business partner. Raised amid the noisy barter of the carpet shop and broadlooms, Avram was educated in a tiny schoolhouse in the Greek quarter, where children sat on carpets and scribbled on chalk tablets the lessons from their primers. As he remembered fondly, he grew into manhood never wanting for the comforts of filial duty or the charitable hand of his Thea Thalia, whose pity for the orphans Karangelos was unequivocal. Theo Christos possessed a manly nullifidian disdain for the Church and admiration for colloquial Marxism, in that order. While superficially consistent doctrinal and revolutionary utopianisms, he thought, it was an obvious contradiction to his namesake and his bourgeois profession as the consummate middleman. Curiosities of a somewhat distant Karangelian kinship on her father's side, thus her exceptional devotion, Thalia bore the brunt of such duty toward her once removed nieces and nephew. She worked diligently, expending most of her noble effort attending to Magda's theatrical pretensions and Lydia's incorrigibility. All of this remained silently juxtaposed against the girls' general malaise over their mother Irsia, her inhumation of their daddy Samson, and their morose taming as children, the tunic and cestus of their father's blood. Theo Christos excelled at ignoring the essentially self-reared Avram, youthfully obedient as he was, and cleverly reinforcing the belief that he would grow to assume the carpet business for the childless couple, a belief neither of them instigated.

Amidst the happiness of a hectic life, a friend of Christos', a Turkish merchant Avram knew only as Sukru, a man of conscience and learning, in that fabled order, issued a grave warning to Christos regarding the impending doom awaiting Christians in the city. A Turkish military campaign to retake the city from Greek forces wisped with exhaled smoke from the lips of Turks and hung from their heavy lidded eyes like a looming confession. Reports swirled that Turks were slaughtering Christians and that Greeks east of the city, even if they feigned conversion, were marched to their death into the lifeless steeps of central Turkey, a cruel and lethal distance from both the sea and the Syrian border where escape and survival might have been possible. Turks masticated opposing atrocities, of course, but Sukru never mentioned this. Christos reluctantly heeded the warning upon Sukru's courageous and insistent third calling to the carpet shop and the arrival in the enchanted port of Smyrna of a harried and undermanned British Royal Navy.

With the city choking in conflagration and the thunderous hammering of heavy guns shaking the resolve of its masses, Christos abandoned his home and business and with his adopted family barely arrived at the port in time. Panic-stricken families jammed onto transport ships and tender boats from atop loading ramps possessing no rails or ropes to keep them from falling. The inability to control the swarm of refugees turned to chaos, the ramps withdrawn as the vessels reached capacity. Terrified mothers and children plummeted into the cold, clawing sea like discarded entrails of fish.

The decision whether to risk escape transpired in an instant, without hand wringing, without words or will. Christo insisted that Thalia and the children take their place on one of the three ramps channeling passengers onto vessels. Minutes later, this second set of vessels again appeared full and his family was not yet on the tender boat. Christos cried out at the top of his lungs. The girls heard their uncle's alarm, turned and looked back, but could not make him out in the surging throng on the docks. Suddenly, Thalia realized Avram was no longer by her side. Now well behind them, he wailed for his aunt. Instead of dissolving the heart with mercy, the cries of women and children fed the cruelty of panicked seamen and the crowd of passengers howling their frightful atonality like a pack of dogs devouring too miniscule a piece of meat. The desperate choice was theirs, risk of drowning or burning alive in the city or the searing slice of Turkish sabers. The crowd thrust forward. Thalia faced the possibility of submission, of falling onto the deck of the ramp. Unrelenting, she pulled the girls backwards, by the hands, the hair, whatever she could grab, tearing their clothes to keep them near as she reclaimed the boy. In the harried instant between life and death, against the movement of the mob, incising its fright, hurling toward the mass of limbs and heads visible at the heart of the ramp, Thalia collected Avram and moved the children to the very edge, placing her body between them and the plummet. Along this tightrope, she shuffled the remaining distance to the boat, seconds before the ropes were drawn and the gate lifted.

Christos braced himself, as other men had, ready to hurl themselves into the pitched bay to save their wives and children from the churning waters, from becoming buoys for others trying to save themselves, from ships' engines or sidling tender boats and the rising surface of the choking sea. Nearly all of them would drown as well. He scanned the deck of the trawler a second time and saw Thalia with all three children, and crossed himself. Then he fought for a spot on the ramp to a small vessel destined for the same transport ship and stood in the center of the ramp, permitting the crowd to push him onto the deck of the boat. As he boarded, yet another ramp dropped. Victims fell upon the outstretched limbs and bobbing heads already in the water, drowning children clinging to mothers desperately lifting them to their last breath. Avram grew to revile everything British.

"The most pitiful sight I have ever seen," he confided to Lambros, years later.

"Salvation has its limits, my boy," Christos had said to him of the Royal Navy as they sailed away. "These saviors are mortal men, but saviors nonetheless. No one else came for us."

Having lost all worldly possessions and regained nothing but traumatic memories of a harrowing exodus, Thalia and Christos still returned to Smyrna to visit and thank Sukru, unburdened with the care of the children Karangelos. They grew and deserted them and their humble four-room dwelling in the outskirts of Thessaloniki, a seemingly endless horizon of corrugated tin and concrete boxes inhabited by hordes of refugees from the furthest reaches of Asia Minor. By then, a decade later, Sukru had prospered in the hotel business. Descending the ramp to the old docks, Christos quivered with rage and a queer feeling of shame. He walked slowly across the same wretched planks of his deliverance where innocents had gulped the piceous ferment of death. Searching for affirmation of her emotion Thalia turned toward him and wept. He looked down at the black waves slapping the hulls of the ships and fishing boats. Sukru greeted them at the port with a taxi and a bouquet of flowers, as if they had been the ones who saved him. They sat at his table with his wife and grown children, a risky honor to bestow upon non-Muslims. By evening's end, he invited them to remain in Smyrna to work as employees at a new hotel he was planning for the newly renovated business district. The man whose desperate warning had saved them was now to be their master, in the land where they once prospered. Christos hesitated. He felt compelled into a decision. Thalia looked at her husband, a suggestion of prudence in her eyes, silently consulting him, but then, he quickly accepted.

Despite being the cockles of his boyhood and a perfect place to appear to be a native, for a fugitive pursued by Greek authorities, Avram declined his own provocation and daydream of returning to Smyrna. The carnage of the past filled his gullet. He stood up from his table, laid the remaining coins from his pocket along his plate and retraced his steps to his craggy hut. The next day he made out for the port again and boarded a commercial vessel from Skiathos headed for the Piraeus.

"Athens is a city where a man can hide from his past too," he thought, "and if not, then onto Alexandria. Perhaps I'll never stop. I'll roam the earth or end up in India, or sail the oceans to Australia, to China and South America." Once on the ship, he remembered a story he had heard as a boy, of a Greek shipping magnate, an able captain of Mitilini or Chios, he couldn't remember, who left his beloved island for Piraeus and became wealthy, shipping dry goods between the great continents. On a grand vacation, he sailed his entire family to the Orient, wife, children, siblings and their children, and all his in-laws. In the Sea of Japan, the able captain struck a reef with his great tanker. The ship split in two and sank in its whirlpools. Avram thought, this is what people must mean when they say that a history of love and blood is lost forever, never uttered among strangers, when no one remains to remember a single face or name. The old story inspired in him a fear of unseen masses, and of the sea, and while the voyage was otherwise uneventful, the sea noticeably tranquil in its blazing blue-black manipulation of light, he spent much of the time with his head over the railing vomiting into the Aegean. The calm of the sea he took as a good omen for his journey. His indigestion, he blamed on the food he last ate.

13

Few other sweets may pass between the lips of the beloved, so enslaved does love become in the imagination of the besotted. Lazaros had announced something of this general import, or at least this was how Andreas remembered the tutorial. He thought it was a commentary on women in general, that there was something there for him to learn. Lazaros saw no need to correct this misconception. He was actually reserving the comment for Danäe alone, a woman whom he could not fathom; more enchanting than he could say, yet for which he developed only a daughterly affection. Lathrans indeed possessed an unflagging fascination with Danäe. She was the entertainment in an otherwise dreary repetition of earthly routines. Tacitly, everyone agreed that such peerless beauty enhanced the experience of its observation when the beauty observed remained oblivious, like an inanimate object. This equally obliging reticence of self-awareness, a trait no one mistook as self-effacement or false modesty, permitted the women who were initially resentful to accept her being celebrated in such thrilling minutia. Regardless of her unpremeditated choices, how she clothed her torso or how little she said in her always less than idle speech, men were ever pleased with the swirl of inquiry and commentary, the endless lathering Talmud of enthrallment that was her every move. Draped about the frame of other women, the same garments, the same gestures might inhibit the abiding pull of feminine charm, but upon her, they were exalted, despite her reserved temperament. Any anecdote or scrutiny of her appearance, any transaction in which she was involved, whether the object of admiration or envy, any concoction drawn from the spittoon of gossip oozing from prurient lips, immediately developed into a matter of public commotion and all-consuming chatter. This apotheosis to each turn of the head and flutter of her luxuriant mane, to every supple, molecular stitch of her indulgent skin innocently exposed to the sun, resulted in a catalog of hoped for indiscretions, fictions manifesting as fantasy, salivation in the younger men, fretful vigilance in the indolent and old. The young had everything to gain from such daydreams, the old nothing better to do than to warn against and ward off the oracular snare of a priestess, with her vaguely mystifying proclamations. Whether procuring a kind of droll reverence or undue foreboding, her every utterance, be it simple or impenetrable, was opined to spring forth from her alleged Magyar origin, a sinuous etching of gypsy gothic and Transylvanian entanglements emanating from her father's ancestry of bizarre rituality. Little in this genealogy was accurate unless one counted her father's most distant forerunner, few of whom the Lathrans knew of anyway.

Dranias family legend had it that a patriarch of old was a traveling apothecary, a popularly harmless alchemist and peddler of dark teas and salves from the Near East. While traveling as far as Lyon, plying his wares, he became one of the few to grace the scaffolds of Pope Innocent the IV. Judgment transpired after a highly publicized *inquiro* into a confessed relationship with a certain Dacian witch, "a priestess of the brew and a traveling companion," as the records indicate, whom the authorities mistook for his sister but was actually his young wife. She, too, was condemned to the pyre, for failing to confess her faith satisfactorily, in part because she could neither speak the vernacular or Latin to understand the question put to her but also for refusing to cease crossing herself in the Byzantine manner and, as the documentary records corroborate, for the ornate calligraphy of scurrying lizards embroidered upon her vestment. The priests mistook this outer garment of Southeast Asian handiwork for cabalism. In the process of punishing her bodily for the acquittal of the soul, in the rabidity of righteousness, in the course of her interrogation the inquisitor discovered that she routinely trimmed her pubic hair and underarms to within a fair shadow of the skin. This unusual hygiene she practiced at her husband's insistence, or so the records suggest, and apparently left a trace of scarring from a few unfortunate mishaps with the blade. These appeared to the prying eyes of drooling inquisitors like "the scratching of unholy beasts upon the gates of chastity." She also apparently perfumed her body with oils so aromatic as to cause delirium and erections in all men, horses and dogs. Not the first wife to suffer for the sexual excesses of her husband, both the moral and the tale ended badly.

Danäe believed not a wisp or whiff of the forerunner's history, whose fame was incanted in his name, Andracos Dranias, and his sensuously pallid wife, Oleandra, her ophidian slither of a walk, the records indicated, likened to a seductive serpent, her long tinseled curls to a she-devil's madness, and her scent to paralytic potions.

Prudery is the art of the idle. The busybody, the moribund *we* of small towns and villages excel in the art of vivid and fanciful rumors and prefer outlandish fabrications regarding the unusually beautiful or the particularly ugly to the typically blanched moralizing heaped upon the brows of common folk. Lathra was no different.

"There are no answers, only the story of men and their crimes and urges," Danäe had warned Pavlos Lourithas on an occasion of his public disrespectfulness. Pavlos, bolstered with courage in the presence of his friends, had come across Danäe wading in the lake on a particularly balmy afternoon. He begged her, malodorously, if a tone of voice could ever achieve as much, to swim with him as his reward, if he could provide her with the answer to whatever it was she was looking for.

"Alright," she countered, "what am I looking for?"

"Well, give me a hint, in the name of Christ and the Virgin," he implored. "I'm not a conjurer." The incident ended with his threatening to wade out to her. She swam deeper into the lake, where none of them would venture, and turned her back, treading water until they grew discouraged and left, or so she thought. Pavlos stayed behind and hid until dusk, when she emerged from the water, lips trembling and teeth chattering, but naked as the eels that swam between her legs. He watched her dry herself and dress. Her perfection became the vociferous legend, from his lips, and his boast that he was the only man alive to have seen the goddess in the flesh.

Danäe's ability to engage in calming, labial discourse with domesticated animals was renowned, even in nearby villages, but it was this same aptitude in favor of the infantile or the mentally deranged which provided proof to the chatterboxes of her inscrutable Gnostic origins and talents. This was especially true of her calming rapport with the prototypical village idiot, Jartzo, whose given name was Ioannis, and his deeply paranoid and unsightly mother, Katerina, ironically named after the wisest of feminine saints. Katerina, as rumor brayed, had engaged in unholy acts with a mule or a bull, no one was quite sure. For this, it was believed, she was execrated and damned to unending labor in bringing forth the infant Jartzo which, after hours of umbilical constriction about the child's throat, culminated in his being severed from his mother's belly in the manner of Caesar, too late to save what was left of his oxygen-deprived mind. No other explanation would suffice according to the imbecilic deductions of jaded men and cynical old maids who could not fathom that any man would chose to commit the sin of so wasting his semen on such an unsightly creature as Katerina.

"Better to spill it on the ground than lie with a beast," they reassured each other.

"A blind Naoditi must have skewered her," the men said.

Katerina was indeed an apelike mascaron, hairy, thick browed, morose, with grossly exaggerated voluptuousness, pendulous breasts swaying to her waist, barreled, barnacled hips and thickly knotted logs for legs, and sporting a large lymphoma on her throat. A lumbering expression and horrible skin condition plagued her unpredictably upon certain changes of season, with pustules and scars spotting her face and neck from past molestations, since she could not resist scratching the irritant. Her body odor, not so unlike that of the other women in the village who labored and had no water available to wash themselves with any frequency, was staggering in its ability to suffocate anyone within a meter. Seemingly a simpleton, when in fact not, she could neither explain nor recall the act resulting in her impregnation in her twenty-first year, let alone by whom. She lacked carnal knowledge to that point even by proxy, and the process neither impressed itself upon her memory nor was, in her mind, significantly different from the host of assaults she endured all her life at the hands of her detestable mother, the difference and only exception of course being the sickly, limp poker of Jartzo's delivery. The shortest pedigree to this ugly evolution was unknown to anyone but Katerina's mother, who died, at the hands of her daughter, some said, shortly after the hair-lipped and initially mute Jartzo was born. This a priori deduction arose from the memory of Katerina's mother apparently gagging upon a vile milky salivation thought to be a potion of poisonous root and hemlock mixed with honey and citrus for palatability.

Upon vesperal ascensions to each full moon, when in the grip of her inspired paranoia, Katerina would roam the village in a creeping, terror-stricken gait and denounce her neighbors with noxious flatulence and matching epithets of the most heretical, lewd and raucous sort imaginable. For the most part, villagers reacted with amusement or simply avoided her, until her venial inspirations would climax into a stream of curses upon their deceased members or some other morbidly creative sacrilege against saints and prophets. Then, when realizing the fear or complete disgust of her audience, or when confronted by mothers, or stones flung in reprisal by their children, she would hurl, in return, her most audacious nuggets followed by "You're Christ and the Virgin that bore him, *panoukla na sas faei!*[51] As if cursing one's face, their race and their god, was not enough.

"Shame on you, Katerina," the women would scream back. "May the devil stuff your mouth with his dung!"

"I'm baptizing your mule's erection next week," she would call back gleefully. "You're all invited to lend your sinkholes."

"Burst you filthy *sourtouka!*"[52] the village motley would screech and snarl, aghast and entertained at once. On and on the fuming exchanges would escalate, until hair-pulling castigation erupted. Finally, the humor would reach its limits and either Danäe or a masculine witness would intervene. If none were available, her opponents invariably retreated and Katerina would stand triumphantly bloodied, but feared for her lunacy and inability to tolerate the contentment of others.

Katerina also loved spiders and collected them. "They keep the flies and hornets away," she explained. The rest of the village was plagued with flies in the summer while her house was an arachnid membrane, alive with webs and nests she refused to disturb. She would find little brown pholicidae and black atypaidae, long-jawed orb weavers and dozens of other species and bring them home to the drawn curtains of her dank house. Jartzo became accustomed to sharing the abode with his many legged brethren. By the age of four, he realized spiders could not

51 πανούκλα να σας φάει – may the plague devour you

52 σοουρτούκα – a transliterated Turkish slang for sluttish bitch

hear his screams and except for scratching the initial itch, barely noticed the bites that covered his groin and armpits. Anyone within three feet of Katerina would witness her as a host. Spiders crawled about her clothing and tickled the cavity of her insensate left ear, which she occasionally exposed to the sunlight. In the functioning and rather obtrusive right ear, she could not tolerate the tickle and gently wiggled her finger through each crevice when one sought a fleshy haven. Each generation of spider had to learn right from left. Danäe tried explaining the health risk to Katerina but she would have none of it.

"The rest of you can live like pigs and have flies lay eggs in your eyes and nose. The filthy pests don't flap a wing in my house."

Danäe found in Lathra and its hodgepodge of Anatolian heredity what appeared to be the fertile soil of her calling, a remarkably honed and gratifying career in animal husbandry. Of necessity, she added midwifery to her valise of mercy and skill, following the death of Maria, who had temporarily assumed that role. She also applied her laconic but fruitful insights to human anatomy and illnesses, proceeding on the assumption that there was not much difference between judging the groans of stolid Lathrans than in construing the growls and bellows of infirm beasts. Soon she developed an uncanny talent for diagnoses in the aid of expectant mothers and sickly or surly children. This left little time for social discourse, limited, for the most part, to wives and mothers who called upon her for assistance, or with the children or the *tsobani*.

The only real diversion she possessed was sampling the leaves of various aboriginal herbs for use as teas. These she gathered from Kythera and on excursions as far as the foothills and mountains to the southwest. She fawned over her intricate little collection of tiny tea sets - three from China and one from Japan - sold to her by a traveling tinker, wiping them clean on a weekly basis and wrapping them in velvet cloth, using them only on special occasions and for her own experiments in tasting. The taste for teas, which Lathrans generally used for medicinal purposes, she had developed as a girl, the product of tutoring offered by her mother and father, who had learned to prefer the leafy brew to coffee while living in England.

She attended Church regularly when Pater Alexi made his rounds, because as she revealed to Lazaros, "I enjoy his homilies and the musicality of his liturgy." Only later when a full appreciation of the diversity of her learning enlightened the listener, did she receive the invitation to engage Lazaros, Pater Alexi and his deacon in the now infamous symposiums of the erudite. Lazaros eventually befriended her, in the reserved semantic sense, he being an ascetic but also her mentor of late, and by association with Andreas, who was the one male acquaintance close to her age with whom her social frigidity thawed, and to whom she dared enjoy relaying the details of her vocation. She appreciated Andreas, and not simply because he did not speak to or glare at her in the manner of other young men. He studied her as well, but discreetly from the vista of heightened admiration rather than voluble desire. He believed he quite effectively subverted his desire in her presence. She found him "intelligent but at once marvelously simple and visibly ensnared by the heart," something she eventually revealed to Elissa. This admission and realization eventually caused in her a singular unease in his presence unlike what she experienced with other men, for as has been noted, that among her most enduring charms was an ingenuous dismissal of her loveliness, a disinterest in recognizing or fathoming the rapt and attentive nature of men and an utter absence of any seductive aptitude. Even the blundering, cajoling repartee of Avram, with his incessant attempts to assist her, failed to evince in her a reason for such kindness. She imagined his conduct to be brotherly benevolence or the product of his miry mood over the loss of his Maria.

Danäe saw herself as unusual, but without intending to espouse any social hypocrisy in connubiality, or any overt desire to resist the subservience and black-booted patriarchy most women endured. Neither did she see herself as a vocal advocate for women's suffrage or as a political revolutionary, nor as having evolved beyond the need to marry, but simply as a girl ill suited for the odalisque of romantic love.

"No man will want me," she confided in yet another young woman whom she knew to be pining over Andreas. "I can't cook very well and I would rather read or roam the mountains hunting for tea leaves than lay upon the divan, waiting to be worshiped." The latter image was one she had heard her father draw with contempt as precisely what streaking modernity and immodesty means for women and why they pursue it with such stridency. But the concept was foreign to most village women. She remained convinced that her love of literature and fondness for the intricacies and vagaries of European culture and thinking would intimidate a toiling man who tended the earth and his beasts, despite her ability to care for animals. Despite the passionate model her parents represented, her experiences in Constantinople, avoiding the horned whims of her lecherous employer, whom she believed drew motivation only from his hashish-corrupted circle of acquaintances and his wife's delusion, inverted in her any girlish supposition that marriage was a noble collaboration without impediment. Among the rumors surrounding her was the suggestion that she had soured to men altogether, perhaps unconsciously, as she herself might have believed of such hearsay, whether men advanced their interests with the antlered erection of a rutting deer or kissed the hand of her apathy with cultivated, Parisian cordiality. Thereafter, she remained the cataleptic, the flame that never burns its adoring moths.

Andreas, for his part, felt compelled to know her and be near her, beyond merely taking note or watching her, and was truly enamored of the fashioned Pandemos of Lathra. He, too, studied the natural, seemingly unaffected, unstudied aesthetic of her every manner and quite easily believed he was as close to the ensconcing magnetisms of love as he had ever felt, having compared them only with such filial dedication as he knew as a boy from his dutiful mother and sisters.

Astonishing in his resemblance to Vasili, who was four years his elder, Andreas was a great classical promachos, his arms emerging griffin-like from the broad-bladed gradient of shoulders, embellishing a scale of vigor the villagers compared to Kythera. A heroic, Attic nose dominated his face, a disciplined sentinel amid the granite of pronounced cheekbones and large, deep-set eyes, shadowed and imperiling, like great boulders about to crush the skull. To women, he appeared more finely cast than any worthy Doric usurper might have sculpted. The only significant differences between the brothers were the incongruity of the proboscis, as if drawn from a wholly other genesis, Vasili having the more refined and deferential to the impression, and the mouth, less sensual in its camber. Among the unmarried women of Lathra and Arnissa, Andreas' paratsoukli was

Theseus, for even those who lacked formal education were familiar with the myths. Vasili's was Odysseus, the brilliant, the sorcerer, as famous for the deep seductive timbre of his voice as for his Apollonian physique - a voice no one ever heard swell in anger and to which maidens apparently swooned in attendance of its graveled whispers and unhurried elocution.

For a moment, Danäe would permit herself the torpor of her narcissus, a feeling of fantasy, the lightheadedness preceding her suppression of any unease she felt in Andreas' presence, the inconspicuous, gentle stroke of his gaze, like a painter's unconscious absorption with the splendor of his subject, eliciting in her a charming blush and the involuntary diversion of her eyes. On at least three occasions, she inadvertently broadcast her alleged disinterest in him to an indiscreet audience of other available young women, whose envy and distrust she unknowingly safeguarded with serendipitous gratuities, favors and advice. The first time occurred when gathering at the lake to retrieve water for the holy font, in preparation for the baptism of the milky little infant, Efthemios Canettas, the newest son of the village mechanic, Petros Canettas, the wizard of all things geared and combusted. The wily young Theodora Triphonas, remarkably large bosomed for a woman so thin in the ankles and haunches, a feature she assumed all men would surrender to, and known for her unvaryingly blunt tongue, complained openly of her failed attempts to ensnare Andreas, the Adonis of her salaciously entrenched imagination.

"I don't see why you fuss so," Danäe said. "He's just a man among others." The comment made abruptly, prompted a hush to the women's banter then a puzzled titter, and the squints and raised eyebrows of disbelief. Danäe had rarely voiced anything even remotely critical of another member of her adopted society, let alone issue what to these women appeared as an unnecessary ingredient to a perfectly saccharine confection. On a second occasion, when gathered together to winnow wheat, it became obvious that Danäe had avoided conversation altogether and cast her gaze down to the threshing floor rather than look up at Andreas. Finally, it occurred again when they were set to work together sweeping chaff into a trough, Andreas crept furtive glances at her twisting torso. And again, she spoke not a word to him when asked to distribute the chaff, mixing it with lime milk and water to feed the swine. Then, some weeks later, captive in the company of the same women, upon the occasion of a minor feast, Theodora, whose father celebrated his saint's day and had managed a brief conversation with Andreas, again announced to her starry-eyed friends that he was her hero, her Theseus, while the others giggled in agreement.

"He should accomplish something extraordinary to ascribe to him so noble a title," Danäe interjected.

"Are you blind?" Theodora asked and turned to the other women. "Why would he have to accomplish anything? Look at him!" The women chided her for an insincere disaffection. Danäe defended herself.

"You wouldn't want to be in the shadow of such a man's myth," she said.

"Why not, for God's sake?" Theodora interrupted. "It's precisely his shadow that I'm yearning for," she said with both hands planted on her hips. The others guffawed and blushed, and covered their mouths.

"You'd forever be on the verge of desertion," Danäe rationalized, her voice fractured with tension. "Women will throw themselves at him; he'll be enticed by the less timorous, someday. . ."

"Stop," Theodora said, agitated with what appeared to her like a clear deception offered by the celebrated augur of Lathra. "You're licking your lips dry over him!" Danäe's eyes widened at the suggestion, but she could only chirp a paltry excuse like an ensnared bird.

"He's all yours, Theodora." She lingered for a moment, a paler shade of mortification, and then politely excused herself from the merriment, walked out of view and ran home, completely humiliated for the first time since she had fled Constantinople. Rumors of the episode wandered the short distance of Lathran etiquette and made its way as a whisper into the ear of Vasili who eventually relayed it in a guarded proviso to his brother.

"Be careful, brother, be sure of what you want," he warned. "A woman like that will never want for suitors. No matter how loyal she may be. Any doubts you harbor will have a life of their own and age you before your time." Andreas was surprised with his brother's caution. He resigned to be patient, to permit the tale its germination and said nothing to anyone else of his satisfaction at the suggestion of her interest. This dormant state of affairs proved prudent, since Danäe would certainly have denied its veracity, abashed and unsure of herself as she was. Suffice it to say he possessed no notion of the appropriate time or comportment to ensure success and so continued to hope for the devise of such a plan. He was obliged just a month later.

Returning a book lent to her by Lazaros, from his now overburdened shelves and strewn across his floor, Danäe strolled down the narrow paths to the overhang below *Mavrotripa*, where one usually found him on hot afternoons. His was the equivalent of the village lending library for the few literates he encountered and for Pater Alexi, who might devour a book or two and then admonish him for possessing such "dribble of the anti-Christ" or for listening to his Victrola, castigating him for his "inebriation with the tri-tone memorialized upon the megaphone of Satan." Of limited use to them, most villagers decried his library as "a worthless collection of paper and ink, and worst yet in unfamiliar tongues." Danäe found Lazaros lakeside, seated on a gracious rock whose depressions and pockmarks, generally the size of a woman's hindquarters, made for comfortable sitting beneath the overhang, as long as the weather was dry and water had not collected there. He was reading from a handwritten, string bound parchment, sampling some cheese, a slice of melon and hunks of bread. Andreas was his guest, having attended the liturgy that morning, a rarity for him, after declining a stroll near the waterfalls of Edessa with Vasili and his betrothed, the pleasingly simple Penelope Halkias, their employer's daughter, and her exuberant mother, Margarita. Andreas was still dapper in his Sunday best, a light brown suit, starched white shirt and thin black tie. For the last year, he had visited Lazaros almost weekly, listening politely and attentively to the caprice of translations of hitherto unheard of literary masterpieces, which Lazaros decanted and wrestled with in the morning hours. These were none too meticulous syntactical, semantic riddles for Lazaros, sustaining his yearning to replicate a particularly profound insight or gracious image of human frailty for a new audience. That day's selection was from *Typee*. A few months earlier he had sped through an abridged installment of *The Last of the Mohicans*, which he also struggled to translate, neither of which any publisher would have considered beyond the first paragraph. His cursive was scarcely decipherable and his Greek too risky.

"I took such outlandish liberties as no one had ever seen," he confided in Danäe.

Andreas listened keenly. He had never heard such tales. Exotic, alien, insular worlds, sailors in barbaric jungles and the nakedness of island women bouncing about like an episodic protagonist. The readings took on an actor's cadence and animation in the depictions of craven violence, brazen and gory. Lazaros seemed to live within the stories and often paraphrased or embellished difficult passages that Andreas candidly admitted he could not understand. Absent the storyteller's zeal, he might have left Lazaros to read to the gliding current and congregating fish, but the manly yarns seemed to fit the audience. Literary source and listener harmonized. When in a less swaggering mood, he read Danäe bits of his erratic translations of Thoreau, James, Fitzgerald and Conrad, she being more suited for this corpus.

Danäe handed back to Lazaros a borrowed volume of *Illusions perdues*, a first edition in the Greek stippled with morsels of un-translated French, purchased and delivered by mail from a bookseller in Athens. After polite greetings, she sought immediately to excuse her presence, but Lazaros insisted she stay, reminding her that she had previously enjoyed his abbreviated rendition of *Billy Budd*. Andreas offered her the most comfortable spot, a weatherworn dimple of rock he brushed clean with his hand. She blushed and declined. Sensing her discomfort, Lazaros abruptly excused himself, and left his scribbles laying on the rock. Andreas retrieved each page, before they blew into the lake. Danäe waited and watched.

"I'll take these up to him and leave them by the door if you'd like," Danäe said, as he handed them to her. "I apologize for disrupting your discussion or reading, or whatever he was telling you."

"He was reading a story about merchant shipman and the islands of another world, but he keeps stopping and explaining what's not written in the book, what's between the lines, as he says. He's a strange parrot, isn't he?" Andreas said smiling, standing between her and the avenue of escape. "Having studied so many great books, I suppose. Perhaps this is what living alone does to a man. It can't be that all Americans are like him." Her mind drifted in different directions, the celerity of a winged messenger darting about inside her. No particular elucidation came to mind, not at first, but she did remember how cunningly he had avoided conversation in their other encounters, the delicacy of his observation and smiling at her. They had never been completely alone. He looked at her this time, waiting for her to say something, or for some dissection of emotion. For the first time, she hesitated before averting her gaze, a habitual insecurity that came naturally. Then, in a flash of insight, she fathomed what others had meant when they said that men were leering at her. Indeed, they always had, even when she was a girl. Suddenly she understood that any redress or apology for a lurid gesture or improper suggestion was the coded expression most men taught each other, something thoroughly insincere, especially when she had not noticed them or requested an apology. Seated on the rock, alone with him, she unearthed the beguiling affect she had upon him, like a lost treasure. She suppressed the elation, the warm and rosy lightheadedness and the blood-infused pulse of the moment.

"I'm very sorry, Andreas," she repeated. "What you must think of me, my being out of place here."

Andreas had waited to see her again during the intervening weeks since the tale of her alleged interest had amplified within him. He hoped, but did not believe the rumor to begin with, not at all, but had also long ago decided that little harm would come with his someday, subtly evincing his affection. For an instant, he resolved, even if it might prove regrettable, to join the league of other suitors she ignored. Looking at her, meeting her eyes, he felt trapped by a vague tutelage of good manners and drew away. The words he sought to retrieve, rehearsed in private, were gone. Instead, he uttered a tautology of his sentiment.

"You already know what I think of you." The sincere but less then deft confession gave the impression of a withdrawn kiss but left little doubt in her mind. She, who had never managed to comprehend the words and gestures of men, inexplicably took this nuance as endowed with admiration. He stepped to the side. She skirted by him, brushing against his shoulder and ran up the path out of sight, the radiance of a hitherto unknown smile, offered with a pleasure that no one would witness. When she returned he was gone. Lazaros descended with her. He bade her company for one of his strolls along the lake, which meant he was in a talkative mood. She felt awkward carrying Andreas' admission and was about to decline the walk when Lazaros noticed her inattentiveness, as he launched into explaining one of his more outlandish theories.

"The consciousness of one's will or perceptions," he was explaining, "choosing one horn of any dilemma over another, occasions the creation of a version of *me* contained in the choice I did not make. I am in the path I chose, and," offered with emphasis, "also those paths I did not choose but am still conscious of. I am all of these, at the same time! What do you think?" He smiled with excitement. She appeared puzzled and offered no response. "The memory of music approximates this phenomenon. I will explain how if you have a moment." At this point, he noticed her not listening. She turned toward the road.

"What did Andreas have to say that has you so pensive, child?"

"Nothing," she answered unconvincingly. He walked quietly with her a few more paces and reached for her arm to gain her attention.

"The old women have an expression."

"Yes, they have many," she confirmed delicately.

"Love enters through the eyes."

"I know that one," she said embarrassed, for they had never discussed the subject. She was reluctant to move the conversation forward. "But quite unlike lust, love pierces deeply, and comes to rest at a different time and place than what we may foretell," he said, patting the top of her head. "And so, as it enters through the eyes it departs upon the rays of light as well, but in a torrent." He turned and walked back to the path toward the lake.

14

Civilizations expose true meaning in their congenial routines. Their sin and habits of hostility divulge in those exhibitionist tendencies of high art, technical innovation and social revolution, or so Alexi believed and often taught from the pulpit. He stressed family life, tending to the needs of children without spoiling them and benevolence to one's neighbors, promoting such values over book learning and high culture. Alexi felt no contradiction in the fact that he was more educated than the average village priest and managed to accomplish both goals of edification and domestication, but often sought to deny others the pleasure and advantage of what he possessed. He took great pains to avoid public comment on the epochal subjects of the learned and politically entwined, but privately urged certain congregants, whom he believed possessed the intellectual accessories to decipher the technicalities of modern debate and to resist what he saw as the enemies of freedom and thought.

———◆———

Having disappeared without a word of farewell to Lambros, his co-founding compatriot and the first to lay claims to Kazvam, Avram Karangelos left behind a seemingly indelible, potted legacy of political intrigue and habituation. This habit rekindled, warped, grafted and malformed through the ensuing years into a philosophical tempest, a bloody cirque of folly between Stalinist, Titoist, Royalist and Fascist renditions of fratric betrayal whose nexus coincided with, and at first appeared to Lathrans as, a comparatively civilized squabble among neighbors at odds over that sapphire elixir of progress - the waters of Vegoritis. The gale of detestation that was England and Germany and the political strife consuming Russia served as proof that such rivalries were not a uniquely Hellenic trait after all. Indeed these were the imported backdrops for the theater that became Lathra and all of Greece.

———◆———

Following the investigation and Mario's adieux to Lydia and her tantalizing embrace, Lambros set about the task of unraveling the headless conspiracy of opposition to his irrigation system, now that it seemed certain the architect of such antagonism might not return. Not wanting to alert Pavlides by using his telephone, he rode his intractable mule to Arnissa to contact the engineer on a telephone in a bakaliko owned by a Greek Jew named Iakovos. The store was a diverse emporium at the edge of town, filled with groceries, fabrics, hardware, wares of the home and shoes. It smelled of silver or some indiscernible metal and the mustiness of damp cloth and had chronically insufficient lighting. Iakovos offered a variety of services in addition to the sale of his merchandise - tailoring, dentistry and banking - as well as a libation-free kafenio for the handful of local Jewish merchants and their sons. It was the first emporium in the region to have a telephone and therefore known to everyone. Lambros called to ask the engineer, Agnostakis, to consider a second trip to Lathra, stressing that, "Avram is on holiday" and would thus not have the opportunity to instigate a reception like the one he had received on his first visit. "Plus I have to return your book of charts."

Lambros had little experience with the hollow ticks and sonic chirping of electronic cicadas, which to him sounded like a distant lapping sea, transmitting an insistent muffle of breathing from a phantom posing as an acquaintance at the other end of the line. He continued his conversation long after Agnostakis had hung up the telephone, the engineer being ungraciously perplexed and annoyed with the audacity of the man asking him to return for a second stoning. Lambros ended his monologue and turned to the proprietor with a wrinkled expression of technical ignorance and awkwardness.

"I forget . . . what do I do now?"

Iakovos sat at a table wiping glassware with a towel, inspecting the prisms of somnific rays pouring through the sparkling facade of his storefront.

"You go home, *vlaka*,[53] or buy something, or have a seat and have a kafedaki. I could hear the humming from over here. He hung up the telephone the moment you said your name."

"Yes, well, I'm sure he is considering my offer."

An hour later, Lambros traveled to, and persuaded, a friend from just outside Arnissa, one Gregorios Rigopoulos, affectionately referred to as Rigos the Phallus, to provide him with transportation for the long drive to Thessaloniki. Rigos was the owner of two mechanical invalids for vehicles. The first, an American-made six-wheeled truck with a large wagon bed, wooden slats and a canvas top, used for transporting both man and beast to Edessa, its engine having finally died after a disgruntled customer poured dirt and barley chaff into its fuel tank. This

---

53 βλάκας - stupid

machine was in a constant state of repair, its parts strewn across Rigos' courtyard, a dusty, grassless haven for chickens, goats, and his six children. The other standard truck was a decrepit affair. Its cab stunk of sour milk and piglet deposits ever since he lost the back door of its enclosed bed while hauling a young bull sold to a breeder east of Edessa. Lambros had accompanied him on that day, and the often-discussed memory served as a bond between the men. The bull had rammed the truck's gate completely off its hinges. Neither man quite knew why but speculated that it was a frenzied arousal while passing a meadow of bovine damsels dragging their burdened udders though the grass, or in reaction to the provocation of a seditious fly up the nostril of sanity, or some other undetermined spur of a bull's rebellion. In any event, door and bull tumbled into a yawning ravine on the narrow winding road to Edessa, and lay in a heap of twisted metal and splintered wood, entombing the now fully decayed carcass. This was a weighty, emotional loss for Rigos, even overshadowing the financial ruin of his previous year and requiring him to use the truck cab to deliver his succulent little scoundrels of the braising spit for sale to butchers throughout the region. Luckily, for Lambros, on this trip, Rigos was traveling to Thessaloniki only to collect a debt from a grocer who had previously purchased piglets and a goat on credit and then possessed the gumption to move his store and household to the Kato Toumba section of the city, presumably to avoid paying Rigos and numerous other creditors. Kato Toumba was a part of town graced with drawn-out dirt lanes and thoroughfares of lovingly nurtured clay roofed bungalows, some painted bright colors, with tiny backyards, in which each centimeter of soil was optimally cultivated with some vegetable, herb or fruit tree.

Being among the literate young men to emerge from his village in Epirus, Lambros sought to beseech the engineer in person or, in the alternative, to enlist the man's colleagues to assist him in a visit to the great library of the University. There, he would initiate his research on how to calculate the fueling needs, piping, pump capacities, and procurement of an Archimedean screw for a pumping station. Delusion being simple, he was prepared to return to Lathra with handwritten notes from what he thought would be his pick of treatises on the engineering and erection of water delivery systems and then planned to proceed immediately from his own delivery to Yianko's kafenio, in order to confront Gallanos and Terzellos with the mechanical wonders of his findings.

"First we get my money," Rigos warned, "before we get your papers and books and then we visit Kyria Kounellitsa."

"Who's Kyria Kounellista?"

"A butcher's wife who likes it anyway I stuff my sausage into her casings."

"Rigo, you've got to stop chasing younger women."

"Younger nothing!" Rigos said, shame contorting his mouth and chin. "This one's a well-used saddle, my Lala. It's actually her appetite that draws one to her, damn it. Not her looks or age. Truth be told, and mind you, I can't have this repeated to anyone, I had a little trouble straightening my aim out when I first saw her naked. A shocking sight it was. But after a few times, I got used to her."

"I don't have time for your shameless jaunts, Rigo. You are a married man with six children, not a buck with a cage full of bunnies. Drop me off at the library and then go back to spread your dirty seed."

"Suit yourself my reputable Lala, but my gypsy will give us both a peek at paradise, I'm sure of it! She suggested as much the last time I was with her. Bring a friend, she said, without an ounce of embarrassment. I tell you she's all tits and fiery pot, unafraid to hear her own groans of pleasure. She lets loose the kind of grunts and carnal commands most women reserve for the men they are accustomed to, if they ever do. And her price is free my friend. That's the beauty of it! She never asks me for anything, no prime cuts for her sons or nephews or dresses, or trinkets. You're not a bad looking worm. She'll like you."

"Forget it," Lambros said. He believed he possessed the compulsive capacity to be like Rigos and for this reason did not judge him harshly. The same lewd images occurred to him from time to time, especially after listening to Rigos detail his exploits, or when he thought of his boyhood curio, and the look of lust on Aphrodite's face as she steadied herself with her two Satyrs, one distended member pointing north, the other south. Yet in the thick of such fantasies, fear always overcame him, flashing through his mind like divinely inspired vacillation. Fear of a wrenching punishment and ignominy that could only transpire here on earth or worse, within the ring of hell reserved for seducers and philanderers. In his vivid imagination, the never-ending burn of repetitive sin might entail witnessing his daughters' condemnation and torment and that they might see him, whether here on earth or down there, and thus know what he had been.

The collection of money from the grocer went fairly well for Rigos, but only after placing the grocer sufficiently in jeopardy of a creditor's violence.

"You thought you could move your shop and hide from me," Rigos told the grocer fiercely as he bent back his debtor's fingers to greet the curly down of his forearm.

"Aaaah, if you break my fingers I won't be able to work," he cried.

"You call this work, fatso!" The grocer proved, upon this second attempt at collection, to be somewhat short of the exact sum owed. As restitution, Rigos helped himself. First, he chose a nicely dressed chicken ready for wrapping and delivery to another patron. He demanded that the grocer keep the gizzards and liver out of sight because he despised the intestines of animals, generally held in high regard by the palette of most men. Then Rigos selected a variety of cheeses, and complained when the grocer failed to wrap them carefully. Next, he moved to the dry goods side of the store and took a pair of nail clippers, a new invention from America well suited for his already trim but flattened and deformed fingernails. After that, he snatched a deck of cards, a tin of imported chocolates and a black and white print featuring ancient lovers in various poses of promiscuity. In lieu of fingering his *komboloi*,[54] the portly grocer stashed chocolates under his counter next to his cigar box with large denominations, regularly popping the chocolates into his mouth and washing them down with cognac.

"That's too much for what you sold me, thief," the grocer chided. "Do you really believe I moved my shop and family to avoid paying for a lousy goat and a few piglets?"

"Interest, Raia, interest," Rigos said, taking a tin of candied almonds as punishment for the grocer's comment.

"Interest!" the grocer protested. "What's that for? I'm calling the authorities."

"It means we're even," Rigos said laughing, pushing his finger into the center of the grocer's forehead, pleased with his barter. The grocer reached his limit and risked a new intimidation.

"A curse upon you, Rigopoulos. May you toss another bull over the cliffs!" The grocer recalled the story of the demise of the bull made

---

54 κομπολόϊ - worry beads

famous by Rigos in a moment of self-pity. Rigos stopped abruptly, just short of the door, his arms filled with plunder. He turned slowly, the enigmatic manly aura that so captivated women filled the grocer with fear. Rigos' overbearing frame obscured the doorway. Momentary inertia provoked the grocer's anticipation into a nervous, nearly girlish laugh. Rigos responded, his voice like gravel underfoot.

"Watch I don't take your wife the next time I'm in town. I'll tie her to your bed face down! She'll have no use of her legs for a week." Lambros was embarrassed for the grocer and felt the man did not deserve this cruelty, but he could not bring himself to intercede or even remark as much to his friend, who had driven him all over creation and never charged him a drachma. Instead, Lambros stood in the corner of the store, stoically, as if he were a waiting patron. With his free hand, Rigos tried to reach a handful of sesame candies from the counter but dropped his obscene picture in the process. The grocer shut his mouth. Rigos kicked the picture away.

"I don't want my sons finding your stained girlfriends anyway. Eh Lalas, put some sesame candies into my pocket, will you? I like them. They remind me of autumn." Hesitantly, Lambros grabbed a handful of candies from the bowl and stuffed them into Rigos' pocket, then looked over at the grocer apologetically.

Rigos begged Lambros again to accompany him to the apartment of Kyria Kounellitsa, conveniently situated behind her husband's busy butcher shop in the center of the city. But his vivid portrayal of her talents and rapacious aptitude were to no avail. Eating cheese and sesame candies while driving, they arrived at the University with ample daylight left to them. Lambros stepped out of the vehicle. Rigos looked up at him, smiling blithely, a halo of adelphic tendresse about his head.

"What fun we are having today, my Lala!

"Yes," Lambros smiled back.

"I'll be back to pick you up in an hour or so, maybe two. My gypsy lives along the boulevard near the big Church."

"I'll meet you before the great doors of the Church when I'm done," Lambros suggested.

"Good idea, my boy," Rigos beamed, digging into his pocket and handing Lambros a few drachmas. "Light a candle for me and ask for my forgiveness, but wait for at least and hour or so. So it counts for all of today's sins."

———◆———

Lambros spent nearly an hour wandering the halls of the University asking whomever he could of the engineer's whereabouts, but with no luck. Returning to the library, he stepped inside with the timidity of a woman peeking behind the closed doors of an altar, or like a student made claustrophobic by the halls of learning just before an examination, dreadfully ill prepared for its rigors. It was Saturday; the anarchists and rabble-rousers were mostly gone. The annals of learning stood abandoned to the settled dust of bookworms and the vacuous entombment of knowledge. He possessed the usual image of libraries. Great repositories, isolated spaces for the study of musty bound volumes and peeling parchments filled with unfathomable secrets, impenetrable taxonomies; intellectual lubrications of the obvious. Until that day, he had never entered one. The doors closed behind him, a hushed and aureate absence of natural light induced the fabled impression he harbored. The experience recalled in him his teacher's allegory for humanity. An icon, a cavern of the imagination meant for exploration, the image beckoned by Pater Sophocles Tzsahnas, the itinerate friar of his boyhood.

Pater Sophocles held a special place in Lambro's gilded memories, his very image of a rebellious hero. Deposed by the archimandrites of the monastery of St. Basil, Sophocles Tzsahnas clandestinely visited Yergola and a half dozen other isolated villages to tutor the children of those parents who wished them to learn the language. They paid him with lodging and hot meals. Unbeknownst to them, he peppered his lessons with anecdotes and readings from the history of his ancient caste of priests, world literature and the mystic poets. "Lest the little beasts morph into centaurs," Pater Sophocles warned.

Like Pater Alexi, he was the rarity of a broadly educated cleric. However, while Alexi relinquished the rising star of his scholarship for the love of his Presbytera Thekla, Sophocles wed his true love from the start, refusing to compromise his overbearing erudition and celibacy.

His stern and deliberate liturgies remained steeped in the medieval superstitions haunting Epirus for centuries. He would interrupt them to calm a wailing child or scold a tardy bachelor making an appearance for the first time in months, and lecture his congregants on the theological implication of a particular sacrament or ritual, or offer God an unsanctioned doxology dripping with the ecstatic imagery of a mystery religion.

"O sacred shroud of wisdom, O savior, whose winsome limb of truth summons my grasping heart." A smoking censor was always in hand, the holy chalice always overflowing, and his offerings of the Word bearing an aphoristic weight like axioms of the Church Fathers. His only notable sin, in Lambro's memory, was that he lacked ecclesiastic authority to perform the liturgy and that he chose not to reveal as much until he was exposed and run off the mountainside by the local bishop and his gun toting entourage. The infamous incident abruptly ended Lambro's formal education.

The great library presented its visitors with an overexerted effort at seclusion and insularity. Its mood and redolence like a musky glass of *mavrodaphne*,[55] absorbed within the sinews of Lambro's memory, like one of Pater Sophocles' lessons, proffered in hushed emotive tones, the meat of the mind and the mysticism of candlelit icons peering back through a haze of incense. For a luxuriant instant, Lambros stood just beyond the doorway, taking in the dark framed stacks of books. He walked a bit further, ran his fingers across the tables and railings, then the bindings and yellowed paper of the older volumes, emitting their musty scent. All of it evoked in him the anticipation and caress of supple, cambered flesh, Elissa yielding on his belated wedding night.

Overwhelmed with its regimented corridors of leather volumes and the catalogue system, a marvel in itself, Lambros attempted to locate a librarian, but had no idea what a librarian should look like. No one was behind the desk near the entrance, so he began eliminating candidates by the manner of their dress, or whether they carried a valise for papers. What would make such a clerk stand out? he thought. Everyone in the place is carrying something. Moments later a woman walked up and greeted him, pursing her lips into a cordial smile lingering long enough

---

55   μαβροδάφνη - a sweet wine like Porto

to provide him with the opportunity to speak. He assumed such a setting to be where a man ought to serve up his best manners.

"Pardon me, mademoiselle." She put her finger to her lips to quiet him. "I'm seeking the assistance of a librarian," he whispered. She coughed quietly, amused at being addressed in so courteous a manner. A malnourished young woman, she appeared well into her thirties when she was actually a bit younger. The pithy dress of unenviable green, covered with a cream camise, invited the keen observer to look lower, below the calamus torso to well-muscled calves linked to smallish feet clad in militant brown shoes, clapping the floor with the snappy cadence of a welcoming gait. Her chestnut hair, which she nervously pulled behind her ear with her hand, flowed back onto her shoulders in waves of youthful vigor. Stylish reading glasses magnified the pale brown of her eyes, a bit frighteningly, perched upon a felicitous little nose with dainty nostrils pointing skyward like a pair of concave depressions a child might draw. The nose, he imagined, was Scandinavian or perhaps of English stock somewhere in her ancestry. He found her inexplicably alluring.

Lambros asked for books he believed necessary for his project. He had rehearsed the question for the last half-hour. The librarian observed him even after he stopped talking. She noticed the worn heels on his leather boots, that his shirt had wrinkled when he took his jacket off, and that his belt had a hole added that was off center. Then she dwelled on his face. She thought it noble, weathered for a relatively young man, no doubt qualities born of hard work, which she found attractive, as she did his conspicuous lack of feminine features. He wondered if her momentary silence was apathy. Perhaps she disapproved of his peasant's appearance, compared with her usually urbane clientele. The library was virtually empty. To his surprise, she continued to dote over him. After a few minutes, he decided it was probably uncharacteristic of her to help her patrons this way. She found the volumes he required rather than merely directing him to the appropriate section of the collection. Among them, she brought him a well-worn but masterful translation of Vitruvius on hydraulics, an excerpt from the *Ten Books*.

"This is a rare book and must be handled with care," she told him, "but I thought you might find it interesting." He was impressed that the Romans achieved such mastery over aqueous conveyance and the calculable angles of concrete irrigation channels, keeping water from fouling or running too quickly. It seemed as if moderns and their advocates in forlorn and forgotten places like Lathra had lost this understanding and needed to regain it by first persuading imbeciles like Terzellos and Machiavellians like Avram. The fact that he was among such a populace, bothered him. He took his seat on an opulent burgundy armchair with a deep cushion, at the head of a great oak table. The chair, trimmed with brass nails bore the imprint of a lion's head and what looked like an inscription that he could not make out without closer inspection. Shyly he turned and signaled her to lean toward him so that he might whisper his comment discretely. She liked the scent of him, like a mountain herb and a distant, piquant fire.

"I've never been offered a seat this comfortable," he said. She smiled and blushed, besotted with his simple manners. Lambros began reading and quickly developed a headache skimming technical treatises whose verbiage appeared circuitously concocted in meaning and whose diagram keys he could neither locate nor fathom when he did. When she returned to check on his progress, he was massaging the back of his head and neck, soothing the discomfort of his failure, a bothersome stiffness that was quite different in its dull, ambient pulse from those sharp spasms he developed after drinking or working for too many hours in the sun without food and water.

"Might I assist you?" she whispered, reaching for the book he was perusing. The delicate filament of ivory fingers brushed his wrist, which she did not withdraw immediately.

"Yes, I'm having trouble making sense of these," he said.

She quickly reduced the number of texts, a simple elimination of those without obvious relevance to hydro delivery systems.

"This is not my area of expertise, but we'll decipher it," she assured him.

"What is your area of expertise?" he asked.

"Besides a librarian?" she replied, welcoming the question. "That's only to pay my rent. Cartography," she said, hurrying to the answer with a twinge of pride. "Yes, I know, there aren't many women in the discipline." She gave him a reprieve from his inquiries and spoke of Gerardus Mercator, as if he were a close relative, his Map and his *Atlas* and *Chronologia*, replicas and translations of which she had help procure for the library. He listened attentively, studied the movement of her lips and the softening impression of her face as she spoke. She became aware of his observation and was unmistakably flattered. With her assistance, Lambros found what he came for. He copied the illustrations of various designs she identified from the texts and which together they discerned as usable. Interrupted only once so that she might attend to another patron, he extended his hand and thanked her for the kindness of her assistance. She smiled and for a moment appeared as pretty as he found Elissa in his midday meanderings, when he felt isolated from her and his children.

"My name is Lara Xenides. Is there anything else I may help you with?"

"I am Lambros Lambrou," he said uncomfortably. Strangers sometimes found his name unusual. Were your parents jokesters or idiots? he would get. The conversation did not end with such dithering pleasantries though. Deriving as he did an increasing consolation in her presence, his headache receded. Inquiring politely, and she answering cordially, they discussed the intricacies of the library's chamber of ancient parchments and assortment of recently translated literature, from the collection in Russian. Few of the authors' names were familiar to him except for Chekhov, for whom Lara made clear her admiration. He refrained from comment even though the name Chekhov again reminded him of Pater Sophocles, who was a polyglot of sorts. Sophocles had bequeathed much of what he read in Russian to his students. An enthusiast of Leskov, whom he assimilated as a young man in his travels through the embattled nation, he had spent years in prison, before and after the October Revolution along with certain condemned Russian clergy.

Interrupted again by someone, Lara excused herself and returned several minutes later with her camise unbuttoned and the top hare bone button of her collarless dress resting intimately upon the crest of an imperceptible bosom, her cheeks flush with color. To complete his tour, she invited Lambros into a dimly lit room with various maps kept under glass. These did not impress him as much as the richly hewn tables they were set upon, gazelle-like legs resting upon vulturine claws seemingly clasping the minds of readers. Under the filtered green lamplight, her plainness faded into an aura of reserved charm, like a graceful carving in jade. He said nothing, nor did he think to express himself in any particular way. She leaned forward to point out various features to the maps, as near to him as good-mannered intentions might have permitted. The topic deflated. The occasion arose for his departure. Turning and innocently blocking the doorway, she gave the impression of being nervous, nearly breathless in her alacrity. It seemed to Lambros as if she were awaiting an embrace or even a kiss, or so he convinced himself as an afterthought. Dumbfounded but resolving to keep from embarrassing her or himself, he self-consciously watched the movement of his hands cupping the bony knobs of her elbows, her hands folded above the tiniest protrusion of belly, and gently moved past her.

"It was a pleasure to have met you, Miss Lara." Warm exhalation caressed her brow as he spoke.

"And you," she whispered, standing in the doorway of the map room, a lingering perfume, a faint trickle of arousal wafting between them.

Exiting the building, he walked briskly to Saint Dimitrios. Sweating a bit from his encounter with Lara, he entered the narthex, placed four coins in a red box to the left of a basket of candles, lit two candles and proceeded to the magnificent sanctuary veneered in gold and ruby and the amber icons of the first faith. He knelt before the icon of the vigilant Christ, to the right of the holy doors, and said his prayers, glancing back once at the worn soles of his shoes as he prayed, embarrassed that Lara may have seen him as a peasant. His prayer flowed without contemplation.

"Christ, forgive me and my friend Rigopoulos for the sins that we have committed today, he with his gypsy and me with my delight in the attention of a strange woman who is not my Elissa. Protect my sons, Stratos and Nikos, and my daughter, Sophia, and my tiny one, Evanthia. Grant me the years and wits to keep Elissa happy and the wisdom to raise these children. Keep them near the mighty arm of your protection, my Lord. Amen."

A moment or two of repose passed. The coolness of the church marble pleased him, the aromatic incense and hum of distant commerce through the open doors. Then he stood and left, staring out into the busy street, assembling his thoughts into sequenced chain links ranging from ambiguity to guilt. Rigos arrived within a few minutes, as they had planned, his face radiant and gleaming, as if he had bathed and combed his hair. Evening trundled along lazily within the hour. They embarked for home. The sun driven cumuli were a milky interstice to the day's radiantly unhindered blue. Each felt the chill of the other, acknowledging in gesture what had overwhelmed them both - the splendorous intuition of a piercing sky and parting clusters. Rigos drove slowly; smoking with one hand, driving with the other, reveling in the lurid details of his conquest of Kyria Kounellitsa, the woman he called his gypsy slut, first this way, then that. The bed squeaked like a sluggish train car. He had performed his sweaty deed three times that day, boasting that the third was a noisy sodomy nearly discovered by the husband.

"Is everything all right up there, wife? the buffo called out," Rigos said guffawing. "I think he knows I am giving it to her, Lalas, but he does nothing to stop it."

"Be careful, he may catch you one day and shoot you and then what a disgrace your children would have to live with."

"No, I think he likes what I do to her. What do you make of that?" he asked, genuinely inquisitive.

"Who the hell knows?" Lambros said, uncomfortable with the discussion. "Men's tastes know no bounds or decency. Or women's, for that matter."

"What did your engineer have to say? How was your reading of the books?"

"Except for these drawings I copied, uneventful," Lambros said.

"Hmm, what do expect from books, answers? Even if I could read I would only look at the pictures," Rigos replied dismissively.

"Books and learning ... to be a man of great intellect is something for our children to aspire to," Lambros said. "It's too late for us."

"Not mine." Rigos interrupted.

"Why not?" Lambros asked, regretting the open-ended question as soon as he asked it. Rigos grew animated.

"I have no tolerance for intellectuals and bookworms. They're troublemakers, always wanting what they don't have and lecturing us on things they don't quite know yet," Rigos said.

"Well," Lambros said, "that's what they're paid to do, to figure things out."

"And to think, someone pays them to read when that's what they like to do anyway. That's not work!" Rigos replied.

"Of course it is." Lambros said with a sigh. "It's difficult. It gives me a headache to read for too long."

"No, Lambros, my naive friend, you're wrong. Intellectuals are like women. They are like women and faggots. Their minds are big holes that need filling with big fat books," Rigos explained, as if irritated. Lambros said nothing and just looked at him pretending to understand his point, suppressing his embarrassment. He preferred debating with academics, he thought, even though he was not one himself. "Wise-ass faggots," Rigos added for emphasis a moment later. "I don't trust a man who can speak to you about every subject under the sun. Somewhere, in all of that gibberish, he has to be a fraud." Perhaps a scholar or priest had outsmarted Rigos in the past, not a difficult thing to do Lambros thought. Then suddenly, the conversation ended. A worshipful silence overcame them. Both looked out their windows contentedly. The rest of the way home was just as quiet, vacillating between this serenity and Lambros having to suppress fits of laughter thinking about Rigos and Kounellitsa or Rigos and a room full of intellectuals attempting to convince him of something, and his finally running from them like a clown with his hand covering his caboose. This was as close to a debate as they ever had, but he still prized his friend, perhaps above all others, a man he saw but a half-dozen times a year. The two men stopped in Yianko's kafenio and bought each other drinks before Rigos headed back for Arnissa.

Returning home later that night, Lambros found Elissa as perturbed as he had feared she might be. Her face was flush. She moved about the room, her nerves fraying with preparations before going to bed. He offered explanations in terse, affirmative grunts, skirting vaguely with insinuations of Rigo's adventures in collecting the money owed to him and exhibiting to her the drawings he secured from the books.

"It took you all day to get this?" Her cynicism drew her mouth in as if by suction. "Roam about at night and all you do is step in the day's shit."

Lambros ignored her. He described the library in vivid detail, bemoaning his parents' poverty and ignorance in comparison with those lucky enough to achieve higher education.

"Like Pater Sophocles," he quickly added, while picturing the librarian.

"What made you think of that impostor?" Elissa injected. So fulsome and charged with excitement was the rendering of his impression of the University that she wondered if his mind might change regarding the education of his daughters.

"So maybe now you'll see the wisdom in permitting our Sophia to learn something other than becoming a seamstress."

"I'm going to bed," he said, ignoring her.

The temptation to speak of his encounter with the librarian was considerable, something he took as a cue to the affliction, the inability to ban Lara from his thoughts. That night he was disappointed in himself for this. A week later, the librarian floated above his ponderous daydreams into forgetfulness, although never disappearing altogether.

15

Elissa arose before dawn on the day before the feast of the Dormition of the Theotokos, the day she traditionally distributed her *eftazimo*,[56] the potion celebrated in the village for its magical propensity to rise flawlessly like the sun in the benignant burn of sky that baked its drenched fibers. Women lined up at the trough of its magical bubbling by late afternoon, partaking of the offering. They blessed her hands and went on their way to bake the ritual bread. Occasionally, a husband and his sons, friendly with Lambros, might accompany a wife, bring along a flask of *tzipouro* in gratitude, drink to the host's health and confer a blessing upon the Lambrou household. The following morning would be devoted to the celebration of the Divine Liturgy and the annual feast of the Most Holy Virgin, commemorated with a procession to the lake, usually well attended by Lathrans and visitors from Arnissa and Perea. The priest's ritual bathing of hands and feet in Vegoritis replicated the tradition of visiting the sea.

---

56 ρεβύθι εφτάζυμο - chickpea yeast

On this fourteenth day of what had been a dry and callous August, few men accompanied their wives to the Lambrou home, adding insult to his already sullen mood and filling Lambros with suspicion. He moved from chair to chair without purpose and supported his head upon his hand like a doleful child. His usual cheerful pride in Elissa's important role was gone. Elissa admonished him.

"If you're not going to help me with the guests, then make yourself useful. Get me some water instead of sitting around with your face sagging like a jilted groom. And get the children out from under my feet before I break their legs."

As daylight advanced unto the sweltering hour, the sun blazing its tonic upon the last of the ferment fizzing in the belly of the trough, and sapping the energy of the weak-willed, Lambros already tallied the year's feast as a failure. He had not foreseen the extent to which he had become the Lathran pariah. Only Barba Ianouli came to visit and drink his ouzo. When Ianouli finally left, thanking his host profusely, he staggered home and proclaimed to anyone who would listen that he was "no shameless Turk, like some around here."

Lambros fingered his crimson komboloi, bead by bead, and watched the old man stumble away.

"What do I want to attend the procession for?" he said rhetorically.

"Do what you want," Elisa said indifferently as if no other comment would follow. Then she hesitated, all her fear of his temper evaporating. "Stay home and sulk, knucklehead!" Lambros said nothing, closed his eyes and napped in his chair.

The fifteenth of August, was, aside from its intended beacon of spirituality, also known for being more or less the exact day of the year when the reprieve from ruthless summer heat would slowly turn into the clemency of autumn. Just as it appeared that absolution would need to wait for another day, a gentle breeze arrived from the Northwest like a symbol of the Virgin's mercy. The day's sudden augury mollified Lambro's misgivings. He awoke from his nap, not to a consuming fire in cramped corridors, but to the clear recollection of a daydream - water poured slowly over his burdens by his daughters and the music of their giddy laughter.

Petty conflicts between men normally resulted in mutual amnesty. This would begin with an initial episode of avoidance, non-attendance to the usual banter of roosters, and then, when a change in seasons offered new routines and its own hurried distraction, acquiescence to some quiet suppression of the friction.

"Grudges are like kidney stones," the old men cautioned, "causing pain to your manhood until you piss them out." The Cypriot's exodus had provided for easy and complete avoidance. The heavenly zephyr stirred Lambros to courage, to renew his quest, if not for the greater good of running water then at least to undo the damage to his reputation, damage accomplished with such cunning by Avram Karangelos.

He decided to try again despite feeling overwhelmed with little time to spare, with worries over weather and blight, with tending his orchards and prayers for the vale of grain in his keep. At the same time, he was battling a new strain of tick-borne encephalitis, afflicting flocks after the import of Caspian breeds by herders in Arnissa, the chronic mastitis of one of his two milk cows, and his hens refusing to lay eggs in the heat. He worked on his drawings late into consecutive, temperate summer nights beneath a shallow, smoky lantern, copying them in a painstaking hand, going so far as to prepare estimates of the increased yields he believed were sure to be the godsend of Lathran growers and farmers. With considerable forethought and as much detail as he could faithfully render, he envisioned a combustion engine or wind generator of moderate size atop a jagged set of rocks approximately four hundred paces from the snaky path leading up to Lazaro's cell. From there an Archimedean screw would draw water up into a pump control system of relative simplicity with submersible casing, a concrete holding tank, a pressure pump of sizeable capacity and a crude switching system for rationing the suitably generated flow, delivering the elixir to its various patients, the grateful citizenry of Lathra.

Deciding favorably upon the advice Lazaros had offered, he next engaged in his campaign *res augusta domi*,[57] an uncomplicated act of diplomacy which proved to be a lesson in humility. Rather than grandstand in the kafenio as he had before Avram ground him into rhetorical mincemeat - an exaggeration and distortion of the event premised on self-pity - he chose as his new tactic the method of discrete persuasion, setting loose the guile of women over the men of influence. An affable

---

57 straightening the circumstances on the home front

conversion of village minds, whose avidity and expedience were well known, might help marginalize the hardheaded old goats siding with Avram, men grazing gullibly upon their grassy archetypes of morality and common sense. The significant women were but three.

The first was Kyria Anna Gallanos, the portly, commanding matriarch of her clan of millers and bakers whose appearance had always reminded Lazaros of the fireplug he had seen in a photograph of Chicago shown to him by Pavlides. Kyria Anna retained an indomitable hold on her husband since her father was the font of his good fortune. Lambros remarked once to Elissa how Anna's voice was the most unbecoming he had ever heard in a woman, manly and hawkish in timbre.

"This must not be so unusual in women who govern their husbands so justly," Elissa reasoned aloud so Lambros could hear her. Lambros ignored the comment, for he felt governed himself, and humiliated by the realization. Gallano's father had been a humble chocolateer trained in Belgium. He had honed an unusual artistry with his confections, both underappreciated and insufficiently remunerated in the Corinth of his day to support a family let alone provide a vocation for his only son. This prompted a series of moves that led to Istanbul. There he entrusted both son and his young wife with the only family endowment Gallanos would receive, the recipes and aptitude for creating the finest slivers of chocolate novelty in the city. Success, however, was not enough to secure them in the city where both politics and survival proved precarious. Anna's family had purchased land in Kazvam and upon their departure ceded it to their son in law as an extension of his dowry, not only so that he would have a place to live with their daughter, but also to ensure that he would take her. Anna had developed the reputation that she might eat them out of house and home.

In addition to his confections, Gallanos possessed a delicate hand when it came to his wife as well, but the effort expended to achieve such patience twisted his natural testiness into a remorseless tyranny over his children and the men in his employ. Vasili and Andreas were obvious exceptions. Their normal response to hand wringing and nervous criticism was work stoppage, which in this instance would have prompted the ire of Gallano's wife. An oft-repeated adage about Gallanos *O demenos*[8]

---

58 δεμένος - the tethered one

was that Anna might someday tie him like a dog to the chestnut tree near the center of the walled compound of his merchant's estate. There she would provide him with sufficient rope to permit him use of the outhouse and enough length to reach the animal trough near the house. Husband and wife slept at opposite ends of the house because he insisted upon keeping goats and chickens beneath the room his bed occupied, apparently developing a fetish for the smell of sour milk and ammonia. In the opposite direction, his fabled tether would reach the small brick oven built into the foundation of the house, adjacent to his wife's busy hearth. This way the poor master of the house could snatch a morsel and not faint from malnourishment.

Next was Kyria Athena Kyriazis, a detached epicure of men's devouring scrutiny. Her elegant, elongated features made her demeanor and vanity even more desirable or irritating depending on one's perspective. The aloof dismissal of her neighbors as mere peasants (when compared with her) provoked smiles in some and pure irritation in others.

"Look at the sultana's hips wave like a flag," the young men brayed. "I'll bet Kyriazis can't handle his sweaty mare," they swooned. "She belongs in a harem!" The women would hear of such comments and respond.

"I would sooner tie a rock around her throat and let her feed the fish of Vegoritis," they snarled back. "Athena and her Athenian standards - like an ass and underwear!" Despite raising four children, Athena indeed enjoyed a somewhat advanced level of education for a married woman in those haunts and in comparison with her neighbors. But she carried on with infuriating pretension, having only graduated from the equivalent of a preparatory school for girls in Athens. She had also attended a year of classes in a private business institute, but left this career after its director made a spectacle of himself, fawning over her girlish splendor. A lost opportunity she alleged to be among the great laments of her waning youth. The most resolutely sensual being in the village, Athena controlled her husband Pavlo utterly with the stingy but perversely creative favors of her boudoir. This sufficed to persuade him of the necessity of satisfying her haughty material demands and dissuaded him from ever demanding an abeyance of her detestable pride. So crazed did he become at the prospect of her favors, bestowed as rarely as she promised them, that any objection to her conduct vanished from his horizon of possibility.

Conspiring along with her conceit were delusions regarding her daughter, who possessed none of her exoticism and actually looked like her father in a dress, and her son, Tasso, who resembled Athena in appearance and was neither a manly brute nor a baron of business, but a simple, pure-hearted boy whom everyone loved. As a result, her dealings with others suffered and caused her general retraction from Lathran society and a loss of goodwill.

Pavlos Kyriazis was among the largest landowners of the village, second only to Lambros. He knew little of the secrets of the land and took no pleasure in its dominance, preferring to hire neighbors and their sons for the labor involved in agronomy and animal husbandry. His herd of sheep was small but among the finest in the region and, barring professional jealousies, often relied upon for breeding stock. His coppice of pears and peaches produced among the most resplendent, succulent fruit in the Balkans. The orchards were nestled in a gentle climb of loam north of the valley and protected from Boreas and Zephyrus by slightly elevated groves to either side owned and tended by Lambros and Praxitellis. His groves also benefited from the soil having been previously cultivated in great, arching rows of lentils and creeping vegetation, nightshades and eggplant. These rotted before harvest when the Turks who planted them hastily moved away, thus enriching the decaying compost and potash sustaining his nubile trees.

These riches abounding, Kyriazis still decided to work unremittingly at two part-time and unrelated clerical positions in the textile factories of Edessa, denying himself the hearth of his peaceable kingdom. All this was to satiate his wife's maddening collection of clothing, jewelry and knickknacks and to nourish her ambition and prediction that her children would one day attain sufficient education in the cambistry of certain voguish business principles, which she claimed to have learned in the Athens of her day, to dominate Lathra. In her most private dreams, this dominion would be over all of Macedonia, and she, the matriarch behind the throne. Reflexively, without consulting her husband's judgment, which she believed was unsound since she was well aware of the real reason for his acquiescence to her whims, she forged ahead with a plan for the realization of her fiefdom. An empire built upon cheap labor and the fission of souls, she had long left behind any idealized accord between her aspirations and a Christian ethic. Consistent with this, she avoided church altogether and never spoke more than a few words to Pater Alexi, which prompted a resurfacing rumor that she was a Jewess on her mother's side.

To this inspired and secretive end, she insisted upon tutors for her children while the rest of the village relied upon the tersely honest learning by rote offered by the government appointed schoolteacher, Evangelis Pantelos. Two hermetically stitched and babushka-hooded marms from Edessa were driven three days a week in their brother's motorcar, at great expense to Kyriazis, thus necessitating his second vocation. One tutor focused upon the language of success, the other on the numbers. The intriguing, machinating Athena was among the first in the region to advocate importing labor from Albania as well. Careful calculations led her to determine the cost effectiveness of human barter and having to hire yet another driver to retrieve such laborers. She felt no remorse in luring and enchaining the often barefoot men and boys emerging from lonely frontier hideouts, illiterates who otherwise walked grave distances through mountain passes teaming with snakes and wolves, without proper clothing or nourishment and enduring months of separation from family and home, all to procure work for miniscule wages and two frugal meals a day.

Last among the triumvirate of matriarchs was Kyria Voula Terzellos, not because she exercised any authority over her household of valor-bloated firebrands, but because both her husband and her three sons admired her more than they tolerated each other. Lambros knew he would have no ear from the likes of Terzellos. They never liked each other much, especially now that he had threatened to hammer his son Spiros into the ground like a wooden post for stoning his hydro engineer. Terzellos and Lambros were at this point not on speaking terms. They ignored each other at Yianko's kafenio and in the fields where their barley shared a common border. Approaching Voula Terzellos might be fruitless and laden with risk. Both men were already at odds politically and Terzellos, as rumor intimated, was a man tending toward violent solutions to problems. He had shot a man dead in Chanakale, amidst the tumult and outrage between him and one Yiorgos Pipinos, whom Terzellos felt had insulted his then young bride of seventeen by impolitely commenting upon her already overfed and weary appearance. Pipino's prattling tongue reached Terzellos within the hour, reports of his licentious remarks regarding her prodigious hindquarters, the butt of jokes and seethe of the hour. Terzello's bride, Voula was indeed born motherly in her visage, a veritable domesticated Martha as a child who grew into the role as a young girl, excelling in household chores and culinary skill, fulfilling her destiny. Her overeager father paid a dowry in hand of gold and domesticated cattle for Terzellos and his generous psalterium, like a ruminant beast. His matching bed and thunderous snores were Voula's only rewards. The farcical Pipinos normally had a mocking temper. His lurid descriptions were infamous. In this instance, he begged Terzellos his pardon, but when met with unrelenting indignation, boldly insulted him, insinuating quite clearly that he would rather indulge his lusts with Terzello's ripened mother, "than your fat-assed wife! So take it easy!"

Terzellos returned home trembling with rage, the laughter of cohorts stinging his ears. He loaded his *pistola Napoli* given to him by his father as a wedding gift and returned to the still unsullied scene at a local kafenio. Luck, occasioned by stupidity, can turn awry and pop up as the weed of misfortune. Having never practiced his marksmanship, Terzellos missed his target and instead shot Pipino's nephew through the spleen. The poor youth, who uttered not a word and was merely seated behind his uncle, required a second day to bleed to death, affording Terzellos, who apologized copiously at the scene to avoid an immediate lynching, sufficient time to flee and enlist as a cavalryman in the Turkish army. He sent his young and prodigious wife to live with his aunt in Thessaloniki rather than subject her to life with her own family, who openly resented female offspring in favor of her two older brothers, earning as they did for their father the fair clime of free labor.

The omoplate of a duly condemned man sometimes bears an unbefitting burden. Terzello's parents and three siblings paid the price for his hasty anger. The opposing clan's arsenal of vintage 18th Century cannon, drawn by oxen before the target in broad daylight, bombarded the home. The barrage killed in one vengeful blast his father, brother and youngest sister and in a subsequent volley maimed a second brother into a legless loathing of his existence. An unquenchable thirst for the blood of any Pipinos seized them. In a few years, the resulting feud decimated both clans, claiming the lives of the remaining siblings and their sons, cousins and even in-laws, leaving only the innocent bile of Terzello's contention, his mother and a few orphaned girls on both sides, whisked away and saved from the foul invective recited before deplorably stupid deaths.

"I fuck the day you were born," the last male of the clan Pipinos said, before he fired his weapon.

In the early hours of the fifteenth, as Elissa had prepared for the veneration of the quiescent soul of the Holy Mother, Lambros confided in her his stratagem for approaching the three matriarchs. In the midst of furious preparations, Elissa still suggested that she be the one to approach Voula Terzellos, using the pretense of presenting her with the day's eftazimo, rather than risk Lambros speaking to her and inciting her husband's bravado. She arrived at Voula's door by early evening, having already delivered with Sophia the last of her eftazimo to a few of the homebound. Lambros had summoned Jartzo with what he called his captain's whistle, two fingers inserted beneath his tongue, an unnatural sound like a winded siren or the piercing whirl of a machine rather than something emanating from vocal chords. He asked Jartzo to confirm that Terzellos and his sons were whiling time away at one or the other kafenio. Elissa handed Voula the yeast and recited a seemingly sincere apology regarding the recent unfortunate difficulties between their hardheaded husbands and impetuous sons, as if her sons Stratos and Nikos had anything to do with the ruckus over the engineer. Wary glances sufficed and the few words exchanged between them prompted Elissa's hasty departure, virtually in midsentence. She walked past Yianko's kafenio and observed Terzellos and Spiros relaxing beneath the long shadows of the affectionately tended chestnut tree, just beyond the terrace. She bowed her head in an unreturned greeting and hurried home to gargle with a glass of ouzo.

"Why are you wasting my ouzo?" Lambros asked as she screwed her face up.

"To wash the lie from between my teeth and settle my stomach." For her part, Voula mixed the eftazimo with water and some weevil-riddled flour and fed it to her swine, emulating the nagging contempt her husband felt toward anything Lambrou.

Lambros fared somewhat better with Anna Gallanos and Athena Kyriazis. He approached both women later that week when they made an appearance in the village square to peruse the wares of a traveling tinsmith and his brother, the bric-a-brac men from Kavala. More than likely gypsies who hid it well, they ventured into the region and each village three times a year. For the occasion, Athena donned a lovely embroidered dress, without its accompanying jacket slung over her arm. She combed her hair into a set of girlish braids and let them fall behind her bejeweled little ears and onto her shoulders. Knowing she would be in the presence of men more apt to barter in her favor with something pleasant for them to pore over, she left exposed her slender arms, taut and pale to her underarms. Elissa agreed to stay away until her husband could attempt some rudiment of persuasion. Lambros drew a few drachmas from his pocket and purchased three meters of burgundy cloth to appease his wife and to glean the cooperation of the bric-a-brac men. Anna Gallanos was gingerly inspecting a porcelain tea set, among the finest commodities on the wagon, when Lambros made his gambit, stepping between spectators in the small crowd and toward the two women as they chatted.

"Good morning, Kyria Anna, good morning, Kyria Athena. The wonders of such manufacture are not uncommon amongst the Orientals," he said, with little more than a vendor's confirmation of facts. He asked the tinsmith, "This is Chinese pottery, isn't it?"

"Yes it is sir, and you are quite right. The Orientals are a far more advanced society than we here in Europe," the tinsmith's brother agreed, putting on airs of expertise, grinning with speckles of bread-crumb between the unsightly tarnish of gangrenous teeth and silver fillings.

"Why should such wonders be foreign to us?" Lambros inquired rhetorically.

"So that I can sell them to lovely ladies such as these," the brother of the tinsmith responded, amused at his own witticism. Then he grew serious and licked his chops greedily, staring at Athena and the obtruding hip with each shuffle of her feet.

"Designed for a man's grip, aren't they?" he whispered to his brother.

"I'll answer that myself," Lambros inserted, "because we have no running water."

"Oh yes," the tinsmith said, winking at him, "running water," he repeated, picking up the line of reasoning, the conspiratorial tone a bit obvious to Lambros and making him wince. "Running water is the miracle upon which the manufacturing arts depend for their creation and refinement," he announced. "An educated merchant ought to possess the skill of utter bullshit," Lambros thought, "if he's selling worthless merchandise." He compared the bric-a-brac man, not as bad an egg, to the traveling photographer, whom Lambros liked calling the occultist. An unsavory character, the photographer instigated a mad, immoral interest the entire village fell victim to, including Elissa, of having their photographs taken and their vanity stoked. An impostor from Salerno, "a half-assed Illyrian," Lambros asserted, who spoke with an Italian accent, the occultist peddled his portrait service to peasants as if it were the key to eternal life. Lambros refused to sit for him. So did Danäe, despite the photographer's begging and offering a substantial sum of money. Katerina threw dung at him, when he pursued her for her extraordinary ugliness.

"No one will believe such a beguiling creature exists, and a woman to boot," he shouted, laughing heartily. Entire families sat for a portrait. Athena Kyriazis posed twice in two different traditional outfits. A foreign woman had posed nude for him, her fingernails as long as daggers, her lips painted to make them appear fuller. In one of them, she was reclining with an arm behind her head and the other across her belly as if hiding a scar, her luxurious brown hair draped across one shoulder, a lit cigarette dangling from her mouth, her left eye shrouded by smoke. Everyone presumed from the photographs that she was a whore or entrapped by the devil, but she was actually a married woman and a mother of two children, thus necessitating the photographer's hurried departure from Torre del Greco, a town on the Tyrrhenian Sea. He sold the photographs of her to incurable masturbators, but this was not the whole truth, for he had also shown a version of them to reluctant men like Lambros and Vasili, and from the more prudish received a scolding.

"I don't want to hear that you showed these to my sons," Lambros told him when he saw the photographs, turning them over in his hand so as not to dwell on the images.

Vasili, on the other hand, did not avert his gaze, but mocked the photographer.

"Instead of luring them with your camera, wouldn't it be easier to breathe in the presence of women if you bathed once a month or maybe cut your hair?"

"Yes, water is the beginning of all industry and invention," Lambros repeated. "It'll be commonplace in Lathra one day, once we have a pumping station delivering water from the lake to every home, with sanitation and bathing stations nearby. Can you imagine that, Kyria Anna? Bathing in one's own home! I hear in America that every home has this luxury. No running to a well atop Kythera or to the lake . . . and who, my dears, who usually does the running if not the women and daughters of the house? And combustion systems to heat the water in the winter! Can you imagine? Those clever Americans. Industrious ants. What more can we say about them?"

"Really, Lambro, that's all very hopeful, but if you'll excuse me I have to go home. My husband is waiting for me," Anna said, offering her goodbyes and walking away as Athena remained captivated.

"Do go on, my dear Lambro," Athena said, drawing him away from the wagon and out of earshot of the crowd and then standing near him, perfumed in a Cyrenaic lathering of a man's senses. "I'd like to hear more," she said, her voice excised and libidinous, her manner suggestive. "It's a confirmation of all that I have argued of late to my husband. You know, he's always away at work," she concluded, her tongue carousing across lustrous dentin, her mouth puckered shut. The bric-a-brac man pricked his ears up, and watched what he saw as an invitation. "Without water, the land is worthless," she went on to say, construed by the stranger as meaning, without tousling my bed, a husband is worthless. Lambros saw and heard none of this in the conversation.

"Indeed, my dear Athena, yours is a correct observation. Your husband would do well to listen to you."

"And your wife," she replied, obliquely suggesting an improper tension.

———•———

A few days later, after finishing his morning duties but without having presented himself at Yianko's in the morning, Lambros sat down to his midday meal with his family, patted his children on the head as they finished and remanded them to bed for a nap. Instead of habitually retiring for an hour to the coolness of his bedroom and the calming rhythm of Elissa's breathing, lulling him to sleep, he made the decision to venture to Yianko's kafenio, to confirm the fruits of his efforts with Gallanos, who sometimes returned to his old haunt to persuade Yianko not to close for the afternoon. Lambros still shared a bed with his wife. The tradition of separate sleeping quarters was mostly for older men and had evolved less from prudery or Christian convention, than the desire to forestall the procreation of children one might not be able to feed, the prevention of birth with a precision of purpose. It was unusual for him to skip this luxury and his time with Elissa.

On the walk to Yianko's he passed Jartzo kicking up dust and close behind him, his mother. Without thinking, Lambros thanked Jartzo again for his assistance in confirming the whereabouts of Terzellos earlier that week. Katerina's agitation swelled like a tempest on the surface of Vegoritis.

"Eh . . . *giagour*, Lambrou! Don't involve my dim wit in your harebrained ideas," she shouted at the top of her lungs, without a care for whom she might disturb. Then just as suddenly, her inflated fury descended upon her son and she began beating him mercilessly with the knotted olive branch she used as a cane, shouting all the while. "I'll break your bones. May a fire consume you! I curse the instant of your conception! May the plague devour you!" Jartzo cowered and howled his pathetic protests, but he had planted his feet and could not move.

"Leave him be, woman," Lambros demanded. "How I despise such mistreatment of the boy!" He stepped toward her, ready to grab the cane or the boy by the shirt, to pull him away. Emboldened, or perhaps requiring the intervention to understand the need to flee, Jartzo just as abruptly broke free from his mother and with grunts of gratitude ran off to hide in the clef beneath Mavrotripa. There he might hear the Victrola grace the placid lake with the resonance of disconsolate lieder or a silken canticle for the piano. Lazaro's recordings arrived weekly by post from America, lovingly wrapped in cloth and mailed to him in heavy corrugated cartons, recordings played nearly every day.

"Come back here you filthy-spawn-of-a-one-eyed-snake[59]," Katerina hissed, her moniker for Jartzo, but until then an unheard appellation of contrived conjunction tickling the tympanic membranes. "He's mine to beat if I wish," she shouted. Fully aware of the repulsion she wrought to the bellies of men, she spit at Lambros, catching him on the pant leg. Then she raised her skirts, displaying the naked fork of revoltingly varicose thighs, spiders scampering into the darker recesses of her clothing, and shouted: "So shut your mouth or I'll have you clean this fish," the ophidian warning darting between tiny sets of moldering teeth.

"Christ and the Virgin," Lambros grumbled as he turned away.

"Them too, for all I care," she growled.

In the season of the Virgin's feast, unaware of the susceptible audience below his cell, Lazaros spun his revolutions of lyric enchantment. On this particular day, he chose an elegant bathing of the spirit in the pure color of dreams, the *Estampes*, subtly, dazzlingly fingered by a nimble young Chilean. Lazaros enjoyed contrasting the Chilean's style with his older Pugno recordings. He had listened to the Pugno in his youth and learned to enjoy their virility and the likeness to what he later discovered were remarkably close to Debussy's own hollow, abrasive renditions, which he had heard in Paris at the beginning of his journey, gramophone recordings of the original piano rolls. He drew the deepest satisfaction waiting for the lyric tipping of balances to a particular phrase or a haunting shift in key, the beauty in the resolution of a leitmotif or a fragmented spool and the unwinding of notes like words in meter, and the musical tête-à-tête between composer and pianist. To experience this fully, he would play the piece four or five times consecutively and only

---

59 Βρωμογόνοφιδώματο - a homegrown conjunction

then move on to something new - on this day, the elusive poetry of the *Valse Romantique.*

When the Victrola twirled, the wolves stayed away, reclining in the thickets, licking their haunches to the crackling melodies. For Jartzo, assumed to be nothing short of a simpleton, who had never seen the Victrola or ever knew of one, the notes evoked a feral world, the reverberations of clever elves or winged creatures in some unseen strata, the resonance of the world's most sublime creations. His agitation would liquefy, like the lake in the midday heat. He would lay still, make not a single sound and cross himself with each unidentified ague of the spine. Liturgical canting induced a similarly calming affect upon him but the sound of the piano evoked his dreams, graceful sea nymphs sailing, sinuous waves, the billow of translucent robes fluttering like sails, images derived from an illustration he dwelled upon for months, before the owner of the book angrily retrieved his stolen property, lissome Pre-Raphaelite naiads resembling the fair Danäe. When she asked him whether he was the one who had stolen the book, he admitted it.

"Yes," he muttered in his garbled annunciate, "to see you."

In the distance, beneath the music, the faint timbre of ephemeral oars lapped through an emerald-blue lagoon, the sound of a father returning home. Eventually the music made the tongue-tied Jartzo weep in tempo. And as the pictures faded in some unfathomed perturbation of his blunted, innocent soul, the desire for sleep would overcome him. He laid his head upon a mossy slip of stone between two great rocks, in a spot where the sun never shone its warming rays, relieving the burden of his unbearable emotion.

Aside from his mother, only Danäe, Elissa and Lambros knew that he could recall or comprehend anything, that he understood the requests made of him, contrary to general opinion, which held him to be innately imbecilic. And in her Spinozist reflections, or on those occasions when Jartzo would fret over moonless nights, or the howl of wolves, or the cruelty of men, Danäe learned to calm his anxious ticks and shudders and the hurdy-gurdy cycle of his childish whimpers with a soothing rhyme of the parables, or her own repetition of the catechist's message.

"They say, my Ioanni - and don't ask me who 'they' are, for I don't know, perhaps the lost Fathers of the Church or the Naodites - but in any event, they say that in Eden there is a spring, and this sacred spring bubbles up in only one place in the Garden. The spring sets upward a draft so pure that it possesses no color at all, even when held in a clear vessel or at a depth lying in little ponds concealed by the velvet grasses of God's manor. Now this water percolates ever so gently between three rocks. The rocks are so smooth with wear that if one leans upon them they bow under the pressure, like something pliable and living. The water tastes like the costliest of nectars when first encountering the tongue and yet leaves no taste in one's mouth after you swallow, the way a thought or memory vanishes. When once sipped, it erases that day's infirmity and aging, and in this way Adam and Eve and all of God's creatures and the angels have eternal life, for there is always a way to God's work that is like a mechanic's explanation for us here on earth. When we return to God, on the day of our judgment, He leads us back to the spring for each of us to sip unto a new eternity."

Jartzo, soothed by her voice, would pantomime the sleep of the dead lying in their grave, as if hesitating to believe her. "The grave isn't the final sleep, my Ioanni," she would say with emotion. "The Gates of Eden will one day glisten before your eyes and open wide. And a divine hand will grace the mute with a melodious voice, the blind with an artist's light, the lame with their stride and dance, the child, the embrace of his mother and father, and the dead will rise in mind and body to sip the water of the sacred spring and live again." She believed he understood every word, because he would cross himself.

As Lambros approached, he saw Terzellos and Gallanos conversing just inside the open doors of the kafenio. His determination palpable, he sat between them and immediately spread out his drawings and calculations from his jacket pocket, arranging them carefully upon the table. Yianko served him an insentient tourkiko.

"What are these, your daughter's doodles?" he said. Lambros shooed him away.

"If you're interested, sit and listen. Otherwise, just watch you don't spill your mud on my papers," he said brashly. Yianko moved the coffee away from the papers and stood by the table giggling. All three men watched Lambros. He blew across the foamless surface and drank in one long, silent gulp, and then set the cup down slowly without a hint of panache. Kyriazis had convinced Terzellos, even before Elissa's apologetic visit, to stifle the vengeful rumblings in his son Spiro's hair-less chest. This was not difficult, wary as Terzellos had become of how little was necessary to ignite feuds and settle scores.

"From what I heard from my fool of a son, the boys threw rocks at the engineer and Lambros was just defending him," Kyriazis had told Terzellos. "You can't blame him," he added. "In fact by my way of look-ing at things, Lambros showed restraint. You would have beaten his son senseless," he told Terzellos, intending to inflate his manly self-esteem.

Yianko sat for a moment but quickly excused himself to attend to his wife, who entered from the back door in a harried state.

"I've told you a thousand times, not to forget the lock on the gate. May a fire consume your hands! Now Pashas and Yero are wandering the village, probably eating Calliope's dandelions again. Who feels like listening to her?"

"What?" Yianko said, frozen with inaction, his mouth gaping with the question.

"Go and find them with your son," she shouted. "Sieve for a brain," the latter uttered under her breath. Yianko raised his palm in the air, as if he would strike her, but then smiled, shaking his head from side to side. She knew him well. She timed her infrequent retorts and insults for when he was with his cronies, what he called his customers. He tolerated the disrespect as a momentary bit of humor. He was not the type of man to posture before other men at her expense. Privately, however, such a comment might earn a day or two of indignation or, from another man, a slap to the face.

Yianko's mules, the first offspring of Lambro's original barter for his land, were the Balius and Xanthus of burden, famous in the village for their immensity and pulling power but also their cleverness, notwith-standing an occasional lack of loyalty and the desire to roam free from the yard they shared with goats and chickens tripping their immense hooves. Yero, the great russet bully of the animal kingdom, was resolute and clever. He perfected rubbing his rump with a maestro's tempo in a figure eight that worked the gate open unless further latched by a chain and clasp. On this day, Yianko forgot the clasp. It was, however, Pashas, the seemingly lethargic colossus, who escaped first and exacted revenge on his master for the occasional excessive prodding, leading the way to the choicest nibbles and the farthest reaches of the village.

"The big devils! I'm going to break them of this habit if I have to kill them," Yianko said as he ran out the door. The commotion vanished with its owner. Terzellos and Gallanos listened carefully, without interruption, as Lambros made a brief presentation. When he finished, a debate arose regarding the logistics of the project - Gallanos rejecting outright all but the most theoretical alternatives proposed. Having tallied the need to refute Avram, Lambros remained amazed at the distrust the Cypriot had sown. Terzellos sat back in his chair and drained a glass of water. He spoke slowly but with confidence, as if he had rehearsed what he had to say.

"Don't think that we don't know what you're doing here, Lambrou. Somehow, you have lured the women onto your side, because women always want what they don't have. There's no way to spread the cost for such a project among the beggars of Lathra. We, the largest landowners, will bear the price of your fanatical enterprise while the rest of them will merely tap into the line at the end, hoping to avoid the cost. So we say, go ahead, build your tanks and canals, or whatever fantasy your engineer has filled your head with, but you have to rely on whatever money you gather from the tightwads in the village. I for one won't help you, Lambros Lambrou, neither with money nor with my labor."

"Nor I," said Gallanos. "Kyriazis is persuaded. He'll probably offer you what he can to have water tinkle in his house for that sultana of a wife of his ... but we will remain as we are."

"And if you change your mind, or drought returns and you ask to tap in later?" Lambros asked. "What should it cost you then?"

"Whatever it costs the others," Gallanos answered.

"We won't change our minds," Terzellos said, "so forget it."

"Yes," Gallanos parroted.

"The price should be a share of costs, from that point back to the pumping station," Lambros answered as calmly as he could, trying to keep the notion of their possible participation viable. "Don't you agree?" They stared without response. Then, interrupted by Yianko's return from his errand, Gallanos stood to leave.

"I beat them with branches as thick as their dicks," Yianko panted, as he pulled up a chair beside Terzellos. "Now, let's hear the pitch, Lala." They ignored him. Lambros stood to leave, rejected again by the likes of men he deemed to be nothing short of idiots, but sought to salvage his reputation.

"Avram made a good point," Gallanos said. "If things go wrong, it'll be too difficult to go back to the old ways."

"So we stay in the same place forever while the rest of the world laughs at us with our donkeys and clay pots?" Lambros responded testily. Terzellos said nothing. He rolled a cigarette, lit it and took two deep drags on it, exhaling from his nostrils and clamping his lips shut as if to prevent his speaking. Gallanos shrugged his shoulders and sat back down. "I'm glad you've changed your minds to the degree you have, gentlemen, but without your help the village will have to wait."

"Then let it wait," Terzellos snapped back. "We always have the springs of Kythera."

16

Avram had not settled long in Athens when he procured a viable situation befitting his skills and increasingly pensive temperament. When he first arrived, he took a room in Piraeus. Interning his mind by day, he scoured the newspaper for any hint of pursuit of the murderer of an old woman and her son. He spent much of his evenings with other vagrants, standing around barrels of burning driftwood, drinking, engulfed in smoke, choking on the sorrows and failures of washed-up men. The rest of his time was spent investigating the scant prospects for employment in whatever part of the city available. Virtually every industry and profession suffered from the effects of capitalist syphilis, economic depression and the illiquidity of common sense. Businesses that had survived managed to function without the assistance of vagabonds and foreigners. He expended his remaining drachmas and, while it pained him, cashed in his two lires and a gold twenty Franc piece, a gift given to him as a boy by Thalia, a great many years earlier. The coin he had kept wrapped in a silken strip of cloth cut from one of his mother's dresses, allegedly saved by his sister Magda.

On a dreary November afternoon, suppressing the recurring image of his hasty dispatch of the old woman, the dyspepsia of a metaphor for his own crazed mother burned in his gullet. He remembered Karpathioti's wife, voluble and green-gilled with terror, and read of her fate in the newspaper. His name appeared in the story. It unnerved him out of his now faded remorselessness. The sensationalism of the writing made him question whether it was the same woman and her "bereft little lambs" that Karpathiotis had spawned. A nuance to his mounting guilt and his memory of the children turned into an unaddressed prayer. He repeated it like an apology to no one, for having made her children orphans, a contrition unembellished by any request for clemency.

The sun had imparted its autumnal ruse upon the earth's torso, brightly lit for most of the day but useless in its lack of heat. In its diffidence, it surrendered by mid-afternoon to a squalid gray cloak of clouds, and then, an unusually drenching rainfall, that beat upon his bare head. Avram spotted what he thought was a kafenio he had somehow missed, or not frequented in the last month, one of the few unassuming boarding houses for sailors and dockworkers possessing a first floor eatery, slightly recessed in the ranks of stucco and clapboard, amid the pilings of nautical commerce adjacent to the wharf. He dodged inside to escape what might become a soaking illness for anyone without a coat and sat between the bay window and a warm coal stove near the wall. He ordered his meal from a sickly looking lad who appeared to need the rations more than he did, waited silently and then, upon its arrival, drowned several pieces of crusted bread in a sumptuous hero's soup of chicken broth, frothy beaten egg and lemon juice. With his face hovering over the steam, he dove deep into the hot white bowl for a bit of chicken and some starchy orzo sinking to the bottom. As he savored the soup, a well-dressed man with a dark complexion entered and sat at a table to his right. He wore a venerable Fedora and long European coat, like one an English gentleman might wear. The formality of his clothing made Avram dismiss his initial reaction and avert his eyes, but the man was someone Avram vaguely recognized. Delicately lined, introspective, the eyes experienced, the well-groomed man had not a single gold tooth that he could tell, nor shadow of a beard. The black-speckled gray of the mustache threw him off his recollection. Avram interrupted his meal for a moment to search his memory, to make sure the man was not anyone he had encountered in Naousa. He glanced over at him twice and finally, assured of his intuition, introduced himself, to be certain it was safe to finish his meal in peace.

"Hello. I believe I know you, sir." The man looked up from his gloves and loose papers, now wet and spread upon the table.

"I'm sorry I don't recognize you, but that's not unusual. I'm in the hotel business and have met so many people that faces tend to all appear the same to me. Like shrimp, as the saying goes," he said hastily, searching for the words. "Forgive me for not remembering you."

"There is nothing to forgive," Avram replied. "Did he liken me to a shrimp?" Avram asked himself. "I've never heard that saying." No, he assured himself, all men look the same, the way shrimp all look the same, all hooked and gray. "That's what he meant." Avram returned to his soup while the man ordered a full meal - fish, potatoes and greens. A third time Avram looked over at him. This time the man returned the scrutiny.

"Forgive my silly analogy, but your suggestion has filled me with doubt."

"Yes," Avram said, his eyes widening. "I'm quite sure of it. You say you're in the hotel business. Where is your hotel? I'm in need of work and am skilled with my hands."

"Well, I have just purchased a new place here in Athens on my own; I have another in Thessaloniki with a partner, a Kyrios Costas Poulides. He's from London. Perhaps you know Mister Poulides?

"No, the name is not familiar," said Avram, "and I've never been to London."

"And a third," he said lowering his voice as Avram raised his eyebrows with his lack of recognition, "in Istanbul." He looked about. "But my first hotel was in Izmir - Smyrna," he all but whispered. Avram's interest heightened.

"Smyrna!" He contained himself.

"Yes, in the old Greek quarter, on Herolimono Street. Have you been there?" The man smiled. Mention of the hotel reemerged in Avram's incautious memory as an expression of sheer joy.

"Herolimono Street," he said elatedly. "Do you know a man named Sukru?"

"Why, yes," the man said smiling broadly. "That's my name!" Avram's eyes filled with recognition.

"Sukru," he crooned as he rose noisily from his seat and walked toward him with both hands spread abreast. "It's me, Avram Karangelos."

"Avram Karangelos?" The man remained seated for a moment and then, in a single, dignified motion withdrew his chair and stood to greet him with a handshake.

"Avram, what has happened to the chubby little boy I once knew?"

"Sukru," Avram said, kissing his hand, embarrassing the Turk with his emotion. "Everything has happened. I'm newly arrived in Athens and looking for work." Sukru stepped back for a moment and looked at him. His appearance was pitiful, his clothes ragged and unclean. He had wasted with hunger and walking, and bore ill the consequence of his hollowed, unshaven cheeks. His wide eyes seemed baked by the sun and made him appear like a desert monk seeing angels and demons in everyone and in every corner of a room.

"Avram, I don't recognize you, my boy, but I remember you. Come sit with me and let me buy you a meal. What has become of you? Where are your sisters?"

"I am a ghost, Sukru, a ghost that should have been drowned in the port of Smyrna." The sentiment gave each man pause: for the Turk, the fearsome image of his city aflame and for the Greek, the howls of terrorized children. Sukru insisted on their sharing a table and a meal. Avram was hungry and did not decline as he might have three short months ago.

They sat for an hour, spoke as they ate fish and potatoes and sipped piquant cognacs at his benefactor's insistence, "good for the digestion and to suppress the taste of the fish, an indulgence I cannot permit myself at home." In the service of memory, the conversation embarked upon the fate of each man's family. Sukru was a widower as well, his first wife had died of cancer, but he had taken a second wife, who had borne him more children. The fair luck and providence of Christos Calphapanaiotis and Thalia and their return to Smyrna to assist him with his hotel became the hub of news at first. In his excitement, Avram inadvertently revealed the whereabouts of his sisters, evading the reason for his having abandoned them. Sensing equivocation, Sukru inquired no further.

By nightfall, Avram had secured a room in the Hotel Voulis in the Plaka section of town and a position assisting in the management of the elegant new hotel, after appropriate training and a fitting, for the attire of a gentleman. Sukru had miraculously appeared before him like a humble utterance of newfound faith, and seized the opportunity to be his rescuer once again. They left the establishment and the pier together and hastily hailed a carriage to the hotel. After vouching introductions to the staff and appointment to his position, they parted ways for the time being. Sukru returned to Piraeus that evening for departure by ferry to Chania for yet another negotiation to establish a foothold in Crete, where Avram expressed an interest in relocating.

Avram entered the room that would be his new home, sat on the feathered bed to remove his shoes and leaned back, his arms forming a tripod behind him, clenching the covers in each hand, stifling the emotion welling within him. He lay upon the bed and prepared for sleep, for the first time in many months confident of its gifts and his future.

"Thank you, my God, whoever you are, whatever you are, for this, my gift from you, for bringing to me a guardian, the kindest man in all of Anatolia."

A merciful sense of calm soothed the knotting at the base of his neck. The relief coursed through his shoulders and in a warming descent settled in the soles of his feet. Then, rising from his extremities, the healing filled his heart, a purfling of contentment only derived in the moment before sleep. In that placid, vacuous, wordless moment, he escaped the vengeful images blinding him in his waking hours. For the first time since Maria's death, after having grown accustomed to her scent and the weight of her body next to him, Avram slept undisturbed.

17

"This thinking, as a profession, has little to do with the art of the gadfly, the principles of the polis or knowledge for its own sake. No, it is far more akin to an insular medievalism from the starry-eyed perspective of the curator," Lazaros said.

"I'm not sure I understand," his listener responded.

"We memorialize our devotion to sedulous regurgitation, the ever more coherent reanalysis and fluent recreation of the history of connections between idly floating ideas." He rambled on. "Mind you, there's nothing to complain of here. It's a respectable occupation to connect things and ideas, but now the whole enterprise seems to be unraveling."

"What's he talking about?" the other man said.

"Humanity's own spiral of complication is becoming a purposeful impediment to anything that sustains a healthy existence. We acquire and expend philosophical problems the way modern painters and architects, intent upon the demise of art, incur their modernism, like a debt owed to the mind's unsteady hand. They reduce a perfectly fine experience of the object of contemplation into the psycho-symmetry of insight and like the symbolists," he whispered, as if everyone understood what he was saying, "create its meaning ex nihilo." Then he quickly added, shaking his head back and forth for emphasis, "It matters very little if the edifice of such adoration comes in the form of the cult of the great mind or the anomalies of its assorted dualisms: mind-body, wave-particle, correspondence or coherence, the absolute or the relative."

Lazaros concluded his little monologue in response to a heated exchange with Sebastianos Ritsas, Pater Alexi's sophistic and devious meacock, his deacon and part-time cantor who accompanied him at least twice a month to conduct liturgies in each of the villages serviced in the region. Also anesthetized were Danäe and, of course, Pater Alexi, always in attendance of such cabals. Sebastianos and Lazaros tired quickly of each other's intellectual pomposities and specious arguments. On one occasion, they nearly came to blows. Sebastianos went so far as to hurl a bowl full of almonds at Lazaros, striking him across the face, propelling them in a fit of indignity at his opponent's apparent submission to a faulty premise.

"Every man resents another's persuading him of his error," Lazaros had responded less than passively. Lazaros was equally as irritable around the man. As preparation for these otherwise eagerly anticipated symposiums of pretension, he would attempt to talk himself out of losing his temper. Rising early on the day of the cantor's anticipated arrival, he would go on extended walks, taking deep breaths and speaking directly to his reflection in the lake.

"When he utters a proposition of abject stupidity or insults you, or criticizes this or that thinker, write it on the bottom of your shoe," he would counsel himself aloud. "Pretend it's coming from the mouth of one of the village urchins."

"Once again your baroque usage is an impediment to meaning," Sebastianos responded, taking his cue from Lazaro's lengthy response that he was not as fatigued with the debate.

"Impediment! Baroque! You're such a boor sometimes, Ano. When professionals tinker with ideas, they call it analyzing a man's work. But all such work, all the thinking that goes into it arrives at its ninth month and its alembic value in the act of its writing down, not as a dialogue, the Socratic tit-for-tat. It is writing a thing out that affords such expanse to our thought. Not the everyday 'give me a banana from the tree,' my dear simian. Socratic emulsions are not much more than the confessions of an ordinary blabbermouth."

"As usual, you've proven my point with your effusive rampage," Sebastianos said, rummaging through his papers for his spectacles.

"I am indeed a glutton for words," Lazaros answered. "If I ask a hundred men what color the sky is today, they'll grunt the same response." No one said anything. "What color is it?" Lazaros asked. Sebastianos looked up and squinted, craning his neck in an exaggerated falcate motion about the sun, appearing nearly above their heads. Alexi and Danäe looked up as well. Sebastianos responded languorously.

"Blue."

"Ha! Precisely! But is it merely blue?" He hurried past the gaping maw of his opponent's response, shaking his head in a circular motion for Danäe and Alexi to note that he was about to commence upon a rhetorical digression of fanatical perspicuity. "I'll answer my own question."

"The hallmark of your character," Sebastianos squeezed in.

"It may be azure, the color of Greece herself, or cerulean on the fringes over there," as he pointed to the East, "like the color of the lake in spring, or the indigo of an impending storm, or in the evening, the sapphire aftermath of the harvests' sallow swept stalks, as a storm dispels the iridescence. So, while blue is correct and your idea of appropriate communication of the fact, quite correct, how dull the world would be like you Ano, my *kojabekiari*,[60] if we could only convey what we see in the sky through the telescope of such paltry descriptions." Sebastianos percolated. Danäe thought the comment quite funny, if for no other reason than many in the village identified Lazaros by the same derogation.

"Lazaros, watch your tongue. It's impolite to offend your guests who visit infrequently and then only to sample your mezedes and wine," Pater Alexi interjected.

"And here I thought it was to exercise the muscle of the brain," Lazaros said.

"It's for that, too, but there's no award for this contest, you two," Danäe added.

"Yes, Ano, you should feel complimented, for if you were a shepherd, or Jartzo or a very young child instead of a *yerondopalikaro*[61] it would suffice for me to merely say blue, but for you, my brilliant friend, in the company of Danäe and Pater, nothing but the best, the most ornate description will do." He inhaled deeply and added rapidly. "Here I go. The sky is pale, absorbing and awash in the color of the previous evening's uncommon autumnal heat, reflecting the fatigue of sunburned mountains and the gray eyes of Pallas Athena, with a splash of the underside of discolored leaves from the orchards. Perhaps it will rain. In short, an interesting shade of blue," the word sauntering into its echo.

"Do you know that you're a jerk-off, Lazaro?" Ano blurted and walked away. Pater Alexi stood, both amused and disappointed at each man's irritability. He rubbed and scratched the lobes of his ears vigorously with each hand, as was his habit after such long conversations.

"My Presbytera is talking about me." He swept his hands down the black robe of his lap un-ruffling creases and dislodging a few breadcrumbs released from the clench of his salted beard. "I'm on my way as well, Lazaros. It was interesting and tiresome all at once. It's good that Ano has met his rhetorical match with the American Gorgias," he smiled sincerely. "If you ask me, you're a victim of your books, as are these two," he said, swinging his finger to and from Danäe and Ano's former spot on the rock. "I pray that God doesn't shake the earth one

---

60 κοτζαμπεκιάρις - an Anatolian Greek transliteration of the Turkish expression for an unmarried man assumed to be an aging queer

61 γέροντοπαλλήκαρο - an aged and unmarried carouser

night and smother you with your wormy pages, the way they're stacked up all about you in your *studiloi*." He stretched his back and spread his shoulders to prepare for his departure.

"God wouldn't do that to me, Pater," Lazaros answered softly.

"I listened with humor to your contest with Sebastianos, now let me say a few words before I forget how to form them with my mouth," Alexi said. "When men think too little, they retrace the steps of their animalism. They reduce themselves to unenviable brutes. When they think too much, they become lunatics, or else whatever it is that Sebastianos and you might be. I, for one, can't even guess."

"I'll take your warning seriously, Pater," Lazaros said.

"And you," Alexi said looking squarely at Danäe, still seated, leaning upon her hand perched atop her knee, "you're living with your head in the sand, without seeing what men do all around you. Open your eyes. They're wolves and will devour you."

"Very well, Pater," Danäe responded softly, her mind splintered with the dull pain of the discussion.

"Not this one, mind you," Alexi pointed to Lazaros, following up his admonition. "He's like the brother you never had." She smiled in agreement.

"The Church Fathers have argued that there is nothing more disgusting than a suspiciously beautiful face," Lazaros said.

"What's that supposed to mean? You're confusing her," Alexi said.

"When a mother begs the emperor for mercy on behalf of her son who has been arrested and placed in chains, she throws off her pearls and adornments and appears before the dreaded judge tearing her hair and bathed in ashes, all to move the judge to compassion. From the twelfth chapter of the *Baptismal Instruction*," he said, knowing Chrysostom to be among Alexi's favorites. "Danäe, my girl, you bear no suspicion. Your beauty, your appearance before God is natural and unadorned and it arises from his grace." Lazaros said. Alexi's eyebrows danced. He wanted to say more but changed his mind. The discussion would have to end sometime. Danäe felt like her head was on fire. She looked toward the lake and had the overwhelming urge to go for a swim.

———◆———

Lazaros realized he might have taken his quarrelsome manner with Sebastianos too far. He relied heavily upon his audience. At first, it was simply to avoid the appearance of becoming a complete recluse. When he first arrived in Lathra, his desire for isolation subjected him to teasing and pranks by the village children, who naturally gravitated to any member of the community displaying any peculiarity, or anyone that would not lay chase or shoot at them when caught in the act of such ridicule. He enjoyed the symposiums. They supplemented his occasional visit to Yianko's for ouzo or coffee, which he originally only partook of to be sociable and of course, his monthly sermons delivered secretly to Pater Alexi's altar. His only other attendance of society was at church on Holy Thursday and for funeral sacraments, the last time being for Avram's wife, Maria, and before that the death of an old widow a year earlier. The widow was a black-draped crow of a creature. He had never met her but had heard that she resented him and obsessed over his presence in the village.

"Who cares if he speaks Greek? He's a foreigner," the old woman had complained of him. The gaseous American, she called him, "bloated with all his money." Her derision incited the children to tease him further and throw stones. He attended her funeral as an act of forgiveness. This had impressed Alexi and inaugurated the overt tenure of their relationship.

It also became convenient and clear to Lazaros that the scheduled symposia of letters were a suited forum for him to propound his more esoteric hypotheses, his intellectual embellishments aroused by sleeplessness and solitude, the metastasis of ideas concocted between translations, between writings and Gnostic emersions gleaned from his increasing magnum of literary libation. He balanced these only with daily walks along the most rugged coastline of Vegoritis, to avoid the heavy-belted obesity of his sedentary activities.

Among these vague ideas - that despite his theories regarding writing, he never jotted down for posterity - was the notion that humanity was destined to become increasingly subject to all manner of disease, digestive defluxion, mental anguishes and psychic manias both individually and collectively, especially the most progressive strains and racial subtexts. This, he espoused, "will arise because of two observable conditions of modernity." The first condition he identified as "the vagaries of finite genetic replication." Increases in food supplies and longer life expectancies would produce a yet uncalculated threshold of population growth, which in turn multiplies a type of genetic imbecility born of the unfettered replication of substantially similar genetic configurations.

"It amounts to a grand scale of inbreeding," he argued. He speculated that this inbreeding would exacerbate despite the rise of the Democratic State, since we all know that Democracies also tend toward economic class allegiance and alliances between forcibly like-minded leagues and trading partners. This economic phenomenon would spawn reactionary notions of nationalism and implausible ideologies of racial purity disseminated both overtly and subtly as premises of fear of the archetypical other. Fear of the Jew, of the gypsy, of the socialist, the Arab, the Oriental or the Negro, a dread and trepidation over the dilution of a perceived cultural ascendancy and intellectual prowess.

"The desire to be one, to be whole, to be unique decreases the potential for the modern version of the barbarian invasion," he insisted. He envisaged if not a conscious deferral then a hesitation over the genealogical need for cross-insemination, the commingling of the races and social classes of Asian, African or South American subtexts. The subconsciously telepathic chitchat of the telephone and other such communicative devices and the invention of moving pictures, with its tendency toward trite conclusions and the portrayal of the stereotypical in all things, even the allegedly innovative, would exacerbate this trend into public policy. All this, he predicted, despite the innovations in travel, which one might think could spur the opposite tendency, would eventually invite us all to view 'the other' as a carrier of disease - physical, social and philosophical.

"Commingling or a mitigated extermination of sameness would do humanity some bloodcurdling but genetic good," he concluded rather coldly. "But cultures and races, even those retaining the habit of curiosity, invariably wish to be alone and left alone, to confirm what they, in their symbolic identities, already know and believe about themselves. Hence, they avoid miscegenation with lower classes with the infiltrating skin color, the languages and unseemly migrants from an uncivilized landscape." He would qualify this point further by stressing its exacerbation in nature.

"Because," he argued, "it's inevitable that the number of species will condense and diminish. This is true in the evolution of both animals and men. I call this the natural propensity of the species for self-loathing of its genus." The duplication of dominant genetic strains would lead to a mathematically calculable reduction in the variety of species, which in men he identified as "the tableau of finite human parts." No invention of industrial novelty or revolution in sexual promiscuity would keep pace with the procreative appetite for this type of replication. Absent this realization, or nations mandating sterilization or infanticide, the only way to deny the trend would be to stop counting.

He believed that the Calvinist prigs to the north, among the most intellectually advanced denominator of the species, were not only poised to reach this conclusion but already in the excruciating clutch of its dilemma and incongruity, openly harboring the enthralling mental masonry of unbridled monolithic procreation, envisioning its aftermath as a Valhalla of their making. "What they'll really be saddled with," he would say gleefully, "will be the plague of genetic purity - the unwitting result being a race of chimerical deformity, beautiful in its own abominable way. They believe that after liquidating all the undesirable mutations of humanity they will possess a race of lofty, heel-clicking Thors and Siegfrieds, with a Goethe, Beethoven and Planck being generational instead of epochal," he said with uncontrolled amusement and then cackling. "A race of depressive, head-heavy albinos is more likely. You see, the error stems from viewing history in too lofty a manner. We can blame Hegel if you'd like, everyone else does - and others with similar philosophical temperaments, as William James once identified," he said facetiously. "Absolute history as forever youthful! He's actually a retired Titan repeating his own asinine refrain, hearing his echo and thinking it to be another voice. Old Chronos stands across the gulf watching the new goddess of time embrace the world like an illicit lover." Space/time was the first truly unisexual concept of science, for Lazaros. "The mystics understood this long ago," he insisted. In his jocose and unceremonious harangue on nature, she is the cognate nymph, her tinkling little trinkets and patulous spaces, nothing like the asexual backdrop of Being portrayed by the cosmologists.

No one understood him. Alexi accused him of forgetting that God indeed intercedes in the machinations of the cosmos, but slowly, because he has infinite patience and knows the meaning of silence. Whereas men, who must die, and feel obliged to keep track of time and all sorts of things they feel compelled to count and calculate, have no patience at all. God works the way a mechanic tinkers with machines, but in an invisible, infinitesimal way, outside of history.

"He'll never let humanity get a hold of the reins of time," he told Danäe.

The other idea, of which Lazaros opined rather fervidly, was what he called his first principle of collective madness, that which propels the conversion of the sciences into mere artifices of invention and complexity, the primary purpose of which is profit.

"Ha! This is it. Man's penchant for gratuitous complexity - the true Tower of Babel," he proclaimed. Science, he argued, is the ideology whose covert and overarching desire is to supplant the supremacy of that which it perceives as the religious tall tale. "Religion, you see has this benign idea of mystical simplicity within its fixed constellation of knowledge and morality. It promotes a universal scheme whose steps do not divulge to us something as mundane as evidence. But not science! Science offers only the evidentiary steps, both miniscule and grand. It postulates its own solution to the mystery of being, that all things are applicable to its method and to the telling. But it will sabotage itself, subvert itself with the most sublime and supreme entropy. And universal madness will ensue, a complication for which we will need a god to unscramble. The more complex the apparatus the more desired it becomes. Poor Boltzmann saw this all very clearly and it depressed him."

In this, Lazaros saw America as the sultry prophetess, a society having commingled science with a theory for the management of human affairs, a maniacal cult of efficiency, which nearly always has money as its end. Lazaros explained that his first principle owed its impetus to Freud and the second vaguely to Marx, but more so to the invention of the Tin Lizzie and to the Anglo-American fondness for selling assurances, which he deemed to be among the most vulgar of human enterprises. He saw credit issued from the very store selling the goods as a financing system perpetuating the slavery of poverty. An analogy he liked using was how doctors administer health and relief with doses of the very disease they seek to eradicate, the difference between dosage and addiction or death being one of degree. It ushers in a unique variety of poverty. Poverty in the midst of possessing a myriad of manufactured trappings to make life easier but that also create a poverty and slavery reflected in the very machinery of their nightmarish manufacture.

"Acquiring what the people do not need today with the false hope of attaining the rest tomorrow," he would say. This apparent contradiction, for a man who in his life never labored for his survival, was a fact not lost on Lazaros and at least once, affectionately pointed out by Alexi. But with his accommodation of Lambros and his water pumping station, Lazaros felt pride in the proof that he was no Luddite, and openly expressed as much.

Alexi's response to these ideas was not the usual menacing stripe across the speaker's back. He grew sullen, appearing to shrink as the words and ideas blossomed.

"All of life is complicated, Lazaro, by consequence, not by design. All strife is concocted conflict for the benefit of a few. So why should we bother with the unsolvable? Even Eden possessed death and rejuvenation. Insects crawled and crept, flew and scurried among the great trees. The birds and beasts fed on them and on each other to their demise and the nourishment of the other. But animals died in blissful ignorance, a kind of dignity and peace reserved for them alone, performing their role without understanding it, without mourning and the torment that burdens a god-mimicking soul. For men, the tree of knowledge, and its confounded good and evil, drew back the veil surrounding the void before the cataclysm of creation. Before this, Adam and Eve were like the lower creatures they had named. But Adam had to bite from the fruit! His taste, at first sweet, became exceedingly bitter and this sublime bliss gave way to an instinct of fear, of being torn and devoured. Slowly, as men tread the earth and shed their cannibal past, they became less and less like their animal brethren. Emotion and passion comes with knowledge, my Lazaro, the byproduct of mimicking one's creator and his angels. This is the curse upon Adam and his progeny, and the entire cast of creation."

On a luminous summer evening, as the stars twinkled harmoniously the light between men and their imagination, Lazaros revealed his theory of collective madness to a small group in Yianko's kafenio. Among them was a visitor from San Antonio, Texas, a cousin of Petros Canettas, a man exuding a healthy dose of nationalist pride and the kind of homespun wisdom offered in his daily newspaper. Tall, robust and as clean-shaven as a man could be, he leaned toward Lazaros and spoke with the kind of direct indignation recognized as uniquely American. He accused Lazaros of being either a shrink or a shyster lawyer, peddling the kind of explanations and *isms* that make men sick for the listening. The drawling English might normally have elicited a bit of nostalgia from Lazaros but curses flung from the Texan's mouth, landing against his bony frame with the ugly thuds of a stoning. Lazaros nodded copiously.

———◆———

Danäe enjoyed the daring and stagy language of such sparring with Sebastianos, as she might any theatrical presentation, both men visibly confined within the cobwebbed closets of their arcane usage and vitriolic yet ultimately feeble attempts to entrap and close the door behind the other. Arguments digressed into fanciful etymologies of too expansive a phraseology that no philosopher or philologist has ever elucidated to the satisfaction of others.

Sebastianos tolerated the debates and their caustic affect upon his digestion only for the concupiscent excuse of catching the faint scent of lanolin and jasmine that was even the un-bathed Danäe. Wolfishly squinting with pleasure, he imagined her pliable, bent over in subservience to his depravity as he fondled himself later that evening in the privacy of his darkened stall, shamelessly deep in the bowels of the Church. Sebastianos managed to keep these libidinous tendencies secret from Pater Alexi, who was a devoted husband with six children, and who never stayed in Lathra or beneath the Church. No matter how long a journey it entailed, whether in snow or scorching summer heat, or the utter blackness of a moonless night, Alexi returned home to his isolated woodland settlement high atop the lake, on the outskirts of Arnissa, home to his *Papadia*[62] Thekla and his waiting brood.

Sebastianos also functioned as Deacon and Cantor on the feast of the three Hierarchs for a priest as far away as Kastoria. That priest's

---

62 παπαδιά - priest's wife

childless Presbytera was a celebrated beauty who frothed the Deacon's fancy as well. Provided guest quarters in the priest's home, with her bedroom just next door, Sebastianos eavesdropped upon her every toss and muted sigh, her insomniac's ritual noted in his corpuscle of craving. He justified his compulsion without any post-flagellant repentance. It overcame him like a pregnant woman's relish for rich cooking. Satiated, with nary a culpable invocation between cravings, he rationalized his conduct as arising from the need to calm the tensions allegedly caused by Lazaro's insolence, the bizarre arguments, and his upsetting theories denying the ultimate spiritual evolution of the species.

"Lord, may you release in him a worm to eat his entrails," Sebastianos would pray.

The Deacon's Lathran visits ended with a single, ignoble yet memorable incident. No one knew that Jartzo loved prancing about the altar, silently pantomiming Alexi. On the evenings after the recital of any liturgy or sacrament, he frequented the Church with its numerous doors, none of which possessed locks. Indeed not a single door in Lathra had a lock. One warm night in June, Sebastianos retired to his chamber after spending the afternoon in his usual subtle scrutiny of Danäe, a keen leer, a vigilant eye peering through an expressionless countenance. She had sat at arm's length from him all that day and leaned over to clean up a plate of grapes which he purposefully let fall, nearly losing his mind with what he imagined he glimpsed. That night, Jartzo boldly ventured into the basement catacombs when he heard what he thought were the muffled moans of the dead. Unhindered by any fear of death or the dark, he crept down the narrow spiral of steps to the cellars, where relics lay chambered in the dust and cobwebs, with a lit candle in his hand. The cubicles possessed no doors at all, being remnants of a hermetic outpost built prior to the region's settlement by Turks, including the cozy burrow Sebastianos occupied. The cubicle contained a cot, a small end table and a coal box attached to a thin flue in the opposite corner, for use in the winter.

Jartzo entertained himself for three days reenacting the womanly startle Sebastianos emitted, having had his emolument interrupted at the precise moment of its magnified purpose. The Deacon flogged away, despite discovery, grunting Danäe's name. The laughter and disgraceful mimicry annoyed everyone in the village. Women took to throwing rocks and garbage at Jartzo, anything to make him stop. His performances so enraged Katerina that she drove her son from her hovel, for fear of beating him senseless, and did not permit him back until he finally tired of his own hilarity and ceased the lurid pantomime. For three nights, Jartzo camped between protective crags and a canopy of pine branches a few hundred paces from Lazaro's cavern and parodied his amusement and Sebastianos' reaction for much of each night, the revolting recital reverberating off the surface of the lake in its raw acoustic splendor. Thus, Sebastianos achieved within the cycle of his rhetorical reprisal, a victory over Lazaros, having in their last contest of minds wrestled three night's sleep from his opponent.

Elissa took the occasion to explain Jartzo's burlesque travesty to Danäe and the meaning of Sebastianos' shameless proclivity. She had received not a moment's education in such delicate matters from her mother. The lesson devastated her. Then Elissa had the bright idea of scolding Danäe regarding her attendance of scholarly symposiums with educated men, stern enough to make her believe she was to blame for the unseemly events that transpired. Even though the gatherings always occurred outdoors, Elissa scolded, it was a practice certain to ward off available suitors. The shame obviously racked her conscience, but Elissa kept talking.

"The rumor might suggest to some that you are promiscuous, since we all know that educated women share this trait. How else can they fare well in such a world of men?" The color drained from Danäe's face. Deeply pained by the comment, she was confused that Elissa would promote such an idea, since she had frequently argued with Lambros the nearly opposite point when it came to Sophia's education.

"Not my mother?" Danäe said, her voice trailing off and wavering with emotion. "She was educated."

"No, my dear," Elissa said, suddenly repentant at having so upset her, "your mother was an exception. There is one to every rule. Don't cry, my girl. She was so proud of you." Her backpedaling failed. She began to cry as well and to disparage the sins of her undisciplined tongue.

Before this episode, Danäe felt persuaded that Lazaro's theories, especially the one about the self-loathing of the genus, possessed a crusty integument of validity and took the time to return home and copy what she could remember from their symposiums, hoping to amass them for posterity. Now she abandoned this mission and succumbed to the discomfort of a new self-awareness, her femininity under scrutiny, the manner in which most men judged her, as if in some unwitting way she had occasioned their shame as well as her own. The result of this insight proved to be as impenetrable a mystery to the rest of the village as the other variants and deviation of Danäe's nature and family history. She cropped her hair with sheep sheers, as near to her scalp as she could, since both Elissa and Macarios Timonakis, each on two occasions, refused to lop off her magnificent flax. She fashioned a loose-fitting shirt and pair of trousers from sackcloth with a linen lining to reduce the irritation to her skin, suffering intensely in the heat. Resented by those complicit in her desirability, she avoided contact with men whenever possible. She spent even more time sampling books from Lazaro's library, but had Stratos and Sophia retrieve them secretly, without permission from Elissa or Lambros, who forbad their children from venturing up to Mavrotripa.

Her usefulness to Elissa fell off, as did the quality of her work. Her duties as a midwife and attention to the domesticated animals of the village suffered since she now attended to them after dark. Everyone considered it madness to risk injury and require the attendees to stand about in the night air with lanterns so she could see well enough to administer treatments. She would vanish from sight each time Andreas, Spiros, Tasso or any younger man was about to pass by the courtyard. When the time came for tobacco to be thread for drying, water boiled for washing clothes, or fires tended for baking and preserving, she became undependable and often retreated into her little apartment in the far corner of the courtyard or into the distant hills, lingering there after tracking a lamb or hunting for teas and wildflowers. The children missed her as well, complaining that she was not available to organize games on Sunday afternoons or explore the caves east of Kythera, or to hike along the shores of Vegoritis and the uninhabited islands leading to Arnissa and beyond.

Matters grew thorny in her reflective misery. On one occasion, missing her parents profoundly, she thought to join them in her childhood image of God's queue before his fearful judgment. More emotive deprecation and melodrama than an actual desire for death, she stood upon a bluff adjacent to Mavrotripa but could not jump for weeping. Walking home, she thought of the women of Naousa who in their time and anguish danced off the cliffs rather than fall captive to Ottoman soldiers. They were her moral superiors, she thought. But theirs was a bona fide reason to die. Continued consciousness carried only the torment to come, a torment inflicted not by the unrest of one's psyche but solely at the hands of heathen captors. Gradually she began to view the purpose of women in more narrow terms that were not completely clear but far less attributable to the nature of any particular woman. Time would mollify her shame, and events outside of her control force her again to find her place in Lathran society, events whose characters might beckon her to a wider world.

18

Love was neither a conqueror nor a bastion for Magda Karangelos. For Lydia though, the departure of Eleftheri Marios eclipsed her concern over her brother's escape and what would have been nearly certain arrest, and then what might pose as adjudication in those impatient and lawless days, and finally execution. Twenty letters later, letters that began as girlish odes to the garland of lotus and fragrance of her deflowering, Lydia's voice and words evolved into sodden, fretful avowals of his desertion of her. She was convinced that Marios had more than disposed of her image in the fosse of his heart. As far as she could tell, he was purposefully evading her pleas for attention. For his part, Marios never received a single letter until he happened to visit the post office on official business regarding the alleged transgression of a young man attempting to mail subversive packages to the enemies of his fellow Macedonian anarchists lurking in the smoky kafenia of Thessaloniki. Postal number 198 Diamandis was confused with Mario's flat number 148 on the same street. The local authorities refused to deliver mail to a non-existent address. In Lydia's case, her handwriting, feminine, ornate and elongated caused the postal sorter to construe her numeral fours as nines. The absentminded postmaster had on each occasion of receiving a new letter, failed to remember that he collected a few similarly posted envelopes every week for several weeks.

"198 Diamandis, the number doesn't exist," he repeated to his staff. "Marios. Where do I know that name? Oh well." He assented to the only authority and judgment he possessed over his fellow men and threw the mail into the postal equivalent of an unmarked grave. Lydia's wayward lore of love ended up scattered like orphans throughout the facility, with five of the earliest letters plopped into a tin atop the postal counter filled with papers and office debris, smothering the perfume of her submissions. Marios entered the office and noticed one of the letters addressed to him next to the tin, sitting beneath a cold cup of tourkiko, and then another, upright and atop its shallow interior.

"These are my letters, you lazy bastard," he scolded the postmaster, confiscating them, tearing the first open and walking the street reading it aloud, irrespective of audience. Reentering the post office, he ripped the cigarette from the postmaster's mouth and berated plebian incompetence. Despite his anger and the discovery of Lydia's ardor, however, Marios could not manage to write her back immediately, nor did he read all of the letters.

At some point in the third month after his lathering kisses both liberated and subjugated her, Lydia determined through the unusual discomforts of her early waking hours and the abatement of her own bloody lunacy, that her first submission to a man's squeeze bequeathed the charm of conception. Oddly, she was neither distraught nor elated, and for a while chose not to focus upon the inevitable confession due and owing her sister. She was instead simply relieved that her brother was nowhere near to judge her conduct. A month or so after the reprieve, her belly ascending in a lovely heightened summons of the navel, Lydia spoke to Magda over tea, munching candied almonds to settle her nerves. She confided that she had written to Marios daily at first, then every week since he left her, and that he failed to respond to her letters.

"But he did leave me this," she said mincingly, stroking her belly, bowing her head, tears dripping onto her knuckles. Magda wept aloud, spit at her sister with contempt and tore her own blouse, exposing her breasts in a spectacle of overreaction derived as much from envy as the shame of illegitimacy and her sister's promiscuity. Lydia permitted herself the momentary luxury of laughing at her sister's theatrics. Then, as Magda appeared ready to slap her, she wept in earnest for the first time, admitting to her sister that she could think of nothing but Marios since he left, clinging to a dreary realization by day and cleft despondency by night, that her affections might forever remain unrequited. Magda's bitterness slowly gave way to pity. She embraced her sister coldly and then, moments later, announced her new mission, like an admiral propounding a naval maneuver or some tactical dogma of seafaring.

"He must marry you immediately, the scoundrel!"

"No, Magda, I can't force him."

"Have you lost your mind?" she scolded. "He fills you with custard, like a dutiful little sweet, and you're going to do nothing? If Avram were here you wouldn't be saying such things."

"Thank God he's not here," Lydia said, resolving to cry again and then suddenly stopping.

"I'm traveling to Thessaloniki and finding this Kyrios Marios myself." Lydia begged against it, fearing aloud the idea of forcing herself upon a man with modern sensibilities and then, confronted with her sister's vehemence, insisted she come along. The practical and moral disadvantages to her parading about Thessaloniki in such a state and the concern for her health over such a long and jarring journey won the day. Together they dusted off the rope-tied trunks of apparel and trinkets brought with them upon their arrival to Lathra. Avram had imagined his sisters' visit would be temporary. They would assist him and attend to the burial of Maria. But for Magda and Lydia, it was always an opportunity to partake of their brother's prosperity, a prosperity that eluded them ever since they fled Smyrna. The trunk was brimming with Thalia's now somewhat dated western relish in garments and accessories and a few articles she had managed to save from Smyrna. The rest she received from a wealthy benefactor in Thessaloniki, a woman who had gained weight and bestowed them upon the less fortunate Anatolians. Thalia in turn gained weight as the years passed, and gave them to Magda and Lydia upon their departure.

"I don't want to look like a peasant at the ball," Magda said excitedly, rummaging through the trunk.

"You mustn't look provocative either," Lydia added, unconcerned with hiding her fear that her sister might succumb to the charms of Eleftheris Marios.

"No, no, we can't have that," Magda agreed. Nevertheless, she chose only those ensembles she imagined would evoke the most influence over him, recalling his flirtation and her flaccid response as compared with Lydia's salacious embraces. Magda modeled one dress after another, rejecting several before a few choice selections arose by begrudging consensus. Lydia obsessed, nearly bursting with envy, but accomplished the necessary alterations to each choice, being a competent seamstress and having taken those particular garments in so that either sister could wear the clothes and bear the caparison of such vanity. Magda accomplished the ironing and packing of her bag. At the last moment, she removed a tight fitting selection in dark blue and shook it out, laying it on the bed. "Once the child is born and your seducer comes to take you and the child away with him, you can greet him wearing this." Lydia sat on the bed trembling, wrapping her arms around her sister's waist.

Magda embarked on her expedition to Thessaloniki within the week, hiring a professional driver from Arnissa to escort her by motorcar to the sparkling city by the sea. Not discussed in the least with Lydia, an abortion jostled onto her mental index of solutions during the jarring journey. The driver, with whom Magda avoided conversation, on three occasions nearly crashed the vehicle while scrutinizing the villous spirals descending below a florid earlobe and caressing her neck, the daring convex to her long fingernails, scrupulous cleaned and polished, and alluring calves, visible when she shifted positions or inclined to her right and the open window.

"If you want to be paid the ransom you've charged me, you might deliver me to my destination without incident, driver," she said on the third near mishap. Abortion would have only been viable if she could whisk Lydia to Flornia, where an infamous midwife practiced her specialized procedure confidentially, and where no one inquired of facts or family names. Most of the midwife's patrons were Albanian and Bulgarian girls, women who would cross the border alone or escorted by strangers practiced in the trade, who often took advantage of the girls' fears and condition, an untidy secret mentioned only in hushed, unseemly conversation of necessity. The abortionist was herself a victim of a cousin's brutal abuse and enslavement as a girl. Years later, she had the audacity to avenge herself on the culprit, and so could not return home to Dubrovnik. She prided herself on having never lost a patient or sent one away ill. Her reputation for calming the fears and disgrace of the girls was unsullied by the contradiction to her particular brand of heretical Catholicism, as was her alias throughout the Balkans: Dracolina the Croatian, the consumer of natal flesh.

———————

The law, or the tail end of any wielding of power, for that is the sum of its reality, is with specific and insidious purpose designed to replicate a labyrinth, even in its most mundane procedures or hierarchies. Finding Marios turned into a considerable enterprise given the bureaucratic embroilment and scolding necessary to obtain a straight answer from any of the sundry clerks within the halls of justice and the police department. It seemed that every destination was the wrong department and every Eleftheri Marios a genetic or administrative replica of one shade or another. The problem of course was that clerks of any government agency notoriously half listened to a query. In the haze and indifference of cigarettes and coffee breaks, they referred Magda to managers, assistants and secretaries from throughout the building and adjacent agencies. Marios Bogatsos on the second floor, Marina Eleftheriou in reception, Eleftheri Papaiannis and Eleftheri Marinakis, who worked in other unrelated government agencies altogether. Nearing the end of an afternoon of searching and walking the halls, Magda began to doubt herself. In her exhaustion, it seemed that Marios had appeared in Lathra as a specter, a charlatan, a lothario under an assumed name for the express purpose of debauching her sister. Finally, on her last referral, she found him in the flesh, sitting at his desk in his office, in his shirtsleeves, mostly unbuttoned, not four doors from where she first inquired of him. Seated next to him was an overtly proportioned matron, an employee from the same building. Her cosmetic application was that of a retired courtesan afflicted with craving for one last galliard of seduction before graying curls might grace the avenue of pleasure. The walls of his office were unadorned and ashen. A clock on a virtually empty bookcase ticked noisily. Lydia's letters lay strewn upon his messy desk in various stages of reading and regurgitation, the final three still unopened. Marios, who was not much of a reader, and even less of a writer, was in the midst of the third draft of a first letter to Lydia, scribbled in his own jittery hand. His objective was to extol his innocence over the last four months and to offer a promise to visit her on his next furlough, this while eating his lunch, halva and an overripe pear, shared with his lusty guest. Magda was shocked to find the matron sitting cozily in a private office with a man not her husband, her skirt pulled above the knees and legs ajar.

"How are you, scoundrel?" she inveigled calmly, her tone a conscious attempt at wit. She dismissed her driver, entered the stifling office and removed her jacket.

"Speaking of sirens," he replied showing his big teeth in a broad smile, adopting an inane look of reconciliation, unaware of the berating about to spew from her lips. As quickly as he introduced the women to each other, the matron sensed in Magda the puissance of disdain. She rose from her seat to leave, nodded, and shut the door behind her.

"Rascal, he must have bedded her, too," she said, passing a colleague, returning to the banishment of her office at the end of the long clinical corridor.

Magda occupied the woman's former seat, her loud fragrance lingering in the room. She crossed her legs and embarked on a distracting, leg-swinging perturbation. The dress possessed a single pleat secured by an ornate pin at the point equidistant to where it wrapped about her and tapered to the waist. A seductive shade of claret, the selection of garment had initially drizzled down her torso and across her hips, but now, even after her recent fitting, draped a bit loosely, her having shed weight in the last week of anxiety. Quite purposefully, she left the pleat fall, unsecured by her hand, well above the long hem, permitting, upon a diffident shift in posture, a certain neglectful hiatus of cloth and silk to peek from beneath a swath of liquid texture. She was prepared to move right to the point.

"I see you have the audacity to leave my poor sister's letters thrown upon this dog house of a desk, like so much rubbish. And you don't even know what you've done!"

"I can explain," he protested. "I didn't receive her letters until recently and am just now writing to her."

"I don't believe you. You're a vagabond who collects hearts! I find you most unsuitable, even disgraceful, but circumstances are such that you must marry Lydia. She loves you traumatically and has not stopped yearning for you since you met." Failing to grasp the import of the insinuation, Marios let out curt, voluble bursts of laughter. He leaned to the right, glanced down at her knees and calves and then stood, looking down at her with brazen expectancy. Standing as near as he was, the pheromones of his black-panted presence evoked in her their first meeting. Already, he thought he had her, and the propinquity of submission. Magda anticipated him in his vein. She had found him attractive and apparently interested in her on their first meeting, but now, the method of her resistance she left unrehearsed. Seeking to avoid her own demise, she remained seated and had the good sense to fill the tension and void with a quick answer.

"Where do you think you're going?" she said, looking him in the eyes as if a knife might be next.

"Nowhere. This is my office," he replied, looking out the unopened window and returning to his chair, surprised at how ferocious she appeared.

"You don't understand, do you? You didn't even read her letters," Magda said, tempering the forte of her sister's secret. She lowered her voice. "She's pregnant with your child, stupid!" Marios sat back in his chair apparently unmoved. Although accusations linked to his escapades never ceased to unnerve him, he did not believe her. This had happened before. A woman from Samos had paraded an infant before him nine months after her initial accusation. In that instance, a lack of a demand for marriage made Marios suspicious. Self-preserving, interrogative police work quickly uncovered the ruse. The child had been the offspring of a first cousin. The woman simply wanted payment for her silence. He opted to believe that this new agenda was no different, discounting the demand for marriage. He had confidence in his tried-and-tested stroke of contraceptive science, essentially coital withdrawal.

"That's not possible, Magda."

"So, you remember my name."

"Of course I do. It's my work to remember such details."

"Is it your work to come into our home to arrest my brother, attempt to lure me with your wavy locks and daggers for eyes and instead seduce my sister . . . out in the world for all to see? You might have ruined her reputation with that alone."

"What are you talking about?" he said, not making sense of the insinuation.

"She told me everything. Against the wall of the courtyard, like a pair of dogs!" her voice tainted with jealousy. "Not possible? We'll see about that, Kyrios Marios." Shifting her weight to face him, inadvertently offering a levant glimpse of stocking, she finally stood, to end his diversion. "I can assure you its quite true and if you deny it again I'll report the offense to your employer and to everyone in this building, for I believe I've met them all. And we shall depose her here for the truth to be known, and when the time comes and the need arises, return with your offspring."

"You'll do no such thing," he said stepping toward her as she stepped back near the wall, the way he remembered Lydia. The most memorable feature of his seduction of her sister suddenly invited doubt in him. Magda stood, silently, in close proximity to the adrenaline of his growing discomfort. He set his gaze deeply into hers, wanting to draw whatever darkness from any well of sensuality. Her lower lip quivered, the cold gray pools of her eyes narrowed and her expression grew tender.

"Eleftheri," she crooned timidly, for she had already thought of him as her brother-in-law.

The intimacy, her intonation, made Marios believe the threat and worse yet the indictment. Skilled in discerning the fabrication of false emotion, his mind raced for a solution. The history of his prowess withered with his miasmic predicament.

"It was your fault I chose her," he said. She could not believe her ears and wanted to respond with incredulity, but could not.

"That's not true," she said blushing.

"You tempted me, just as you are now," he said, "and then made it quite clear that I'd never have you." Shame mingled with her pleasure in the concoction. She turned away for a moment and then returned to find his expression kinder than noted in her first impression. He perceived her genial little smile as her being ripe for plucking and endeavored to kiss her, a reflex ignorant of any purpose. How might a kiss expunge the fact of fetal flesh and blood? She turned and acquiesced to a peck upon the cheek, stopping him with a hand to his chest as he moved closer. She looked in his eyes briefly and then reached for her jacket.

"You're a talented liar, Eleftheri Marios. I'll expect your answer regarding my sister by tomorrow, at which point I will be returning home. If you have it in you to do the honorable, manly thing, I'll be quite surprised, because I consider you to be a complete and utter rogue unworthy of taking my sister's noble name from her, unworthy of spawning in her a child, even if it becomes a child of her sorrow."

She left the office, walking briskly down the maze of corridors and out of the building into the sunshine, gathering her composure, discarding the mesmeric affect he had upon her before finding the driver and returning to her hotel. Marios sat quietly in his chair, his head propped in his left hand, twirling his pearly komboloi with the other. He lit a cigarette. His mind moved back and forth between the sanguine call of fatherhood and the fantasy of running from sister to sister in the same night. He remembered a fleeting sense of apprehension overtaking Lydia, standing upright, her full weight upon him, making it difficult for him to time his withdrawal. He rose from his desk, the pleasure of the image recurring and surmounting his realization that Magda was telling the truth, confirmed in Lydia's last letter to him, which he finally read. The day's episode had made sickly sense to him. She asked for no money. His mouth dried and his mind raced. He stuck his head out into the hallway and called the matron to return to his office.

"Shut the door," he said as she entered. She obliged him eagerly and locked the door before ingratiating the staff in adjoining offices with her muffled moans and a jaunty rhythm upon the desk.

———◆———

Magda returned to Lathra without a response from Marios. She went back to his office on two occasions following the unsettling yet exciting encounter with him. On the first occasion, a bureau clerk advised her that he had just departed on assignment to Florina that morning and would return late that evening. She decided to stay one more day. On the second day, early in the morning, she learned he was en route from Kavala.

"You said Florina yesterday. That is in the opposite direction of Kavala," she questioned the matron. The woman raised her eyebrows.

"What do you want me to tell you, Miss, he's a nimble fellow ... in more ways than one. One day in Florina the next day in Kavala, who knows where Mister Marios will be tomorrow. But, I'll tell him you asked for him." Then noticeably lowering her voice she asked: "May I inquire of the subject of your business with him?" Magda sensed some envy to the diminished tenor of the question. Before arriving on that second day, she resolved that if he still avoided her, as a last resort, she would be content with mere injury to his reputation. But when the opportunity arose, the matron intimidated her. She decided to bide her time and let the birth of the child work its effect upon the louse, what she called him in the matron's presence.

Marios was actually hiding from her, behind the closed door of the Magistrate's office, across the hall from the bureau headquarters. He had never left the building. She requested permission to leave him a letter before departing Thessaloniki. After a polite but evidently manipulative discussion regarding the smartness of the matron's outfit, the matron permitted Magda to sit at Mario's desk, under scrutiny of course. The woman swung her crossed leg with so incessant a rhythm it distracted Magda, deflating the anger she sought to convey through the swagger of her penmanship.

"Any animal can dip its pink sausage," she wrote. "Be a man about this and come to Lydia and what will be your son or daughter. Tend to your obligations as a father even if you have no intentions as a husband." The terse letter ended with the bold scribble of her initial and surname. She desired to persuade him of the merits of attendant fatherhood. Even if it meant subjection to his lurid propositions, or that she serve as a surrogate for her sister's affections, a notion caustically censored within her but materializing in her imagination in all its stimulating possibilities. By now, she made her mind up that the alternative to bearing the child was impractical for Lydia's lachrymose constitution.

"Lydia will falter," she said aloud, persuading herself. "Like our mother", her thoughts trailing off in avoidance. "She'll blame me for the fate of an aborted child and pine over the likes of the father even worse than she has." She believed that the child would be a daily reminder of her abandonment and convert Lydia's love into a healthy resentment and finally, a loathing for the man who violated her, and in this instance, loathing might ensure her sanity. Unwilling to abandon or sell her brother's holdings in Lathra, she devised to send her sister back to their surrogate parents, Thalia and Christos, for such assistance in raising the child, as Lydia would certainly require, and until a story of her marriage and widowhood was invented for local digestion, after which she might return from Smyrna with the child.

Upon her return to Lathra, exhausted and disheartened with her failure, but her mind racing with the plans she had envisioned on the drive home, Magda proceeded to pass by her brother's house, where Lydia remained a virtual recluse for fear of detection of her perceptible bump. Instead, she carried on to the doorstep of Lambros Lambrou. It was just past midday. Elissa was removing a generous tray of what was to be the afternoon meal from the brick oven on the ground floor of the home. Lambros had already arrived from a morning of pruning trees with his sons. The children sat sedately about the table inside the veranda doors, waiting for their meal. There was a chill in the air. A small plate of salted filets, a little fish like a herring, a meze extracted with some labor from the lake, smothered in oil with onions and parsley, and a loaf of bread was set on the table to occupy the children. Elissa noticed Magda and ventured out from the alcove beneath the veranda. The oven was still hot, the tray of food in her hands.

"Magda, how are you?"

"Elissa, may I speak with your husband?"

"Yes, Magda, yes," she said cordially. "Is everything alright?" she asked and then immediately shouted, "Lambro, you have a visitor," and then turned to Magda. "Please join us for a meal, dear, we have plenty. I've cooked *yemistes*.[63] The peppers and squashes are still crisp from the cold cellar. You know I wrap each one in cloth, right on the vine, to absorb the moisture. It keeps them free from pests, from spots and blight and they last longer in storage." Magda was indifferent, if not bored with what Elissa imparted.

---

63 γεμιστά - stuffed peppers and squashes

"No, no thank you, Elissa. It's very generous of you, but I'm exhausted after a long journey from Thessaloniki and seek your husband's counsel on a delicate matter of family business."

Lambros emerged on to the veranda in his stocking feet, saw that his guest was Magda and retrieved his boots from inside, returning with them on but untied, just as Elissa and Magda ascended the staircase. Elissa retreated into the adjacent room with her yemistes and set them on the table, but left the glass-paned door ajar so she might overhear the conversation.

"What does Lambros have to do with her delicate family business?" she grumbled, unable to control herself in front of her children. Sophia blushed. Stratos sought to leave but Elissa stopped him. Lambros immediately felt the unease that more often than not possessed him in the presence of Avram's sisters. He found her mannerisms and eagerness distracting. Magda appeared different to him - harried, vulnerable and as comely as he had ever seen her. He ascribed this observation to her ensemble, somewhat tight fitting about the hips, with stockings darkening her enticing calves. She reminded him of a woman he saw in a magazine, a woman from Madrid; sultry, haughty yet wanton, her stance, leaning upon one leg, suggesting hips like the curvature of a guitar, a mantle for a man's hands.

"What's wrong, Magda? You look worried. Have you news of Avram?"

"No, no, Lambros, it's not Avram. May I speak with you in complete confidence? I can't trust any of the riffraff in this village. May I indulge your kindness?"

"Yes, of course," Lambros said. Noticing the door ajar, he closed it without thought.

"Riffraff," Elissa muttered, "who's she talking about?" Elissa moved Nikos from his seat near the door and took his position at the table, where she could pull the laced drape back and at least observe the conversation and hope to make out an occasional garbled word. Magda looked like a townswoman in her dress, sophisticated and younger, with her silk stockings and leathered heels. Her jacket was open, inviting, and her ruffled white blouse unnecessarily, scandalously unbuttoned at the top, the long skirt rising high above her waist, accentuating an ample bosom. Elissa mulled over the perceived implication.

Lingering in her dark heart, in a voice Magda dared not cognize as her own, lay a perilous secreted emotion, an arousal, an expectation of favor. Her inexplicable infatuation with Lambros had remained a covetous secret, except to Lydia. Influenced by the encounter with Marios, without realizing it, she came closer to Lambros, with each chapter and edict of the tale she told, a tale portrayed completely as Lydia's despair, as her innocence and Mario's insidious lechery. Motivated into using her sister's gullibility to glean information regarding Avram's whereabouts, Marios had seduced her sister and impregnated her in the process. Shock registered upon Lambro's face like an unanswered question, expending his breath between his teeth and lips. Magda took another step closer and looked up at him, a wisp of the reticent doe.

"Is it too much for me to ask that you visit Eleftheris Marios and speak with him?" His mind went blank and voiceless. The scent of her filled his nostrils, a musky mingling of lavender and several pungent days of her perspiring over an uncomfortable journey. Lara appeared before him. One of the few times since his return from the library, that he recalled her.

"I don't mean to take you from your family, Lambros. Perhaps on your next visit to Thessaloniki you may try to persuade him to stand by Lydia and the child. Otherwise, she will need to go far away and hide her disgrace. She's not a young girl anymore. Tongues are wagging as it is. She'll need a husband and a father for the child."

Magda took yet another step closer. Lambros retreated and stepped to the right to offer her a chair by the railing. She declined.

"Yes, I'll visit him for you, but it may be a week before I travel in that direction." She took immediate pleasure in his seemingly unconscious choice of wording. He would pay the visit for her, not for Lydia's sake, but for hers. Unaware of Elissa watching them, Magda abandoned caution, stepped toward him, touched her fingers to his arm and traced her other hand lightly across his back in a feeble, momentary embrace.

"Thank you, Lambros, thank you. I cannot ask for more." Even miniscule gestures such as these were unheard of between men and women of casual acquaintance in Lathra or Apollonia. Elissa had had enough. Audible from behind the door, she demanded that her children move away from the table and swung the door open violently, bursting out onto the veranda, pushing Magda away from him.

"What are you doing, hussy! Get away from my husband! And you, idiot, letting this woman rub on you in front of your children!"

"No, Elissa," Magda said nervously, "you've mistaken my gesture of gratitude for your husband's advice in a sensitive matter." Her face quivered now. "I meant no disrespect to you or to him." Elissa held her breath as Magda spoke and then erupted.

"Liar! Bitch!" she screamed.

"Elissa," Lambros squeaked like a guilty wheel. "Watch your tongue and your temper." Elissa stood between them positioning herself with her back to the door.

"Shut your mouth, *manga*,"[64] she snarled, pointing her finger at him, yet with a cowing gesture, as if still concerned that her children might witness the blatant disrespect of their father or that he might strike back. "Who is my husband to give you advice on a delicate matter?" she shouted at Magda. "Find a husband like the rest of us and rub your foreign tits on him. Now go home to your brother's house and pack your bags because you'll not be able to stay in Lathra! I'll make sure of that!" Embarrassment and a normally feverish temper sweltered in Magda. She grew faint and pale for a moment, just short of ire and indignation. She contained herself and descended the steps before succumbing to a flood of fury and turning to respond.

"Your husband is a good catch. If I weren't a woman of honor he would already be in my bed." Elissa exploded: "Filthy sultana, I can smell your whoring from here!" She leapt down the steps as rapidly as her children might upon the arrival of a favored visitor. Magda froze, in awe of the ferocious flush to her rival's rage, rousing the same in her. They exchanged very firm but free-wielding slaps, instigated by Magda. Then, as Elissa was poised to extract fistfuls of her hair, Lambros interceded, squeezing the tendon between her thumb and index finger and dragging her back up the staircase.

"Wife, your children are watching this disgraceful catfight."

"I'll pluck your eyes out, like a crow pecks at grapes," Elissa screamed. Magda had escaped her grip took a few strides and looked back at Lambros. A look of pity softened her face for a brief moment. Mucus glistened from her nostrils. Lambros stretched his neck to see if

---

64 μάγγας – macho man

any neighbors had walked by the courtyard and either seen or heard the ruckus. "Christ and the Virgin," he thought, "what the hell have I done now?"

Magda returned home trembling uncontrollably, Elissa's handprint showing like tentacles across her face. She had failed to persuade Marios and had undermined the assistance so easily wooed from Lambros, making it unlikely that he would assist her even if he still desired to do so. She walked into her brother's house and asked Lydia, who was full of burgeoning anxiety to hear from her sister, to wait until she had rested before discussing her mission in Thessaloniki.

"What happened to your face, Magda?"

"Nothing," she said. "Let me be. I'll tell you later." She undressed in the privacy of her bedroom and prepared to bathe with the large porcelain bowl of water Lydia warmed and set down on the small night table by the window before exiting and leaving her sister alone as she had requested. She sat on her bed; covered with fresh linens and a blanket her Aunt Thalia had gifted her for her dowry. Shivering, she covered herself.

"You have been overpowered by your desperation for a man, old maid," she said aloud as if speaking to her sister.

Three hours later, having bathed in the timorous delirium of her mortification, having sipped a cognac and napped, utterly exhausted, a fatigue exacerbated by the sudden realization of her apparent fate, she awoke, sat at the table with Lydia and informed her of the need for both of them to leave Lathra immediately. She admitted that Marios would not be coming to make of her a bride. And that she, Magda Karangelos, true to her mother's troubled legacy had, under the guise of eliciting assistance from him, embarrassed herself with unseemly conduct toward Lambros Lambrou and that she had "slapped his hysterical shrew of a wife and unraveled every benefit that we have received from our brother." All of this would make life in Lathra untenable, she explained. The idea that someone might stay behind to maintain the land holdings vanished in an instant. They would have to sell the land and the house and move elsewhere, perhaps returning to Smyrna with Thalia and Christos, perhaps to Nicosia or a village on the far coast of Cyprus where the Karangelos name meant nothing more than a black angel, somewhere in the cold oblivion of forgetfulness where there might be peace. They could not warn their brother for they had no idea where he was, nor whether he was yet a fugitive. Magda sat in her chair and that evening, with carefully chosen words, not revealing the full extent of their downfall, wrote to relatives in Nicosia and to Thalia and Christos. Lydia took the news with unabashed emotion and wept until the wee hours, when she finally felt sleep unraveling the filament of her heart. Fervently, she prayed to awaken only if she might live in the embrace of her mother and father. Even if such embrace was in the moment before the doom and derivation of madness, within the circle of their destiny.

19

Time whispers by, like the master's first Nocturne, Danäe thought. The words had a fading ring like the tuning fork of her somber tonic. By master, she meant Chopin. She felt as much after learning that the sisters Karangelos had quietly repacked their legacy into the overburdened trunks that accompanied them to Lathra. She mentioned as much to Lambros. He asked what a Nocturne was and received an explanation halfway through which he walked away fighting consecutive yawns, his eyelids drooping. The sisters had slipped out of the village with the same hired driver who had driven Magda to Thessaloniki. Thankfully, for Lydia's sake, the man spoke not a word to them during the two-hour jostling of kidneys, sitting three abreast in uncomfortably close quarters. Lydia noticed the adamant arousal to his right pocket but didn't quite know what it was. Her hip and thigh had unwittingly pressed against his. She thought it looked similar to the bulge made by a pouch of tobacco he eventually removed from his left pocket, a stiff crease in the pants, but the right pocket remained wood-like, even after he withdrew the pouch to smoke.

"You are not smoking in this compartment," Magda said sternly.

"Very well," he said, acquiescing. He pulled over, shut the engine off, got out of the truck and walked deep into the patch of trees along the road.

"Now where's he going?" Magda said loudly, so he might hear her.

"He's not carrying two pouches of tobacco, is he?" Lydia asked her sister. The driver returned a bit winded but apparently relieved and got back in the vehicle, stinking of his cigarettes, his right pocket miraculously deflated. Lydia made Magda change places with her and looked out the window the rest of the way. She was miserable and her neck had cramped from constantly staring to the right.

Athena Kyriazis, who shared the sisters' passion for couture and the breeding afforded by a post grammar school education, was one of the few women in the village the sisters had befriended and confided in with their plans, except they permitted Athena to assume that Avram's permanent absence from home was the reason they were now departing as well. Magda arranged for Athena's husband, whom she and Lydia had spoken with only when they had first arrived, to purchase the equivalent of a life estate in the property. He was to deposit an undisclosed sum in the National Bank, in a pre-existing account established years before by Thalia, at the time of the sisters' original move to Thessaloniki. If after seven years possession of the real property remained unclaimed by either sister, title would revert to the Kyriazis name, with all costs for the transfer of the estate payable by the fortunate grantee. And with that, the sisters departed for a life unknown.

By Christmas, Elissa finally forgave Lambros for accepting the embrace of another woman. This included a reprieve from self-banishment from their bed. She had spent weeks sleeping on the floor with her children in their room, which contained not a stick of furniture. Her jealousy, however, etched its tarnished motif in the shape of constant speculation and doubt on those other occasions when no sanely counseled woman would shudder with suspicion. Lambros found it difficult to attend to his affairs with the other growers and the tsobano, who refused to enter any home in the village, being an Albanian and a Muslim otherwise tolerating Greeks, and who would usually meet the owners of his flocks at Yianko's kafenio. Yianko's was now a no man's land of anxiety for Lambros. The litany of tensions obliterated his kafenio routines, first his row with Avram, then his discomforting and inconclusive discussion with Terzellos and Gallanos, and now Elissa's incessant questioning and insistence that Stratos accompany him everywhere. Not wanting Stratos to witness his dejection, Lambros resorted to accompanying his son to Pavlides' kafenio, where the younger men attended to their manly twirls of the komboloi and ouzo sipped over simmering politics, available maidens and the price of commodities. At Pavlides', it was ouzo with ice, like the hint of shade between two trees on a scorching summer afternoon, or with water, the way an adulteress might partake, diluted, like pale milk with the essence of anise that nearly skips the palate and lingers only in the nostrils. Yianko's kafenio, on the other hand, was longer, slower gulps of ouzo or tsipouro straight up, the latter, like a man's pulse after a brush with death. While this routine sufficed him to break away from Elissa's scrutiny, he felt out of place and unimportant at Pavlides', often being the oldest patron to have a seat and commonly addressed as barba Lalas, a barba before his time. Lambro's attendance was nearly mandatory, since Stratos thoroughly enjoyed his newfound interest in dancing to *zeibetika* [65] for the coins thrown at his feet by the young mangas who appreciated his freewheeling, youthful style. The music was provided by Avgitas Kirithos, affectionately dubbed "little Homer" by the younger men in the village. Avgitas owned a bouzouki and through the years taught himself how to play the wailing standards. No one quite understood how he earned a living, but they all agreed he was a masterful player of his instrument, handed down to him by his father. Once a week, on Saturday evenings, he would play and sing along with Tassos Kyriazis, a superb crooner, and Pavlos Lourithas offering isaaci drum rhythms, inspiring the passions of otherwise reserved men with dancing, and the prying eyes and ears of local girls. The boys increased business for Pavlides, who on nights of full capacity charged the performers nothing for their drinks and an occasional meze, and ushered in an era of burgeoning tolerance of female customers. Strato's dancing also proved its value in helping to dissipate and deflect much of the ill will associated with Lambros and his irrigation mania.

"What a palikari Lambros has sired," they repeated. "The old man can't be all bad to have given us a son that dances like a deity."

"The dervish of Lathra," Lazaros once called Stratos, watching him spin in a Dionysian frenzy, arms swinging out like wings, legs carousing, squatting and kicking out like a Cossack, balancing on one foot, and

---

65 ζεϊμπέκικα - Anatolian war dances of Zeybek origins

sweeping down like a vulture to a glass set on the floor, holding the glass between his teeth and swallowing the swirling libation.

For the most part, the rest of the village was unaware of such tumult in Lambro's life. They were busy, stoic as usual, preparing for cold weather, hoping to prevent the need for mid-winter barter with other isolated outposts along the Macedonian frontier or retreating to Edessa to purchase survival fare. It was only in Lambro's distressed and sleepless psyche that his fortunes ambled or disappeared with the choice between the waters of Vegoritis or the errant springs of Kythera and his troubles with Elissa.

———————

Lazaros in the mean time grew increasingly reclusive, avoiding the intricacies of society and virtually all commerce since the night Jartzo had discovered Sebastianos in the cellars of the church. He was eerily aloof during the two visits he received, one by Alexi and the other, at Alexi's request, by Andreas. On report from Andreas, the priest speculated that Lazaros suffered from melancholy or some associated mortification over the whole affair with Sebastianos.

"I think he pities the cantor, and Danäe," Andreas reported to his brother and the priest. During the months that followed, Lazaros developed a mild discomfort on his right side that soon became chronic. He ignored it as his having pulled a muscle or favoring the right side while sleeping upon his hard cot. The doctor had attended to him a few months earlier, retrieved by Lambros at Andreas' beckoning, for an ailment of the mouth, an abscess, which all but caused him to cease taking nourishment. The doctor chastised his patient for the severity of his living conditions.

"You can't live on words," he said. Lazaros in return summarily dismissed the doctor's credibility when he proposed a mildly invasive treatment, in that instance the removal of flesh around the abscess in order to uncover a potentially decaying molar beneath. Lazaros believed the procedure to be unnecessary and a typical response by a man with a scalpel.

"I like you, doctor. You're an interesting and clever fellow, even if you are a bit arrogant in your cloak of scientific deduction. But don't give me the attitude! As if the ability to memorize body parts and concocted Greek conjunctions makes you infallible."

"Cognac won't cure this problem," the doctor said without humor in his voice.

"Then I'll gargle with *Raki*,"[66] he responded. The doctor appealed to Andreas and Lambros. They shrugged their shoulders. They had led the doctor to Mavrotripa, but had little control over the patient and his quandary.

"We're very sorry, doctor," Lambros said, thinking he had once again delivered a professional to no avail. The doctor complained as he rose from Lazaro's bed and began packing his medical bag.

"Yes, I enjoy being hauled by a donkey cart for an hour or more to have a failed Cenobite remind me that I'm a demon with a surgical motive. I've a Caesarean to accomplish in Perea, if you'll excuse me."

"I've never been a Cenobite, doctor," Lazaros said. "If anything, my hermitic, idiorythmic tendencies are wholly secular in nature, may Christ be amused and not condemn me."

Lazaros never mentioned the discomfort on his right side. Now three weeks later, Andreas, who would not visit him as often since Danäe all but suspended her social attendances, found Lazaros on his cot in excruciating pain, sweating profusely and drained to the skin with dehydration and a high fever. He could hear the plangent moans as he approached the columbarium, echoing off the rocks and across docile Vegoritis. He tried coaxing him to his feet, but Lazaros could not stand with his agony, let alone walk. Lifting him in his arms, Andreas carried him down the steep precipice to the dirt road, laying him there to rest as his groans increased in intensity. Even the bony weightlessness of the infirmed became heavy over such a precarious distance.

"I'll come back with Danäe," Andreas said, failing to hide his concern. "I'm afraid to carry you the whole distance to Lambro's house. I'll be back, my friend."

"Christ and the Virgin. Hurry," he mumbled. "It hurts very badly." Andreas darted to every place where he thought he might find Danäe, but could not. On his way, he beckoned Elissa to attend to Lazaros and ran by Calliope's disheveled shack, a dried mud, straw and thatch-roofed

---

66 ραχί - Cretan version of tsipouro (τσίπουρο)

structure along the same stretch of dirt thoroughfare. She had functioned as the village midwife for years before Maria's murder, but was in disfavor, having killed a patient or two with her misdiagnosis and for overcharging villagers for years with scathing demands for eggs, red meat and chickens in addition to cash payment, unconscionably withholding treatment in a barter for woefully little nostrum and medical skill. She was retired now, living on fish from the lake, discarded fruit and what bread she could buy. She could scarcely see beyond her hands, nor remember anyone's name and had developed a hunchback, her body shrinking to half its size, and her skin looking like an orange rind. Andreas mobilized Lambro's children to locate Danäe and then ran back to where he had left Lazaros.

"I'd have been better off carrying him after all this," he said. Calliope discovered Lazaros writhing in the dirt, his face pressed to the earth, muffling his howls. She removed her shawl and listened to his back, laying a hairy ear on his cold sweaty skin. Andreas turned him over gently at her request. She pushed gingerly against his chest, on his back and below his ribs, but could not distinguish between the intensity of his appalling cries, summoned by any pressure on either side of his abdomen. By then the pain prevented him from speaking coherently. A swelling appeared about his waist, an inky darkness, even for his normally murky Alexandrian hue. The old woman felt the burden of her medical duty, but could not discern what ailed the patient. She became anxious and flustered, starting a sentence and then leaving it unfinished for her growing audience to interpret as panic. She turned her head abruptly and complained to Andreas.

"I can't think with his bellowing like a beast."

"The man is in terrible pain, magpie! What do you want him to do, whisper for you?" She was offended, but dared not leave.

Elissa, who arrived at Lazaro's side just before Calliope, covered him with a thin blanket and wet his lips with a cloth dipped in water from a small pail she brought with her. Then, suddenly the pain seemed to subside. He became quiet. Lambro's children made the rounds of usual village haunts announcing their quest for Danäe. Children from throughout the village congregated by the roadside, kicking up the dust in their scurrying tension, the dust landing softly on Lazaro's hair, coating his beard and contorted face, belaboring his breathing even further.

Barba Haralambos Calphapanaiotis walked by and satisfied his curiosity. He lived in the valley to the southwest of the corn and chickpea fields and routinely walked to Lathra to visit his childless daughter, who had married Pavlides' eldest son. That day he didn't stink of garlic, which he usually ingested in quantities great enough to turn a dog's head to heaven, believing it warded off the evil sneer of Naodites, whom he despised even more than he did Turks. The old man took a single look at Lazaros and offered an immediate diagnosis of hernia, a condition he had suffered in his forties, being eager to reminisce of his Promethean endurance of its agonies. Calliope brashly concurred; keen on anyone offering such deflecting guidance, anyone who could actually distinguish Lazaro's facial features from a distance of two paces.

"It's nothing fatal," she opined. "Now get away from him you filthy children. The poor man's going to choke to death before he has a chance to be treated." Lambro's children finally arrived, having located Danäe. Danäe appeared harried and tousled. Her short-cropped hair, recently trimmed again nearly to the scalp, was uncovered to the elements. She wore a ragged gypsy's sackcloth dress. Her legs were bare, the pale down exposed, her feet crammed into short leather boots borrowed from Stratos earlier that year. She had grown vivacious since last seen in public, with less labor and living on yogurt, honey, nuts and the most saccharine of fruit, and was even more pleasing to the men. She had run as fast as she could from the eastern flanks of Kythera, where Stratos and Sophia found her tending to one of the tsobano's dogs that had tangled with a wolf earlier that week and developed an infection in the crease of purple flesh covering its teeth and gums. Panting, her legs burning with the exertion from the long sprint, she understood the gravity of Lazaro's condition even before reaching him and called out to Andreas as she approached, imploring him to find a vehicle, her voice fractured with emotion. Andreas had already asked Lambros to secure one of the two available vehicles in the village, one of which was not operational on that day, Petros Canettas having disemboweled it for diagnostic maintenance. By then, Lazaros was emitting low rumbling moans, mimicking the sounds heard above Vegoritis, like creaking oars left dangling over the water.

"My God, listen to him, we've got to take him to the hospital in Edessa," Danäe called out, her fear patent and raw and inciting others to the same nervous panic. Moments later Lambros arrived with Terzellos, driving his truck. She looked up at them, pale and haunted with fear. "His appendix has burst," she said. Andreas prepared to lift Lazaros up into the bed of the truck.

In the time it took to shuffle children a few meters away from the patient and back the truck up to that side of the road it was too late. In one final, plaintive gasp, Lazaros expended his ghost, his head cradled in Danäe's arms. A nearly imperceptible wisp of dust spiraled up from the wry contortion of his mouth, falling lightly upon the ashen mask of his face. The apparition frightened the children and the tale went forth from that moment that they had seen Lazaro's spirit rise up to heaven, that he had been, "raised from the dead . . . but not like in the gospel."

Danäe sat by his side in a stupor, flushed of color, just as she had attended to her father. Elissa consoled her, lifting her beneath both arms and walking her back to her room where she lay still upon her narrow cot into the night. Exhausted with grief, she slept to near noon of the following day. She remembered crying for so long over the death of her father that her throat and chest seemed on fire. She worried she might never stop and asked her mother whether anyone ever recorded a daughter weeping herself into blindness, to oblivion, a pool of salty tears.

Terzellos suddenly refused to place the body in the wooden bed of his truck, which he used for hauling livestock.

"The sheep will smell death and rancid sweat in the wood," he said apologetically. "They have an uncanny nose for such things. The truck will be useless to me then." Lambros leveled his disgust in a single glance and then turned to Andreas. "Don't look at me like that! You said we were taking him to the hospital not the catacombs," Terzellos said, regretting his cooperation with the likes of Lambros.

"Then we must carry him to the church," Andreas said quietly. "Vasili and I will make him a coffin." While the departed was still pliable and warm, Andreas, with a wave of his hand, signaled Apostolos Timonakis, the barber's son, who stood around nursing the drooping lip of sorrow deforming his face. Together with Lambros they set the body upon their shoulders and carried him, arms folded upon his breastplate. Andreas struggled mightily to contain his tears, constricting his chin toward his lower lip, biting his tongue, coating his clenched teeth in blood. They carried him past Yianko's kafenio where the curious gathered in the square, observing the procession.

"A few minutes ago the dimwit would have driven him to Edessa," Andreas said to Lambros. "Now, with God's breath sucked out of him, the Americano is too ripe for Terzello's shitty truck."

———•———

Everything about Lazaro's death was inapposite to his public life in Lathra. His friends laid him in a chamber beneath the church, the only tomb-like structure in the village, to forestall decomposition until preparation of his body and burial and until Pater Alexi could arrive to chant a threnody. Lambros recruited Jartzo to keep vigil beneath the church and mind the body, which he did, pacing about the place with an agitated sense of mission. But he howled and sobbed when he first saw the body, for he knew the music that had soothed him all those years came from Lazaros. Unpredictably, Katerina did not object to her son's participation. She simply and quietly locked herself in her house.

Pavlides, with Lambros by his side, called Pater Alexi that day on the telephone, the kafenio noisy with talk of the death.

"I can't hear you well." The priest said. "Who died?" he said, uncertain if he heard the name correctly.

"Lazaros!" Momentary silence accompanied the buzzing on the line. "Lazaros Zervas, the Americano, the Neyorkesos' nephew," Pavlides said. "You know, barba Andoni was his uncle." The silence continued on the other side of the line.

"What's wrong?" Lambros asked.

"He's going senile," Pavlides complained as he held his hand over the phone, too late to mute his voice. "He doesn't know who I'm talking about." Lambros took the receiver from him, pulling the cord taunt.

"Pater . . . it's your funny friend that died, the one who lives in Mavrotripa, the fellow with all the books and papers," Lambros continued.

"Who am I speaking with now?" The priest said calmly.

236

"Lambros Lambrou."

"I know who he meant, Lambros. You needn't say more," Alexi responded, his voice trailing off with emotion. Alexi cleared his throat and swallowed as if taking a drink. "Of what? Did he finally fall from that God forsaken cave?"

"His appendix burst," Lambros said, secreting regret. A brief silence again.

"Christ and the Virgin, what a pitiful waste," the priest said with quiet disdain. "So treatable a condition. What's wrong with you people?" The breach in the conversation drew a sigh from Lambros.

"I'll come immediately. Make accommodations for me please, and for my family as well. Presbytera and my children will come along and stay until Sunday. And Lambro," he asked, "please, I don't want my family to stay in that dungeon beneath the church."

"That goes without saying, Pater. You'll all stay in my home."

The grief generated in those who witnessed the death of Lazaros Zervas was as deep as any the village ever witnessed since its renaming and their trickling exodus from Anatolia. Lazaros was their orphan. Pater Alexi arrived with his Presbytera and their two children a day later, and stayed in Lambro's home as arranged. The entire family slept in Danäe's room while she took up in Mavrotripa. She did not find the sepulchral recess of Lazaro's amusement to be the thoughtful and organized atelier of introspection she imagined. The decision to stay there quickly became for her an act of contrition. She had failed to visit him and perhaps prevent his death. While there, she began the arduous process of searching through the thousands of strewn papers, letters, musical scores, bound documents and notebook tablets piled high along the cold stone, at first merely for something to indicate a testament of his wishes. She found nothing in this vein, but did uncover a flotilla of half-embarked voyages of novel fancy, inquiries into art, literature, philosophy and music, starts and fits of translations and erratically argued excurses on a variety of texts in a host of disciplines, all of which mystified her, defying her belief that she knew Lazaros at all. It would take her months of compiling and collating these scattered papers to piece together the most complete works accomplished in the years he occupied his hermetic vault. Among them were his translations of *Typee, Billy Budd, The*

Last of the Mohicans, a handful of Emerson's essays, two untitled stories apparently of Henry James and a few essays of the naturalist, John
Burroughs, the later a volume bearing an inscription by his mother from
that very year. She found a singular, remarkable treatise he had prepared
on the vicissitude of the art of polyphony since its high water mark in
the Renaissance, a work that remained untitled and unfinished as far
as she could tell. Additionally, she uncovered outlandishly translated
snippets of Mallarmé and Verlaine and extended passages of *Jacques the
Fatalist* and *Gambara,* works sounding to her as if he consulted English
translations before the secondhand rendering proposed in Greek, copies
of which she found well abused in his stacks.

Besides his transcriptions of Palestrina, Dufay and other Renaissance
masters, he continued to compose music. This was a complete revelation
to her. Danäe deduced that this had only occurred immediately after his
arrival in Lathra. Predominantly chamber works for strings and a few
orchestral miniatures, each piece was a highly condensed study, perhaps
underdeveloped or meant as an etude in color and dramatic impetus. The
primary problem with all of the manuscripts was his failure to number
pages or title the works in ways that made reconstruction meaningful
without significant musical insight. The manuscripts were marked up as
well. Many pages had large sections crossed out. Others were black with
scribbles between and over the staves, mostly set down in pencil. At the
unfortunate creases along each half of a page were faint and faded passages appearing as if the tiny-toothed voracity of devouring pulp mites
had consumed them. Other impracticalities were, for example, an oboist
or bassoonist languishing with an infrequent note of yearning or a single toot throughout an entire piece, only to have a solo in a works' final
utterances - or perhaps not - depending on how one combined the pages
with similar instrumentation.

On or about the week of his death, or the last time he could pain-
lessly concentrate or take pleasure from any text, Lazaros was apparently reading Byron. The book was set open in the midst of *The Siege of
Corinth,* and sat atop an open copy of Origen's *Exhortation to Martyrdom.*
Beneath the Origen was a commentary he was preparing on that treatise,
in English. The first thirty pages dealt with the implications of the
title Εισ μαρτύριον προτρεπτικόσ. Danäe thought the work marred by
the ravaging pain he must have been suffering, which made her want

to weep again. The introduction to the first draft of this commentary precipitated quickly toward Part IV of the *Exhortation*, The Criminal Character of Idolatry - The Cult of Demons, and focused on the passage:

". . . demons, in order to exist within the heavy atmosphere that encircles the earth are always on the lookout for the savor of burnt sacrifices, blood, and incense." Beneath his commentary on the *Exhortation*, on a clean sheet of paper, was probably the last string of words Lazaros ever scribbled. The note to himself said, "Speak with Lambros Lambrou, who maintains a similar fear of lingering in places where the pious gather, lest a demon cast her evil eye upon him or inhabit his interiority like a bad dream." Below his work on Origen's tractate was an open copy of *Die Theologie der Logomystik bei Origenes* a polemical treatise by Aloysius Lieske arguing in favor of Origen's dogmatism, and below it a closed copy of Paul Koetschau's *Des Gregorios Thaumaturgos Dankrede an Origenes.* Danäe previously thought his German not proficient enough to absorb such study. Beneath these two were open volumes of Chrysostom's *Homilies on Genesis* and Lazaro's handwritten notes on the *Baptismal Instructions.* His notes were, again, in pencil and quite faded, decipherable at points only with a magnifying glass, laid alongside the pile of papers and books. This, she reasoned, suggested that the notes were a much earlier effort. Finally, at the very bottom of the nine texts was a copy of the *Instructions* themselves, covered with Lazaro's copious scribbles in the margins and between the lines. These jottings were in ink and somewhat easier to read.

During his last days, he apparently was listening to a recent Koussevitzky recording of Sibelius' *Seventh Symphony*, the final disc gracing the table of the Victrola. The set had arrived in a handsome velvet-lined box, each disc held within paper-covered sleeves. Danäe found nothing identifying the sender except a slip of paper crimped over the first sleeve with a note.

"I hope you have a peaceful hour in which to enjoy this. It disentangles the incessant jabber, for me. Perhaps it will silence the voices that haunt you." The note, written in English, was in an explicitly feminine cursive with daintily trailing curlicues at the end of each "p", "q" and "y" but not the "j". Finally, he had been working, wearily as it appeared from the documents strewn on the floor around his chair, on another commentary, completing a lengthy presage of the meaning and implications found within Origen's *Commentary on the Gospel according to John*, a work as self-castrated as Lazaro's intellect. To Danäe, he seemed to struggle with fending off anti-Gnostic allegories to Origen's diagnostic, his analyses of Job and Genesis hovering like ghosts above tortured trees. The commentary upon a single line of Origen rambled on for forty pages before he seemed prepared to retire the text, presumably exhausted. The single line:

"This is the beginning of the Lord's creation, made to be mocked by His angels."

Then, he seemed sidetracked, for an additional twelve pages, with a panegyric upon the beloved apostle's propinquity to the Master. His treatise stated:

"How can it be that John did not succumb to his grief at the thought of his head having reclined upon the breast of the Christ? And when his grief subsided, did not his pride swell at having heard the lullaby of the Lord's heartbeat?" Lazaros apparently relished asking such questions but the exhaustion in attempting to answer them must have resigned him to move on to the *Exhortation*. Danäe thought it a simpler, more tractable work and thus ascribed this motive to his shift as to which text he would analyze.

She found it interesting that few, if any, letters surfaced from his mother. The ones she did find, she read carefully, discerning between his mother's eloquent poetry of thought, a distant draw of maternal loneliness, tenderly pointing to some enclosed work of literature, a pressed wildflower or leaf of a grand old specimen of tree, or in one instance, a tiny fossilized seahorse. One letter included a lengthy discussion of her mailing him, in response to a specific request, an old tin beer and ale tray of John Hohenadel Brewery Incorporated of Philadelphia. The serving tray, a feature of Lazaro's daily life in Mavrotripa, depicted two friars of the brew marketing a mechanized smoking dog to a red-coated proprietor with a blissfully bulbous nose. Lazaros used the tray for serving food and beverages to his infrequent guests as well as for storing his recent letters from home. She found no letters from his father, but numerous envelopes postmarked Philadelphia, each with different philatelic specimens, neatly tied in a bundle, envelopes addressed by a virile hand resembling his own.

Verbosity had clothed his asceticism, she thought, and obscured the deep spirals of sentiment in which Lazaros moved through life. It lined his walls and insulated his castigating scrutiny of all writing. She was mistaken perhaps, for Lazaros himself said in a letter to his mother that it was the serried texture of words, the grain and grit of them, as he put it, not just their power of suggestion that overwhelmed him. Lazaro's books and papers provided evidence of his constant battle between reading and writing, learning and creating, the discovery of anything new. Even a single sentence or image taken from a lengthy text propelled him away from his own summation of thought, his writing and the burying of everything in the past deep into his idea of the psyche. A sea of whirling words had tossed and turned inside him. This sleepless eye of lexis drew from him his youth and worked to divest him at times, even of music. For Lazaros, music ascended or descended, depending upon one's perspective, into a Thrasyllusian analysis of its elements, far more frequently than unfolding an aesthetic significance. "Music is the great reminder of consciousness," he had written on a slip of paper. Danäe remembered how twice he had repeated to her: "All non-fiction is bullshit, but it keeps the world guessing and congratulating itself in its search for some squalid truism." Nothing of him fit with what she found left of him. Sadly, she concluded, his tendencies deprived him of the love of any woman, which she assumed was the owner of the feminine hand of the note, perhaps with the exception of maternal love.

On the fifth day of her librarian's labyrinth of bereavement, with what Lazaros would come to mean to her, Danäe discovered, beneath his bed, a small bundle of letters. She read all of them, as she had his writing. From the start, composed by what appeared to be the same inclined, feminine hand in elemental English that mailed him the Sibelius recording, the letters unfolded as the sweet and happy consequence of a son's musical accomplishments, a grown Lasso Krohn, on his way from Helsinki to Philadelphia to study music at the Curtis Institute of Music, and to live with Lazaro's parents. The salutations unerringly read, "Love, Niina."

Elissa, Danäe and Yianko's wife, Persephone, prepared the body. They washed his exposed skin, caked with dust from the road, and coated the limbs and torso in a mixture of fruitful oil and the essence of fragrant dried blossoms and berries used for dies, gathered by Danäe from the valley below Mount Vermion on one of her searches for brewing herbs. Stiffening his long hair with oil and lanolin, they combed and parted it on the right side, making him look a bit stodgy but also more refined than the way his follicles had determined the growth of hair while living, wildly ensnaring the thin frame of his head like tentacles and hiding his large ears. Persephone manipulated his jaw, which had distorted mildly at the instant of his calling, relaxing it in an attempt to return to him the aloof expression of a contemplative, so that the son of Erebus and Nyx might recognize him. (Lazaros, in a half-finished essay, intimated that he might dissipate from this life unrecognized by a single soul.) Clad in one of Lambro's white shirts and an old brown suit given to him three years earlier when he was not as thin, and with a tie, he appeared like an American to the women, curiously distracted.

"Let's make him look dapper, the poor lost lamb," Elissa said, knotting the tie donated by Andreas.

Three days later, on the morning of his funeral, the coffin remained undelivered. Vasili had taken the news poorly. He returned in the evening from the workshop in Edessa with his betrothed, Penelope, driven by Thomas, her brother and chaperone. Penelope and Thomas were to stay the night and return with Vasili and Andreas the next morning. Vasili was startled to find Andreas at home instead of tending to the final touches on the job they started earlier that month, helping Yiorgos Doxiades add a room to his tiny house to accommodate his pregnant and now widowed sister Dimitra, a young woman from Florina. He hired Vasili and Andreas at a particularly busy time for them, necessitating their splitting efforts to complete various projects. Doxiades was the only farmer in the village to earn his living completely from growing tobacco and raising swine, the former of which he sold directly to Italian cigarette makers for a lucrative sum each season, angering Greek distributors in the region. Dimitra, his younger sister, had moved in with him and his wife and children, abandoned as she was by her husband, a furrier, upon the inconsiderate errand of his demise - driving off the highest precipice of an ancestral highway near Kastoria. He and his mink and rabbit hides littered the six hundred meter canyon with no safe way to retrieve the body or the pelts. A season's work rendered irretrievable. Her foolhardy brother-in-law attempted to retrieve the pelts and the baptismal cross around his brother's neck that kept winking at them with the glare of the sun reflecting its gold and suffered injuries, nearly falling to his death as well. Dimitra was penniless and provided little incentive by her husband's family to hope for support from them. As a result, she sold her husband's home in Florina, to the chagrin of his family, and gave what little proceeds she received from the transaction to her own brother, to affix an additional room to his house, accommodating her grief. Yiorgos Doxiades hardly knew what a plumb wall meant let alone how to construct one and thus had hired the brothers Lambrou.

Vasili, Andreas and Thomas spent the evening at Yianko's kafenio, which remained open because of the day's turn of events. Speechlessly, they drank between them a bottle of raki, by the last few drops addressing everyone as effendis, but never much mentioning Lazaros. Hung over, work began slowly the following day to complete the project of accommodating Dimitra and her uncomfortable enormity, which yet unknown to her was the domicile of the spitting image of her now bird-and-beast-scattered husband. Traveling back to the shop in Edessa by early afternoon, with lumber in tow, graciously permitted the use of the shop and its full array of recently sharpened carving tools by his future father-in-law, Vasili worked feverishly to expedite his homage to Lazaros. Normally, it would have sufficed to slap together a simple pine box and adorn it with a raised cross or one embossed upon the lid, since the boxes were often reused a few times before being burned, and the remains and affects laid in a marble or concrete sarcophagus. Instead, he and Andreas chose to honor their friend and patron with a creation befitting their affections. Using oak dovetailed and joined for strength, Andreas built the hull of the vessel without metal fasteners or nails while Vasili embarked on carving the lid of a more malleable specimen of wood.

By mid-morning on the day of the funeral, the body still had no skiff to plot a course upon the River Styx. Pater Alexi sent Nikos to remind Andreas of the urgent need for a coffin. Andreas appeared at the church in his black suit, sweating, with his shirt unbuttoned at the top, and assured the priest that the body would not require a shroud or display upon its bier "like the carcass of an animal," as Alexi insisted might be necessary without the benefit of a coffin. Pater had solemnly embarked upon the service as planned, with Tassos Kyriazis performing as cantor and Nikos Lambrou acting as altar boy and deacon, for which the church possessed a matching set of vestments. Vasili worked into consecutive nights, sleeping at the shop to complete his work and finally arrived late that morning with Thomas and Penelope, interrupting the Orthros briefly to entomb the body in its stole of oak and rosewood. Lambros led his cousins and son Stratos, carrying the heavy casket through the doors to the sanctuary as congregants gathered outside the church for the liturgy.

Alexi lingered over Vasili's work, mesmerized by the richly detailed relief depicting the events of John 11:1-46, beginning with the attempted stoning of the Christ in Bethany, unto the end of the story, encircling the words at the center of the gate announcing the blackness of the underworld: "Lazaros come out." Each of the four corners was bedecked with the only recurring image, a lion balancing upon a stack of bound volumes, roaring, straining upon muscled haunches to attain the heavens, the vanity of its splendid headdress descending beyond an earthly inferno and into the mouth of Tartarus.

———◆———

Alexi offered one, from among the unused of his collection of Lazaro's short but esoteric homilies from years past, that he held back, not because of its difficulty or because he previously considered an element of its spirituality or turn of phrase suspect, but because he took it as meant for him alone. This was also one of the few such offerings wholly unmarked by some celebratory function for a saint, a church father or a martyr. Alexi remembered and had dog-eared the corner to bear in mind that Lazaros delivered it to him after a particularly long deliberation with Sebastianos. The subject of the debate was Alexi's youthful decision to marry rather than pursue a career as a scholar and theologian. In retrospect, Sebastianos had tipped his hand, joking over the idea of wedded bliss and extolling his admiration for St. Basil's ascetical works and the decision to devote oneself to scholarship. In all likelihood, Alexi was fated for a bishopric. He heard the rumor repeated enough in those days to believe in his grooming by the patriarch of Athens himself, a mentor from his seminary days. Lazaros sensed the difficulty the priest still had with the choice from his past, between ambition in the service of God and his youthful Thekla, whom he married and with whom he had children. On that occasion, empathizing with Alexi, he responded with a homily offered the next morning, as always, in an envelope on the table in the altar.

"How unhappy is man. He realizes slowly, through the strained trial and error of reason and sometimes not at all, what an honorable woman tastes of wisdom. Even while she is a young maiden, she seeks such happiness in the possession of her other half, in the soul of another, embarking upon the search and completion of the tapestry to her soul. This is the mark of the divine in her. So a man should seek as much in a woman. For while others strive to find in the pure contemplation of God that which men identify as wisdom, the intimation, the very declaration of Ecclesiastes signifies ever so alarmingly that such pursuits are as meaningless as the lust for money or the shallow longing for mere comfort. All things lead to the dry dust and granules of corruption and death, fed upon by worms, upon which subsequent generations not only trod but also sow and expel their sustenance. While we may, for a moment, scoop happiness in the hand like a dip of quenching water, most of the elixir slips through our fingers, God's sacred sieve, before we raise our hand to the mouth for a drink. All that remains is the empty palm of thirst. Therefore, my brethren, we castaways from Eden must have deserved our banishment. Not for the occasion of our nakedness and shame, or mere disobedience exhibited to an intolerant Landlord but, instead, for the sacred awareness bestowed upon us by our disobedience. The emblems of authority and the hallmarks of our knowledge are many. And while they are impotent to change the verity of existence, which is the tricky, unfathomable handiwork of the Father, we must be wary, for these idols rouse the conundrum of our unhappiness precisely as the unquenchable, nagging fear that we will never find, or, worse yet, lose that which is our other half."

No one understood a word, but the women wept and the men swallowed hard and scratched their heads in suppressed sorrow. Faith felt amplified for Alexi, as it did in the intense solitude of the empty sanctuary. Everyone knew that his favorite service of the paschal season was not the metaphorically dramatic liturgical recreations of holy week but the shadows and mystical hues of Holy Vespers initiating the Great Lent.

"Pure Monday, purest of Mondays, most luminous day of ascending prayers," he would proclaim, as if celebrating a birth instead of a march to martyrdom. "Parishioners are plentiful, always filling the church like begging dogs," he once uttered tetchily to Lazaros, but on this day, this one time of year, he preferred whiling away the evening hour in solitude. He confided to Thekla that this was his retreat from his own sin, occasioned by his contact with men, the moment of his truest confession, the frightening but peaceable crucible of reflection that drained him of all pride, covetousness and any remorse over his history.

"Oh, come now, Alexi," Thekla would whisper and press her head on his shoulder. "Your life is not as bad as that, that you must hide from us to speak to God." Through the years, the anecdote of their suffering of his desire for solitude worked to dissuade his congregants from coming into the church immediately on the evening of Holy Monday. On that night alone, he would burn enough incense to choke any attendant and the mice regularly habituating the church and its cellar. Only a few barely breathing souls (heavy smokers, perhaps) refused to be driven out. But even they stood near the entrance to the church as far from the altar as possible.

"He's going to burn the church down," Calliope exclaimed each year.

"He's invoking the devil, if you ask me," Voula Terzellos once snapped back.

"Move from your spot," Anna Gallanos said, "so the curse and the demon's ogle don't latch onto us." Alexi simply desired a quiet hour to collect his thoughts, to hearken to the readings, and cursor the canted triplets into his soul, entreating Christ for His mercy and in an otherworldly undertone singing to himself the prayer, "Lord Jesus Christ, have mercy on me, a sinner."

"Prayers materialize in the ascending incense only if they are let loose from men's mouths," he instructed, encouraging the cantors, who by the end of the service covered their eyes and mouths with handkerchiefs. The women would wait outside until they would hear him proclaim the reading from *Revelations*. Then, with the doors thrown open

246

and the smoky prayers clearing from within the church, they would rush in to light a candle, listen to the reading, kiss the gold cross and his hairy knuckles and receive his blessing, his pupils still dilating from the incense-drenched hour of incantations.

———◆———

"Atropos awoke in anger that day and snipped the stamen shamefully short." Danäe mused aloud and twice, so she would not forget what she said, as she rummaged through a pocket in the flimsy sheathing of her jacket for her utensils and wrote the thought down on a small slip of paper with a stub of one of Lazaro's pencils, wetting the lead with the dew from her tongue. She did so in the presence of her cousins, before Pater Alexi and his Presbytera. She wanted to remember the thought as her own. Then she sat quietly waiting, as if time were a speechless specter, passing through her body and leaving it behind. Everyone watched her, eyes darting behind retinal prisms bending the light with cognac. To Lambros, she appeared gripped by a throbbing anguish, something that must run its course before letting its victim go in peace. Elissa finally had the opportunity to sit at one of the tables borrowed from Yianko's kafenio. She looked at Danäe, not understanding what she had said, staring at her as if she were an invalid but also in no mood for one of her cousin's indecipherable trances. With the help of Yianko's wife, Elissa had prepared the memorial feast in honor of the deceased and felt drained of all energy, overworked and in grief for a man whom she had no chance to know but whom everyone inexplicably admired.

"If a man does not marry and sire children, of what value is he?" she said to Lambros that morning, awakened early to resume her preparations.

"I don't know," Lambros said, deflated, "but look, nearly everyone loved him. Of whom else among us can we say that?"

Pater Alexi took note of the pagan import to Danäe's comment. He worried for a moment that she might assume the model of indifference to what he had once assumed Lazaros perceived as pedantic Byzantine traditions in favor of what Alexi, when speaking with Lazaros, exaggeratingly called the blasphemous arrogance of secular knowledge. But wary as he was of her despondency, instead of chastising her, her comment prompted a confession. His old views of him, mollified with the years, could not have been valid.

"No one knows this ... in fact, I didn't realize it until another sample of his writing came into my hands and I noted the similarities in style, but Lazaros was the author of many of my homilies." Presbytera arched her eyebrows up into the veil of combed tassels covering her hair across her forehead. "He never confessed this to me, nor did we ever discuss it, but I know it was his work." Danäe did not look up. Alexi interpreted this as her already suspecting.

"He would leave them for me on the table in the altar," he divulged shyly. "They were never signed. The handwriting was irregular; I suppose to mask the author's identity. That's when I suspected him and began engaging him in our little debates, to thank him in a way that might prompt his admission and not embarrass him. Unfortunately, that disgrace of a deacon drew from poor Lazaros his otherwise well suppressed temper. 'He who is in a body must unwillingly succumb to bodily things;' he used to say, quoting the Alexandrian school. But that's another matter." His audience said nothing. "Now what do you make of that?" he asked, looking at Danäe. No one responded. "I often whisper one of his prayers, among the first things he left for me." Then suddenly he looked to the ground and swallowed. The women seemed moved by his attempt to conceal his emotion.

"Recite it for us, Pater," Danäe said, her lips drained and trembling. He cleared his throat and extended his arms before him, palms raised.

"Oh Lord, thank you for this day of humble labor and for this day's meal you shall bestow upon me and the peace you will grant my sleep tonight. These are the certainties of your blessing. I cannot think of a better place to be, my Lord, than in the silence of your heavenly manor, with the incense of my thoughts, with the watchful, temperate saints of your narration and the hearts of the martyrs to soothe my restless memory." The prayer ended. The table fell silent.

"Was he a priest in America?" Presbytera Thekla asked, and then rose to attend to her children.

"I don't think so. Other than what we gathered in our little symposia, does anyone know much of his life?"

"I'll write to his parents. They're still living," Danäe said, wiping her cheeks with a handkerchief.

"If you ask me," Andreas said in a diminutive voice, "he wandered the earth and found it small and wanting, with no place to call home until he came here. He read books as if words were an ingredient of the universe, the way others think of water or fire. He understood something about the music on his Victrola without judging the simple tra-la-la of our songs and dances. I liked that about him. Although once, he told me that he found it odd how men found the serious music he enjoyed, to be feminine, yet they thought nothing of listening to sappy love songs on the radio. What to me sounded like so much screeching was to him like having a woman in his arms. It was good he had someone to share this with, Danäe, otherwise only the rocks and poor Jartzo were witness to this, his short life. You were like a daughter to him. And Mavrotripa and Vegoritis, they were his alcove in paradise. I'm sorry for the way he died." Danäe had never heard Andreas string together so many words.

"Who knows such mysteries as the length of a man's day?" Alexi said. "None, but God." He rose to his feet to join his Presbytera. "What does it matter now, if he was happy?"

20

The death of Lazaros and departure of the sisters Karangelos cast a pall of ill omen upon Lathra. Seeing what he believed to be a gentle inhalation of the lungs and an infinitesimal movement of a half buttoned eyelet on the deceased's jacket, Vasili, who otherwise slept soundly, lay awake for several nights imagining that they had too soon laid Lazaros in his sarcophagus. He imagined the creatures of his labor, the figures in his carvings, awake, writhing along the surface and boring down through the hard wood in response to a tapping from within the casket, tormenting the nimbus of its tenant's sleep until Judgment Day.

"Dreams like these are bad omens," he told his brother.

As winter arrived, after years of cyclically consistent drought from Kastoria to the Aegean, clouds amassed like the frown of an infuriated deity. It rained steadily for eight days, enough to quench the deserts, exposing the roots of trees and the bones of creatures buried long ago in the crusted sod, rotting the hooves of the living and concluding the emollition of the dead. Hundreds of thousands of swollen worms rose to the surface and sprawled themselves about to escape drowning, but drown they did. After a respite of three days, it rained intermittently for another seven. Spurts of angry downpours belabored the mood of men and beasts as they peered out from any retreat of confinement they could find, awaiting pardon. Violent thunderclaps shook the earth and fuscous, anarchistic storm clouds fed into the mouth of a great black fiend to the west. Lightning spiked across the tin of the heavens like nerves engraved with loathing, lingering in the sky as long as a soul might fear to look, ghostly outlines of fire charging the lake and the indigoid menaced horizon. Pavlides' kafenio lost its electrical generation, but no one was willing to venture out into the deluge to restart the dampened engine. Lines of communication to the north became knotted whips of cloth and copper and the roads impassible by vehicle or horse cart. Kythera, the Momus of desiccated demons, added to the woe and continued to pour its pagan torrents from overburdened springs for days after the rains ceased. By the twelfth day, villagers began invoking the story of Noah and the Great Flood. Some blamed the Naodites for casting a spell upon them, but news came that other parts of Macedonia and Thrace were faring no better. Fear and remorse for their many transgressions frayed the voice of prayer as Lathra swam in its rueful fen of misery for nearly a month.

The rains claimed but one life in the region, a hapless youth from Arnissa, the youngest son of a man known to most of the villagers in the region, as he was a renowned harness maker who sold his products throughout the Balkans. While traversing a steep roadside torrent, the boy slipped and struck his head, and fell into the surging waters. They found him a day later at the bottom of a ravine created by the rushing waters emptying into Vegoritis, his body bloated, his mouth agape and filled with dark gray pebbles. The boy's death, however, was less renowned than his father's despondency. A midget of a man with a household full of daughters, he wandered Arnissa for years wearing his son's decorative vest, embroidered by the boy's mother in happier times, until it tattered into shreds from his picking at it and pulling the threads. An emulsion of grief and weariness bade him the desire to join his son. He was walking in the village square, headed in the direction of his home when the remnants of the vest finally fell from his body. He stared at the garment as if it were a dead animal. A moment later he lifted it off the ground, dusted it off and flung it over his shoulder. Then he turned in the opposite direction, walked for most of the day to Edessa, and without apparent second thought proclaimed before witnesses, "I'm tired of pretending to be alive." He turned toward the precipice in the twilight and told a bystander, "My boy died a useless death, before he could know all the pleasures of life," and then flung his unraveled soul over the cataract. Everyone attended his funeral and mourned the entire unhappy episode as if it were their own. The church mercifully abided full burial rites for him, since his wife and children had always attended liturgy in Arnissa. But Elissa could not help feeling that he was a selfish fool.

"What of his wife and daughters? she told Lambros once they were at home. "What happens to them now, without a father?"

"You don't know what condition his mind was in when all this happened," he said. "I heard his business was faltering. Cars and trucks replacing harnessed horses and mules in Thessaloniki. The future must have seemed a dim prospect for him as well."

"Well, I hope he likes the dark," she said.

In Lathra, the dampened period of dejection lasted all winter, draining more water than anyone ever imagined possible into the bottomless bowel of Vegoritis. While miring each effort and footstep in misery, the deluge did manage to rout those other vivid memories of the season's mournful beginnings. By the floral grace of May, as roads and fields finally drained and dried, misfortune forestalled its baneful poison and thereafter, for nearly four years, the village flourished without dearth or famine, or litany of the heart's interment. Ixion spun within the arc of its magical spoke a serene reign of domestic bliss.

Lambros reveled in the simple cadence of his duties, moving instinctively from task to task, day to day, recanting his reputation, taking percipient pleasure in the mundane magnificence of the vital, but usually ignored things in life. The dappled shade of trees, the distant bells and bleating of sheep, the minutiae of Elissa's often surprising gastronomy, the budding verdant view from his boat, and the hint of dark worlds beneath the brim of his hat as he peered down at refracted eels swimming in the lake. Most of all, he counted himself blessed with the dutiful bond and playful felicity of his offspring. Once, while assisting him as they would with his labors in the peach orchard, shearing the tall grasses strangling the sun-yielding trunks of trees, pale pink petals showered his urchins' head and shoulders, inveigling their unceremonious darts and scampers and softening the usual quibbling with his emotions. He discovered a deep tranquility in his children's distinctive laughs and metrical panting, as they ran about him, inhaling swathes of fragrance, blown free within the gusts of wind turned away by unyielding mountains. Breezes carried for impressive distances on the swelling clouds of spring. Nomadic petals flew past them, like ambrosial blessings bathed in myrrh. In the clutch of such indescribable joy, brought on by as little as fair weather, his heart would beat without dreams, without remorse, and utterly lacking in the daily disenchantment belaboring men's ideas.

Elissa's gratification in having prompted the exodus of the sisters Karangelos evolved into a gnawing regret. She did not yet possess the courage to confess her offence, rashly interpreting her rival's admiration of her husband as evidence of actual or even platonic intimacy. To pacify her guilt, she befriended Athena Kyriazis, an apparent surrogate and friend to Magda, and carried with great labor the full burden of the alliance. Her prickly distrust of Lambros, in such excess of prudence, finally dulled and faded away. The maddening surveillance of his every strut and manner evolved instead into a fixation with her role as a mother. Lambros was pleased, despite the fact, for the time being, that his children had to suffer the torment of her ceaseless doting.

———◆———

During the happy half-decade that followed the flood, there was a wedding each year as some of the first generation of daughters came of age and discovered that, miraculously, the young men had not succumbed to the patrimony of nomadic lust. Spiros Terzellos, the first, and as of yet, only available young man to break away from Lathra after Avram's sisters vanished, married his foreign charmer, Rina Philemon, a mechanic's daughter. Few from the village received invitations to the rather unremarkable urban wedding. Old man Terzellos had objected to his son's choice of profession. Spiros had apprenticed as an auto mechanic, first in Lathra with Petros Canettas and then in Thessaloniki with a Chioti named Heracles Seras. A power broker of a man in his part of town, Seras grew to love the boy as if he were his own son and convinced him to move there. Rina's father worked for him as well and introduced him to his daughter. Spiro's father, on the other hand, stewed under the pretense of his son's choice in brides. He held nothing against the girl, but insulted by his son's lack of respect for his wishes, abstained from making the trip to Thessaloniki. As a result, his wife Voula and their other children attended without him. The marriage occasioned a temporary rift between the old man and his wife and pitted Spiro against his brothers and strong-willed sister, Amalia. These tensions, in turn, infected the new union, providing the young couple with a yet uncultivated topic for bickering, peppering the already prolific acrobatics of newlyweds with anger. Son and daughter-in-law felt unwelcome at the Terzellos homestead. Voula monthly made the trip to Thessaloniki to cook for her son in the oil-laden convention of her kitchen, since Rina could only mimic her family's gourmand, what Spiros called "the potato boilers." He also despised his in-law's inclination toward tedious, colloquial jokes and indecipherable taxonomies using words they often mispronounced.

"And here I thought we were the *horiates*" (hoi polloi). "As much enthusiasm as a callus," he complained of them to his mother. "But at least my Rina is pretty and I don't have to prune trees like my father's barefoot field hands."

"Shut your mouth ingrate! Terzellos had scolded his son once. "Who are you to begrudge these men their work, even if they're heathens? All these years your bread has been laced with another man's sweat."

"Bread," Spiros snorted, "from beggars who wipe themselves with the hand that holds their bread!" The ill will instigated by such visceral arguments made blood increasingly irrelevant for Terzellos and his son, until the announcement of a pregnancy. Then suddenly, for the old man, it was "my Rina did this" and "my Rina has that." Growing in girth seemed to augment the bride's nobility in the old man's mind. By the time the grandson was born, Rina was all but the Terzellos family crest and Spiro's savior from himself. "Good thing the lazy bum married such a good girl," Terzellos crooned. "She knotted his tie good and tight."

Incredibly, Apostolos Timonakis married one of the Maenads, the Petalouda's daughter, Martina Praxitellis. Leggy, but just shy of comely, in a toothy sort of way, with a wanton air about the simplest of her facial drawings and an impertinent way of suggesting her superbly pointy breasts, Martina, it was soon realized, was the most pernicious and crafty of the bee keeper's hive. She was the last of the three sisters Spiros attempted to corrupt before finally succeeding. Martina invited him on at least four other occasions to return to her in the leaf-less thickets between her father's unkempt tract of apple trees and the lake. This went on even after Spiros met and was courting his fiancé in Thessaloniki and was quite unlike the one-taste-of-honey-is-enough tendered him by Martina's sisters, who permitted themselves to be kissed and groped but otherwise resisted his attempts at erotic suggestion, if only because they had only the vaguest idea of what else he wanted of them. Martina, on the other hand, being the most curious of the three, had, as a young girl, studied the coitus of herding dogs, of sheep and donkeys and understood at least the mechanics of physical affection.

Convinced of Spiro's ultimate defection of attention in favor of his Rina and quite certain that his circle of friends would eventually be privy to his bawdy exploits, Martina was smart enough to know that once her submission was common knowledge, she would never find a husband. Gambling on his kind nature, she confessed as much of her escapades to Apostolos, playing the veritable victim, cunningly placing a wedge of resentment between the two friends and managing to evoke Apostolos' pity. Even in her weepy retelling - the story never being the same twice - it appeared as if her favors were obtainable yet again. Vivid descriptions of each dip of Spiro's wick into her waxy hive of feminine imprudence, which did not abate until Spiros moved to Thessaloniki, provoked Apostolos' curiosity. Speculation swelled the prurient skin of his pride and he soon found himself no longer wondering what it was about this dubious, corruptible damsel that Spiros found worthy of such risk. Apostolos' fascination turned into adoration, his adoration into conspicuously desperate desire.

The typically doltish Yiannis Praxitellis caught wind of very little of what delinquency his daughters conjured until they wanted him to notice. He approached Apostolos one day, as the young man was walking back to the village from the orchards and a rendezvous with Martina. Salacious pleasure in his conquest floated like a halo about Apostolos' face. Affronted by his daughter's haggard exhaustion and the less than credible denial of her shameless antics, her father sent her home with a backhand across the cheek. A ferocious welt appeared immediately, copper with walnut overtones. As he did his cocked fedora and the hand rolled cigarette dangling from his mouth even while he spoke, the old man wore his nicked and rusted rifle from his days in the Turkish military with typical panache, astride his shoulder, the butt of the rifle pointing skyward. Suddenly, any trace of effeminate mannerism, what in him was a pretense of modernity, disappeared.

"I understand you're interested in my Martina?"

"No, no, no," Apostolos stammered as Praxitellis let down the rifle from its perch.

"That's not what she tells me."

"Who tells you this, Kyrie Yianni?"

"My oldest daughter tells me this, Apostolos Timonakis," he said calmly. "You know; the one whose skirts you've already peeked under."

"Not I, Kyrie Yianni," he said, the lie drying his mouth within seconds.

"It's better for you to tell me the truth," Praxitellis said; smoke streaming through the dark hairs of his nostrils and into his face.

"I'm telling you the truth, sir," Apostolos said, his words like nerve-racked chords between fits of coughing and choking as he scanned Praxitellis' chin, his nose and forehead but not his eyes. "It wasn't me, Kyrios Praxitellis, I swear to you . . . ." Praxitellis noisily spit a piece of tobacco from between his teeth.

"Now you've irritated me, Apostolos," the old man interrupted. "I'll tell you what's going to happen," he said with impregnable authority. "You will return home to your worthy father, who I understand labors like a slave, and is still recovering from his cantaloupe disaster, and you will announce to him that you are going to marry my oldest daughter.

He will be very pleased. Her dowry will be worthy of your manhood and the prospects for your future achievements. Hopefully, she will give you sons, on top of everything else she apparently bestows."

"I can't do this. My mother will not permit it!" Apostolos said anxiously.

"Your mother," he laughed heartily. "What does your mother have to do with it? You're a man, aren't you?"

"Yes," Apostolos acquiesced, miserably.

"Good. Then it's settled. You know, I read in the paper that a man in Mani shot his son-in-law in an unfortunate hunting incident. He thought he was pulling the trigger on a boar. Maniotes, damn them, they shoot first and focus on what they are shooting at afterwards. You know how the blood feuds go down there in Mani and in Crete, don't you?" Praxitellis laughed again. "They're lucky they have boars to shoot. What do we have up here?" he said rhetorically. "An occasional rabbit and some mangy wolves; wolves, afraid of Konya's even shabbier dogs."

"Yes, I've heard," Apostolos said apprehensively.

"Heard what, boy?"

"About what you just said. The Maniotes and their famous feuds."

Praxitellis drew the bolt half the way back on the rifle and blew across the bullet lodged in the chamber.

"This infernal dust gets in everything." He smiled broadly, displaying an array of sturdy teeth, pleased with the young man's consent.

———————◆———————

Vasilios Lambrou finally succumbed to the dower of his fate as well, and wedded the devoted Penelope Halkias, his employer's daughter. The sacrament would take place at the local church in Edessa on a sumptuous May afternoon, just after Lent, amid the elation of her family, who lavished the orphaned Vasili with a dowry fit for a prince. Gold liras, china, a chest of linens and lace doilies, a fine draft horse, some productive grapevines southeast of the city and, surprising to Vasili, a full third expectancy in the church pew business, all promised to him by the girl's exuberant father. The business had grown to employ more than twenty men and included in its product line fixtures for the homes of wealthy urbanites, as well as the ecclesial trappings for which the company had become known. Penelope's mother, Fotini, was especially happy - no mother-in-law for her daughter to contend with. She had expended much venom in the previous year upon her own daughter-in-law, the wife of her eldest son, Theofanis Halkias, nearly destroying the marriage from its inception, until the first grandchild, a daughter, was born and named Fotini. This happy consequence aside, Theofanis wisely moved his young wife and daughter a convenient distance away to Kilkis to ply his trade as a toolmaker.

Penelope's younger and unmarried brother, Thomas, with whom Vasili would share in the business as well, trusted him as if he were a brother. He had worked with and befriended the brothers Lambrou for seven years. Being a benevolent and contented fellow with little ambition, more comfortable in the kafenio talking politics than in the wood shop, Thomas did not protest the sharing of his inheritance, and had actually suggested the idea to his father and brother. Vasili was the one with the artist's eye, by far the most talented carver in the shop and the region, but also possessing business acumen, something that Thomas lacked. The brothers Halkias and their father met well before the betrothal and raised a toast to Vasili. They agreed that he would be included in the plans for the business and for the sake of Penelope must become an equal partner.

"I pity the father that let him go, and let's face it," old man Halkias said, "your sister is moody and her bloom isn't getting any fresher. I'm offering her hand to the palikari as soon as possible."

In her insular imaginings, the world of her paintings and her poems, which she hid beneath two floorboards in a corner of her cluttered room, obscured from everyone in her household, Penelope developed a deep affection for Vasili soon after her father hired him. Her father boasted of his many skills, and often referred to him as a master crafts-man, but he proved most impressed with the steel of his character. She had many occasions to visit the shop, assisting in the bookkeeping and in cleaning the office. One day, after a year of hearing such continual praise, Penelope confided in her mother her impression of Vasili, and then her affection. At first, her mother thought the match untenable and suggested a tailor's son from Arnissa as a better choice. Penelope, however, made it clear that she would rather become a nun than live without Vasili, whom she believed cared for her. She, for her part, loved him wholly and desperately, and not only because every cleft and cleave of his masculinity thrilled her. He was a kindred spirit, she believed, a primitive artist, and, unlike her deprecating view of her own undisclosed talents, an artist of superior skill. She believed that he instinctively understood the categorical elements of substantiality, of line, color and light, and that this insight made him an enlightened man, a seer with his hands and the mythic imagining of a poet's eye.

After confiding in Vasili, he asked to see one of her drawings. She resisted for months. She explained that her family might view anything of this nature as an elicit escapade, as her being prone to giving herself over to immodesty or bohemianism, a life without marriage and child rearing as its purpose. He asked her how she came upon the pastime. She evaded the question, for she honestly could not recall the spark to her creative impulse. Finally, after repeated requests, she acquiesced to showing him something she had recently created, but only with the pledge that he never reveal as much to her parents or brothers. The work was an untitled painting on paper, an allegory of insistent brush strokes upon a page of indigo nothingness, something one might imagine as the complete and utter absence of light beneath the waves, a stepping into the Heraclitan flux. The painting barely depicted three spectral gray dolphins tearing through a fulminating, teaming sea. It was all gradations of blue, a limit imposed by the colors of paint available to her and her one small brush, and gnashing Vegoritis, her model, a body of water she had only seen twice. Utterly surprised by its lack of the tangible and the conspicuous, Vasili thought it marvelous, like nothing he had ever seen before, for aside from Lazaro's books on art, he had no opportunity to visit a museum in his life. And while she would never show her work in public, or study a mentor's technique, or suffer the competitive sting over the work of peers, or sit in coffee houses and talk of art until color and light muffled the words of others into sterile glances, or ponder the influence of a school of painting, or move to Paris to be corrupted for her art, she would, throughout the years to come, enjoy her work openly.

The entire Lambrou brood attended the festive event, as did Danäe. She spent months of morbid isolation amid Lazaro's effects, reading his letters and manuscripts, hiring a solicitor from Thessaloniki to administer his estate, and writing to his family in America and to the boy whom she surmised was his son, living in Sweden. Nine months after his demise and at the end of the rains, with nothing resolved of Lazaro's testamentary disposition and having heard nothing from his son or the mother of the boy, the tedium of her studious existence and the neck-stiffening slump of her shoulders compelled her to return to the attendance of her veterinary skills and other interests. Elissa, in the mean time, had already persuaded her, in anticipation of attending the flurry of weddings and baptisms, to grow her hair to near its former splendor.

"What a sin it would be for you to attend your cousin's wedding looking like a porcupine."

The acuity of meaning Danäe ascribed to recent events forced the question of her place in the Lathran social order. The process of answering this for herself matured her in an indescribable but perceptible way, to anyone who cared to observe. Still shy, mystifying, inclined toward obliquity and introspection, by most standards, she quickly revived Lathran interest in her every endeavor, first by attending liturgy again. Slowly she increased her dealings with villagers over their long-neglected domestic fauna. The change in her was especially evident at home, in her newfound appreciation of Elissa, whom she rightly assumed resented her upon her arrival years ago. Now they saw each other as sisters. She offered again her invaluable assistance in raising Evanthia, who, being the youngest of the four children, was, out of shear parental weariness, left to her own devices. In her plan to present Danäe to the wider audience of the wedding reception, Elissa borrowed on her behalf a dress from Athena Kyriazis, whose long-limbed elevation most resembled Danäe's figure and stature.

"No bodice and peasant's blouse for you, young lady," she said to entice her. "In this dress you will be the elegant orchid." Danäe thought the fit too bold. She studied herself in Elissa's small oval mirror, hanging on the wall. She remembered when she first arrived in Lathra, making faces in the mirror for Sophia, primping and parodying the urban women she had seen in Istanbul, seemingly standing before the vales of vanity, and remembered the scolding Elissa gave her for lampooning and promoting such giddiness in her daughter. Nothing else came to mind. The dress fit very well except for the length of the sleeves and the hem, a centimeter or so short, but this did not bother Elissa. The sleeves unadorned as they were, could ride up her forearm anyway. She pulled her still growing hair behind her ears and stared for a moment at Elissa and finally at herself, without reaction. The color of her hair had darkened. Her eyes appeared like polished pebbles she would find on the beaches of Vegoritis. She grinned and saw nothing but awkwardness.

Athena would also be an invited guest at the wedding, with her husband, her sons and young daughter, along with any Lathran who ever contracted for the skilled labor of the brothers Lambrou. Yiorgos Doxiades, his wife and children and his widowed sister Dimitra would be present as well, but without her cherubic though not yet baptized son of a furrier, the last of whose corporeality was now the molecular fodder for all manner of colubrine and the digestion of worms slithering about the crevices of the cliffs. Her mother kept the boy at home so that Dimitra could attend the wedding and potentially turn an unmarried head. Her mother, also recently widowed, arrived from Florina to live with her son in his appended domicile, now overcrowded again because of her, despite the room added by Vasili and Andreas. Dimitra emerged from the turmoil with her dead husband's family, the lovely young widow, her grief short-lived. An exotic etching, with the pale cherry of faultless fictile lips, she lost the weight of birthing, which at first lingered upon her hips, and regained the nubile, untarnished waistline and slender calves of her adolescence while retaining a milk-burdened bosom made all the more decorous by the accentuating taper to her black dress of reluctant widowhood. Long, raven curls reclined luxuriously about her shoulders and a small bonnet scarf provided cover for the top of her brooch-combed head, her bangs pulled back beneath it.

Pater Alexi conducted the wedding ceremony with the assistance of a foreign priest, a novitiate he met, oozing with the mystical rites of his Transylvanian pedigree, recently ordained after spending two years at various largely unoccupied monasteries at the foot of Mount Athos. A Greek-speaking Romanian whose accent was listlessly similar to the inspired way Russian intellectuals enounce English, like a march through mud, he was seeking a home amid Hellenic splendor.

Vasili asked Lambros to accept the honor of *koumbaros*.[67] Lambros not only accepted but also took the role seriously, consulting with the

---

67 κουμπάρος - best man

prospective in-laws beforehand about the number and nature of the wedding favors and details regarding the sacrament and the reception to follow. After much debate and hand ringing, the Halkias clan, fearing the loss of limelight but also desiring not to assume the entire expense for what they assumed was the village riffraff of his large contingent, agreed to extend the celebration for a second day in Lathra. They would use Lambro's large courtyard as the setting, and local cooks and musicians as the entertainment committee. Thus, many of the guests who could not attend the ceremony in Edessa, which would have required ferrying everyone with repeated trips in the village's three untidy trucks, or the hiring of a caravan of sorts to accomplish the feat, were able to dance with the bride and groom on the second day without leaving Lathra. Feeding everyone was potentially less expensive than the steep price of petrol needed for a hired caravan.

The first day's revelry was joyous, the second, hotly Dionysian. The majority of Halkian guests had never laid eyes on Lathra. The village was not on a single map of the region and, as one of the Halkian guests had said, "As godforsaken as the devil's mother, as the saying goes." In fact, Penelope's grandmother, a discourteous but stylishly dressed spindle of a woman with no hindquarters to speak of, pearly teeth for her age and very shortly cropped and dyed hair, an unheard of convention among horiates, knew nothing of its existence, so vague and unrecorded was its reputation in non-agronomical circles. The old woman fancied herself as sophisticated in comparison and seized the opportunity to inquire of her hosts as cynically as she knew how, desiring to inflict the painful anonymity of ignorance.

"Lathra . . . Lathra, what kind of name is that?" she squealed during the first night's reception in the only moment of tension between the clans. "What does it mean? It sounds like the name of some pagan sourtouka or dingy-dong prancing about a stage." Pater Alexi overheard and interrupted.

"Madame, please. It is a holy reference. I chose the name myself. In fact, the koumbaro was among those who conferred upon the choice."

"Excuse me, Pater, I meant no offense, but I've never heard the name before." Her apology tinged with incredulity. Imbibing the evening's merrymaking, the local tsipouro sweating from his pores, Alexi abandoned his usual reserve and his motto in such settings: never offer biblical exegesis to the herd while grazing.

"The Epistle to the Romans," he said, unable to contain his annoyance. "The patristic version of the word: in the day when God will judge the *secrets* (pronounced emphatically) of men by Jesus Christ according to my gospel; or, Psalm number ten: he lies in wait *secretly* as a lion in his den. Oh, that God would reveal the *secrets* of his wisdom, for wisdom has two sides. The book of Job ... shall I continue?"

"I'll tell you a *secret*, Pater," the old woman said as she rose to leave for another table, insulted by his didactics, repeating his emphasis on the word with less than a retraction. "It's still a foolish name," she snapped. His temper flared. He stepped close to her so others would not hear.

"Know this: God has even forgotten some of your sins," he said, curling his lips to conceal his irritation. "The rest of the verse," he added.

The Halkians forgave Vasili his origin. They admired his integrity and had no quarrel with his father-in-law's judgment. And while they saw themselves as town dwellers, and all villagers as country bumpkins, many of them proved charmed by the iambic jewel and its setting, the long, lush valley of cultivation punctuated by the rocky ugliness of Kythera and the blue emulate of sea that was Vegoritis. Before the end of the gala, a few inquired of the availability of land.

"There's no land for sale here," they heard repeatedly, "unless you want to live in the quarry," meaning the wasp crags just north of Lazaro's property, or, as Lambros suggested cynically, "you're willing to build a water pumping station to benefit the entire village with indoor plumbing." Sarcasm drew the visitors back into their pretense of sophistication. Electricity and indoor plumbing were amenities long accustomed to in Edessa.

"These people live like Arabs," the grandmother mumbled.

Wine infused, the dancing and singing lasted until early morning. The dexterous bouzouki of Avgita Kirithos, by now practiced to a level beyond mere competence, made for him a local reputation and occasioned his accompaniment by four professional musicians, friends of his from the taverns of Thessaloniki. This included a singer, a woman of nearly mannish appeal, corpulent in all the correct places but vaguely intimidating, with a mutinous expression as if the words of the songs sweltered in her mouth and would detonate from between her lips, whom Athena, wine absorbed as she had become, ogled with flirtatious abandon. When confronted with her husband's jealousy,

Athena assured him that she was inquiring on behalf of her remaining bachelor son. The singer however, was married to the able percussionist, an Alexandrian who thrilled the crowd with his *santouri*.[68] Along with them strummed a youthful guitarist, fluent and beguiling, with a Spanish turn of phrase, and a clarinetist, an older *Chioti*,[69] who doubled as a singer, with an appropriately abrasive baritone and pockmarked face. The Chioti drank as if his insides were on fire but never seemed to bear the effects until the celebration finally ended, upon which he suddenly blacked out. Finally, there was the slim, handsome violinist and *outi* player, Gregorios Narlis. His Anatolian and Pontian drones and double stops raised such *kefi*[70] as had not been witnessed since the marriage of Tassos Kyriazis to his Nomia Timonakis.

By mid-evening, the entire village had attended the festivities. Intoxicant, ambient delight seemingly suspended time, with hours skipping and taking wing in a riotous floating of joy. Temperate weather continued past nightfall, a warm gentle breeze and tawny moonlight followed the eager May sun. Above the heads of enchanted revelers, a string of lights, powered by a groaning generator on loan from Pavlides, illuminated their every step. A long spine of wire permitted the placement of the generator far behind the house, the noise dissipating over the placid head of Vegoritis. The courtyard had become a veritable constellation on the clearest of nights, a mood-altering marvel to spectators and dancers, glimmering light upon wine glistened smiles like the tail dust of comets. Sweet spacious melodies traced the heaven of nightingales, satiating them, the rite like an elliptical passage into marital bliss.

Narlis was instantly spellbound with Danäe, his zeal mounting as the sky drained its daylight behind the mountains. He seemed to be playing for her alone, following her every move with each *marcato* and *sul ponticello* across an unraveling hank of horsehair.

"He's captured the walk of a woman on his fiddle," the men said as he accompanied a familiar tune of forlorn love and the sea, singing along in happy inebriation. She noticed him as well; the intensity of his gaze, his emotive dexterity and a sequence of double-stops more common to

---

68 σαντούρι - hammered dulcimer

69 Χιώτης - from the island of Chios

70 κέφι - spirit of revelry

Paganini than the carefree harmonies of *laika*.[71] Blushing as she walked near him, she noticed the nearly feminine flawlessness of his beardless face. Having nearly reached its original length, her hair she wore back, in a double braid.

"You must look available but avoid competing with the bride," Elissa had said incautiously, as they dressed on the morning of the reception.

"I'm not a ewe. You're mocking me with such exaggeration," Danäe interrupted. Her complexion smoldered. Its winter frailty yielded to tresses pulled and tied behind her head, exposing a sensuous bough of neckline and protruding clavicle. Pallid lilacs of linen draped her body like a rain of petals. As she danced with the bride and then Vasili, the weave of braids loosened, unraveling in stages until her hair fell to her shoulders completely. Narlis lost his mind, stopped playing in mid-phrase and abandoned his post. Carrying his violin beneath his arm, he approached the girl he presumed would play the aloof and icy goddess, not a breath flaming the coals of his hope. Embarrassed by his overture, she hardly looked up at him, casting her eyes out toward the gathering. Elissa caught sight of them and quickly intervened.

"May I introduce to you my cousin, Miss Danäe Dranias?"

"Yes, please do," he said above the swelling music.

"I'm the woman of the house, Elissa Tiros . . . Kyria Lambrou. And you are, sir?"

"Gregorios Narlis, a friend of Avgitas, the bouzouki player. I'm very pleased to meet you both," he said vaporously, as Danäe would later recall, and without taking his eyes off her.

"Excuse me," Elissa said as she hurried off, smiling shrewdly but gesturing for Sophia to act as chaperone.

Narlis spoke without pause. They inched their way to a table on the veranda, and sipped mavrodaphne, the music and commotion dissipating above the house. Sonia Halkias, sister of the bride, also fascinated by his legato, quietly joined them. Rambling about a profusion of topics, the conversation finally began fighting for air but then resettled upon music. Danäe inquired of his training and tastes. Eagerly, he revealed that he had spent three years in Paris studying under Joufroy Tascher, a largely unknown provincial violinist who sacrificed a promising career

---

71 λαϊκά - the people's music

for love of his Madonna and the seven children that followed. Tascher otherwise earned his living teaching and performing in chamber ensembles and small orchestras throughout France.

"He's spent the last eight years learning to play the lute and its predecessor, the vihuela. He's enthralled with the work of Dowland, Bésard, Dufat, Cabezón and a host of others, sometimes transcribing such tablature into violin and viola duets," he explained with pride, as if accomplishing the task himself - "a true master of the trills, mordents and appoggiaturas of living, if you ask me." The roving theme of conversation then shifted to what he perceived as Macedonia's cultural isolation. He meandered, describing for her his visits to the great capitals of Europe and to New York, Philadelphia, Boston and Baltimore, occasioned by his profession, the good fortune of his family with its summated wealth, and his education.

"I can't survive indefinitely in a place without a great concert hall at my beckon," he said with tempered immodesty. "I'm going to leave Thessaloniki one day and return to roaming the great centers of art," he caught himself saying wryly.

"A musical Erasmus," she inserted. He had no idea what she meant.

"Unless a reason of competing loveliness arose here," he added quickly. "Then I may discover my own Dowland to transcribe." The smile that followed was silly and self-satisfied and compelled her to change the subject to Lazaros and his musical predilections and eccentricities.

"His sheet music is predominantly for piano," she said eventually, "but there are a few scores and a manuscript or two in his library for strings as well. I suspect he felt much like your teacher, but for different reasons. He, too, retreated from the world to pursue his happiness, closely and intensely, but alone." She went on to wonder aloud if he might play for her a piece from Lazaro's collection of scores before his departure for home. Confident, Narlis invited her to retrieve a sample. She excused herself and ran from the party to Mavrotripa, bounding off with candid excitement, nearly falling into the lake from the very rock where she and Lazaros last sat together with Andreas.

Andreas did not fail to notice her fascination as she listened to the musician speak. Twice he arose, intending to join the conversation, but precaution and the scent of his jealousy restrained him. Seeing Danäe rise from the table and run off, the effervescence in her gait, as if she were playing with children, made him decide not to permit his disappointment to sabotage her pleasure or disrupt the elation of the day. He followed her from a safe distance, to ensure her safety, he told himself. Danäe had returned from Mavrotripa excited, breathless, scanning the gathering for Narlis, who again stepped away from his playing and met her on the veranda. When Andreas returned, he saw them there again and turned his chair away from the canvas of his envy. Having realized the musician's fixation, Sonia Halkias went back to the dancing as well.

"I've found a few here; they're mostly for piano," Danäe said. "It was a bit dark in his cavern and my lantern was flickering. Perhaps you can choose one and transcribe a few phrases for me." Narlis perused the selection, denied his ability to sight-read very well but proceeded to bow a few bars from a partita he recognized as having been for violin, previously transcribed for the piano, impressing her with this adroit reading. He passed over a single page of feverishly scribbled manuscript entitled *Volaverunt*, without comment, and settled upon a worn copy of the Dvorak *Trio in F Minor*, a lyrical piece he counted as somewhat familiar to him, although not strictly of his repertoire. Danäe summoned Sophia and Evanthia as chaperones and they all slipped inside the lamp-lit house to listen to his disjointed but courageous reading of various fragmented violin parts from the work. The dance from the second movement pleased her immensely, as she later confided to him, but the Adagio moved her - a levitating counterpoint soaring above the defiant dance tune blaring in the courtyard, reminding her of the music her mother loved.

Sophia excused herself between movements and Evanthia fell asleep exhausted after two days of festivities. Even to one who did not know her, Danäe appeared transfixed to Narlis. He concluded his disjointed performance abruptly, placed his violin down next to the sleeping child and taking no chance of a missed opportunity, took Danäe by the hand, caressing a stray strand of hair away from her cheek and kissed her, stepping back clumsily to gauge her reaction. A delicate bloom of momentary surprise preceded an unconscious approval, an ascending wisp of daring, her lips sodden with black *daphne* and a nervous dart of plum. Narlis was so besotted, he could manage nothing but to stare, his comrades bellowing above the now vacant hum of voices, calling him as they became weary of playing ditties without the melodic escort of violin.

Narlis turned, lost his balance, stumbled, apologized for his clumsiness and appeared ready to trundle away when she interrupted.

"I'm told that upon moving to Lathra, before his collection of recordings arrived to keep him company, Lazaros would listen to the few recordings he purchased in Paris and the ones he had first received from his mother, over and over again, a habit that never left him," she said, making Narlis hesitate. "When I finally raised enough nerve to speak with him, I asked him why he did this. It seemed strange to me that he would risk tiring of the music. He explained that he wanted to subject each work to the unbridled scrutiny of his soul, to sear every note in his musical memory, so that he might have them for his voyage down the river Lethe, along perhaps with the sound of his mother's voice."

"He sounds like a fellow I'd have liked," he said, sensing her sorrow. He thought to kiss her again, but offered instead the drooping lip of indecision, since Evanthia was by then awake and yawning her displeasure with the continuing noise.

"Go to sleep, child," Danäe said sweetly, "I'll take you."

"Danäe, I'm very delighted to have met you and wish to visit you again."

"Yes, of course ... if you bring your violin with you," she suggested bashfully. Narlis returned to his playing and departed early the next morning, engendering before his departure a planned occasion for an embrace and private kiss on a walk in the direction of Mavrotripa. He had convinced his fellow musicians that sleeping on a blanket on the floor of Yianko's kafenio, rather than driving in the darkness for home or the hotel in Edessa, was for a worthy amorous cause, "An infatuation that only the poets can fathom," he assured them. Then, while walking with Danäe, sensing that anything more than a quip of his affection might embarrass her, he waited for her to entwine her forearm in his before pulling her beneath the shade of a densely foliaged tree, pressing her next to him just long enough for a kiss. The second kiss alarmed her less, a taut, tracing quiver of restlessness coursing along her spine. Until that time, she dismissed the pleasure of such intimacy as a mirage, having encountered them only in the lyric poets and the maudlin imagery of wayfaring dance songs. Narlis returned to Lathra on several occasions, solely to convince her that his love was the Aegis of her fortune. The slow pace that was his courtship eventually convinced her of the same.

Elissa took credit for the introduction and promoted the relationship as fated. Thus, with nothing but a handful of sheet music to offer as a dowry, the unconquerable vixen's betrothal to her appoggiatura became the season's peroration of scheming Eros.

21

On one of their infrequent but memorably long walks, in the midst of discussions of many subjects dear to his heart, Lazaros instructed Danäe upon the general demeanor of the locals.

"Greeks are never optimists," he said. "It's not that we're pessimists, or melancholic, mind you, we're just not all that hopeful. Nothing of happiness lasts as long as the light glistening in the glassy eye of hindsight. Others forget sometimes that the wheel rotates ceaselessly and always turns within the arc one tick too many. Our extraction among the myriad of mortals is born from sacred hubris. Tamers of the rock-strewn earth, of horses and all the docile beasts and the raging sea, forever outnumbered, chronically forlorn in the stall of happiness, we are faithfully suspicious of any prolonged elation, having long understood that existence is another name for Agon and that revelry, music, poetry, art and conjugal favors are all welcome and necessary distractions."

After a suitably long season of weddings and blessings of the earth, Ares returned and fired the furnaces of the underworld. The reincarnated cankers of Domitian proffered atrocity as a public spectacle, spilling the ocher dye of civilization in an obscenity of violence, witnessed and indeed made possible through the cloudy convolution of man's weary lens. Where the cooperation of his envious neighbors failed Lambros, the helping hands of foreign civilizers, the harbingers of convenience, and so, of water and sanitation, granted him his heart's desire, albeit with a perverse twist. The water pumping station and irrigation project came to fruition, but without local benefactors or supervision, completed by the water wheedling of foreigners in the span of four months. And not just any old swarthy *Romios* engineer in love with the idyllic Lathran landscape but the modern Italian army and its corps of engineers, exacting credit where it is due. These nascent, *facta non verba*,[72] Romans surrendered their catguts, swallowed their cantatas and buttoned their pants long enough to accomplish an engineering feat worthy of their ancestors. This, of course, after dropping the same pants about their ankles in a humiliating defeat some meager months earlier to an invigorated Greek ragtag, half their size. Il Duce's ultimatum discourteously answered with Metaxa's sleepy yawn and then a fisting.

A petrol-fueled water pumping station dotted the top of Kythera like a fez and another rather untidy looking slab of concrete despoiled the shores of Vegoritis just beyond Perea, part of a larger engineering campaign providing electricity to most of Macedonia along with the pre-existing hydroelectric plant in Edessa. Kilometers of pipe lay below the frost line of Greek resentment, unknowingly side stepping the dispute that tilted allegiances away from Lambros. Thus, the Italians delivered what would be the most costly quench of thirst ever sipped by Lathrans and their recently untended valley.

In consideration for their labors, the masters of such engineers, those clever, astringent racial prudes, insisted that the locals till their fields once again, so that their Prussian brethren preparing to catch their death of cold in Orthodox Russia might die with Macedonian wheat bricks in their paunches. And so the innocent wards of greater Roma, suffering from the feeling of a different kind of fullness, might relieve the bloat and indigestion of any political pledge offered by Benito of the-on-time-trains.

As is usually the case, such an arrangement comes at the expense of an impoverished non-beneficiary, subject to confinement in prison camps or asylums or, as in the soviet experiment, wholly exterminable. In this instance, a half million Griechen would starve, be shot, burned or else interned until the same litany of starvation, bullets and a fiery death could be arranged more efficiently. Everyone in Europe was hungry to some extent or another, but like the Poles and the Finns, those infuriating Byzantines needed punishment for daring to say no to an emblematic recreation of the fourth crusade. As the story goes, everyone waited for a spiteful division of gray goosing boy scouts from the 40th Corp,

---

72 in deeds, not words

sporting occult little lighting bolts on their lapels. "Panzers, not pan-sies," Danäe said, turning the phrase in a wry stammer. The Huns were camped on the Yugoslavian frontier with their Bulgarian lap dogs, one of the most comically lopsided alliances in memory, or at least Lambros thought so, the Bulgarian bone of reward being Thrace. All of this would begin just a scenic tank-waddle from Vegoritis.

Whenever envy, debate or deliberation does not paralyze Greeks, death and valor usually follows. Their curled and amber page in his-tory had the motley, battle worn 20th Division take its stand against the fearsome Panzer Abwehr, across the rim of Vegoritis and running East to Edessa. A veritable handful of New Zealanders and Australians under Mackay would help sustain the second utterance of nationalist negation in as many years (carrying the same patriotic and moral weight as Churchill's oratory without the eloquence) trying to hold something resembling a line of defense from Veria to the Aegean coast.

Fifteen days later, the dead at their feet and truckloads of battered defenders from another continent sent north to detention and labor camps, Macarios Timonakis stood outside his home and stuttered an offer to his unwelcome guests, explaining that he planned to plant can-taloupes for them. He went on disdainfully, thinking not a one of them knew a lick of Greek.

"Do you even know what a cantaloupe is, shit heads?" Rifle bolts rattled. "If they come here, I'm going to play a trick in kind on the sigma stigma boys," he had previously mentioned to Vasili. He and Andreas had just returned from the frontier, shoeless, feet wrapped in rags, uni-forms in tatters, wooden faces etched with defeat, a defeat preordained by tanks and ruthless numbers. Vasili had a flesh wound just below the fourth rib, the rather large extraction of shrapnel and his torn shirt car-ried in his pocket, the wound sanitized and bandaged well by an army field medic who later died of his wounds.

"Don't talk like that, Poponaki (little cantaloupe), just go about your business," Vasili had warned Macarios. "Haven't you heard what they're doing, turning women and children into the devil's soap?"

The sauerkrauts grudgingly declined Macarios' invitation. One par-ticularly pale rider, his cropped strands of blond madness standing on edge with pomade, instigated his commander's wrath, his recrimination barked with a villainous croup, presumably to instill fear.

"This filthy gypsy is mocking us, Colonel, with his ridiculous melons." Macarios' lack of sincerity was clear in any language. He had not surrendered his weapon nor obeyed the newly imposed curfew, the pretense. After an hour of hapless indecision and torment, Macarios received a tutorial in authority that included a rifle butt to the forehead. He woke up a few minutes later to his burning abode. His wife, their unwed daughter, the now pregnant Nomia and her husband Tasso all herded into what would turn into a heap of charred rubble. Macarios lost consciousness more than once as they prodded and roused him to blistering cackles, so he could hear the last agonizing cries of his race. Chin trembling on the breastplate, his head split, blood dripping and sizzling on the stones and hot crusty dirt at his feet, he sat up and spat curses between sobs and chafing swallows of smoke. Before the fire had consumed itself, the embers still glowing hot, arising like a cinereous ghost from the remains of his house, Macarios Timonakis rummaged through the baked and naked stone and called out each of their names. When a soldier removed his helmet to wipe his sweaty head, Macarios lost no time heaving a large stone from the house, striking squarely the quadrangle of a well-cropped Teutonic skull, promptly oozing its ruddy pulp. He bent to lift another and raised his eyes to a dozen rifles.

"Fuck your Fuehrer," he said with all the scorn he could muster. The stark rhetoric of bullets ended the whole ordeal. A few partisan were eyewitnesses. They had been making their way back home, crouching a safe distance away in the tall grasses that eventually caught fire as well. The flames consuming the house had been visible from the terrace of Yianko's kafenio, among other vantages, the piercing shrieks of fiery consumption heard down to the concave heart of Vegoritis. Athena Kyriazis paced in circles outside her home, lamenting her son's birth, tearing her hair and dress, spinning and falling into a heap, cold to the touch, knowing her Tasso would not have let harm come to his bride.

"My son, my son! The flesh of my heart is consumed," she cried, pushing her weeping husband away. Years later, she told Elissa that she had discerned her son's defiant cries above the others. "That's how I knew he was gone," her words rattled with grief, deep black wells of tears clouding her eyes.

The following day the locals gathered in the church basement, terrorized but persuaded in whispers to gather the remaining weapons distributed to them a year earlier for use in the Albanian campaign and months earlier upon the Yugoslavian frontier. A few rusty, heavier weapons came to hand, previously provided by their absentee allies, busy digging out London and kicking up sand in Tunisia and Algeria. Gallano's nephew Aristoteli and Lambro's friend Rigos had died in those engagements - Ari buried in a shallow grave beneath the hoarfrost-covered floorboards of a roofless Albanian outpost and Rigos captured by Reichstag intellectuals on the third day of fighting and savaged for information before escaping and returning to the front to kill more of them. On the eighth day, the unit returned Rigos to Arnissa in a pine box, pulled by a donkey cart, his unsecured head thumping against the container, a hero with his metals nailed to the lid because his chest had been detached from his limbs - an exploding telegram of a shell caught between the teeth of suicidal courage. Rigos, the one they called the phallus, was the only man in whom Lambros confided his having suffered from sinister dreams of conflagration, admitting to him that as he aged the nightmares made him whimper like a child before waking up. Rigos responded by disclosing that he believed his nocturnal erections and fantasies were to blame for his rutting by day. Now his escapades were the object of marvel and legend.

"It was good that he died the way he did," his nephew Omëros, who had fought along side him, told Lambros. "He started to like killing better than what he was famous for," he said, a knowing sadness piercing his grin. "What would have been the point of living?" The question pinching a resolute wrinkle at the bridge of his nose, as it did on Rigos when he knew the answer to something.

"The Italians are coming," the civil administrator had announced over a year earlier, handing Lambros and Stratos each a vintage rifle and four containers of ammunition. "After we make short business of them, the real murderers will follow. You wait and see," he prophesied. "You'll need these to shoot them when we call you to defend your nation and your sweethearts."

"What about our wives and children," Lambros said.

"What about them?"

"We will be defending them as well."

"Suit yourself," he said.

"No, you don't understand, mister clerk for the King. I want to wait here and kill the invaders if they get this far. If they walk up to my door, of course I'll shoot them, but I'm not leaving my wife alone with four children."

"It'll be too late by then," he responded.

"Too late for what?"

"For the living to shoot back." Annoyed with the conversation, the administrator caught a glimpse of Nikos. "Here," he insisted, "take one for him, as well. He's old enough to spill an opera singer's blood," and handed Nikos his own rifle.

"What about my bullets?" Nikos said.

"He's a child," Lambros scathed in response, the administrator ignoring him.

"Don't be greedy, you can share with your father," he told Nikos. "Now teach him how to use the thing before he accidentally shoots one of you in the back," he blurted officiously, climbing into his vehicle.

"Peasants," he said to his associates. "They need to be told how to pee and wash, let alone save themselves. It's a good thing we have them, though, someone must be the vanguard."

———◆———

For several nights after the Timonakis inferno, Olga Stoyanova reappeared to Lambros. Sleepless and weary once again, over the next few days he stole away into the mountains and heard preached a revolution he did not fully understand, pleading the overfed concept of armed resistance before the Italians received their invitation back into the region as pipe-laying day laborers, intending to put a stop to any poetic fraternity among Greeks. Before this frame of mind, he failed to understand that Greece, with her shining seas and bevy of ports, might be an Avenue des Champs-Élysées to the crude oil of North Africa, and thus a perceived line of defense for Fascists. The concept of invasion had little meaning to him. Greece had always fought like a stubborn slave trying to free herself, but somehow he had forgotten this. It came naturally to him to resist entrenched authority. Soon he parroted the opinions he read in the comrade-in-arms weekly, a newspaper, delivered religiously to Yianko's kafenio, filled with petty metaphors for Lenin and Trotsky's venomous tryst and Stalin's theology of slaughter, sterilized and serialized for the common reader as a noble political cleansing, an allegedly true conversion of souls. The idea retrieved from such fervent propaganda, was that the Russians would save Greece.

"I don't believe the Fascists will risk it," Lambros said. "Anyway, what army will want to get where it's going through these mountains?" Alexi laughed at him.

"You're naïve, my boy. Conversion is rarely like Saint Paul's," he warned. "More often it's the consequence of an importunate diet, a one-book doctrine. Everyone north of here has had their noses thumped and disjointed by men who can barely understand Marx, an insightful man, who wrote as if he were permanently constipated."

"Are you trying to be funny, Pater? Complaining about a one-book doctrine! What book does your boss try to sell us if not a cure for every ailment under the sun?"

"Yes, that's true. Christ is the cure for the ailments of the soul," Alexi responded testily, "but you dare to compare such murderers to the Church."

"Speak clearly if you want to persuade me that the voice of the peasant hasn't been heard for a change! The meek will inherit the earth. What horseshit! When is that going to happen? The meek must take what they deserve before they're crushed or pushed into a pit with a lime blanket."

"Do you really think giving power to poor people will help them, or make them live better, Lambro? Who is heaving the horseshit now! Your credo is no different from telling ignoramuses a bit of humor. They laugh for the moment and show their appreciation, but when the humor passes they go back to despising you, resenting you or, if you're lucky, however they felt about you before you told the joke. No, Lambros Lambrou, give them a piece of bread because you want to obey Christ's appeal to all men who have a piece of bread to give. Do nothing to harm them, but offer them nothing more than bread, for ideas like these are curses."

A year earlier, Lambros had ignored the shadowy, nauseous insights accompanying his usual intermittent epiphanies of involuntary memory. All he remembered was his mother's voice whispering to him to pack up his family and leave Lathra. He resolved to visit Yergola and his mother and the graves of his ancestors, but never acted upon the sleepy notion, permitting the day's habits and duties to postpone the discussion with Andreas and Vasili, who would also have wished to make the trip.

On an endless December morning, anticipating a snifter of menace before season's end, as they retrieved ricks of straw left in the fields, the rumble of vehicles and the grinding shuffle of booted footsteps echoed in the distance. With Lambros was the entire brood, including Danäe, assisting in piling up the straw onto mule-drawn wagons. Behind them, beneath a lone mulberry tree, Sophia and Evanthia played and tried catching stones they threw at each other. To the east, in the loll of thigh that was the valley, others in adjoining fields were hurriedly working to the same end. Mechanized squeals and growls lurched across dirt roads. A specter of dark red dust rose into the bright sky. Everyone scurried home, the women and girls chattering and weeping, men distilling wrath and panic already churning from their month on the spit of retaliation along the Yugoslavian frontier. Lambros had also fought there with most of the willing, suitably hard-bitten men who walked home in defeat, cold, hungry, feeling nothing of the brawny theatrics of bards and historians. Now he hurried to the edge of the field and hid his scythe in the beaten down grass behind the tree. As the people began to congregate on the path and approached the village he speculated aloud why this army would want to camp in Lathra, isolated, unserviceable and unconnected to anywhere but Arnissa, and at that by a rugged, narrow road unsuitable for heavy vehicles.

"Listen to Lalas, pretending he's Jartzo! They're here to take our food, to fix our women, and good, and to find new ways to punish us, Lambrou. Why else do you think they've come all this way?" one of his neighbors said behind his back. Lambros turned away, embarrassed and perturbed, but did not recognize the voice. The women's voices subsided. No one else said a word. Arriving in the village by cart and on foot, the mechanized convoy nearly overtook them on the road. Immediately ordered to gather in the square, the dearth of men became obvious to the already incensed skull and cross bones legion and their entourage of uniformed doctors, engineers, guards and cooks. They were tall, gray, fit but hungry looking men, walking and speaking with a kind of confidence and arrogance they had never seen before, not even in Turks. Death tainted the skin, the shape of the mouth always slightly agape, and the tongue between the lips, as if the task of killing required some great concentration. They had walked from Paris to Belgrade, someone whispered, sniped at and throat slit for weeks by starving Serbians, kindred mountain goats whom the enemy could neither find nor kill sufficient numbers of their clansmen to lure them out into the open. Now they were corralling Greeks. In no mood for hide and seek, the Lathrans were given until dusk to reassemble en mass or suffer the consequences. Not a word of vulturine guidelines and cackles was understood, except by Danäe, whose tongue stuck to the roof of her mouth and whose teeth chattered.

The Lambrou home became the Colonel's quarters, Elissa his personal maid, and the children, like wretched urchins of another woman, made to sleep in goat stables and inside the empty *ambari*, to eat scraps of food normally left for the pigs and to witnesses their mother's humiliation and abuse. The Colonel, a generally preoccupied man, an optician by training, constantly cleaned his glasses and inspected the integrity of the wire frames. An amateur violist, the Colonel was stuck on Hindemith's Opus II *Viola Sonata*, humming the theme repeatedly, between denouncing the serialists as "goddamn noise makers," the Russians as propagandists, the English as plagiarists and the Americans as propagators of the musically lewd and formless wailings of the Negro promoted by the usurious Jew. To his men, he was a prototype of the famous Reichsmarschall, sharing in the rumor of degenerate inclinations because of his violent intolerance of rapes of Serbian women. He had personally executed a seasoned soldier for the depravity of removing a woman's breasts with a bayonet. The *Gelding* his men called him.

"He has no rifle to unload," they whispered among themselves. His immediate staff knew better. His wife was dapper and his two children with her in Stuttgart, Erwin and Madeleine, whose photos he posted next to where he laid his head. His wife's photo was of a painfully thin flapper, short-skirted, plunging neckline and the optical illusion of spikes beneath a beaded blouse taken at a cabaret frequented in Berlin, a useful photo in his loneliness, the only image that worked for him. He also read poetry avidly, reciting Holderlin, Trakl, Rilke and others.

"Gibt es wirklich die Zeit, die zerstörende?"[73] he projected as if on stage.

"Listen to the crazy ass-trimmer," his men would tell each other on hearing him.

———◆———

Privation and fear of severance from family and home caused the natural rebelliousness and angst of adolescence to hide its normally hideous head, not only for Nikos, but also for the late-blooming and somewhat more coddled Stratos and Sophia. Even amidst the stagnant tempo of a provincial existence, where whole years vanish from memory like blank, unnoted faces in a crowd, Nikos subjugated his puberty and its hormonal surges. He resented his father and brother for vanishing into the mountains and leaving him behind but, as intended, took upon himself the duty of watching over his sisters and mother, especially his mother, to ensure in his mind that she was not more than a housemaid for their captors. He began by intercepting and interrupting the Colonel's private directives, any commands that seemed to take on an unusually aggressive or improperly flattering tenor, usually delivered with a combination of Greek stippled German and gestures, offering to complete the demanded task himself. As the days plodded on and boredom set in, the Colonel's mischievousness turned to leering. His tastes seemed suddenly to incline toward the exotic terra of Elissa's Anatolian textures and he began making comments and suggestions regarding the terminus of a neglected mother's needs. Nikos understood the remarks through the redolence of tone in the lurid responses of the

---

73 Does it really exist, this destroyer, Time?

Colonel's subordinates. He laid awake at night beneath the veranda, adjacent to the room in the house where his mother slept, deprived of sleep, exposed to the elements, straining to distinguish between the creaking floorboards of her insomnia and any surreptitious footsteps crossing the floor and approaching her bed mat. He heard none, but had fallen asleep on more than a few occasions and was never quite sure and accomplished his tasks by day, barely awake, snatching sleep when his mother made her way to the lake for water. He suffered the panic of his imagination and remorse over his failed vigilance. Elissa reassured him, but this was no help. She wept for her weary son as she watched him work. No one learned whether the Colonel acted on his compulsion, but one night Nikos heard the floorboards crackling. He could not tell if they were in the room his mother now occupied or from his parent's room. The noise reminded him of the ballast in the fishing boat, like ropes pulled taunt against a wooden frame. The sounds lasted long enough to fuel his fears and followed with lighter footsteps. He lay hopelessly awake that night.

In the morning, Nikos quietly worked his way to where an axe was stored in a wooden box, where his father had kept an old assortment of tools hidden, behind a barrel below the veranda. He hid it himself, near where he slept. That night the sounds in the house repeated. His mother betrayed nothing the next day. The following morning the Colonel awoke first and was alone at the latrine his men had made of a small tree behind the house, well beyond the shaded outhouse.

"They hate us so much they won't even use our shithouse," Nikos told Sophia. He walked toward the barrel, grabbed the axe, tucked it beneath his shirt and hurried behind the house. He spotted the Colonel and hesitated for a moment standing by the outhouse, watching him pee facing the lake, turning in profile and smiling as if he were enjoying the view. By now he could hear that his subordinates were awake and descending the steps to the courtyard. He heard his mother calling for his assistance. He would have to kill him without making a sound. He placed a good size rock in his pocket and waited for the Colonel to stop shaking his pecker. He would have to bury the axe in his skull and stuff the rock in his mouth to keep him from making noise. Then he would drag the body by the legs the twenty meters or so to the edge of the cliffs above the steep descent to the lake and push him over. He would circle around the back of the neighbor's abandoned house and come running down the dirt road toward the courtyard, as if responding to his mother's calls. They would not find the body easily. It would wedge in the dark shadows between the large rocks. When finally they would find him, they would assume the assassination was the work of partisans and likely shoot every male in the village to avenge his death. Nikos quietly slipped to the far side of the outhouse and waited. The Colonel walked by. He was taller than he first appeared. Nikos did nothing. When questioned, Elissa insisted that the sound he heard was the Colonel's insomnia, his suffering by night for his murders by day.

———◆———

Danäe and Dimitra aroused immediate interest among a handful of the soldiers, along with three much younger girls. All of them stripped, deloused and then, before sampling, made to bathe in frigid Vegoritis. Shivering with cold, they waded into the lake. Dimitra held fast to Danäe's shoulders, pressing herself against her back for what warmth she could find. The captors stood by the shore laughing, ogling the refraction of floating breasts. Two of the younger girls cried uncontrollably, one feeding off the other's terror, a third, wide-eyed and simply numb to her torment, fainted. A soldier waded in fully clothed and slapped the younger girls, who were afraid to venture too deep, demanding that they stop. The faint one, no more than a malnourished thirteen, was dragged away and not seen until later, in the back of a transport truck. Danäe suggested that at some point they make a run together for Mavrotripa. Dimitra, who developed the beginnings of a warm and promising bond with Andreas, after appearing so lovely at his brother's wedding, could not.

"No, Danäe," she whispered, her susurration of lips a barely audible tremolo. "I'm afraid to run."

"Not now, in broad daylight, silly," Danäe replied, her teeth chattering. "At night, when they're asleep," she said turning her around and embracing her, looking at her as if she were a child, wiping the blemish of her tears. The soldiers, now drunk and impatient, howled in entertainment.

"Look at the lovebirds," one of them crooned.

"What happens until then?" Dimitra asked her.

"We'll have to endure what they have in store for us today, but as darkness falls we can escape, we can hide and then make our way into the mountains to find our *andartes.*"[74]

"I can't leave my son and go hide in the mountains," Dimitra said, haunted by her predicament and the choice being offered to her. "If some harm befalls him, what would I do? What would I be?"

Danäe made her escape before nightfall, alone. A dilute and violet haze had ascended from the lake. Nerve-rankled trigger fingers fired at ricochets, discharges echoing into the hills and along the spine. The soldiers had left her unattended for a moment as attention fell upon the young girl who fainted and a weepy, shivering Dimitra.

"We'll take her first," the ringleader had said of Dimitra. He was a Bulgarian, an officer who had rounded up a handful of obsessive types among the more beastly regulars. "She still has some meat on her bones and nice milky tits."

"She needs warming up anyway," another said. "Look at her shaking like a leaf! Don't bite me with your chattering little teeth, my winking doll, with your big mouth and those luscious lips."

"We'll save the giraffe for last," the Bulgarian said laughing, fondling Danäe. As he rambled on, the most brutal of her captors bit Dimitra on the lips, drawing blood. When she yelped with pain, he slapped her across the buttocks, pulled her to him and planted a trail of cognac and stale tobacco bite marks across her face and shoulders.

"The giraffe could raise the cock on a dead man," a third agreed. The cool evening air placed the gang of them on the move. Naked and trembling beneath the blanket draped about her shoulders, they dragged Dimitra from beneath the arms into the rear of the transport truck, parked out of earshot and prying eyes.

"Leave the damn doors open so we don't sweat to death," the Bulgarian said. Facing the scene, Katerina and her Jartzo had huddled beneath the far corner of the two wooden steps to their hovel, hiding and watching what the girls suffered.

---

74 αντάρτες - Greek partisans

"She resisted and they gave it back to her." Katerina later told Doxiades of his sister's ordeal. "What's the point of resisting? The younger girls squirmed and winced and put their hands in front and behind them to protect themselves, but mostly they cried for their mothers." The next morning, pointed back in the direction of her brother's house, Dimitra stumbled home, feverish and coughing, her body and clothes sullied and caked with blood and feces.

Danäe hid in Mavrotripa for eight days. No anadartes came for her. The lack of food and water induced apparitions of her parents. Bats and rodents tore at her clothing and hair and bit at her wounds. She staggered into the courtyard and collapsed, dehydrated, starving, virtually unrecognizable. Elissa and Sophia put her up in the sheep stalls and nursed her. She wheezed and coughed into a pillow to keep from drawing attention. She had a fever, deep bruises and open sores about her arms, hips and across her back, from her abusers and having fallen from the grotto at night attempting to climb down in her delirium. Every hacking expulsion traumatized her emaciated body, but her consumptive appearance deterred the type of curiosity reserved for Dimitra, who within days found herself returned to the truck.

Clever kobolds as they were and not fooled by her disappearance, the band of rouges obtained permission to discover where Danäe had concealed herself. Late at night, they burst into the stable where she was sleeping and confronted her. She refused to speak. The interrogation lasted over an hour. Danäe believed her end had come. Batons to the buttocks, nipples and orifices, the shoulder blades, elbows and kneecaps firmed up before she fainted, then dragged by the hair before Elissa and the children. A more enraged beating would have followed but Elissa intervened.

"Tell them what they want," she begged, "or my children will be next."

"*Onlar orada saklanıyor olabilir!*" (They may be hiding there!) Danäe said in stymied Turkish, terrified but defiant, her face already swelling, an airborne backhand making pottage of her mouth before she could finish. The interrogator pulled a knotted plait of hair, twisting her neck unnaturally. The other pointed his rifle at her heart. *Die dritte schnauzer* pulled at her lower lip with his forefinger and thumb, and dropping his baton, pulled out and plugged his Lugar between her teeth. Elissa betrayed the secret of Mavrotripa straight away and was herself subjected to the black leather tendril.

Two Herculean farm boys from Perea were indeed hiding in Mavrotripa. They had known of Danäe and volunteered to retrieve her but arrived a day late. The firefight for Mavrotripa lasted for more than an hour. The boys killed six of the Huns, with nearly double that wounded, before mounting their last stand and dying with eyes spitting fire and hands wringing the bulging jugulars of their enemy. The great door of Mavrotripa vanished. Many of Lazaro's books and papers were rudely thrown into the lake. But the impetus for the search ended and the interest in Danäe had defrayed, bruised and emaciated as they left her.

Narlis, her violinist, who by then had frequented Lathra weekly to be near his betrothed, eloped into craggy anonymity with the rest of the younger men from the village. There, the andartes planned and conducted ultimately futile guerilla raids, like gnats about the tired eyes of a lizard sunning itself, which with the flick of the tongue not only alleviates the irksome buzz but also manages a quick morsel. Nevertheless, the pests (the loathed *Heide*) succeeded in waylaying the plans of those vacationing Knights of Acre, whose desire was to leave Athenian puppets dangling under taunt strings and then exit gracefully to join their comrades for some vocational pillage from the Carpathian steppes through the plains of Belarus. For their part, the andartes, as Greeks always have, undermined their own splendid efforts, and quarreled over whether to furl or wave the flags of doctrine garlanded by Josip Broz, summoning a fury and bloodlust from all sides. Civilians suffered the usual accusation of harboring and feeding one side or another when all they really fretted was whether enough trahana was on hand to fill the swelling bellies of their children. The few words sputtering from the mouths of peasantry became the curse of their contention. Humble servants of proffered flesh found punctured by the pincer, set upright and then aright in the iron maiden of ideology.

Elissa managed well to stave off abduction and starvation for Nikos and her girls, Stratos being with his father. When they complained of their meager rations, she reminded them that the Lacedaemonians of antiquity viewed drinking the broth of boiled bones as a source of potency, the holy marrow of a warrior's nourishment.

Lambros occupied a mysterious cave called *Parthena*, difficult to find in the midst of a formidable rise of mountain moonscape. Allegedly named by early Christians who hid from pagan mobs and later Muslim avengers, the cavern prompted prayers to the Virgin, by anyone daring to scale its barely navigable bluffs, or for the strength and courage to attempt the seemingly suicidal climb from the north face. Vasili, Andreas, Yianko, Praxitellis, Thomas Halkias and Gregorios Narlis (who knew nothing of Andreas' affections for his betrothed), a half dozen other native sons and a few like-minded partisans from Arnissa, Perea, Farangi, Agios Panteléimon and Drosia joined Lambros and fashioned a competing guerilla front in the epifocal of a staggered formation running southeast, along Vegoritis. Terrzellos, Pavlides, Gallanos and the balance of Lathran and other regional fighters aligned themselves with a troop of royalists and republicans and joined a larger contingent, the remnants of a previously decimated battalion of the regular army taking position along both flanks of this arc of resistance. Not really at its center, but tactically the most concealed position, Lambro's partisans could only be exposed in Parthena under the ripe circumstances of perfidy or stupidity, the latter being the more common variety of treason.

The republican command loosely coordinated its miniscule battalions engaging in any harassing actions along the roads, where the enemy seemed wedded for its own safety. The partisans had been quite successful destroying bridges to slow the German advance. As luck concocted, the center of the arc consistently drew the task of the less clandestine daylight missions, exposing their maneuvers to detection and intense retaliation by artillery and tank fire, forcing them to retreat into Parthena and its skeletal haunts. On the twentieth day of their Faustian gambit, after a failed assassination of two enemy guards assigned to detain a group of hapless women returning from the fields with their aprons full of a dead neighbors' discarded belongings, a series of skirmishes sparked, further fracturing the resistance movement. Among the casualties of those skirmishes was Savas, the strong-willed middle son of Menelaus Terzellos. The boy had argued violently with his father over their respective political and ministerial affiliations.

"I disown the mongrel," Terzellos had said and spat at his son, hitting his jacket pocket near and dear to that myocardium of ideas where he kept a copy of a celebrated epistolary to the trodden laborer. The boy's mother, Voula Terzellos, preferred indifference on such subjects but felt obliged to remain loyal to her husband, a type of tail-wagging faith in his blind rage that usually cost her dearly. Naively, she joined in the tirade against her son thinking the consequences would be harmlessly temporary, as they always had. She pulled his hair, slapped and humiliated him.

"Did I give birth to this boy?" she lamented theatrically, in public, rendering her son hopeless for his galactorrhea, the interminable queue for his birthright. Only peripherally involved in the military maneuvers, in this, his very first campaign, Savas officially fought under the command of his father but counted himself a rabid Titoist. A more than adequate tirailleur and thus meant to be reserved for long distance assassinations, Lambros, appealing to his philosophical affiliations, asked Savas to move forward on a bluff of bosky boulders in support of the center position. A splintered slither of granite from an indiscriminate mortar bounced off the bright back of Parthena and struck Savas in the eye. The pebble penetrated through the cerebrum to a vortex unknown and darkened all that swam before him. His heart, however, beat again, as the scullion of his father's remorse. Crazed with anger, perhaps more than sorrow, over what he perceived to be the ineffectual tactic of the center, Terzellos tore his hair, vowing revenge upon the "*koproskila*[75] that lured my Savas to his downfall." Lambros lost four men in the brief skirmish with the reincarnate reduviids[76] and arranged for a fifth, Thomas Halkias, having suffered a wound to his pelvis and left leg, to be smuggled back to Edessa. Thomas survived, but treated as he was in his father's untidy factory, on a bed of fermenting sawdust, his leg became infected and required amputation. In the gangrene of his delirium, he also blamed Lambros and his tactics, a quite expected conclusion. He could not believe that orders had been issued to hold the inescapably defensive position, the orders no more the fault of the lieutenant upholding them than the dead lying around him. Fortunately, for Vasili, whose reputation and Halkian inheritance might have been at stake, the guide accompanying Thomas home contradicted his bitter version of the battle.

---

75 τά κοπρόσκυλα – literally the dung dogs or the dirty dogs

76 hemipterous vampires, creeping, crawling assassins pining for Jutland

While the loss of his leg certainly burdened Thomas Halkias, it was his apparent inability to obtain an erection, something never spoken of, for which he needed someone or something to blame. A lesser man with so illustrious a past as a womanizer might have undone himself, but not Thomas. Soon fitted with a crude prosthetic leg, dangling next to his once celebrated member, he wistfully dubbed his new prop his "instrument of destruction." Thomas was short by any standard, and his rather narrow, ill fitted appendage hung from just above his knee to the floor. If he leaned to the right on his cane, the prosthesis swayed fitfully from beneath his long coat. Spurred by his misery and resentment, in a pantomime of vulgarity quite unlike the man who had once taken his steps carefully but confidently with two feet, he would remove the prosthesis, his flying buttress, for it bowed a bit, and set it between his legs beneath a piece of cloth or his buttoned coat.

"I think I'll go to Moscow someday and find myself a Bolshevik she-devil that can accommodate my new instrument of destruction," he would say caustically to the men at the factory.

"What will you destroy, Thomas?" the men would ask in a singsong riposte, already knowing the answer.

"Asses," Thomas would respond with the nip of cruelty in his ouzo-fleeced vocals. "Stalinist she-asses." The men would roll with requisite laughter no matter how often repeated. Vasili, having taken Lambro's lead, abandoned the breadbasket of leftist propaganda. Short of removing the yoke of slavery, he believed that the whole notion of revolt was nothing but political juvenility and eventually persuaded Thomas of Lambro's innocence. He reminded him that his survival depended upon Lambro's decision to order needed fighters away from the front to escort him home.

"Lambros is not a man who joins with others lightly," Vasili told him afterwards. "The pursuit must have some ante for his kin," he explained to his dour brother in-law. "He cares less than you think about the hounds of doctrine."

Terzellos reacted swiftly and caustically to the death of Savas. He befriended the local republican commander from Edessa and persuaded him to order another synchronized raid, at dawn, when the enemy would not yet have stirred, he argued, but also when they would have all of daylight to track their attackers. The audacious plan was to bomb two fixed depots, small, heavily guarded buildings where munitions were stored, with one narrow dirt lane in and out. The mission required a small contingent of men to feign a frontal attack between the two depots, less than a half-kilometer between each, long enough to permit the flanking partisans to drive vehicles loaded with previously confiscated explosives and steer them in the right direction.

Preceding this second raid was the capture of three partisans, two locals and a Serbian mercenary, somewhat familiar with the location of the center position, if not the cavern Parthena proper. If Terzellos knew of their capture, he did not understand the consequences. At least one of the captured might try to save himself and betray Parthena's existence. Immediately, he moved his flanking troops on the right to higher ground and notified the left by messenger. The center never got the news of the capture, not that it would have made much difference. As the blood of dawn pierced the indigo of the sky, Lambros initiated the planned incursion, the action designed to draw the enemy away from the depots. He expected to conceal his men once the pressure-relieving raids and explosions from the flanks occurred. The flanking raids never transpired; the depot not approached by the partisans to the left, and the right never getting the vehicle close enough to detonate its cargo. The center was exposed and quickly enveloped, making escape back into Parthena a treacherous affair.

After interrogation and before the three tormented andartes were to be hand-and-leg bound and taken to the wall of Yianko's kafenio, the oldest prisoner, a farmer from Farangi, wishing to save his second eyeball from the hot poker of extraction, confessed the correct coordinates of partisan positions including, roughly, the passage to the womb of Parthena. For what malady of the flabbergasted and speechless does glowing iron not provide a cure? That same day, the tortured confessor, conspicuously absent, saw the two remaining captives shot in the compulsory presence of Lathran elders and a handful of women and children. Beaten mercilessly, the Serbian could barely stand and indeed had fallen over twice before being propped against Yianko's wall. For some reason, the Colonel seemed compelled to shoot both men at once. Death appeared to the observer to be the true reprieve. Neither of the partisans was Lathran, producing a less animated expression of pity in the women, already hardened with the spasmodic trivium[77] of violence and mayhem, dragged along like a big dog on a leash. The lack of reaction puzzled and infuriated the captors.

"These people deserve to die," the sergeant told his officers. The interrogation of the two men extracted specious coordinates mapped from the blood-coaxed avowals of those who knew they would die anyway. They knew nothing of the one-eyed farmer having already extorted from him the nearly perfect crosshair for Parthena.

All but obliteration resulted, a merciless, sunrise artillery barrage; *ich bin der Geist der stets verneint,*[78] the infantry meeting the column of scurrying ants as they attempted to escape caverns and hideouts collapsing upon them like the endless wrath of volcano gods, Goethe's pagan, a clever croupier at the gaming table for men's souls. Most of the contingent from Edessa and all of the cortege from Arnissa vanished, melting into sartorial rags, untreated wounds, exposure and dehydration in the cold graves of Parthena's weft of crevasses. Some of Lambro's immediate contingent hid deeper in the rocks, weathering the bombardment, gambling that their pursuers would not enter Parthena's unplumbed pit merely to confirm a body count.

A full day passed before Vasili and Lambros ventured out of the burrow to scout another, less obvious route leading down the most precipitous footpath to the north and spilling onto the road to Arnissa. Continuing the stunning bad luck, they encountered a patrol passing near the base of the descent, revealing that otherwise secreted passage and making retreat a harrowing ascent as they climbed for cover amid vitreous rocks and sylvan crow fodder. The main trail was all granite, roughly the width of the dead mule rotting across it, and as hotly disputed as any fight in such close quarters. Vasili argued for immediate withdrawal, a bold attempt to escape under darkness, the idea being that the unfamiliarity of the terrain would neutralize any advantage in guns. The enemy accommodated, dug in and erected machine gun nests, showering bullets on each egress they had discovered, drizzling mortar rounds on the supposed coordinates for the cave and as was apt to happen, on the correct ones as well.

---

77 The medieval study of logic, grammar and rhetoric.

78 I am the spirit that ever denies (Goethe *Faust*, i.)

No stay of fulminations and recrimination occurred that night. A debate renewed between Vasili and a Perean partisan who had wished to remain in the lair for as long as they could and then escape to the south, along a route the enemy had not seen yet, a route requiring rappelling down twenty or so meters of cliff when they possessed but one rope, measured at only fifteen meters. Vasili thought the partisans would starve or grow desperate for water very quickly. The enemy could wait them out before reducing their numbers around their position. Even if the ammunition lasted, the end was certain. Neither option was good. Lambros was visibly fretful, aggrieved at having included his son in the dismal affair. They slept that night with death as a sentry and awoke the next morning to the sounds of crows and vultures circling about the mule's carcass and fighting over the bleary eyes and swollen tongues of dead men. Lambros awoke realizing that he had slept through the night. No fires raged in his mind's eye. All of his trepidation was there before him, balanced upon the razor's edge of the cave. Indeed, the only thing he remembered was a voice, his own, he surmised, but an unknown voice nonetheless, proclaiming authoritatively commanding the choice. In the morning, the debate resumed. A cold, fitful sleep changed no one's mind. Lambros grew sullen and unapproachable, but when the deliberations intensified again, he finally stood and offered his verdict as the official commander of the unit.

"Stratos, you will remain behind," he said. He was not prepared to raise the knife of his son's sacrifice. "Keep what little water and bread remains. We'll lull them into believing the cave is empty. Whatever happens in the end, they'll assume all of us have died or, if any of us make it through, that we've slipped into the mountains. One of you must stay with my son," he said, addressing the whole body of his troupe but looking directly at the Perean. Suddenly, the Perean changed his mind and stepped among his local comrades, who all opted for escape.

"Two of you can last here for another few days. Then, with any luck, you can make your way to Arnissa unmolested. Whatever you do, don't go back home. They'll take revenge on Lathra after this fiasco. If they are still searching this godforsaken hole after our bones are scattered by the birds, then you must decide whether to hide your weapons and surrender or to turn southwest and head for Maniaki and those parts. If you surrender, grab a tool and make them think you are villagers on the way to work, stumbled upon by chance." Then he turned to Stratos and lowered his voice. "If you chose this route, my boy, you have to adapt to survive their wrath," he said, each word weighted down with the cadence of dread. "At best, they'll send you to a prison somewhere up north. It will be cold. You will be hungry. They will mistreat you."

"I don't want to stay in this tomb," Stratos pled. "Let me fight my way out with you."

"Stratos, my son," he stuttered, "I can't let you do this."

"Why?" Stratos implored. A confused and frightened look shed the years from him. His father shook his head. "Please, baba," he begged, ignoring protocol and his father's rank.

"Listen to me!" Lambros said firmly. "This is the better chance for you." Stratos looked at him with an expression his father had seen only once before, when he had beaten him believing he had hurt Sophia in a quarrel. Stratos wanted to mask the panic he felt. He stepped away and adopted a distant attitude, ignoring him, walking to the mouth of the cave, peering up about the cliffs towering above him. But he couldn't contain his emotion and tears filled his eyes. Lambros now adopted a more insistent tone.

"Andreas, it's my preference that you stay behind with Stratos and return him to his mother. You're the strongest among us. God preserve me if her son doesn't return to her." Andreas suffered the decision before he spoke. "I leave this decision to you, but I am asking you, cousin."

"I understand that you want to save your son, but I also prefer to fight with you and my brother," Andreas responded, dispensing a pained sigh into the sunless echo of the cave. Lambros looked at him with hands plunged into his pockets, as if searching for the last coins of a pauper's plea.

"As you wish," Lambros said with patent disappointment. "Who'll stay with my son?" No one responded. "Andreas," he repeated, "Vasili can also stay with you if he wishes, but you'll have less to drink, less time to last. We're down to a few swallows of water as it is."

"That won't be necessary, Lambros," Vasili interrupted, moving closer to Andreas, laying his arm on his shoulder and offering him a cigarette, which he refused. "Brother, what do you say? We have followed our cousin halfway across the continent and back again to come to this end. Someone of our clan and its tarnish on this earth should survive all of this, don't you think?" He hesitated. "Do this for me." Andreas set his weapon down, but said nothing, always prepared to listen to his normally taciturn brother. "I'll see you again, my brother, on the shores of Yergola, or perhaps laid out by the boatman on another Vegoritis," Vasili said, valor swelling his voice. Andreas relented and turned his head away. The men emptied their pockets and knapsacks. The few morsels remaining to them they left for the two that would remain in Parthena to tell the tale.

The starlit night strained its rift of cold across their necks. Lambros led his men and crept down the footpath toward the narrow mouth of the pass and the mule's carcass. Approaching midnight, fatigued with stooping and crawling in a slow, snaking progress, Lambros risked rising to his feet as he neared the road, entering a thicket of leafless saplings, thistles and waist high thorns. The thorns made an unmistakable sound scraping against cloth. At first it was quiet but as the last of them stood, the plucky leader of the runic echelon detected a whinny of an uncontrolled cough from poor nerve racked Praxitellis, who was shot by a sniper and given a third nostril. A mêlée ensued. One of the few pitched spitting matches anyone survived to recollect in such honeycombed terrain, normally abandoned to partisan lazars. The battle raged uninterrupted and at close range. Rifles dry-fired and the matter fell to knives, fists and rocks splintering skulls. Lambros dispatched two attackers at once, a gory affair, maiming the first with a bullet from the man's own pistol, a shot through the jaw, and then a second shot between the shoulders. The other man he killed with his sailor's stiletto thrust beneath his arm, twisting and lacerating the lungs. When the man did not die and kept trying to get to his feet, Lambros applied the steel to his throat. Bruised, bloodied and exhausted, Lambros, Yianko, Vasili and a wounded Narlis had escaped and crawled their way to a grove, arriving at the cemetery near the entrance of the village by waning moonlight. By night's end, the rest of his men had laid in contorted heaps, men whose names were engraved in the memory of their comrades but otherwise were lost. No one counted how many of the enemy had been dispossessed of their light, but the enemy command reconsidered its plan to leave the region unscathed, to be content with simply controlling the roads running southeast to Thessaloniki.

A coordinated castigation of the region followed, unprovoked sentences and summary executions, old men, women and boys as young as Nikos Lambrou, even the tzobano's sheepdogs, the indiscriminate torching of houses and stables and the undignified lopping of any remaining burgess of local governance. For Lathra, this was fated to be Yianko. After digging out from under his rocky shroud in Parthena, fighting and crawling his way to survival, he hid his rifle and returned to his wife and children to risk reopening the kafenio. Vasili and Lambros tried to dissuade him but he put it bluntly.

"Living a little is more valuable than the honor of braggarts whose courage always surfaces in the past tense." He returned to his wife and daughters, squeezing and hugging them until they insisted he bathe. His own children may have inadvertently given him away, innocently squealing with joy when their father appeared, resurrected, black-bearded but in one piece, or Katerina may have betrayed him. No one knew. She despised Yianko for an affront from the past and refused to speak to him. He had publicly mocked her long ago, for appearing in church with wetness on the business end of her dress, and then when she confronted him, accused her of having spiders for lovers. That morning she had motioned a local youth toward Yianko's door, a youth later thought to have been a collaborator simply because he survived, having not fought with either camp of partisans, a boy, who along with his name, disappeared from the hieroglyphs of Lathran memory. Barely a day passed for Yianko, returning to the bosom of his contentment and a sequestered cask of cognac, before a handful of soldiers seized him without discussion or interrogation and tied his hands behind him, while his wife and daughters pled for his life. Yianko craned his head back, searing his last moments into his wife's testimony. Shot impatiently, as if they had somewhere to go, he fell in a heap next to the wall of the outbuilding a few meters from where Avram had discovered Maria. Having nowhere to go, the soldiers lingered over his body, smoking, laughing, and drinking his cognac. News of Yianko's execution spread within hours.

"Not even a cigarette or a drink as a last gesture." Umbrage made its way up to the ears of andartes. Lambros was despondent. He waited a few hours and then in a gamble for survival, made his way by nightfall to beg for Calliope's assistance, asking her to instruct Elissa to leave Lathra for Arnissa in a specific manner.

"She should leave openly, by daylight," as he and Elissa had discussed in hushed tones on the starlit evening just a few days before he left with Stratos for their rendezvous in the razor-toothed craters of Parthena. Lambros had fully expected his own to be among the corpses satiating Teutonic appetites. Now, he was unsure whether to stay and risk rescuing his son and Andreas or flee and hope his original plan would work. He had faith in Andreas' skills and courage, but sleeplessness brought on indecision, sapped his strength and clouded his judgment.

Everyone predicted the impending struggle between partisan leagues, deducing that it would fuel itself into a blood feud far worse than any known before, and they all expected its eruption, without reprieve, as soon as the current occupiers would tire of the region. Terzello's zeal also reached a furious pitch. In his more scathing retelling of the circumstances surrounding the death of Savas, he gauged his own resentment on the ill feelings festering in others and cast all the blame upon Lambros. When he failed to convince whoever listened to his rants, he read more malice into his own biting exchanges with Lambros over the waters of Vegoritis, more than had existed at the time, since these episodes went largely un-witnessed. Finally, he recalled the incident involving Spiros, if only to justify his regrets and being talked out of retribution. In a drunken fit of anger, after contradiction by Gallanos on the issue, he offered a sizable bounty for Lambro's head on a pike. "So I can piss in his mouth and shit on his scalp," he said, deranged with hatred.

The following afternoon, Elissa hurried Danäe and the children into packing a tiny donkey cart with provisions and winter clothing and shouldered a satchel of food and effects for their missing father and brother. The overburdened animal sensed their anxiety and once hitched, brayed uncontrollably. Elissa whipped him into submission and finally embarked upon the escape to Arnissa in a disheveled state and with her nerves frayed. Danäe, still recovering from the wounds suffered in her fall and interrogation, resisted leaving at first, wishing not to desert Narlis without word of his wellbeing or demise, but interest from a less than timorous suitor, a salivating, bushy-eyed Prussian, helped change her mind. The Prussian had along with the Bulgarian selected her from the start, and now crowed gleefully at the sight of Danäe up and walking again.

"I'll split her like a log," he boasted. Seeing him hanging about the courtyard quickly convinced her to abandon her station. In the meantime, her sojourning violinist, Narlis, collapsed of his wound, and while not affecting a vital organ, his injury remained untreated. In the midst of preparations for transport, he nearly succumbed to his fever, his sweaty, lovelorn head resting upon a comrade's lap. Surviving the transport to Thessaloniki, Narlis did not return to Lathra or to Danäe, and so lingered the missing motif to her heart, the undeveloped lyric of Eros.

Elissa harried her brood in an effort to comply with her husband's message and instructions. She rushed about looking for her gold coins, but in her haste could not remember where she moved them, after years of their lying behind the same stone cranny in the foundation. She had relocated them, years earlier, because a niggling Jartzo had learned where she hid them. While mostly ignored, the movements of refugees prompted an occasional interrogation or reprisal depending on whether the contraband was human or commoditized. On this day, among those who owned no land in Lathra other than the piddling plot on which their houses perched like bird droppings, who all but gave up hope of obtaining safe passage to their work along overrun roads and sparse rail routes, few if any families were departing. Elissa waited nervously until midmorning when finally, prepared to risk the attention, she found herself following Kyria Arianna Devazoglou, a quiet woman who lived in a cluster of three homes just beyond the schoolhouse. Arianna and her mother, infirmed with a nagging cough and a color to her complexion betraying illness, and two malnourished children, entered the village square en route to Veroia where Arianna's husband had found work but from which he had failed to return. Her evacuation comprised of a small horse pulled wagon (the horse having returned alone a week after her husband failed to appear) loaded with nothing more than the old woman, the younger of her daughters, a large cloth wrapped about enough bread for the journey, an urn of water and a carpet bag full of clothing and spare shoes. What was left of Arianna's family progressed unnoticed.

Elissa and her party lurched out into the square. As they passed before Yianko's kafenio, the soldiers gathering for a drink and something to eat glanced over at them. With an abrupt swipe of his hand, a young captain ordered them detained. Elissa watched Kyria Devazoglou trundle out of view, beyond the bend in the road. A few women passing by looked on with apprehension. Cloaked from head to foot in black, the soldiers nevertheless recognized Danäe. Her lips quivered and face turned ghostly as batons pressed beneath her chin and below the small of her back, tilting her gaze toward the blazing sun. The Colonel was occupied, sitting inside Pavlides' kafenio with his adjuncts and generally unaware. Danäe's ardent Prussian was at that moment predisposed on the shores of Vegoritis, hammering other maidens among the rocks. The interrogation ended as quickly as it began when the captain, failing to understand garbled pleas, interpreted black scarves and dresses as a sign of recent widowhood. Permission to leave finally came with a diversion enacted by the widow Tasoula Praxitellis and Yianko's eldest daughter. Until then, Tasoula had been as quiet as a church mouse but within days of her recent widowhood, she was emboldened and uncaring of her own safety. Both women called the officers over, one right after the other, hands trembling. Tasoula lured them to the terrace with chinking tumblers of cognac. The women's eyes met.

"Goodbye, daughter," Tasoula said.

The journey took the rest of the day. On the way, they passed a blot of burned-out cottages and mangled vehicles smoldering with dead patriots striking posthumous poses and stragglers wandering around carrying water and looking for food, but the passage ended without harassment. Once in Arnissa, preoccupied with a ferment of partisan executions, Praxitellis' brother provided them a place to sleep in the backroom of his leather shop, where they would anxiously await the return of Stratos and his father.

A month later, the grapevine provided Danäe news of Narlis, of his recovery and return to Thessaloniki. She neither wept nor sought solace in prayer, but lit a candle for him in the vacant church, the only candle she could find, a nearly wickless finger on the floor of the narthex. Bulgarians had shot the local priest a month earlier. As a result, no one attended church and no candles were on hand. His replacement took one look at the condition of the church and a shaggy greater Arnissa and retreated to St. Gregorios, a lovely chapel overlooking a quiet little cove along Vegoritis' northern shore, along with some roaming fugitives he sought to hide and feed.

Starved and dehydrated after four arid days and cold nights, having resorted to drinking the muddy drizzle and dew from a trickle between the rocks, Andreas and Stratos agreed between them to make a run for the lake rather than permit a bile bouquet of urine to be their next day's hydration. They had lasted a whole day and night longer than Lambros anticipated and fled unnoticed, since, as Lambros gambled, Parthena appeared abandoned to her nocturnal snakes and rodents. Reunited with his father in the forests to the northeast, after messengers alerted the partisans of their whereabouts and before a foolhardy rescue was necessary, Stratos greeted his father as if he were the resurrected Christ. Unlike Stratos, who as he grew rarely acknowledged his militarisms or his captivity within the clutch of Parthena, Andreas was never to be the unflappable, affable Promethean again. His nerves over the safety of his ward unraveled the psychic protuberance of the experience. Soon, as nearly everyone observed, he adopted the impatience and volatility more often attributed to his cousin, which indeed only fit Lambros in his youth, but lingered on as his reputation. Gone in Andreas was his friendly smile, his warmth and sincere curiosity in what one had to say to him. He appeared to look past the speaker now, even when addressed casually, reserved his comments nearly completely and grew cross if one insisted he participate in this or that conversation or activity. He observed Danäe as if she were a wisp of smoke from a man's pipe, his brother as if he were looking indifferently into the mirror and at Lambros with something less than gratitude as if he had saved his life, for his intuition told him as much. He repeated, when asked, that the odds were that he would have died in the fight to escape Parthena. Even his face appeared changed.

"He looks like an insatiable wolf," Theodora said, an andartisa now, but still enamored of Andreas and still accusing Danäe of entrapping him for no purpose, to no conclusion and to the detriment of other available young women. From then on, the andartes called him Borzoi (a Russian wolfhound).

———◆———

Lathra wilted and festered in her vacancy, abandoned by all but the innocent, the frail and those collaborators in name only, who returned to the village by attrition and the realization that for the sake of their manly credo and desperate resistance, they had reigned down the fury of their captors upon parents, wives and children.

"My men still have bullets in their rifles," an enemy captain said, deriding the Lathrans. "They can't all be widows."

Katerina, at once pitied and reviled by her neighbors, swallowed the ugliest of regurgitations offered to her, and was advised in hushed, tension racked tones that in addition to the Jews, partisans and Xorachi,[79] all cripples and mental incompetents were subject to deportation. Rumor had it, in order to extract a bit of dental gold, to make alkaline fertilizers, to make soap and hairy blankets or to proselytize the inferential god of their science or simply to rid Europe of its Untermensch, the insane and bestial other that could not otherwise work as a slave. Katerina usually responded in kind to the malicious intent of her neighbors' warnings, but she had seen enough slaughter to take heed and panic. Wringing her hands with uncertainty, she thought at first to hide her son in Mavrotripa, but gave up this idea because the door was now missing and she knew he would invariably become noisy, grow cold and lonely, or they might follow her when she delivered food and discover him. Lambros, upon whom she sometimes relied for straight talk and advice and then curse him as an afterthought, was not available for consultation. In the meantime, the now dejected Kyriazis was among bona fide reporters of atrocities against foreigners. Pronounced and consumed weekly, news wagged in undertones of sheer gossip, making its way from mouth to mouth like a village mascot or a shameful anecdote regarding a disfavored acquaintance. No one openly condemned the evils described, motivated by preoccupation more than fear, even though it reminded them of what the Turks had done to Anatolian Christians. Privately though, they shook their heads in unspoken gestures of afterthought, and asked whether the analogy with the Turks fit or not, cringing with disgust at such stories as were reported. In the midst of hunger and the stench of death hovering about them like their own odor, pity still bored a wormhole into the conscience. Kyriazis had learned as much of the enemy's medical and psychological experiments through contact with andartes fleeing Florina, whom he met while he

---

79 gypsies

could still walk to Arnissa and catch a ride to his factory job in Edessa. These men were in turn privy to the news and tactics from as far away as Belgrade.

Gallanos and Terzellos waited for enemy attention and their foray into Perea, a recent hotbed of partisan activity, before consulting with Kyriazis and weighing the risk of returning to Lathra. They blended in among those feigning passive collaboration, acted as if they had never taken to the mountains and stayed close to their homes, venturing only to the fields and back. Both men suffered brief but terrorizing questioning when the enemy returned to Lathra en masse, but they were set free. Gallanos, who spoke a bit of their language, had the fingers on his left hand broken but before more could happen, swayed his interrogators with a bit of humor, stating that their presence confounded his plans to escape from his wife, whom he portrayed as a miserable ogre. Terzellos and others insisted they not advertise their release, for fear of inducing other andartes to return home and drawing attention to a suddenly changing population of males. The execution of Yianko, who his murderers assumed to be the magisterial archon of the village, satiated or at least distracted them and made possible a Lathran return to fields and orchards to resume work. Under these circumstances, upon his return, Gallanos whispered to Kyriazis what he heard about the fascists' deadly antics in Spain, in Poland, in Serbia and in Russia. He in turn spoke of such things to Athena, in the shadows of nightfall. Athena, for the first time concerned about others in the village, counseled Calliope in a frightened undertone, by chance, as she met her on a walk to the bakali, with its sparsely stocked shelves. Calliope in turn went to Katerina with such warnings. In the end, it was Kyriazis who provided Katerina with a contact, a certain one armed Titoist from Kragujevac. Katerina contracted for transport services through him and he translated from the Serbian for her and found another man to escort her and Jartzo. The Serbian agreed with the general gossip and, proportional to his fee, agreed that the boy, being the equivalent of a circus freak, was particularly at risk. He would protect her and her son from the calamitous piercing and rupture of the times, and what appeared to others as a peculiar dependence upon each other, or else from deportation to Birkenau, the recent destination of locals of allegedly debatable genesis, the purblind or those with psycho-medical iterations.

"You'll follow a man named Czeldic, a man with a mole below his left eye. He'll help you and find you a place to hide in the mountains," the Serbian advised.

"Why can't we hide in the mountains here?" Katerina said.

"And eat what, and sleep where? The men I have met in the Pindus are likely to skin you and eat you themselves," he said, hyperbolically. "The Krauts are finished desecrating churches and houses in Serbia, Despinis Katerina," he said turning his face away at the sight of her. The hardened boils, the enflamed pustules and cratered carbuncles, the spiders scurrying about her hair and neck, anxious as she was, fascinated and repelled him at once. "They're all here now, the pale devils. They want to smack their lips on some Greek mutton, too."

Katerina bit her nails so incessantly that her fingertips became sore and bled. She paced about her yard gathering trinkets of significance to her, sorting and counting them, attempting to talk herself into a decision, to raise the courage necessary to leave all that she knew since the death of her ghastly mother. The day after making her decision, she dressed in her finest ensemble, a daintily threaded stole and traditional Macedonian dress with lattice woven petals and geometric keys and a contrasting cream bodice. Behind her ears, she pulled the loose strands of her washed and perfumed hair, exposing a flecked elongated neck and a contorted right ear that had shrunk with deformity and age. Jartzo, with his tenebrous eyes, widening, softening a normally doltish expression, wore a brown jacket with a tan tie and a pair of baggy pants given to him by Lambros after Nikos had outgrown them. He stumbled about in Strato's old black shoes and used some hairy twine for laces. Katerina brushed the spiders off him before they embarked and spoke to her arachnid wards, asking them to mind the house. Calliope relayed as much. Yianko's widow swabbed tears back when she saw them, decked out for their exodus.

"They look like they're going to church to light a candle," she said sorrowfully to her daughters. "Where are you going Katerina?" the widow implored. "They'll want nothing you have woman, or from your Ioannis. Go back home, dear, please. You'll feel lost in the mountains with no goat to milk, no chickens to curse for shitting on your stoop. Go home to your spiders, dear; no one wants you to go." Katerina smiled warmly, pulled her son close to her and waved goodbye, the rancor of her history in Lathra having been frightened out of her.

The escape arranged for them was to be by foot, to the west, toward Florina. From there she and her son's whereabouts remained a mystery until a year later, when her mountain escort returned with the news that they had secured transport for her by vehicle through Serbia but unfortunately drove directly into capture. There, the human load was mistaken for escaping Roma, redirected and sent west. Mother and son were in the end consumed in the Croatian pogrom extinguishing Serbs. Katerina perished, virtually at the doors of Banja Luca, hysterically rebelling against her impending separation from her Ioannis, clenching his hand, nearly crushing his fingers, wailing her protests in garbled Pontian, and what little she knew of Slavic, Croatian and Turkish, anything to make them understand. The lurch in the queue caused by her antics enraged the Ustashas captain in charge at that point in the line. The man was a sadist, with hair like fire, as the story evolved through Czeldic's driver, "a demented Croat with ice for eyes."

"He went berserk, the unholy maniac," the driver said mimicking the barbaric expression of his tormentor. "They say he ate the livers of little ones," he said covering his eyes with the depravity of what he had uttered. Captured as well, the driver explained, he fumbled his way out of the predicament by pleading in rustic Kajkavian, a dialect he had learned living among his enemies, and by luck, he was wearing a Roman crucifix about his neck, a bauble on a thong of leather taken from the throat of a dead girl. "The sun caught the silver of Christ's naked limbs and twinkled at me," he said, the girl and her cross lifelessly inverted in a heap of still clothed corpses outside a camp near Zagreb. "The little girl saved my life," he said, venerating her memory. "She'll never know it, though. The look on her face, what a sight it was, all pooled blue and gray. That is my penance," he said. "Mother and son stood face to face," he went on, "entwined by the arms, but separated by force. Damn my luck and my eyes for seeing it!" The Croat, he explained, pulled Katerina by the hair and beat her mercilessly, ordering her stripped naked to humiliate and expose her freakish pendulousness, proclaiming at the top of his voice the sub-humanity of the spectacle. When she howled for Jartzo, he pulled her to the ground, spread her legs apart with his hands and feet and fired a bullet into her womb.

"Now you won't be dropping cripples like calves, will you, bitch?" the Croat shouted, staring back and forth between her, and the onlookers and Jartzo, who was on his knees begging his captors, a confused stricken gaze contorting his face.

"By then the sky grew thick with clouds and it began to rain lightly. This annoyed the godless piece of filth even more." The driver went on to tell in vivid detail that while her body had been damned, the rain kept her pitiable fortitude from diving headlong into the blackness of death. She kept cursing her tormentor, between horrendous cries, calling him *djavo*. "It was all too much for the unsown brain beneath that red hair," the driver said, "a son of Satan, as he was. It pushed him into a fury. Then, as if he were trying to decide what to do next, he raised his pistol and shot at her twice from a short distance, striking her thigh with the second shot."

"Be quiet! Shut your mouth!" he screamed at her. The driver explained that the Croat's shriek was bizarre, envenomed, with a queer theatricality to it. He kept pressing the pistol barrel against her cheek. "You worthless excuse for a head and ass, he yelled at her." The Croat's voice crackled as his words devolved into hideous laughter. His men began laughing with him, for they feared him, although a few remained quiet and turned their eyes away. Then a prisoner at the rear of the queue raised a surly protest.

"Maggot," the voice said. "She just wants to die with her son." Czeldic's driver remembered that the comment was audible enough to hear but not to pick the man out.

"Who said that?" the Croat shrieked and fired a shot in that direction, striking another man in the front row. "Shut your shit-filled mouth." A second shot followed as the man fell clutching his chest. The prisoners backed away. Katerina had coughed up her bloody phlegm and closed her eyes, when a spider apparently crawled out of her ear and across her face, startling the Croat. He yelped and another gunshot muffled into her face. Blood ran like a bubbling spring and stained the gray gravel with a misshapen silhouette.

Where normally he might have wailed and leapt about tearing his hair and clothing, or screeched a minimalist's refrain until he was hoarse, poor Ioannis, pathetic, dismal, childlike Jartzo, the so-called son of a bull and his mother's bestial impulse, slumped into a ball of quivering helplessness and cried out for her, whimpering at the annulment of her savage voice. Katerina's ribald refrain was finally sweetness to him, the strange triviality of her habits proof of an inestimable affection and the shades of her cruelty an atavist embrace. Ioanni's deformities and stunted growth cosseted his true age. Canine collared, the Ustashas threw him in a truckload of children doomed for Sisak,[80] augury to the triumph of death and bone-grinding labor. What the driver described, one envisioned only for the most fearful sphere of hell, the gibe stone upon torture's craven crown. There he had witnessed Jartzo among the dead. Perhaps they beat him, because he could not center his attention on the toil demanded of him. Perhaps he starved or died simply because his dysenteric heart was, for the first time in his life, left unattended.

"But I am quite certain it was him I saw through the wire in the yard. He was lying on the ground fully clothed in their dirty rags. His head was titled back, his mouth wide open, his legs splayed unnaturally in opposite directions." The driver handed what remained of the money back to Czeldic.

"Take it back in case an avenging seraph is watching me," he said.

22

Avram's fate frittered no differently than most of the citizenry trapped in Athens. The bequest in Lathra remained yet unclaimed. His sisters' whereabouts were unknown to him. He could neither receive a letter nor beckon them for assistance. The hotel where he discovered solace and employment burned to the ground on the eve of foreign invasion, a fire thought to be intentional, a reprisal incited by gossip because one of its owner's was allegedly a collaborating Turk. Sukru, however, had long ago returned to Turkey and sold his interest in the hotel to his Greek partner. The partner in turn sold it to a merchant shipping magnate from Syros desirous of a grand citadel where he could entertain his Athenian harem. Throughout this period, Avram honed a credible talent for inoculating himself against regret and despondency, warding

---

80 a Croatian manned, Waffen inspired children's camp within Jasenovac

off the kind of desperation and despair he felt after Maria's murder. Among the dreary riddles of his subverted personality, whenever bad news arrived or lingered in men's mouths, was his complete avoidance of the commerce of men and his trundling about for days, shaman-like, in a trance of forgetfulness. Then, as if having been administered an antidote, he would take some particularly sun drenched nourishment - an orange from a tree growing in a secluded courtyard of a nearby home, or some halva with slithers of almonds, among his favorite tastes - and suddenly, he would climb out of his stupor in a wash of genial emotion and speak to whomever he found before him.

Homeless, without employment, having lost his few possessions in the hotel fire, he reverted to pilfering, begging for food, and the kind of petty crime he rationalized with the times. Carrying a clawed hammer tucked beneath his belt, he smuggled wood at night from military depots and abandoned office buildings for the benefit of a widowed laundress, also previously employed at the hotel. The woman had three children to care for. He befriended her and gained permission to stay in her apartment on the outskirts of the city, sleeping in an anteroom adjoining her room to the tiny quarters for the children, whom he ignored except for her eldest son. He initiated the boy as a partner in his crimes, teaching him to fend for himself. The boy reminded him of his days in Smyrna. He was quick witted, a slippery dodger in need of guidance and clever with adults, whom he manipulated without effort with the cursive pout of his lips and guiltless eyes brimming with questions. The two of them spent enough time together for Avram to feel burdened with caring. He would carry him on his back to his bed, at the end of the night when the boy was exhausted and falling asleep on his feet.

This arrangement lasted for a year through the mournful dirge of famine plaguing the city, the supplication of horse-drawn carts bearing swollen-bellied plebs, until an ironclad hoof to the head felled the widow as she stooped to retrieve a tumbling morsel of bread dropped by her youngest child. Meddlesome neighbors passing themselves off as distant relatives demanded that Avram take leave of the apartment. The motive, of course, was to devoid the house of anything of value and scatter the widow's children like chaff to the wind. Avram resolved to avoid the sallow of such tribulations and to live alone, content that the horse had spared him, since he, too, had bent down into the street to retrieve the same morsel of bread. But he missed the boy terribly. He had taken to calling him *kleftaki mou* (my little thief). He missed their evening routine, the feel of his fleece jacket draped about his neck, his feet dangling by his sides, the weight of him on his shoulders.

One spiteful morning a month later, with his pilfered wood coals consumed and his aching belly distending below visible ribs, Avram found himself awakened from his shivering bedroll in an abandoned livery. The cold poke was from a baton in the hand of a uniformed Eleftheri Marios, surrounded by an entourage of his privates, civilian ruffians and informants. A recent appointee and officer of the military police for the puppet government, Marios had officially moved to the beleaguered metropolis to further his career. Unofficially, he was escaping the wrath of a besotted wife, rotated on his spit and abandoned to her husband like a hand rag, the husband eager enough to skewer Marios in return. Quite unexpectedly, he learned of Avram's whereabouts through a Naousan, whose recall for faces evolved into real or perceived associations between disparate sets of eyes, jowls, moles, scars and noses from the past, the man's phenomenally synchronous mental gears turning with the steady tick and clank of a noisy wall clock. Slowly, inexorably the informant deciphered what it was about one face or another that nudged his sleepy but remarkable memory. He had regularly noticed Marios at the military police precinct, next door to the hospital where he worked as an orderly. He recognized the policeman immediately, but never thought to speak to him until after repeated sightings when he began to put the two men together, remembering Avram's essential, albeit withered features in increments, observations made of him while he stood in the doorway of the livery, surveying the comings and goings of a desperate society.

"Do you remember Thanasi Karpathiotis, officer?" the Naousan said, initiating the conversation with Marios.

"No, should I?" Marios said with an involuntary look of curiosity about him.

"The Rumeli, the Turk from Naousa, the Karpathioti or whatever the hell he was, the one that was murdered along with his mother," he said, running his finger beneath his throat, surprised that so stark a memory was unfamiliar to the investigator. Marios tensed, the muscles of his face failing to conceal his unease with the name. A torrent of fragmented images culminated with Magda confronting him in his office, and then Lydia, his arms straining below her contracting thighs, her mouth pressed against his, her hair sticking to the coarse stone of the wall of the Lathran courtyard.

"Yes, I remember the investigation, if only for what it occasioned," Marios said as he arched his eyebrows.

"Which was what?" the Naousan asked impatiently. "You obviously didn't apprehend the perpetrator."

"None of your business, hook nose! Now what do you want?" Marios said poking him with his baton.

"His assassin is right here in Athens. I've seen him on many occasions, just a short walk from here. He's starving like the rest of them. He stands about watching people come and go."

"You don't say," Marios said with a dissolute smirk.

"Might there be a reward for such information leading to his capture?" the Naousan asked.

"A reward?" he laughed. "Listen to him," Marios said to his cohorts jovially but with his mouth contorting and betraying his disdain, pushing the baton to the man's temple. "The reward is your civic duty, carried out in lieu of your own arrest, Jew!"

"I beg your pardon sir, but I'm neither a Jew nor a Gypsy. I only lived in Naousa for a short while. I'm a native of this city and proud of it! My ancestors date back to Demosthenes."

"Bullshit," Marios injected. "Stories so old they may as well be a pack of lies." The conversation ended with servility. What passed for a negotiation was an exchange of the fugitive's exact location for a tin of cigarettes.

Avram said very little. He vaguely remembered Marios; a receding hairline and whiskered lip further distorted his appearance from the one seared into his memory. Marios recognized Avram even less, until he pressed his prisoner for news of his sisters, to discern whether he knew of Lydia's corruption and her child.

"Do you have any news from Magda and Lydia?"

"How do you know my sisters?"

"Why wouldn't I? I met them in the course of my investigation."

"Is that what you call it, stumbling across me after all these years?" The men snickered. "God help us if our great administrators are as competent as you. Tell them to make you the mayor after your new bosses leave town. You'll be a good fit, a protégé, as they say." Marios obliged him his insolence, being yet unsure of whether he knew of his involvement with Lydia, as if this might translate into a type of power Avram could sway over him.   Instead, he placed him in the custody of interrogators who prodded him with bayonets and burned him with cigarettes to extract the answer to the single question of importance, whispered to them by Eleftheris Marios - the whereabouts of the sisters Karangelos. Avram repeated the harried assumption that they were still in Lathra. Marios knew they were not.   Avram looked at him as often as he was in the room, without hope, the bare walls of a punished man, nothing more in the untrammeled eyes or expression, and realized that he had no idea of their fates. The interrogation fizzled. He stared down at his prisoner sitting on the ground panting and cringing, a man long ago exhausted and used up, he supposed. 'I should give him what he wants', Marios thought. Without arraignment or adjudication, Avram was placed onto a convoy of trucks and then a prisoners train traveling north, along with a contingent of Jehovah Witnesses, some Vlachs and a handful of Jews, the later mostly from a single textile manufacturing clan.

Depravation and hunger had aged Avram, but he remained a spry, talented opportunist, inventive when necessity bore upon him. On the train he mostly stood. Room to sit was at a premium. The men permitted women, children and the ill and elderly to sit instead. Sleeping upright is like sleeping with the eyes open - an art, and the unguent of a sage's soul. He spent the first day thinking about anything but his lot, the efflux of his mind like a sinless confession. He lingered on the pleasures of impaling Maria each night of their brief marriage but felt nothing in his loins and then reflected for hours upon her boar's breath of a brother, Karpathiotis, and his gurgling death. He pondered Lambro's obsession with Vegoritis, Danäe's leonine mane and flawlessly long legs, the smell of the tourkiko at Yianko's kafenio. He considered sadly his haughty, cloying sisters, the strip of his mother's dress no longer in his possession, the idea of a father he knew only from photos. Christos and his carpet shop came to mind and the ramps at the port in Smyrna. Thalia's *keftethes*[81] and then, for the first time, he remembered

---

81 κεφτέδες - meatballs

her rewarding him, for reasons long forgotten, with a bowl of *risogalo*.[82] He dreamed of a glass of tsipouro by the sea, on a moonlit night, and of the sleep of peasants that followed. The laundress and her starving children haunted him, his kleftaki, Sukru and his benevolence, the view of Kythera from Yianko's transom, the ripple of wind through his wheat fields below Lathra and the drama of the cherry blossoms on the hillsides above them. Between heavy eyelids, Vegoritis appeared before him in her winter dress, like the marble casing of a fleshless goddess.

The second night of travel proved more exhausting. The burning ache of his legs and feet made such meandering reflection difficult. The clacking tracks annoyed him and his thoughts turned to dread of the unknown. By now the trainload was a mass of huddling heads and drooping shoulders. They had survived without food or water, many for days. They were swimming in sweat and unbearably rancid odors - vomit, urine, excrement and the rotting carcass of an old man who died in his sleep within hours of being on the train, all degradingly deposited at the same end of the car, the old man's shirt and pant legs torn into strips and used for sanitary purposes. Earlier that day, the train had stopped at a station and transferred prisoners from two of the cars, young Slavs sent by another train to blood camps in Czechoslovakia, transfusions to invigorate the bloodletting. During the transfer, two youths burst out of the adjacent car and ran in opposite directions along the length of the train. A sharp batter of consecutive bullets gunned them down. Avram could see the commotion from between the bars on the little window above his head and noted their error. There was nowhere for them to escape to and take cover. He wondered if they knew or even considered this. To the weary inhabitants of the car, the shots sounded like distant hammering against metal, but a man's voice suggested that they were probably executing prisoners. A few of the women began sniveling feebly. The chorus grew slowly and finally the children began wailing with fear. Avram shouted and explained to them that their transporters were repairing something, and then convinced the dead man's wife, a wretched, failing collection of reeking rags, to rid the car of her husband's body when they had the chance. He had made his way to the woman to speak with her privately.

---

82 ρυζόγαλο - rice pudding

"We've no way of knowing how long we'll all be kept in this filthy box, or where they are taking us," he reasoned with the top of her head as she stood wan and sobbing. "Perhaps if we let him out, they'll at least bury him before he begins to melt away in this heat and sickens the children. You wouldn't want to frighten the children any more than the already are, would you?"

"You may discard him," she agreed grimly, "but strike me here," she said pointing to her head, "and throw me out with him." The train, which had changed tracks numerous times and now seemed to have spent more time idle than traveling, having changed tracks again that night, came to a stop outside what they believed was a yard in Bucharest for a reason unknown to anyone, but presumably to pick up more prisoners. Distant shots echoed again. Previously, Avram noted they had been herded onto the train roughly in the middle of a length of thirty cars, but had no idea of how heavily guarded the yard might be in broad daylight. Waiting for nightfall was out of the question since the train could embark at any time. He could see conifers towering above the tops of adjacent trains on nearby tracks.

"The trees must be nearby," he reasoned aloud. Unknown to Avram, two guards assigned to the middle of the line approached their car. An unusually shrill ruckus designed to agitate the inhabitants of the car, including the old woman's change of heart and protests regarding her husband, prompted the guards to come to the doors and begin shouting. Avram waved his arms in the air for more commotion, promising a breath of fresh air. He and a young Vlach, whom he had leaned upon throughout the last leg of the journey, had worked their way to the door, the Vlach following him about the car as best he could, tacitly privy to the moving parts of his intentions. Avram had drug the body to the door from beneath the arms, the Vlach and others lifting the legs as it passed. The door opened slowly. Grasping an arm and a leg, Avram and the Vlach threw the corpse out and what little remained of the man's clothing, smeared with death and feces, onto the unsuspecting guards. Along with their discarded cargo, the duo leapt to the ground and daringly rolled beneath the train car, running the breadth of the train yard and rolling beneath a second and third set of cars sitting idly on their tracks. Three other men jumped to the ground and ran in other directions, but were shot by guards further up and down the line. While the first guard followed them under the train, Avram and the Vlach were already crawling beneath the second train. The guard that had opened the door dove to the ground to shoot just as the second soldier dropped his rifle. The rifle struck the iron rail and discharged into his comrade, splattering his medulla onto the tracks and stones. Whistles squealed along the ranks. Shots rang out from either end of the rail yard but neither escapee was stung. Avram and the Vlach disappeared. Conifers lining the rail yard's eastern fringe proved of excellent density, obscuring the direction chosen for their escape, east of Bucharest. Within the hour, both men bathed in a farm pond, fully clothed, drank their fill of fresh water from a well and ate bread given to them by the farmer. All causes possess conditions that both hone or obviate their effects. The hunt for Avram and his comrade delayed the delivery of human cargo for another day, the effects of this delay on the captors and prisoners, an etiology unknown.

Within a day, Avram bade goodbye to his comrade, whose name he never learned, and made his way across Eastern Romania, probably to Braila, surviving for two days in a dilapidated harness shop, where he discovered some stringy horsemeat, fully cooked and stored in a cloth satchel, and a bottle of rag-corked wine standing erect between a water wheel and a few rocks in a nearby stream. He made his way beyond Galati, or thereabouts, resting a few more days in a cluster of abandoned farmhouses. Everything was intact, as if the owners would return at any moment, except with no food anywhere, not a garden or grain bin with anything in it nor a chicken or goat that he could kill, as if voracious men or beasts had come in and devoured all the flesh and bones of every living thing. Even the birds, rabbits and squirrels had fled, as in Xóros, a place with a conspicuous vacancy of the living. He walked on and saw a large mound of dirt and tracks from an earthmoving tractor no longer in the vicinity. His walking eventually took on its own meaning, for it was remarkable how few people he encountered. But this only lasted until fatigue and dehydration set upon him. A week and a half later, he lost his bearings and crossed the border into Moldavia, north of Reni. Finding the region as habitable as a forested lunar crater, he turned into the setting sun, back through the Carpathians, and embarked on an arduous trek of stark and relentless sameness, finally ending his uncounted weeks of walking in Uzhgorod, the frigid crisscross of Slavs and Huns along the Czechoslovakian border with the Ukraine. He thought about walking unto a state of bliss, walking as prayer, never to stop, to see everything and nothing but his feet, stepping lightly upon the earth, to be an apparition to others.

Then, just as suddenly, lacking warm clothing and stamina, his will to walk expired. He spent most of a day and a night trying to regain a body temperature that kept him from shivering. In the morning, he found an old coat draped over a fence that fit him well. He spoke to few people, not knowing the language, and then only to beg for food when he was unable to steal some bread or find a rotting potato. Resting his calloused feet for a day, he resumed walking through the town, striding ahead without purpose, drawing attention to himself, for he looked like a man who had escaped an ordeal, a dead man come to life. He stumbled across the Church of the Holy Ghost in the rundown end of the settlement, spotting its budded cross, high above the diffident bubble of a dome. On the second day in that vicinity, he bathed himself and his clothing in a trough, ate his last bit of rancid turnip with a handful of dried beans and seeking some warmth, attended the liturgy. Inhaling the incense of his youth, the familiar chants and poetry of the Evangelists corralled his senses, and calmed him enough to feel a moment's peace. No man would hunt for him beneath the vacant cross, he believed. Legions of saints and martyrs would arm and protect him. Providing the only warmth in the church, the congregants shuffled by, staring at him. The priest, recognizing a disquieted soul lurking in the corner of his nave, signaled two burly ushers stationed at the entrance, and had him brought forward, before he could slip away. Avram understood and obeyed and waited for the priest while he completed his truncated Sunday socializing, distributing a large, dark-floured host to his flock, who ate it as if it were their only meal for the day, chewing and catching the crumbs beneath parched lips, crossing themselves fervently. The cleric's proto-ecclesial Greek was enough to make him understood. He offered Avram three pieces of the host. Avram sat for a moment and ate. The priest watched him chew and swallow without speaking. When he finished, Avram felt enough need to acknowledge the compassion of a stranger to grasp the priest's hand, contort his thumb and first two fingers into the sign of the cross, and then lay them upon his own wrinkled forehead, his chin and the hollows of each cheek, having not seen a blessing since Maria's burial. Forcing the presbyter's blessing moved the priest rather than arouse suspicion.

An hour later, he escorted Avram to a busy sector of town where a small Greek contingent of more or less six families and various orphans lived. Avram found ready lodging with these exiles. The victuals, while starchy and bland, were sufficiently plentiful to share and at dusk, a comfortable cot with blankets awaited him. Lanterns were doused by night, to dissuade searches by uniformed thugs roaming the city looking for trouble. In the morning, a small cranking window above his head, reminding him of the train car, permitted the room some brisk air, since it adjoined the main part of the house containing its large hearth and oven, often reeking of stewing cabbage, beets and onions. The priest's gift he received without hesitation, as if he deserved it for walking what now felt like halfway around the earth, but also in exchange for performing various labors for the commune, as there were more women and children. His hosts were Thracians, recanted communists displaced from their home along the border with Bulgaria before hostilities erupted, having fled to Thessaloniki to live near relatives and finding themselves persecuted and hunted by loyalist henchmen, forced to flee Greece for a tutorial in the bedlam that was the Stalinist utopia. Avram kept to himself, worked hard and never ventured to engage any of the women or girls in even the most discrete, let alone direct conversation, his avoidance appreciated by the men and women alike.

By night, in his idle hours, unbeknownst to his hosts at first, he roamed the streets with a small band of petty thieves he met by first being their victim. When the thieves realized he had nothing to his name, he asked to join them rather than suffer the boot of their dissatisfaction. The gang stole and trafficked in the occasional bric-a-brac of value, village vodka, what was called Odessan tobacco, actually a finer Turkish blend apparently rolled in Moldavia, repackaged and bearing a mimeographed pencil sketch of the Amalfi coast, and other contraband. The most valuable booty included sacred utensils and artifacts from Roman Catholic churches and icons with gold leaf or silver plating from the Orthodox churches and homes. While he found the Catholic churches foreign, with their sculpted idolatry and what he considered maudlin symbolism, the simony disturbed his conscience. To climb his way up from behind the sorrowful veil of water, (Dante's idea plaguing him after learning what it meant) he decided to award the value of any of his share of pilfered gold and silver to the poor, wherever he found them. Once, after bestowing a large sum upon a woman and her hungry children, his comrades ridiculed him and the leader complained.

"Have you lost your mind, Cypriot? I can understand saving for your own kind, like the softhearted nanny that you are, but pity is for queers. They'll live and you'll starve if you keep this up." The commander of the band of thieves was one Maksim Niérve Kolas, a Belorussian from Polotsk whose father had claimed to be a relation of the poet Yakub Kolas. His mother's extravagance was to claim being a French national. Both embryonic contentions of his boyhood overwhelmed his adult life. Tall, square-shouldered and handsome by all accounts, Maksim Niérve was a splinter of soreness to every man in the commune, and indeed to nearly everyone on the fringes of the city. Crass and forceful with his cohorts, he was nothing short of eloquent in his native idiom when circumstances warranted. Legend had it that he could plead away a woman's possessions unto her virginity, regardless of age or position in life, convincing her of the sweetness of surrender, reveling in the inveigling of women without succumbing to the intemperance of love himself. The other celebrated spice to his colloquialisms was the occasional French tarragon to susceptible usage of the mother tongue, his mother being Gallic and from the valley of the Niérve tributary and Loire River, La Charité to be exact, or so she prided herself.

"But this was a lie," according to Maksim Niérve, "since she was nothing but a slut laundress from Troves when my father met her," he said, reciting the opinion shamelessly. "La Charité is too delightful a piece of heaven for anyone to leave willingly for this heap of human puss. She was a stubborn witch," he added, making a face that seemed to hurt him. "While she raised me, she begrudged speaking Belorussian, but spoke it fluently with the vagrants she fucked, always saying they were handymen or paying boarders. What do you expect from the daughter of a Bolshevik who ran from his country the first time he heard his name whispered in anger?

She loved correcting me about the Kolas name, always saying, "Your idiot father concocted it. He thought it would make him something more than a bootlegger. He and his stinking emperor's brandy!" She insisted my dad had stolen the name from a daffy Pollock who thought he was Baudelaire or something. She drove the old man to drink, and drink he did, his own sour merchandise, until he drowned himself in the toxin. Wasted away, my poor old dad did. There was nothing left of him but his jealousy and the stink of the distillery. The very smell of France to me," Maksim Niérve said bitterly, with the only incalculable emotion anyone ever saw in him.

Avram hit it off with Neri, as friends called him. Even after their first meeting, he quickly surmised that Neri was the primary purveyor of the gang's victims. It was Neri, who on their first encounter, kept the others "from kicking the shit out of you," he reminded him, "with your fucking empty pockets." Everything Neri said made Avram feel welcome, even his insults. "You looked like a hook on a wall, with your clothes hanging from your collarbones. You're lucky I found you, so don't let me down, Rumeli." Neri's fascination with Avram had something to do with the freewheeling nonce of his diction and ringing accent, which made him laugh. Neri came to trust in Avram's abilities and went out of his way of late in avoiding the Cypriot's dark moods, especially when they stole from the homes of impoverished Orthodox.

Their friendship only cooled when Avram grew weary of the howling laughter accompanying his every word. He came to feel that Neri and his band were laughing at him over far more than his accent. Then he made the egregious error of suggesting to Neri that the name Kolas sounded similar to the common Greek word for an ass, an intentional stretch born of the compulsion for vengeance.

"Just change the *alpha* to an *omicron* and you've got it, brother!" The thief grew somber and pouted. Avram added insult to injury.

"You can't take a joke?" No one laughed. They argued briefly then Neri banished him with a wave of his hand and utter silence. "All my life," Avram's mind raced as he spoke, "all my life I just wanted to find a place to live, with a wife and some children. Here I am, in the rectum of Russia. What am I running for?" he repeated to one of the women, the first from the community he had ever spoken with at length. "There's not another Maria here or anywhere else."

"This is not the rectum of Russia, stranger. If it were, you'd be sleeping on ice," the woman said jadedly. "All of Europe is a bad joke, if you ask me," she said, her daughter pulling at her skirt. "You should go home. At least the smells and the weather will be familiar." She went on without sympathy. "The smell of this place is what bothers me most." The little girl smiled at him.

Avram's career as a thief ended. Neri left him with two cartons of cigarettes, the last of his earned contraband. Avram kept to the commune and to himself, inhaling ideas and then setting them loose in a haze of smoky resolutions about time and love and the meaning of being someone who loiters through life. The woman he spoke to listened in an outwardly preoccupied way. Then one evening as they spoke, pity, like a fleeting glow of moonlight, softened the grimace normally occupying her face. Later in the night, on the pretense of having heard voices in the yard, she invited herself to his bed by candlelight. The door creaked open. He heard her bare feet barely touching the floorboards. In her cotton gown, she slipped beneath his blanket and placed her leg between his. She returned like this twice but after that sunk back into her indifference. Finally, when he inquired why she had not returned, she walked away from him.

This chapter of Avram's lamentable odyssey lasted until Einsatzgruppe commandos dragged the entire commune out into the street as part of a larger pogrom against foreigners and refugees that had been congregating in that section of the city. Shots rang out far down a line of raised arms that, while not all visible, stretched as far as the eye could see. Women and children wailed piteously in a begging, high-pitched tone catapulting everyone's fear. Then after an interlude of relative silence, shots sounded from just around the corner of the neighborhood. Rumors scattered like frightened birds. The Einsatzgruppe were ordering hands in the air and waiting for what seemed like an eternity to shoot their victims as fatigue set in, or when they scratched an itch. As the officials in charge reached the street of the commune, they ordered the men and young boys to drop their pants and expose themselves, examined for Semitic snipping. An older man from a neighboring apartment refused, was dragged and beaten into submission, and quickly went along with the rest. A bayonet wielding Amazon conducted the inspection, a long nosed, bespectacled fräulein with cropped brown hair and brass buttons cascading between heraldic breasts and a hero's rib of medals. Afterwards, the prisoners whispered among themselves that every officer in the command would take his turn with her. But for then, she performed her caricature of authority, arching her back at attention, villainous in her tight leather gloves, slapping her stiff little horse whip on burley hips, uncovering the youngest of the boys like a fondling demoness while her black-shirted bosses stood on, madly entertained. Avram's circumcision was the only one unsheathed.

"*Juden*," the lieutenant shouted with his boot kissing Galzien accent, trying to impress his son of Mannus counterpart. "*Der grosse Heide*," he added a bit unsure of himself. "*Zwischen uns sei Wahrheit, Juden.*"

"*Drickeger Hund*," the Grenadier said. Two more soldiers stepped forward. Avram understood that he was marked and finished. There was nowhere to run. His nostrils burned with the scent of his fear. He reached for the cross normally hanging about his neck, but it was gone, removed by Mario's aides upon his detention in Piraeus. Struck across the head and arm he dropped to his side, begging in swift bursts of contrition that he was a Christian. Meaning to have fallen to his knees, he righted himself and drew a distorted cross in the dirt, the pair of relentless black batons flaying like pistons. No converted Esther stepped forward to utter inspiration in a prayer of martyrdom, to divulge her imperiling faith for Irsia's lonely Mordecai. Successive brindled blows made him want to let go. He rose to one knee and turned his face to his abusers, speaking between smashed teeth. "*Drickeger Hund*," he mimicked. The bludgeons counted dozens more until he lay still in a swollen orb of tissue and wool. Some say the likely dead reconcile the mind to their beginnings, a race of images dissolving one into the other until the first memory. Then for him, it was his father's gentle hands, cradling him on his lap and his own pulsing heart, rooting at his mother's breast.

The balance of the commune were hauled away to Lviv, then to Syrets, with hundreds of others, as if their keepers did not know what to do with their human cargo, and were finally made to stand at the rim of a previously hand dug channel, awaiting deliverance from the fear of that which always comes last. Even in the clarity of such daylight, no one knows the truth. Perhaps the people of the commune, the soon to die, did not view such sudden dispatch as condemnation. Perhaps they did not stand above their dead and writhing brethren as a people judged, but rather in that moment of utter desertion, as a desolate chosen few.

Among the dispossessed was Eleni Kalonis, a petite and precocious little starling, less than a week past her eighth birthday, thrown by her mother's synchronicity into her parent's uncovered grave, just as the chorus of triggers whistled their discordant notes with a bang. Practiced in games of concealment, knee-socked little legs draped in the indigo of a party dress embroidered with a gardenia *mamá* had planted over her heart, Eleni hid within the piles of putrid limbs and blood-matted hair, and waited past nightfall before she turned her face skyward to take a deep breath. In the hour before dawn, as she heard distant tractors and lime trucks plodding toward her, she climbed out and with unexplainable grit and bearings made her way to the Church of the Holy Ghost. Thereafter, she was smuggled back through the human conduit that delivered her to Uzhgorod in the first place. Eleni provided such testimony of what one imagines was from then on her lifelong affliction, including, not so incidentally, the fate of Avram Karangelos, whom she knew well enough to name and describe by the shape of his head and his thick lips. Even the disinterested possess loose tongues and the dead, a barbed psychic ration of reprisal against the living.

Now Kyria Kounellitsa, the wife of the butcher from Thessaloniki, distracted with sorrow and penitent upon learning of the death of her paramour, Rigos the Phallus, Lambro's friend hailing from those rustic haunts between Arnissa and Lathra, who had satisfied her every carnal whim, was a beloved cousin to the mother of Eleni Kalonis. Her only surviving relative, Kyria Kounellitsa, unhesitatingly took the child in. It was in this way that Rigo's little sausage casing of a demirep learned the name of the man from Lathra, the Cypriot, whose "knobby, purple *lilí*[83] made the soldiers so angry as to want to shoot us all," the little girl said describing her family's execution. From there, the story of Avram Karangelos wormed its way through the viscera of interested listeners, including, eventually, the authorities, who sought by proxy the whereabouts of the dead man's sisters.

The Lambrou tribe could not return to Lathra to reclaim their vacant houses and neglected fields. The enemy had planted itself in the region

---

83 λιλί - little dick

and the house. That day found Lambros towing stone from his landlord's demolished proprietorship, a wall having finally fallen under the weight of its age, when Eleftheris Marios drove into the square in Arnissa and parked his vehicle before a dilapidated kafenio. Evanthia summoned her father, who sat with the investigator and heard the unfiltered version of Avram's fate while they drank chicory-laced coffee served by the proprietor's twelve-year-old daughter, her playmate. Lambros was downcast and subdued and grew remorseful as his memory settled upon his old rival and he thought of the early days and their hungry descent upon Lathra. He listened to Marios, scratching at dribbled specs of dried honey on the corner of the table, trying to focus on the story and not become annoyed with his interrogator. The use and abuse of Vegoritis, the ordeal of change that so vexed Avram only a few years earlier, bore little significance to the sorry tale Lambros heard.

"Do you know where his sisters are?" Marios asked guardedly.

"Magda and Lydia?" Lambros asked, surprised to have to think of the sisters again. "I have no idea. Why do you need them? Their brother is long lost to them anyhow. What's the point of telling them how he died?"

"I remain curious, Kyrios Lambros, because this man, like no other I have ever investigated, managed to escape from me twice." Lambros stood.

"So what will you do, tie a heavy stone about their necks in honor of their wily brother? I'll never understand men like you, Kyrios whatever your name is, inspector."

"My name is Eleftheris Marios," he interrupted. "Now sit." Lambros remained standing, annoyed with what he took as a prying indifference to Avram's death and their plight. "Please sit. I need to find Lydia."

"Why?" The tone of his plea and the surname, Marios, suddenly seemed familiar to him.

"I have some private business with her," he said in an unusually mortified way. Lambros took note and an instant later remembered what Magda had confided to him.

"What kind of business?"

"I can't say," he responded. Lambros added nothing more. "So do you think it's worth my while to drive on to Lathra to inquire of her and her son?"

"Who told you she had a son? This is a rumor, nothing more," Lambros said, hoping to illicit a confession from him.

"An informer," Marios responded placing his hand on his baton for effect. Dark looks shot between them.

"Then may a fire consume the faggot," Lambros said, knowing that an accusation might garner an arrest. "Lathra is no more. There are only a handful of skinflints and old women there now. We have lost our home and our place in the world, Kyrios Marios. I have no idea where she is. Go find her yourself." Lambros walked away, removed a handkerchief from his pocket and blew his nose free of the dust of old stones. He waited to hear his name called out, for the command to raise his hands. Marios watched him, sitting, thinking, smoking his cigarette. A son is born, a son is lost, he thought to himself.

Two years later, Lambros, Elissa, and the children quietly slipped back into their house, now a virtual shell, like Lathra herself, a silent, stagnant host to rodents and snakes.

23

A schism between the earth and the sky quaked and quivered the briefest of omens, so pithily, that some of the people behaved as if they might forget it all the next day. But the epicenter, kilometers from her languid heights and the subtle shimmering refractions of her darkest waters, spread a monstrous subterranean tentacle along the fault line of Hades, fissuring a splice of granite beneath the eastern banks of Vegoritis. At first unknown, the throes of re-creation slowly drained a full third of her body, as if to satiate the thirst of a gargantuan sunder-beast, a covetous underground dragon thirsty from having heaved so much lava and brimstone upon Anatolia. At least, this was what some came to believe. As days passed, numerous shudders and aftershocks thundered west of the epicenter cracking the foundations of the oldest parts of homes, like the old Turkish quarters of the Lambrou home (another omen to Lambro's enemies) but also to several other buildings straddling Vegoritis. The crudely fashioned rails of the tsobano's herding yard north of Kythera tumbled. The hand dug well outside the Petalouda's homestead collapsed and filled with rocks and dirt. Foundations and verandas shifted and resettled. Doors came off hinges. Glass windowpanes to iconostases, in both homes and churches from Arnissa to Edessa, shattered. Away and to the south and east of Anatolia, where men lived but left no mark on the earth except the fire pits around which they pitched their tents, the desolation was negligible but noted in the call against profanation of the faith. In Anatolia, the imams blamed the earthquake on the fallacy of progressive Islam or the presence of the few Christians still living among them, sowing choices between faiths and such contempt as they could muster meaning. In the Churches of Macedonia and Thrace, the cry went out that God was repaying the Orthodox for providing sanction to foreign doctrines and the evil designs of masons and freethinkers. Others in the region blamed it on the Naodites, somewhere smelting unnatural ores and pouring the waste into such crevasses as could make its way to the entrails of the earth.

Upon seeing the dramatic drop in water levels, another assemblage of the imbecilic panicked. Prone to invoking ancient rites, races and rhythms of the earth as etiology, they swayed an unlikely ally in Haralambos Calphapanaiotis to give up an old horse of his for the purpose of a sacrifice to Poseidon, as if the lake owed the vacant deity a carcass. The poor nearly blind animal was moseying on its last leg anyhow, in the grip of intestinal founder and oozing gum legions. Danäe had been unavailable to assist of late, so the horse was content to snip at weeds and leaves around the village that it could rip with its callused lips and rotting teeth. Ridden hard to a flange of boulder plunging abruptly into a deep pool of Vegoritis, nearly succumbing to exhaustion, the animal staggered toward the precipice. The fearful partakers of this idolater's sacrament fed it a handful of oats, like offering a cigarette to a man dying of consumption, an unmeant final torment. When the last soggy oat fell from its mouth, Poseidon's mount revolved one last circle over the edge, the perpetrators chanting a refrain claimed to be from the *Theogony*, a hymn of galloping dolphins and flesh feeding tunnyfish.

"All creation groans and travails, until now,"[84] a traveling cleric warned when he heard the report, "and these Neanderthals are drowning horses."

---

[84] Romans 8.22

"Hold fast to your faith in Christ and repent of your own sins, not your brethren's transgressions," a listener inserted beneath the exhortation. Lambros had just finished remodeling parts of his house with his sons and with Andreas' help. Some of their work had split and shifted with the quake, but the paneled glass of three new windows to the world, framed amid the stone of the house, remained remarkably unscathed.

By midyear, the evidence mounted that regardless of prodigious winter snows and saturating spring rains, water levels had dropped to their lowest ever. What was once a spectrum of green and lavender along an unencumbered vista of pebbly shores to either side of Mavrotripa was now a banded cavity of bone-like rocks competing with an encroaching nostoc and an emerging thistle of unknown and unnatural origin, excreting a prickly slime of seed and flora upon the slippery stepping-stones of diminished Vegoritis. Until the hypothesis of the subterranean fissure was propounded by a few curious and enterprising young Pereans digging around the shores of the lake in an attempt to repair a dock, a competing and less primordial explanation of supply and demand was propounded, namely that the dozens of small village pumps and irrigation stations were simply using up the water. It never crossed the minds of most villagers - if indeed this was a viable explanation - that it might be the hydroelectric demands of the wider region centering about an expanding agriculture from Edessa to Thessaloniki. In the ailing hearts of some of her returning citizens, the inevitable search for blame settled finally and preposterously upon Lambros, who, having been a partisan lieutenant, was now alleged to have encouraged the fascists to tap into Vegoritis. Every manner of explanation persisted, often ignoring the fact that the springs atop Kythera had mysteriously dwindled to a trickle as well.

"It was his idea to use the lake," the rumor growled in the paunch of its antagonism. Terzellos and his cronies were especially adept in promoting this notion, easily sold to the riffraff and cynics congregating at Pavlides' kafenio for the latest rage, wagering until after midnight on *kzserḯ*[85] and backgammon. Rumor spread regarding the mimicry of western mores, enticing unmarried young women to ensconce themselves in the phallic fray and lascivious pleasures of smoking in public and dancing the *chiftetelli.*

---

85 ξερή - a card game

On one such bacchanal summer evening, Elissa asked Andreas to go to Pavlides' kafenio and escort Nikos home, increasingly outraged as she was by each hour of his unauthorized absence. Even as he arrived, Andreas could overhear Terzellos bellowing, repeating the theory regarding Lambro's complicity, and responded in what was for him an unusual tempest of resentment.

"Have you ever heard such a dim-witted thing?" he remarked, sitting amid the regulars outside the kafenio. "Lambros never got within fifty meters of a goose-stepper without shooting him first. Nose hair! In the same breath that you indict him of leftist instigations, you now dare to accuse him of collaboration! And for what purpose? For the sake of an old disagreement over irrigation, over a pump you use like the rest of us." Terzellos, too, had festered and reached the end of his patience with all things Lambrou. His anger had boiled over when Lambros returned from Arnissa and resumed his role as the Lathran center of gravity. All afternoon he bored his cohorts with unremitting condemnations, accusing Lambros of responsibility for Sava's death, of draining Vegoritis, for the exodus of the sisters Karangelos, for the deaths of Katerina and her imbecile son, even the assumed frigidity of Danäe he blamed on Lambros, despite contradiction and others reprimanding him with the vote of reason. Terzellos threw his chair back and onto the floor of the terrace as if to announce his ascendancy and the acceptance of a challenge. His face was red and contorted into a diabolical visage, the unholy unity of humiliation and rage.

"The last man to speak to me this way lies sleeping in his crypt!" A minor inaccuracy to Terzello's aggrandizement since everyone knew from his innumerable retellings that Pippino's innocent nephew had paid the price of a fool's ire. Before anyone could react, or promote equanimity, Andreas strode forward, hammering an iron fist between Terzello's eyes, leaving a knuckled imprint above the bridge of his nose, and rattling the brain into a transitory seizure. For a moment, Terzellos appeared to teeter between life and death, but afloat upon the Acheron of his hashish-anesthetized imagination, his mouth foaming its milky venom, he returned to the living, eyes rolling and lids flittering in their dim, rekindled light. Andreas placed a foot upon his neck, while holding off the youngest of his sons, Panaiotis, who had just grown into ample manhood himself. After a second series of frothy spasms, Terzellos labored to breathe again and Andreas refrained from imprinting his sole upon his neck.

"You've killed him," Panaiotis screamed.

"Calm down, he's not dead. He'll be fine!"

"Look at the demon's gate you've opened now," Gallanos said as Andreas walked away.

"Why don't you pee on his face, Gallanos? That'll revive him. Otherwise, shut your mouth or you'll be my footstool as well," Andreas snarled and turned away. Convinced that his father would survive, Panaiotis left his side and hurried after his father's attacker. A handful of witnesses quickly evolved into a mob. Andreas had reached the wall of the terrace in front of Yianko's kafenio, but did not turn or acknowledge the gang stalking him. He already regretted his overreaction. Mumbled taunts and suggestions of reprisal reached his ears just as the men encircled him.

"Assassin," Panaiotis howled, dashing toward him with a bottle in his hand. "This is for my dead brother and my father." Grabbing his shirt, his belt and hair, the throng wrestled Andreas to the ground. Panaiotis broke the bottle across the back of his head. The others exhausted themselves punching and kicking him. The Lathran Ajax struggled to his feet, desperately repelling his attackers, breaking one man's jaw with a blow to the face. Nikos sought to intercede, but was tussled to the ground as well, barely escaping a crushing grip about the throat by a youth he counted as a boyhood friend. He scurried to his feet and ran the short distance home to fetch his father and Stratos, who, in the waning light, were pushing Lambro's uncooperative Massey into the yard, the first tractor in the village and another source of envy.

Nikos had witnessed compatriots murdering each other "over which page of ideological purity to wipe their asses with," as Vasili enjoyed reminding everyone. Now his cousin had rekindled those same aggressions. The unburied dread and hatreds had revived and the surefire gates of hell opened once again. Nikos returned in minutes with Stratos and Lambros, at a full sprint, roaring like lions, shooting rifles in the air above the heads of the assailants. Bruised and bleeding, Andreas had crawled as close to the wall of the terrace as possible, causing a few of the assailants to land grazing blows and to strike the wall, injuring themselves. The throng swelled to twelve men, their sons and nephews, and, in the midst of them, a few frantic witnesses - Yianko's distraught daughter and her two girlfriends walking by and carrying baskets against their hips filled with herbs and greens - pleading with the men to stop. Pavlos Lourithas stood by the Judas tree to the left of the square, a rope draped over his shoulder and dangling into his hands, fashioning a noose to string over the gallows branch.

"Bring the criminal over here. We'll stretch his neck a bit." Children ran excitedly to their mothers as the shots rang out. Lambros made his way among the crowd. Reaching Panaioti, he grabbed his hair with one hand and pressed the rifle barrel to his forehead, demanding that the mob relent. Panaioti stood stiffly at attention. Knives were drawn, but no one moved.

"Away, cowards, away!" he thundered as Stratos and Nikos lifted their bloodied cousin to his feet. Danäe had run close behind and stepping between them confronted Pavlos, who was boldly swinging the noose just as she stood before him.

"Burst, you bag of wind," she bristled, standing face to face with him, outraged that he aspired to command the mob and hang a man. "You would do this to the man who carried you to safety when you injured your foot?" Pavlos stared lovingly at her golden tresses, then her hips, twisting his head to look behind her, emitting a silly whine and lurid grin from an otherwise affable face.

"Not to you, Danäe. Never, my love," he crooned, making the youths laugh nervously. Maria had saved his foot, but he routinely attributed his healing to Danäe, one story contriving the other, of how she inspired and frustrated the groin of his formative years. Someday, she would pay him for that, tenfold, he had promised his friends. She grabbed the rope from his hands and threw it behind him.

"Take the rope back to the goat you stole it from." He stepped toward her defiantly, prompting her to think quickly. "You think you are a hero because you slit the throats of a few soldiers whose backs were turned?"

"Watch your tongue woman," he said, but still leering, wiping saliva from his lips with grimy fingers, his ogle ascending from her hips to her breasts swaying with each gesture beneath the drape of ill-fitted garments. He sniffed the palpable fear and herb of her scent wafting by and then reached out to touch the taught curvature of her underarm.

"Become a man and then look at me like that," she recoiled. "I speak with your mother each week. She still washes the shit from your pants, boy!" Pavlos could not believe his ears.

"Bitch!" he yelled. "Making us all hard as rocks and never giving us a dip." He lunged at her, swinging feebly but still slapping her across the face.

"Give it to her, Pavlo," an adolescent voice rose from the mob. A few protested less volubly. Lambros rattled the bolt of his rifle, stepped toward him and pointed from the hip toward his heart. The others backed away until Pavlos stood alone.

"Pavlo, son, are we beating women now because we can't have them? Do as she asks," Lambros said in a soothing voice, unruffled by his predicament but aware that he was not in a position to shoot anyone. "Your father, God forgive his soul, wouldn't like such carrying on." The lilt of parched mouths ensued in perturbed silence. Hardened looks gave way to Pavlos nervously fanning the air.

I ate beans today," he said chuckling, and fled with his rope dragging behind him. The others looked at each other nervously. The young boys howled with laughter, unusual for Lathrans of any age, who prided themselves on not shedding public tears but never laughing hysterically either, both considered an abdication of decency and manhood. As quickly as resentments swelled, they deflated.

"Yes, Panaioti, why don't you go hunting with Pavlo again," Barba Ianouli said in a reference to a famous winter hunting trip Panaioti had taken years earlier. He and a friend had gotten themselves lost in a patch of forest southeast of Lathra and through sheer luck found each other before stumbling home days later, having repeatedly pissed their pants with fear. Panaioti saw the advantage slip from him and said nothing. With a few parting comments from Gallanos, the mob slowly disbanded and Lambros and his battered clan retraced their steps home.

Danäe administered her salves and bandages tactically along Andreas' bruised limbs and torso. Before a reprisal could mount, Stratos drove Andreas to his brother's home in Edessa, where Penelope and her nieces nursed his recuperation. Andreas was more concerned about with the bruises on Niko's neck than his own wounds and apologized copiously to Lambros. Lambros remained silent, justification settling across his face, in his recent mistrust of Andreas' judgment.

"I don't know what's happened to him since Parthena. He's not the same quiet palikari we once could count on." Andreas walked thereafter with a slight limp and limb-coursing pain in each stride, an untreated chink of the femur being the culprit. He became preoccupied, amphibiously emerging and submerging among the speaking and the mute. Within weeks, he sold his land and house to Lambros and moved his meager belongings to be near his brother and his adopted family, using the proceeds as a down payment to purchase Thomas' share of the Halkias factory, which reopened and began prospering again.

Thomas, no longer interested in the family business, returned to his jovial self when, within a year of his amputation, he regained the full panoply of penile function and hoped to marry a girl from Edessa, who hobbled about just as he did, her right leg being significantly shorter than the left. Lambros bought Andreas' house and land for Stratos and his new betrothed, Anna, a dark haired, small boned milkmaid from Perea, by way of Bursa, an orphan whose father had also been a victim of a dispute over water rights and whose mother mysteriously disappeared, speculatively, the victim of a partisan kidnapping by ungracious Balkan hosts.

<hr />

It was shortly before this time, unbeknownst to her parents, that Sophia had taken up the mantle of her father's now nearly abandoned political zeal, and joined one of the myriad of organizations regurgitating Lenin, siphoning the suckle of Greek youth. Mostly, she spent her time proselytizing in whispers a creed whose consequences she understood in only the vaguest terms. She attended secret meetings organizing the confiscation of food and clothing for rebels hunkering down in the mountains of Macedonia and Thessaly. The leftist rebellion occupied the same crags that kept partisans safe during the struggle against the *psihofagani*,[86] a coronet reserved for the blonde ghosts born between the Ems and Ober. Now that Greek rebels and republicans were mutilating

---

86 ψυχοφάγανοι - the devourers of souls or soul-eaters

each other, both sides picked on the few unaffiliated who might act as mules and carry loads of provisions into the mountains. A government or army accusation meant summary execution. When an unattached villager refused to be a mule for the rebels, he would disappear shortly thereafter. Sophia left meetings where death sentences had been issued with a cynical slip of the finger across the throat. She had heard such callous decrees issued by and against men that she knew well. On three occasions, she warned the intended victims of their fate, leaving the meetings as late as she could, taking roundabout paths to the homes of the condemned, who wanted only to mind their own business.

The third time, she slipped past a known rebel named Alekos Tsihlidis, a transplant in Lathra, the only known survivor from a village southeast of Florina that had been thoroughly demolished two years earlier by the psihofagani, who burned or shot every living soul for brazenly supplying partisans in that region. These had been among the most effective andartes. It was not enough that they simply destroy a bridge or some other strategic site: they had become renowned for harassing and killing truckloads of invaders while crossing bridges, or ambushing them while they camped in what they believed were hidden ravines, or on cold nights while sleeping in abandoned farmhouses that would blow to bits beneath their heads. One of the few survivors, Alekos wore his violent history like a scowl, walking about armed like a silk-road bandit with multiple knives and pistols tucked in his belt, his mouth and neck covered with a bandana. He spoke with the brittle drone of a rasp on metal, his vocal chords ruined by fiendish smoking and chronic coughing and having his throat slit by a republican who inhaled a bullet from Aleko's pistol just before he could finish him off. Sophia walked past, not seeing him in the dark, and then into the house of his neighbor, a young lad she only knew by a first name and by his paratsoukli, *Iakkhos* - the pretty one. Iakkhos was a handsome boy but a loner who never played with other children as a child. He rarely attended school and his parents kept to themselves, never setting foot in a church or a kafenio. Speculation was that his mother, a feared Pontian witch of a woman, had poisoned her daughter-in-law, wife of her eldest son and Iakkho's brother, a young man known to everyone as Phidias. Phidias had fallen madly in love with a sultry, melanic jezebel from Thrace whose eyes shimmered with the blue steel of indifference. He insisted on her hand

and planned to move east to farm the land granted with her dowry. His mother wished to keep her son close to her breast.

"Only a gypsy whore or a Naodite has eyes like that," his mother confided to the rest of the family with indistinct coldness. "It's unnatural." In the third month of betrothal, she plied her tongue-tied bride-to-be with venom-laced tea, which the girl drank despite its bitter taste, to please her fiancé's mother. Phidias mourned the girl's death as an accident and went to his death on the Yugoslavian frontier a year later, but rumors of his murdered bride lingered.

Iakkho's father permitted Sophia to enter the house, for he knew why she was calling on them. They listened attentively. She stood inside the front door addressing the boy informally as Kyrios, even though he was only a few years older than she was. She warned him of the rebel double-cross, and that he ought not to agree to carry food into the mountains since she believed they had decided to kill him even if he complied.

"Save yourself, my Iakkho, and leave as soon as possible if you want to dream of love someday," Sophia said. Iakkhos looked at her warmly, a faint smile drawing across his face as if he found her pretty. His father had already packed a satchel for him. Iakkhos thanked her, and his mother gave Sophia a cloth filled with dried chickpeas and salted sunflowers as a gift, kissed her cheeks and sent her on her way, whispering that her boy did not lower himself to pursue girls and for Sophia not to get any ideas. Once outside, she threw the chickpeas and seeds into a depression in the road and covered them, scraping the dirt with her feet. Alekos Tsihlidis saw Sophia and began to follow her nervously scampering home. When she was alone and out of sight of any lantern or nosy traveler, he accosted her, knocking her to the road and demanding to know what business she had in the house of traitors and dead men. Frightened and whimpering, she nevertheless thought quickly and told her stalker a tale of being in love with Iakkhos and wanting to see him one last time, but could not remember his surname when asked for proof of her affection.

"I'll show you love, my little turncoat. Love like a fist," Alekos said as he drew a knife, tore her clothing, and told her he would splay her like a rabbit if she shouted. Iakkhos's father emerged from the dark and buried an axe into Aleko's skull, stripping him of his weapons as he groaned. Sophia ran home terrorized. A day later, with cold compresses dripping water into her eyes, she revived enough to tell her parents of her narrow escape and the killing she had witnessed. Scolding her like a child, Elissa slapped her daughter across the legs and buttocks, bruising her, punishment for her deceptions, and forbad her to leave the house. Sophia never returned to school, let alone a meeting. A week later, Iakkho's mother found his father beheaded in the horse stable, the horse roaming the village. Sophia wept bitterly at his funeral, which only she and her mother attended. Still unknown to them, Iakkhos, on his escape to Edessa, had already been murdered by rebels. When her comrades inquired of Sophia's lack of attendance at school and their meetings, Lambros decided to send her to a distant relative's home in Volos where, because of her superior literacy, she might find work as an office clerk in the tobacco factories. She earned no such position and instead did housework for her unappreciative hosts. Homesick after a year's absence, she left the house and walked back to Lathra, a dangerous and arduous but ultimately uneventful journey.

———◆———

Terzellos recovered from his thumping, but complained of headaches and blurred vision until several months later, the day Andreas returned to Lathra. Andreas, wearing a black-handled pistol tucked beneath his belt, a knife to its side and a blood red kerchief around his neck, arrived in the morning to secure the sale of his land to his cousin by midday. Then, despite pleas for patience and assurances that Terrzellos had vowed no reprisal against Lambros or his children (an avowal he had really not made), he ate a midday meal of Elissa's benefic fish stew, drank an aperitif, waited until near three in the afternoon and walked out into Lambro's courtyard, squinting as he checked the position of the sun. Resolutely, dragging his aching leg to Terzello's house, he passed Barba Ianouli on the way. The old man turned to watch his martial stride across the square, offended at the lack of an acknowledgment or greeting. Lambros had attempted to accompany Andreas, with his rifle. Stratos and Nikos emerged with weapons as well, but he refused their assistance and reproached them for attempting to intercede in what he insisted was his private business.

"You must continue living here, Lambro. I, on the other hand, have lived here long enough." Danäe returned a bit later from the lake and a day of wandering about for herbs, unaware of his intention. She went straight to her room to rest. By then, Andreas had arrived in the dreary, narrow rectangle of Terzello's courtyard, littered with equipment, bird-cages, crates of fruit and ladders inclined upon the walls at impossible angles, set forward from their place of rest for the application of fresh whitewash. Chickens and goats wandered about in an aimless quest for weeds and crumbs dropping from the mouths of sons and other glut-tons. He untied the red kerchief from around his neck and tucked it in his back pocket. "Terzellos," he shouted, "show yourself and bring your sons out as well, what's left of them!" When no one responded, he again called out for the inhabitants to present themselves. Panaiotis emerged alone, armed with a rifle and waving his sister and parents away. Then a moment later, Terzellos and his only daughter, Amalia, emerged, each with pistols drawn and pointed at Andreas. Voula Terzellos stood in the doorway, cursing her husband and the intruder alike.

"What have you brought down on our heads now, *teras*?[87] Tongue-monger! Fool! I'll strangle you if you survive this!" Bawling with self-pity, she reentered the home and drew the curtains to the veranda doors.

"We have business to settle from the not-so-old days," Andreas pro-claimed. The blazing sun backlit him with jaundiced light, making it difficult to discern where his aura began and his body ended. Terzellos raised his free hand to shield the sun and look his enemy in the eyes. "Do your cross," Andreas said as he handled his weapon.

"Those days will never end as long as you pester me," Terzellos responded coolly, unflustered, pulling the trigger as his voice trailed off. The rattle of gunfire split the somber firmament and echoed off freshly painted walls. Andreas dropped to the ground, emptying his pistol from a kneeling position, watching Panaiotis and old man Terzellos fall. A shot pierced his cheek. He spit a tooth out with corpuscles of gum and what felt like slithers of bone. Then he rose to his feet and strode up

---

87 τέρας - monster

the steps toward Amalia, her mouth gaping wide with shock. She had run out of bullets.

"Twenty bullets and Satan is still walking!" she screamed to her mother. Andreas appeared to her like a gutted beast, his face and white shirt splattered with blood, the flesh of his wound smoldering. Voula Terzellos came out and knelt by her wounded son, moaning her guttural *amanes*.[88] An arm's length away her husband garbled his dying mouthful of words, perhaps begging him to spare his son. His stare agatized. Andreas pulled Amalia by the hair, forcing her to her knees, and drew his long blade, turning her face toward Terzellos, dragging her a few steps closer to him. Fainting, limp in his hands, he let her fluid weight fall upon her father. Terrzellos reached his arm toward his daughter before his mouth opened, setting loose his pulse to the uncounted oblivion. Andreas studied Amalia for a moment, deciding whether to slay her, and then looked back at Voula Terzellos, who sat caressing her son's hair in her lap. He remembered that Terzellos infamously directed the doctor in Arnissa, who helped his wife give birth to the breech born Amalia, to "give the little rodent some strychnine; I don't need another mouth to feed!" A furtive decree issued before the mother knew whether her infant would survive the slap of life, a common refrain in those days of scarcity and fatuous postulation regarding the worthlessness of girls. Amalia grew to be the old man's eyes and ears, the only member of the household who would read and write for her father and ultimately, the rose budded darling who managed his affairs and could bring tears to his eyes. "Not like the numbskulls and ingrates my sons have become," Terzellos complained to Voula. "Except of course, my poor martyred Savas."

Suddenly aware of the intense pain to his face, Andreas tucked his pistol in his belt, descended the steps and walked toward Lambro's home, clotting the wound in his cheek and mouth with the red kerchief. Shots rang out throughout the village. A signal. Men hurried to arm themselves along old lines of allegiance, but few strayed from their homes, waiting for word of what had transpired. As he passed through the square, a din of children gathered at his back. He staggered into the Lambrou courtyard and leaned against his truck.

---

88 αμανές - Turkish - stylized, bewailing laments

"Lambro! Lambro, come out!" he called. Lambros emerged with his sons. Elissa and Danäe followed, all of them surprised to see him alive. Elissa commanded her daughters to stay indoors.

"What's happened, cousin?" he answered without seeing the wound clearly.

"*E poustithes me fagane*,"[89] Andreas said and slid down the side of the vehicle. Lambros and Stratos helped him upstairs and sat him in a chair at the table. Nikos stood guard at the boundary of the courtyard, facing the road. Danäe knew nothing of Andreas' earlier arrival. She had not spoken to anyone in the house before reclining and had slept deeply, dreaming of a snake slinking up her torso and removing a ring from her finger, a ring that her mother had given her. She awoke to the sound of gunshots and ran out to the veranda where Elissa told her of Andreas' intention. Danäe turned on Lambros for not waking her, for not stopping him, but by then Andreas had returned. Elissa enlisted her for pity's sake. Danäe knelt facing him, cleaning the wound with tsipouro, probing for bullets, her hands trembling. He sat still most of the time, with his eyes closed, emitting guttural groans, but a few times grabbed her wrist to prevent her probing too deeply.

"What has become of my sweet Andreas?" she whispered to him. The entry wound was already showing signs of festering. The hot lead had disfigured and burned his flesh. At first, she believed it ruptured the integrity of his cheekbone, but a gentle cleaning convinced her that he had spit the bullet from his mouth along with a splintered tooth and that the jawbone remained intact.

"Make the pain ease a bit, Danäe, please."

"We can pull these two teeth, they're as sharp as knives now, but you must go to the hospital to repair the tear to your face," she said. "I can't sew such a wound."

She removed his bloodied shirt and gave him a clean one of Lambro's. Then, having Sophia retrieve the ingredients, she applied tobacco paste and leaves to stop the bleeding. After a few minutes, Andreas shut his eyes and rested as she worked. Quietly, Lambros asked Stratos to load the truck with provisions and then to keep watch with his brother. Then he broke the silence.

---

89 οι πούστηδες με φάγανε – the faggots have devoured me.

"Stratos will drive your truck," he said. Andreas opened his eyes. "I can drive myself. They'll be hunting for me."

"You will not drive yourself! I will drive you," Danäe said adamantly.

"Elissa, speak to her," he begged unintelligibly, blood and small bits of tissue spattering from between his lips. He bent forward to the bowl she had used to clean his wound and spit, clearing his mouth of fluid.

"You can barely stand from the pain," Danäe protested. "Look in the mirror," she persisted, and reached for the oval mirror Elissa had set next to the bowl.

"It's not as if I have a wife waiting for me, to mourn the loss of my looks," he mumbled, holding the kerchief to his face. In his first encounter with Panaiotis Terzellos, she had salved his wounds so tenderly as to have made clear her affection.

"You might have had a wife, had you asked," she said softly, her lips quivering. All of them remained silent, listening for his response. The pain stabbed through his face and head. A sense of his untenable future surmounted his usual inertia regarding her.

"Then I'm asking you now," he said, his mouth filling with fluid again. She darted a glance, his face relaxed for a moment, then she turned to Elissa for her reaction, not knowing what to expect, perhaps a caveat, or her face drawn up as if disapproving or in pain. The girls held their breath. Elissa proved unpredictable. She suppressed her enthusiasm, her eyes awash and lower lip drooping ever so slightly with emotion. He suffered a smile and muffled a groan. Blood coated his teeth. Danäe poured a glass of water for him. Then she reached up with a clean handkerchief and blotted his cheek gently. She looked him in the eyes.

"Give me the red one," she said, "its sopping wet," she said, her voice trailing off.

"Where will you go?" Elissa asked. "Amalia will have Spiros hunt you. They will follow you wherever you go. You'll do nothing but get my cousin killed."

"They won't follow me to America." They fell silent for a moment.

"America," Elissa said calmly, waiting for Danäe's reaction. He cleared his mouth again.

"Yes. Kyrios Halkias has a brother in Philadelphia who paints bridges. He's a foreman, with work to offer any man not afraid of heights, and has already agreed to sponsor me as a relative. I made the arrangements when it seemed you might marry the musician." He spit into the bowl again, slavering another comment indecipherably. "I'm sure he won't begrudge me a bride." Danäe looked at him without wavering.

"And what a bride she will be," Elissa said, accepting for her cousin. Evanthia and Sophia leapt in their places. Danäe sank into the depths of a chair next to him and reached for his hand. For the first time since Narlis disappeared, she felt the strain of her affections pushing against her. But Narlis had not entered her mind. Andreas sat by her, covering his wound, and then reached for her hand, pressing it to his neck behind his unblemished ear. She leaned toward him and caressed his brow. He shut his eyes again, inhaling the fragrance of her ascent.

At dusk, after the tumult of having discovered Terzellos dead and his son lying gravely wounded, Danäe drove Andreas to Edessa. Before they drove off, Lambros placed three gold liras into the palm of her right hand. Into her left hand, he placed two old photos, after rummaging for them through a box of trinkets, one of her with his children when she first arrived in Lathra, and another of his clan posing on the top of Kythera, as well as the letter she had sent him years ago, begging for rescue. Lambros stroked the lid of the box. It was where he kept mementos and was one Vasili had carved while still in Apollonia. Vasili had given it to Elissa and Lambros as a wedding gift. It bore on its lid two birds hovering with a laurel garland. Elissa also gave her a miniature icon of the figure of Christ in the Garden of Gethsemane. The letter emitted the aroma of its aging yellow hue, but also faintly of Istanbul and the banker's house, permeating its fibers, trapped after all those years. She looked up for a moment, embraced Lambros and then sobbed into his shoulder. In all those years, she had barely engaged in conversation with the enigma of a man who had saved her, a man she once confided to a perturbed and jealous Elissa as the type of captain that never abandons his ship. She wept again her goodbyes to the children, who were excited for her but fretful of the journey she had longed for in secret, ever since Gregorios Narlis described the continent across the great ocean. Lastly, without words, she held Elissa tightly and lingered in her arms. Then, choking back the heavy dust of the exodus, Elissa and the girls ran out to the end of the courtyard and watched the truck rumble across the square, into a tangential string of clouds that was the hush of a bloody sunset. Shots rang above the echo of the truck. Elissa crossed herself as it swerved past the square and onto the road beyond where one could see.

"O my girl," she repined, "like a little sister you've become. When will I ever see you again?"

The word spread quickly that Danäe had eloped with Andreas. Amalia offered her father's truck as a reward to any man who would give chase with her and kill the fugitive and his accomplice. Despite the truck's value, no one volunteered, just as no stranger would approach the Lambrou homestead knowing the whole clan was armed.

"I'll give you the gun to shoot them with, cowards!" Amalia shouted bitterly, standing among them in the kafenio. But the agitated account of her story contained the truth; her father had fired first. The children, who heard the shots and encountered Andreas stumbling through the square, crowed with gruesome fascination over what they had witnessed.

"Andreas is a beast with half his face blown off!" they cheered, gleefully horrified. Quietly, some felt a quantum of mercy for him, more than they pitied the dead man. No one called the authorities, not even Terzello's wife, who did not need to forbid her daughter to call the police in Edessa, since Amalia vowed to have the elopers killed. Days later, mother and daughter buried Menelaus Terzellos without fanfare. At the request of the widow, no eulogy was given. A young priest from Naousa had arrived to conduct the service and did not know the deceased. Nearly every villager attended, a few uttering the Lambrou name beneath their breath, like an affliction.

For a season, the Lambrou home appeared like an armed camp. Lambros and the boys did not venture out into any setting without a weapon, and never alone. Elissa and the girls confined themselves to the house and courtyard, a tiresome circumstance, setting ill upon her nerves. Holy week, in its entire liturgical splendor, came and went without incident and without much majesty. The village was in no mood. Yet another priest on loan, retired, from Edessa, had little reason to know which villagers were skipping the feast. Using the foreign priest as an excuse, very few of the men attended. The old cleric, vine ripened for over seventy-five years, had a distinguished silver beard matching the royalty of his paschal vestments. His canting voice was still haunting, but he could no longer remember the words to the weeklong celebrations, requiring an altar boy or a deacon to suspend the holy books before him, while entreating the sacred, palms pressed to heaven. The paschal liturgies drug on for so long that by their final stanzas the church was virtually empty. The old priest had been told the story of the recent gunfight and referred to the Lathran flock as "cowboys" and "a tribe of heathens" when reporting to his superiors at the archdiocese. Business for Lambros carried on at great cost, mostly upon the legs of the tsobano or errands run by barba Fourgos's grandchildren, who had come to live with the old man since becoming orphans. Giorgios Fourgos was a foul-mouthed endopeeos who had migrated south to the village Maniakion many years earlier, but recently returned to Lathra. He had lived among the inhabitants of Kazvam whom he routinely referred to as *malakes* (jerk-offs) and *vlakometra* (morons), sometimes as terms of endearment, then moved away after a bitter exchange with Avram, an argument over the old man's allegiance to the King, whom Avram despised as "a gold-digging tsarist and a foreign usurper."

"The African will kill me in my sleep," he once warned Lambros years before the issue of water and irrigation arose. Of late, Fourgos reclaimed Katerina's shack, which was originally his home, but refused to live in it as it had come to be.

"It's worse than a tomb," he said with revulsion, "with all those spiders and cobwebs!" He had sold it to Katerina years before because he liked the fact that her newborn son bore the name Ioannis, like his own father, and precisely because she was ugly and mistrusted. "She reminds me of my wife," he said, amused with himself. "All that remains is for her to be a stomach retching cook. She already has an ass like a wheelbarrow." At the time, he wanted to punish his neighbors for siding with Avram, by making her a permanent resident, since until then she had only squatted or rented homes.

"Let them control the spiteful wench," he was said to have exclaimed regarding the sale to her. "I'll give the malakes what they deserve." Just before the shootout with Terzellos, he hired Andreas to build him a small dwelling out of the old stone and timber strewn about the village and from abandoned homes. Then he ceremoniously burned Katerina's house to the ground. Nearly the entire village watched. After hearing the story of their falling out, repeated to him by Yianko's daughter, Fourgos kindled, in the wrinkles of his prior apathy toward Lambros, a new admiration. He behaved as if he had never left the village, treating

Lambros like a long lost friend, as if he had always been in antipathy to Avram Karangelos.

"They argued over how to get water to the houses and fields," she told him. "Everything turned tragic after that, Kyrie Giorgo, as if the saints are punishing us for taking sides over so trivial a matter. Now look. We all have water and no one cares how it comes to our doorsteps. And the lake dwindles every summer."

"How bad can Lalas be if he proved a splinter in the African's hide?" Fourgos proclaimed with a kind of satisfaction in the victory.

"He wasn't an African, Kyrie Giorgo, he was a Cypriot," the girl instructed.

"That's the same damn thing if you ask me," Fourgos snapped back. He never discussed the history of Avram's animosity with Lambros, because he had heard him praise their common foe for his insight regarding the desiccation of the lake. Instead, Fourgos simply cultivated his friendship and reminded him of his own row with Karangelos from time to time.

———◆———

Lambro's only school age child, Evanthia, did not return to the recently reopened school either. In fact, she outright refused. Evangelis Pantelos, the old schoolteacher, had taken up the diversion of an able street proselytizer for the socialist cause and moved to Kastoria, a hotbed of Slavic enlistment, where he was assassinated just as the occupation waned, in a lover's spat, the local gossip had it. A student, a young man rumored to have been an immoral protégé, was allegedly the assassin. The new traveling teacher for Lathra was the middle-aged Zoltan Serak. Serak was a shortened name. He was a Bohemian, like his mother, with as prolific an array of ticks and mannerisms as he had talents and an encyclopedic knowledge of Greek language and culture. His neurological condition (for one could not doubt that it must have been) was a baffling ballet of arching appendages, sways, dips and facial exaggerations, at first appearing random and endless in variation but upon scrutiny, quite limited in choreography and obeying a very rote blueprint of spastic dispossession. The ticks and twitches frightened Evanthia and some of the other children, who openly feared he might eat them if they disobeyed.

"We have a madman for a teacher," some of them bragged to their counterparts in Arnissa, whose female teacher had her own set of eccentricities. An Argus-vested mademoiselle with a pensile bosom and a negligible harelip she felt the need to disguise with copiously applied foundation and lipstick, she apparently had a snarl as frightful as a guard dog, thus making the marriage of the two educators the forgone theme of childish lampoonery. Apart from these mannerisms, though, Kyrios Serak was quite brilliant and managed to teach every student in the village more in a year than Evangelis Pantelos could in three. Fascinated by him, Nikos published the results of his observations of the man to Evanthia, among others, in part to calm her nerves. His efforts were unsuccessful, but Zoltan Serak for his part inadvertently influenced one of the only intellectuals the village ever produced in Nikos Lambrou, whose ultimate profession proved impelled by readings and discussions of the phenomenon of psychomancy, and what turned out to be the placebic effects of the teacher's disorder, resembling epilepsy.

———◆———

Elissa, in the meantime, carried everyone upon the strength of her will and inability to admit defeat. She intended for all her children to survive and succeed as God saw fit, but resolved to help Him along as long and as well as she could. She entertained sparingly. Athena Kyriazis was an occasional guest. She became one of the few women Elissa trusted, much to the dismay of the Medusa's husband. After the death of her Tasso, Athena had ceased being the vetted, ciphered siren of the village. Once the friendship with Elissa blossomed, her sobriquet fell from favor. Pavlos Kyriazis had returned to his jobs in Edessa in earnest and preferred his wife to stay at home and out of sight while he was away. Athena stayed quiet throughout the occupation, and even more so during its violent aftermath. She disagreed with her husband's politics, and in the month before her son had been killed, risked growing faint with yearning for a certain debonair officer of the engineering core, a Roman. While she likely refrained from any improper indulgence, Athena had mentioned the charming Roman once or twice to her husband and assumed that this was the origin of his rabid jealousy. In fact, and unknown to her, her husband's distrust had spawned during those dangerous times when he stayed for days in Edessa rather than risk trouble on the hours long walk home. There, the coy and hesitant Kyriazis embroiled his loins in a brief but torrid liaison with the youngest daughter of the loom, a robust, sunburned filly of Eros half his age, a girl reveling in the stiff smell of sweat beneath her and whose orgasmic vocalizations brought any man a sense of accomplishment rarely achieved at home. He lost weight, kept his hair trimmed, took better care of and attended to his attire. The affair ended abruptly when some months later he saw her, skirts riding high, breasts bobbing in the moonlight, his churlish mistress violently abusing the yet older but apparently, more ardently endowed floor supervisor.

"There he sat, bare-assed on my suit jacket," he had told an associate, covering the very chair where just the night before he, Kyriazis, had been the servitor of the same greedy girl.

Kyriazis had risen through the ranks to become a partner in one of the businesses, helping his cause along with a few cleverly tendered payoffs and token gifts to subordinates and employers alike. He even received a ringing endorsement from the floor supervisor, who was now regularly debauching their eager seamstress. Having achieved the power to end the girl's sensual liaisons and both of their otherwise entombed careers in the factory, Kyriazis decided not to escort the couple to the permanent egress and quite certain unemployment, disgrace and poverty, mindful that work was scarce. Instead, since necessity became a habit of separation from home and Athena's bed, and he often slept on a cot in his office, to protect his business interests, he learned to delight in the knowledge, and at times spied upon the lovers' less than covert midnight couplings a floor below. With each vociferous thumping, he realized that it was precisely her rigorous and audible coaxing that in the first place aroused in him the profane musings of his imagination. Ultimately, although never learning why, and while it fueled her husband's distrust in her, Athena became the beneficiary of this amorist's turn of events, whenever he returned home.

While the fratricides were still in full swing, Lambros, Elissa and the children indulged in the risk of occasional excursions from Lathra for matinees at the outdoor cinema in Edessa; their preferred fare, American Westerns. These day trips made a deep impression upon all of them. Their travel was plagued with tension. All of them crammed into his new red truck and were fearful of being followed for no good purpose, but once there, enjoyed themselves. Lambros loved the cowboy hats and flagrant characterizations of good and evil. He liked that the men never cursed, a spiraling trend among Lathrans spurred on by the return of Fourgos, who sprinkled nearly every sentence with his resourceful swearing. He vowed to emulate the Americans in this self-control after each outing, but failed before the end of the drive home. He also enjoyed how the women, one of whom reminded him of Lara the librarian, were intelligent, impertinent, even mouthy, but somehow remained subservient to their husbands, whenever they managed to snag one who had not been shot in a duel or dragged by a horsewhipping band of drunken outlaws with some indeterminable grudge incapable of translation into grocery Greek.

"Why are they angry with him, patera?" Evanthia would ask innocently. "Who knows, my koukla? I suppose because the farmers and husbands are not outlaws like those fellows in the dark clothes and black hats. Perhaps they're all jealous of what the other has."

"What is the moral of the story?" Elissa would ask on the trip back home.

"The saying of Socrates, that someone taught me, mana," he imposed upon each film. "To become wealthy, a man should diminish his desires."

Eventually, in his newly inspired self-image, Lambros resembled and walked about Lathra like an unaffiliated lawman wearing a creamy gray Texas long brim, ordered from a Sears and Roebuck catalogue that Pavlides received each year, and a rust-spotted, olive oil lubricated Lugar, for which he possessed only a handful of bullets. He kept the Lugar in honor of the man he had killed with it, strapped to his hip with a thong of leather, always on the ready to stare down the menace and glare of death in a test of speed and mettle, the only way to draw on one's manhood it seemed. Rather than alarm his Lathran enemies, it made them want to see the films. Had they not seen enough mayhem to last a lifetime, had he not appeared like a jester, his swaggering recreations might not have proved endearing to the village republicans, and the old hatreds and thoughts of avenging Terzellos and his son Panaioti may have rekindled. Eventually, everyone came to know that Lambro's political alignments were halfhearted. He had only enlisted with the first group of partisans (aligned to the left) to combat the invading Huns and Bulgarians. All he cared about was his family, the lake and his ouzaki, they thought, precisely what he always wanted them to think.

"An andarti is an andarti," they remembered him saying in those days. "Who cares whether he's right or left-handed."

———◆———

Panaiotis Terzellos survived his wounds, but as an invalid cared for by his ever-weeping mother. No one had the appetite to promote the tenure of bitterness over the feud, narrowly perceived as a repercussion to the rankling with Avram. Privately, many men traced the animosity to the gunfight with Andreas, with Panaiotis being a not so innocent victim in that affair. Others blamed Andreas and his knock to Terzello's head, or revived the hard feelings over the siege of Parthena and the death of Savas, but most saw it as a history worth burying. Surrounded by death and famine, the usual liturgical treatment for the dead was the first reverence sacrificed. There had been no time for a funeral for Savas, only a hasty forty-day memorial service. This apparently had disturbed old man Terzellos.

"Savas, Savas, Savas" barba Fourgos carped at the mention of his name one too many times. "Enough already for blessed Christ's sake! What's the death of one kid with all the appalling things that happened around here? Not much, I say. Not even a single teardrop in God's eye, if you ask me."

"It's true. The earth soaks up its drink like a sponge," Lambros said, "but a son is a son. A man's ticket to eternity." This was one of the few times that Lambros contradicted Fourgos, appearing, to the old man, to have forgiven Terzellos his faults, and disturbing him greatly.

The opportunities for reprisal and conjectures regarding the lake's condition soon dissolved into cold indifference. The whole affair regurgitated and then was finally laid to rest with the news that Spiros, rather than do Amalia's bidding and slaughter the Lambrou clan en mass, crashed his new sedan on the road to Larissa. Perishing along with him was his young wife and his sister, who died nine days later, after awaking from her coma and finding no one by her bed. Spiro's daughter, who was not in the car, went to live with the bereaved in-laws. The Terzellos name thus expunged, Voula Terzellos scribed an impassioned plea to Spiro's in-laws and asked permission to raise her grandchild, "to quiet the dirge in my soul," she wrote, begging for the remnant of her race. But the in-laws ignored the letter and she never saw her granddaughter again.

"What a useless death, to die in an automobile. An error that spans the blink of an eye," Lambros said when he heard the news. "There's no purpose to such a life but its sorrow," he said thinking of Terzello's children.

Rumors continued long afterwards. She had distracted Spiro with her rage, Amalia had apparently whispered to a nurse in her last moments of head splitting lucidity.

"He lost his steering . . . the poor boy."

"A real Antigone," Athena said of her. Lambros felt pity for Amalia, caught up in her father's furies, but could not believe his luck either. No Terzellos men to deal with, he thought. He counted Amalia as dangerous as any man. No new generation to fester resentment, "I can sleep without a gun under my pillow," he confided in his cousin Vasili.

Following a seven-year absence, Pater Alexi returned to Lathra. At the onset of the political incivilities and bad blood between brothers, he found himself arrested as an instigator of seditions and defender of anti-government sympathizers in Filótas, a small town south of Vegoritis where he had tried to establish a new combined parish for the town and for neighboring Lakkiá. At first, because of his civilian clothing, the locals thought he was a Jehovah's Witness and threw stones at him. Betrayed to the authorities by a novitiate, a cunning worm vowing celibacy but turning out to be a young man Alexi would confront and scold for exhibiting a circumspect predilection for boys, the incarceration began on the heels of a fashionable Falangist frenzy, ever after causing Alexi to amble with a bamboo cane. From then on, Alexi's habit was to ask "where's my *bastouni*⁹⁰, I misplaced my *bastounaki*." Spared execution by the grace of God and the intercession of the bishop of Thessaloniki, he accompanied certain unidentified authorities to Athens, who then imprisoned him without a trial. Awarded the parish Alexi sought to initiate, the novitiate was eventually run out of town as well, in a failed ambush, a reprisal allegedly perpetrated by parishioners whose violated sons goaded him with long astringent flashes of memory and even longer knives of retribution.

There had been no public announcement or any publication of Alexi's prison term. He received nothing by way of visitation rights with his wife or children. During his internment, his Presbytera's letters went unanswered and, as she rightly assumed, undelivered. After more than a year of inquiry, she received notice from an Office of Criminal Sanctions for the Incarcerated that Alexi received all her letters but had been denied the privilege of pen, paper and postage to respond, officially, as the letter made clear, due to his "intransigence and continued instigation of the inmates with politically subversive ideologies. Therefore, all communication is hereby revoked until further notice."

"They can't possibly be talking about my Alexi. He knows when it's best to keep his mouth shut," she cried to anyone who would listen. "Why would he do this and risk a life without his wife and children?"

As years crept along Alexi adopted the customs of ascetics. He thought of Lazaros often and prayed in mantra-like repetition for the welfare of his family and the alleviation of his ailments. His feet ached with poor circulation and were always cold. His shoulder felt as if a well-meaning mechanic had left a bolt inside him, the sound clinking against his spine whenever he turned his torso to the left. His Presbytera meanwhile, grew weary and years later, migrated to Australia with their

---

90 μπαστούνι – walking cane

children. Her older brother and his family had preceded her a year earlier. In her loneliness and the uncertainty of her husband's sentence, she bigamously married an officer she had met in Edessa years earlier, an elderly and refined Australian attaché and physician for the General of the Army at the time. In a tortured rationale, she believed that a marriage in the Orthodox Church was essentially meaningless in the eyes of the Anglican Church. Zoë, Alexi's eldest daughter, renounced her mother over her decision to marry the Australian and abandon her faith. Once of age, she returned to Greece to wait for her father's liberation as a political prisoner.

Alexi learned of his wife's elopement in the fifth year of his incarceration, with the first letter set in his hands after his imprisonment, postmarked Melbourne, in the juvenile hand of his daughter. Upon his release, he recognized Zoë from a distance, waiting for him outside the gates of the prison, grown, blossomed, recreating the figure of her mother as a maiden. She kissed his hand and face and wept into his musty, moth-riddled robes, returned to him by his captors and now draping upon his arthritic-fastened frame, like a tent. She addressed her father as "my Presbyter and Pater Alexi." He sank to his knees and kissed her sandaled feet, her tears falling like dewdrops upon his shaved and furrowed head. Thus baptized, Alexi believed he knew what it meant to be reborn, to be a man truly set free.

Zoë accompanied her father as he tended to his former and now ailing parishes, which still had not seen a permanent pastoral appointment. He finally reached Lathra in time for Spiros and Amalia Terzello's forty-day memorial service. Alexi attempted to consol the widow Terzellos, who had but one child left to her, Panaiotis, dead beneath the neck, a mere ingesting and expelling body mumbling *neró neró* (water water) in the same dirge-like pitch for every supplication. At first, his mother offered water for his every utterance, frustrating him further, until he foamed with anger.

"Who knows the mind of the damned and damaged?" his mother would say of him. Voula Terzellos understandably remained perpetually inconsolable, bitter in her judgment of life and men, reduced to a caricature of the lunar-prone old woman, cursing Alexi as he approached her, saying "the emissary of the grand sadist," and spitting at him. In due course, she sold her Lathran estate to Pavlos Kyriazis, for half its value, branding him the following morning as "a foul breathed thief with the smell of another woman about him." She moved to Edessa where her son could be cared for with the help of paid strangers, as she could no longer lift him onto a toilet or to his bed. Andreas arranged with Vasili, who further arranged through Thomas Halkias, to deliver to her twenty drachmas a month for the care of her son. She never learned of the trail of mercy that laid the sum upon her table, but suspected. Vasili likened the blood money to Lazaro's sermons. Panaiotis eventually died of the tedium that was his fate, but the money continued to arrive. The widow remained the most pitied among the annals of Lathran matriarchs, exceeding Rena Papachristos.

Pater Alexi never got the opportunity to speak with Andreas. At first, he sought to chastise him in a letter, espousing the meaning of the commandments, the need for confession of his sins, aberrant and egregious as they were, and of reconciliation to one's enemies. But the letter's intent grew into a merciful elegy and sounded more like parting advice to an old friend.

"The essence of faith is to be able to wait for answers that God may never provide," he advised in its last lines. Andreas never saw the letter. Vasili, however, did, although unfortunately he misplaced it, having stuffed it into a box he made years earlier, shortly after Lazaro's death. He imparted the gist of it to his brother a few years later when they reunited in America for three wondrous weeks. Andreas listened mutely to his brother's rendering. Contemporaneous with his first reading the letter, Vasili had traveled to Arnissa and bowed his head before the altar upon which Alexi presided, but confessed nothing to the priest's liking. The tension between them was palpable.

"My brother wears a beard to mask his deformity, Pater. I miss him still and unless I follow him to wherever it is he has escaped to, for which I will hold my tongue, even under the knife. . . ." He stopped, unsure that he should continue. "Well, let's say that his confession is from my lips. May the man who made him what he has become, make amends with him in the afterlife."

"As you wish, Vasili," Alexi replied. "Or should I say as he wishes." The priest could not help believing that they were glad they had laid Terzellos in his grave.

The encounter generated some misunderstanding and a brief resentment, which spread like a tumor. Alexi was unaware of it until he spoke with Elissa at the conclusion of another liturgy on the feast of *Agia Varvara*.

"I suppose your husband is happy now that water is running everywhere in the village?" he uttered innocently, almost inattentively as he extended the cross in his hand for veneration.

"My husband is happy that he is alive, that his children possess their limbs and their wits and that his God has not abandoned him, Pater. Give my regards to Presbytera and your children." She kissed neither his hand nor the bejeweled cross he presented, her remarks made knowing that his wife had absconded with his children. The comment pained him, visibly, but the old Alexi was gone. There was no anger or pinprick of pride creasing his face. It was Zoë who looked as if she was restraining herself from rising to her feet to confront her insolence, and who might slap Elissa. But her father's voice remained composed, and calmed her.

"Do not let your disappointment in whatever it is I've done to offend you, daughter, turn you from the cross of redemption," he said to Elissa. Raising his arm closer to her face, he offered the cross once again, his hand extending from the black hole of a rubescent robe. She took a step toward him, kissed the cross and crossed herself, then looked up. "Had you only spoken when my husband was as good as a leper," she wanted to say, but the words stifled in a contortion of her mouth. She glanced back at Zoë, whom she had not recognized at first. Suddenly she was embarrassed to have the daughter witness such treatment of her father. She bowed her head deferentially and looked back at Alexi.

"Forgive me, Pater," she said politely, stepping away. Alexi attended the next person standing before him, but looked back up at her and then to his daughter.

Elissa stood outside the church for a moment, atop the steps, not wanting to rush home, watching the people disperse and shuffle about their business. A few greeted her as they passed by. Lucidity, like immersion in cold water, made her mind stop and then thrash in a whirlpool of pity. She sat on the steps for a moment leaning to her side, on one arm, her hand cooled by that portion of the marble shaded by a tree. Alexi had not spoken to her with an air of authority, she thought. He had done nothing wrong. He was not a mind reader, nor obliged to have spoken up for Lambros if he did not agree with him. She stood up again.

"This is the power of the cross," she said taking the first of many steps down to the road, a refrain in the deepest agitation of private prayer. "For mercy to live in the heart of a man wrongly accused." She reached the road and walked home.

———◆———

Casualties of the fratricides, for Lathra, were her orchards and fields, a few dozen sheep and all of Doxiades' pigs, consumed by starving rebels. Besides the murders of Iakkhos and his father, Petros and Efthemios Canettas, the mechanic and his son, had died in the same battle, fighting for Vafiadis. Their story persisted; the father (Petros) killed first, had led a limping frontal assault; an hour later his young son charged the same fortified position, tears blinding him, explosives strapped to his chest.

"Canetta's wife boils her brain with black scarves and never lets the sun see her face if she can help it," Lambros would say, relaying the tale of their sacrifice. Sebastianos, the lurid cantor, also distinguished himself in death, arranging his obeisance for his comrades in arms as they huddled for warmth after a fight, catching a bullet in the throat while leading them in prayer. In honor of him, his comrades fought again, in a skirmish west of Florina and killed many of the enemy. One of them carried the rosebud cross the cantor had volunteered to bear in each engagement and died as well. Sebastianos left a sister and his mother in Thessaloniki, penniless and without testimony. Shameless inclinations aside, he was the only child of his family to have been educated, and to stare at death like a man, no mere mactation for Christ. His last word, as his larynx frayed and severed from his tongue, was to complete his prayer with a garbled "Amen."

The wife of Praxitellis had a nephew from Kavala who moved in with them just as the fighting erupted. His name was Dionysius Varnalis, like the poet, except this fellow could not read. Him they found along the road, impaled by bayonets, his hands removed after an accusation of theft and Republican sympathies. Innocently, he had confessed to both, appearing to understand the first admission but not the second. No one

knew who did the accusing, but it was common knowledge that his assassins removed his hands before killing him and that as an alleged informant he held a level of repute completely unbefitting. The locals counted
Terzellos and his son as among these casualties even though they knew
that the whole episode was more a matter of personal vendetta and a full
season after the great feud over the revolutions had subsided.

The only other presumed casualties were Dimitra Doxiades and her
son. Dimitra recovered well from her mistreatment by her Nazi and
Bulgarian tormentors but never remarried and reverted to what she was
like when she first arrived in Lathra, speaking at length only to her brother
and his wife, Marina. Of late, she had spoken to her sister-in-law about
her son, about the months before he was born and still nourished within
her body. He must have heard his mother "from within his cocoon,"
she explained, wailing for many nights over her dead husband, the baby's
father. Because he could hear everything, Dimitra was convinced that the
experience affected her unborn infant's temperament and his feelings
regarding what life must be like on the outside of his wet, warm haven.

"I begged him not to drive so fast, his father the daredevil. Always
driving like a maniac. While he was laying in pieces in the ravine with
his precious furs, may the fire consume them, I was crying and not eating, and wondering what would become of my baby," she admitted.
"It must have traumatized my poor little son to hear his mother cry
like that. It must have, because he moved about in my belly as if he
was desperate to cover his little unborn ears. You could see him rumbling in me, from one end to the other like a storm cloud rolling across
the sky. He must have thought it was all weeping and walking, swaying and walking atop weary peasant's legs, on rocky paths to fields and
to church and to the miller's for flour," she said pensively, "because
my child turned out disturbed, in the head and the heart." Indeed,
the boy emerged at birth as dark as night and congenitally angry. As
he grew, so did the great circles beneath his eyes until they became
ominous crescents, magenta and black, unusual to her family and for
so little a boy. "And he was always angry," she said, "always livid, cursing at passersby and any creature that came near him." As long as anyone could remember, he seemed tormented, and at every turn running
away from everything, even from his mother. His mother would find
him alone, at first not far from the house, then all over the village and,

eventually, high in the mountains, blaring and howling at the trees and rocks in his uncanny way. Once she found him screaming, standing upon the banks of a rivulet whose frolicking water was too cold and fast. "He must have been afraid to cross," she told Marina.

One day, during the thick of the political feuding, when it was dangerous to roam the mountains regardless of whose side you were on, Dimitra went out to look for her son and never came back. Doxiades searched for a month for his sister and her boy, whom he loved dearly, not in spite of his anger but because of it, because of how pathetically it debilitated mother and child. While searching, he nearly lost his life in an ambush, but never found his sister or her wayward son. These were the ones counted as the human losses of the political strife. Other villages in Macedonia, Epirus, Thessaly and Thrace fared much worse.

24

Lambros eventually returned to the benison of his routines, effortlessly, imperturbable tourkiko in the early morning served by Yianko's sullen eyed daughter and garnished by the gifted hands of his confectioner widow, who immersed herself in her various labors. "Or I may as well expire with grief for what I have seen of life's endings," she said. She baked each day, except Sunday and Friday, in honor of Yianko, who in his heyday indulged heartily of her syrupy creations. Lambros tended to preoccupation with his animals and from time to time walked up the stony steeps of Kythera and the hills beyond to spend an hour or so with the new tsobano, Philipas, whose company he enjoyed. The old tsobano, Konya, was among the locals to have disappeared, presumably deported into a work camp or gulag in the final, bitter days of occupation, but no one knew for sure. He simply never returned. Lambros adopted the convention of the tsobani, favoring God's four-legged conversationalists by day, preferring their bleats, brays, growls and moos to the whining and boasting of former cohorts who were now aging and feigning deafness whenever they had no answer, or wished to avoid a topic.

Occasionally, in the evenings, Fourgos and Yiorgos Doxiades would meet him at the kafenio, now that Yianko's was open late. On Saturdays, they would loiter until near midnight, litter and tilt the tables of fabled fortune with assorted political and agronomic nonsense, and twirl their komboloi into the night, honing a particularly mythic recollection of their alcohol absorption while nursing the same glass of ouzo or beer for hours. Yiorgo aggrandized the beauty of village maidens and smoked away his allowance. Lambros reminisced of Apollonia, fishing the lake there and the ease of living. Yiorgo could envisage this well, since he was the son of a Maditos fisherman. Yianko's photo, taken in the year before his death, adorned the wall of the kafenio. Distinctive even in his middle age, his proud jaw and nose drawing out a gregarious grin, he stood poised with his hand raised to the forehead, but not obscuring his profile. The photo made him appear larger than life, when he was of average height. He looked the hero, caught in mid-smile without his weapon, slinging his jacket over his shoulder at that moment. Lambros crossed himself before the photo each time he arrived. Whenever Yianko's daughter saw him, she would retreat into the kitchen, her eyes welling with tears, gain her composure and then return to work.

Pavlides' kafenio, where Gallanos became a regular, not only flourished but also beckoned a competitor along the same stretch of sponge-soaked, unnaturally aqua-pearl waters of Vegoritis. The new establishment bore the name Kafenio Macarios, named by the inheriting heirs of Peponis, in honor of his defiant legacy. It boasted more tables, a dimly lit dance floor and a record player housing and mechanically twisting and plopping down the popular minstrels of the modern poets. Most importantly, both saloons were able to make and serve ice with their refreshments, since coolers accompanied electricity to each establishment. Yianko's wife would purchase the ice from them to keep from loosing her loyal clientele. For the first time, young women graced evening revels in calf-length skirts and fitted blouses. Some would smoke and drink incognito, behaving with a piquant audacity only dreamt of a few years earlier. This of course lured the jaded youth of inland villages, who were in need of escape from the rituals imposed by land and church, and summoned them to taste that most urban of addictions, the night. Lambros voiced himself vehemently in opposition to a second building facing the lake.

"The Turks knew what they were doing when they pointed everything toward Kythera and not Vegoritis," he argued vainly.

"Sit down, count your komboloi and twirl your mustache, Barba Lambro. Our kafenio is not your concern," they answered him. Even Stratos and Anna debated the matter with him, while Elissa warned him not to embark upon another crusade.

"You drove them all crazy with the water and look what happened ... machines swallowed up the lake. Stay out of it and let the palikaria deal with this."

"The palikaria are fools and asses; when you're old, you realize that this is what it means to be a palikari," he replied, wounded by her relegating him to extinction. Avram was right, he thought, reverting as he did in his youth to broad, unblemished distinctions. Everything men try to turn into a system, or try to fix for all time ends up as a desert or in a tangled pile of truisms, and then the system fails. Everything they try to explain away smells like arrogance with the rot of finality about it.

"There is nothing wrong with noble failure boys," he said talking into the mirror, as if he were in a conversation with the young men, "but cowardice is unforgivable and forgiveness granted in order to gain financial advantage is nothing but a type of cowardice, the worst kind of hypocrisy." He disliked that young people had become opportunists, fleeing for work to Hamburg and Berlin, cities filled with vagrant Turks and Bulgarians and other enemies.

"They've forgotten the cast of devils that dipped their hands in our blood and picked at our bowels like vultures," he said aloud, as if Elissa were following his thoughts. He looked her way. "They like our sea and sunlight to tan their pale faces and forget their fathers' cruelty." On the other hand, he also believed that Greece had become nothing but its myth. But there was food to eat and no one was shooting at them. They were poor but unceasingly on the verge of happiness, the whole race of them living in the moment, perhaps as no other people on earth ever had. Who cared if they needed help rebuilding? "Who wouldn't need a helping hand after being cut down at the knees?" he said as if confessing to unmanliness. "Even the fascists got help." Elissa had lived and endured her husband long enough to know what his drooping jaw and averted stare meant and sought to enliven him, if only for the moment.

"Sleep nurtures the child, the sun nurtures a growing calf and a little wine profits the old man, who becomes a palikari again," she said warmly. "Have a glass of wine and keep your wife company for a while. Forget the lake."

———◆———

Within two years, Stratos and Anna assumed management of the fields and orchards, which now required a swell of foreign labor for the harvest and greater attentiveness than Lambros could manage, by virtue of the sheer increase in his land holdings. Kyriazis, much to his wife's chagrin, since his eldest had died in Macarios' inferno and the other children had forgone the desire to plunge their hands into the soil, rented some of his land to the youngest son of Haralambos Calphapanaiotis. Haralambos persuaded his son to move to Lathra and live with his sister and father. For a time the son reluctantly tried his hand at farming, but then abruptly left one night to join the military. He said nothing to Kyriazis, nor did he offer farewells to his father. While sailing across the Pacific, he wrote to his sister once, the letter filled with promise and hope for some intangible contentment. A month passed and Haralambos received notice that his son had died during a bombardment on a frozen hillside in Korea. Haralambos expressed Greece's business in so distant a land as tantamount "to a cruel game of Chinese checkers." Thereafter, without explainable connection, and quite abruptly, he adopted a tyrannical intolerance to noises, both external and anatomical. He was especially sensitive to metal on porcelain and his own mastication of certain hard foods. He lost weight precipitously. Coughing, sneezes and clearing one's throat bothered him immensely, wood being sawed made him cringe, the sickle through wheat, the bleats of sheep and barks of dogs, the pouring of liquids, the cries of infants, the swishing sound made by a woman's petticoat against her dress and the rustling, crinkling sound made by paper of any sort all perturbed him. He sat beneath the great chestnut tree on his property, as if tethered, summer and winter, and never ventured far away again.

With a sense of fiscal desperation, Kyriazis next offered the lease of his land to Stratos, who liked the sound of shuffled paper and signed immediately. With this decision, Kyriazis' remaining son realized an opportunity to abandon Lathra just as Nikos Lambrou was about to. Nikos had made his application and, amazing everyone, passed his entrance examinations to attend the university in Athens.

"And here I assumed the flame had never been lit in my younger boy," Lambros confessed with pride, "at least not the one at the end of the spine. Who's the dim one now?" he said, pointing at himself. In consideration for payment of his expenses, Nikos promised to return home after having become something useful, like a dentist.

Kyriazis, all the while, grew to dislike Lambros more than ever, but like Avram, envied the constancy and respect of his wife and children. In this paradoxical vein, Kyriazis willingly provided business assistance to Stratos, whom he coveted as a son and very soon treated as a surrogate for his slain Tasso. He rallied in assistance of Stratos in creating a cooperative of Macedonian fruit growers, affecting positively the prices received for their demanding labors. The organization flourished and Stratos soon became among the most successful agronomists in the region and an able organizer for the cooperative system, although he was condemned by his opponents on the right for promoting the idea of water rationing, since the lake was dwindling. Stratos had visited villages all around Vegoritis and from Florina to Kavala preaching conservation. Kyriazis ignored all of this, despite being opposed to conserving anything. Soon Stratos was farming all of his land and managing his orchards. Their friendship blossomed beyond business. Stratos commonly referred to Kyriazis as "my uncle, the benefactor" and Athena, who retained her appeal well into middle age, "my sultana of an aunt."

"What does he see in that man?" Kyriazis said once to Fourgos and Yianko's widow, having stopped in his old haunt for a drink.

"It's his father, for Christ's sake," the widow responded.

"What does he see in you, *hamali*?"[91] Fourgos added. "Working like a slave in those god-forsaken factories."

"Yes, what's so different between you and Lambros?" the widow came back.

"He's the kin of assassins and the crony of Trotskyites," Kyriazis said without anger.

---

91 χαμάλης – lout, porter or lowly laborer

"Oh stop," Fourgos said. "Good thing Andreas had the balls to rid us of the fathead, Terzellos. The man could not pronounce his own name properly, for Christ's sake! May the Holy Virgin spare us such imbeciles for neighbors! And if everyone accused of being a Trotskyite ever existed in the flesh, Stalin would be a drunken desk clerk instead of Lenin's testicles!"

"I'll bet you don't talk about his father in front of the boy," Yianko's widow said to Kyriazis, adding to the reproach.

"It's true, I love him like a son, my *yavrim*.[92] I can't hurt him," Kyriazis admitted, speaking of Stratos with emotion, "even though I hold my piss until I reach his father's fields."

———◆———

The speedy departure and betrothal of Danäe and Andreas ended with their marriage in Edessa two days later. Vasili and his wife Penelope, witnessed the civil ceremony, visibly stirred by the most subtle symbols of affection - the single kiss, the way Andreas held his bride about the waist and her hand, as if it were an ornament of glass. That same day, the couple immediately embarked for Thessaloniki and a planned surgery for Andreas' wound. Along the promenade by the sea, in the shadow of the White Tower, an Australian army surgeon, who stayed behind to woo his Macedonian sweetheart (later believed to be Alexi's Presbytera), reconstructed Andreas' cheek, his jittery patient convalescing in a private makeshift clinic. Without a hint of nuptial ecstasy and barely a second kiss between them, the couple rode a rickety bus south to Athens, nearly losing their lives at the hands of a distracted driver, smoking without cessation and arguing with his business associate, blowing smoke in his face and accusing him of pilfering bus fares.

Awaiting the authority and papers to travel abroad, Andreas and Danäe slept for weeks in separate rooms with questionably distant cousins of the same sex.

---

92 γαβρίμ - Turkish transliteration for a young male loved one

"In which church, were you crowned in marriage?" the matriarch of the house asked them.

"We were married in a civil ceremony," Danäe confided candidly. The old woman gave her verdict.

"Then you're neither married nor can you sleep in the same room." Her unwed son, in the mean time, was routinely sneaking gypsy girls into his bedroom and pounding his tempo atop the bed boards, with neighbors routinely complaining of the nuisance into the wee hours of the night.

After weeks of such ardent censure, they departed for the port of Piraeus, fully credentialed and packed for a transatlantic voyage upon hundreds of feet of luxurious American engineering and accouterments beyond their imagination, all of which they could see but not partake of in third class. The twelve-day journey, with its chronic seasickness and sleeplessness delivered them to the stone feet of liberty. Danäe lost a great deal of weight and appeared on the verge of fainting for lack of nourishment and dehydration. Andreas was a spasm of worry over his ability to care for his bride in a strange world, and waited for her to announce any day that she wanted to return to Lathra, a thought she admittedly entertained.

She anticipated New York to be a city of prospect and hope, a land of the future, ever since Narlis conveyed as much in his vivid depictions by proxy, stories told to him by his mother, filling gaps in those memories from his only visit as a young boy. Mostly they were renderings and descriptions of an idyllic drive from Brooklyn to Boston and south again to Baltimore. In his short time with Danäe, Narlis had described America with the vitality of a realist's portraiture, one she longed to immerse herself in and understand. His depiction had contrasted sharply with Lazaro's paradoxes. Lazaro's was a critical yet enticing sense of being an American, and beneath all its lack of subtlety, a sentimental indictment of his own choices, not so much his home.

"I am a citizen in America, a born and bred, fully tolerated citizen, but forever a stranger," Lazaros had told her when they first met. "I love America," he said with emotion, "but she can be deceitful, and in her peculiar way, may not love me back."

"It's a blessed and beautiful land," Narlis promised her. "The city is exciting and startling at first but then, after a while, it becomes a cold place with an onerous wind that seems to be generated from between the dominion of concrete giants, the buildings are so tall. I imagine that to live there all the time would render you feeling quite alone. The sun is so weak in the cities it fails to warm your skin; one feels forever in the shade. But in the hillsides and meadows and the small tree-lined towns, all of which seem to have rivers and streams running through them, it is a place of poets. Dark green mountains brood with mists and rainfalls and countless creatures crawl and prance though dense, hardened forests the size of Thessaly. And in the West, which I have only seen in photographs, it is a wild place, Danäe, a place for barbarians to flourish and become nobles and kings. The people are friendly to strangers but also suspicious, like peasants everywhere. They are an industrious and hard-working people, a land of inventors. But work and money are nearly a religion. I believe Americans are this way because they worship death, without grasping it, of course."

"A morbid thought," she had said.

"They worship time and dread it, all at once."

"Oh," she said sadly, believing she understood the thought.

"Yet, my lovely rose petal, they're a people drunk with freedoms and leisure. In the cities, wealth lavishes upon great endeavors of sport, art and learning, presented to everyone, regardless of who one's father may be, or so they boast. Like Rome must have been, at its height. Someday I'll take you there, Danäe." After the precipitous events of the last months, her memory of Narlis already detached and dissolved in her heart. Reminders of him had blurred into simple compassion, unsentimental, without erotic nuance, without pining. Now that she was in the place Narlis had prophesized he would someday show her, but adored and needed by another, she clung dearly to her husband's arm.

Processed in haste as husband and wife, in what for them was wide-eyed confusion, they had decided during their intrepid escape to Edessa to adopt her surname, Dranias, to avoid detection and detention. Not only in Piraeus but also in the new land under such records and circumstances they assumed might be harbored, and fearing the discernment of a black mark upon the name of Lambrou. Upon official release, a few hours later, carting cloth bags beneath their arms, they found their way from the port of New York to the street, eating stale sesame bars stowed from home and apples bought from a street vendor. They walked until dusk and until they resolved to stop. Then, for the first time, upon the manicured lawn of a great public building paying homage to Doric temples, beneath a prodigious leafy maple scalloped with a charming stand of hibiscus, without the leer of prying eyes, they made love in the chilled, fragrant air and the clement cloak of darkness. In that moment, Danäe came to believe a child had been conceived in her and in earnest felt inspired by the scar-brandished Promethean upon whose chest she laid her head and fortune.

The following morning, making their way to the grandiose train station and mustering the broken English cultivated in her by Lazaros, they made their way to Philadelphia. In time, after living with Andreas's sponsor and employer for a year, with the help of the local Greek Church, they made a home in the middling industrial city of Chester. Their hearth was a welcoming little duplex near the edge of town, on a maple-lined street buttressed with idling vehicles and noisy children scurrying and carousing across tiny lawns and down narrow alleys.

Andreas painted bridges. His workday began at six, retrieved by vehicle after a mile's walk from his doorstep. He retuned in the evening to a smiling Danäe and their drooling pink azalea, Eleni Dranias, named after Andreas' grandmother, Vasili having named his first daughter after their mother Ioanna. He worked with Greeks from Philadelphia, from places as far as Tarpon Springs, from the Bronx, from Baltimore and Camden and Fall Rivers, Massachusetts, mostly gamblers and boat jumpers, men who were looking for ways to stay in the country legally, and with hard drinking Seminole, Creek, and Cherokee Indians. All kinds of men, with tribal names he could not pronounce, men with given names like Sam and Jack coupled with objects of natural significance to nomadic warriors, like the ones in books that Lazaros had read to him, things like colored clouds, crooked rivers, the tassels and tails of hairy varmints and the fangs of wolves. One man in particular intrigued him. An untamed man named Ulysses Four Feathers, a Choctaw by his reckoning, whom they bailed out of jail at least once a month for having such a good time at local taverns that he could no longer stand on his feet and whose face retained an engorged and thus unsociable quality from the frequency of punches he endured. He felt that Ulysses Four Feathers understood something of life that he perhaps did not, an understanding based on a different set of illusions or mysteries than his. Some of the men had families to care for. Others had nothing to their name, flirting with a fall from a bridge because the pay was unheard of, risking hitting the road or the water "so hard you'd not see the body for the blotch when you looked down," men who spoke of the river and its roiling current as if it was a ravenous beast. Andreas spoke to few of them, befriended none, but respected them.

All day, Danäe would put her husband's work out of her mind. Then in the evening, she would wait for him in front of the house and watch him walking down the street as he approached, stiff with fatigue, grateful for the earth beneath his feet, and in that moment she would become afraid for him. She would kiss his bearded face speckled with dry paint, his gaze as cold and sharp as barbed wire, his inhalation imperceptible, as if he had been in a trance. Then she would wash her hands with his over the kitchen sink, entwining her fingers in his under the warm lathering water, sit him down without speaking and serve him the meal she had cooked. By evening's end, with each touch of her hand and the sound of her voice, his face would yield up its kindness and his breathing take on the rhythm of a contented man.

Danäe filled her days with the work and pleasures of home and eventually drew a small salary working two days a week as a seamstress for a local dress shop. She embroiled herself in the social machinations of the local Greek Church, with its compulsive women like the froth of harnessed horses. She exercised her hitherto dormant compulsion for literary composition by reading fluidly in English and writing pages of lucid, occasionally maudlin diary entries, accidentally lost or discarded in a springtime house cleaning. She inquired of every gratis or discounted exhibit and odeum in the great metropolis nearby, to which she might extol upon her daughter the vessel of her premonitions and the subtlety of her absorbing intellect. An annual Christmas tradition for them was Wanamaker's department store and its grand organ, remembering Lazaro's description and his wonder at the power of the instrument. Throughout her daughter's adolescence, her answer to the trundling moods of a young girl was to take her daughter to the gardens and great arboretums, exhausting her questions and the calculations of origins and endings. For herself, Danäe embarked upon a journey through the renaissance of Greek literature, studying Cavafis, Seferis, Ouranis, Elytis, Kazantzakis and the generation of poets who lost their epic virginity and orthodoxy to the wide-hipped harlot of free verse and the coffeehouse rapport with avant-garde nihilism. It aroused her Greek into a seemingly new language and a delicious devotion to the hyphen and the conjunction.

Daughter Eleni's birth preceded that of a son, Gregorios Dranias. In an effort to fund the expense of a growing family, Andreas had begun working through the end of each week on private construction ventures, purchasing tools and garnering sufficient customers and projects by word of mouth to leave the heady danger of bridge painting altogether. This proved fortuitous because he had had words with the surly Irishman promoted to foreman, and because the company was to move with a job painting bridges in Connecticut, which would have forced him to live away from home for at least two years. The Irishman had always seemed angry when Andreas spoke to anyone, because he could not understand him, and grew impatient when Andreas balked at the Connecticut job.

"We all know why you came here, muscles," he said.

Andreas tried answering him. "To be able to live and work with . . ."

"I don't wanta hear any fleeing for freedom crap," the Irishman retorted rapidly. "You're here for the money like anyone who comes to this country. Everybody wants to shoot his dice on the fantasy, a fat wad of dollars in his pocket. So cut the crap." Andreas became anxious at his job.

"You may throw this man off the bridge someday if he keeps at you," Ulysses Four Feathers had said to him.

So began Andreas' prosperous career as a carpenter and cabinetmaker for affluent Main Line families, often working day into night building and adorning the interiors of mother-in-law suites, at times sleeping at the job site and waking the following morning to resume his hymn with the saw and hammer. Eventually, he hired a Puerto Rican named Eduardo Rueda. He trusted his worker's skill but never asked the man to visit his home, with Eduardo's throat clutching brood of children, his corpulent wife, his mother and in-laws all living under the same roof lest their procreative folly ossify in his home and Danäe begin demanding more children, or companionship from Greece.

<hr />

A year later, on a humid Sunday afternoon, while the family Dranias enjoyed the sleepy hum of an electric fan, reclining after their midday meal, as they had grown accustomed to from the old country, a forceful knock rapped upon the frame of the screen door, rousing them in unison. From the other side of the gray mesh, Danäe observed a tall, lean young man in a smart suit, a white shirt and polished shoes, with wavy hair and an eerily indistinct resemblance to Lazaros Zervas.

"Pay Danäe and Andreas a visit, before you leave Pennsylvania," Niina counseled in a phone call to her son, speaking to him in English now that he seemed to respond only in that language. "They knew your father well and loved him."

Lasso Krohn had studied at Curtis while living with his grandparents northeast of Wilmington, Delaware, and then moved in with his leggy girlfriend Amelia Everett, a student of sculpture who lived in Philadelphia, near the city's iconic Museum of Art and the smaller homage to Rodin. Influenced perhaps by the concept of line and color in music, in painting as well as in sculpture, Lasso found nothing more comely in a woman than long, slender thighs. His motto was, "find the holy grail of such thighs and proportioned calves are nearly always a given." A tiny waist is often a bonus in the same woman, observations committed to innate memory. He found that the aesthetic journey from the waist up was often worthwhile too, but also that the countenance of a sylph, a dangerous drawback, was common in these feminine types as well. In Amelia's case, there were candid thorns for breasts, oblique illiquid shoulders, a fearsome snaking neck, and eyes and lips with an air of suspicion about them, as if she would succumb to nothing short of heaven itself. He never searched beyond Amelia Everett. She captivated him in every way, introduced him to the worship of her contortionism and the linearity of her soul by means of a contagious obsession with art - Monet, Van Gogh, Cézanne and Rodin the music of Bartok, Berg, Ravel and Stravinsky, among a host of others. Lasso found it unusual that anyone could dichotomize a single obsession, but Amelia did it without difficulty and with fully persuasive enthusiasm. A week after they stood mesmerized before the *Women Bathers*, Amelia returned from having visited her parents with a recording of Bartok's *Divertimento for String Orchestra* - Antol Dorati and the entire Minneapolis Symphony pressed onto an RCA saucer. They lay in bed one afternoon, listening to it repeatedly, making love each time. The following day they returned to the *Women Bathers*. Amelia stood before the painting and wept for joy, "Time so perfectly defied," she said later, explaining her emotion. Lasso knotted his face into an obscuring smile, concealing his emotion at seeing her so happy. He had already fallen in love with her, daydreaming of her legs wrapped about his neck on a quarter hourly basis, but it was her intensity, the melodrama of youth and its emotional aesthetic that made the deepest impression upon him, and affected his playing, making it more fluid and daring, according to his colleagues.

"If I can play like the trees above the bathers, arching into a single miraculous line, I will have understood my birth and death," he said. She kissed him violently and seduced him in a prohibited corner of the art museum.

A week later, lying in bed with her, listening to a radio broadcast of Berg's *Violin Concerto*, Lasso revealed that he was obligated to leave Philadelphia for a time. Being an American citizen by birth, he received a completely unexpected summons to report to the United States Army. And so Lasso Krohn left his long-legged "goddess of the mole-less derma" as if existing in a painting, in the throes of her passion for him, and from her perspective, in the lurch. Amelia promised to wait for him and his newly adopted aesthetic fanaticism.

Leaving his fiddle at home, he traveled by bus to Louisiana for basic training. He wrote letters and received responses every week. Then on to Japan for more training and next to Chosan Korea, to win his sharpshooter's bars for picking off more than his share of rag-footed Koreans and Chinese hurling themselves toward his ever-roving foxhole. Then on a brilliantly icy February night, where crystals crinkled lashes and clamped the larynx of any mammal not suffused in fur, a mortar shell knocked him to the earth in a state of senselessness only a drunkard could envy. He awoke on a cot in a still cold field and met a cheerfully demented doctor festooning his surgical tent with lewd photos of women in all manner of receptivity, introducing them to him as his real nurses. Among the photos, hung from clothespins, were letters to his wife he never mailed to her, after discovering her deception of "the boy who loves you," as his letters always ended. "I got a letter from her sister, warning me," he said. "She felt sorry for me." The doctor transferred Lasso to a hospital in Japan, for his gimpy leg, a hell of a headache and his healthy disdain for shoveling dirt. Lasso spent twenty-eight days in the walking ward, poked, prodded and questioned, dreaming of Ameila's legs spread in her inimitable way, like victory, imagining his performance (as first violin of course) of the Bartok *String Quartet Number Two* - mute on, mute off as quickly as he could - before General Macarthur and Chairman Mao.

"A puny day dream if I ever had one," he mentioned to Amelia in a second or third unanswered letter. Unbeknownst to him, the Bartok was among his father's favorites in the repertoire. Depravity is the human condition he thought somewhat disconnectedly of the piece, especially when subjecting children to cruelty or bad men's fascination with brutality. Better yet, he would play them Stravinsky's *Pastoral for Violin and Four Wind Instruments*, invoking the memory of their childhood, melting the heart into a pool of virtue. He had played it once, fell under its spell, and hummed it incessantly during his time in the army and while overseas. He hurried back to Korea, lying to a captain about his state of healing and by returning to the front, earned the rest of his frontline points and the right to go home, his personality anesthetized by the carnage, frostbite deforming his toes and the same persistent headache plaguing him day and night. On his last day along the 38th parallel, he mentioned to his Sergeant Kingfisher (adopting the name of his hometown) that he "studied music in a pretty good school" and that he could play various instruments "better than average."

"Hell, boy," the Oklahoman said as if actually regretting something, "you coulda' had a cushy stretch playin' waltzes for the top brass in Hokkaido instead of shootin' Chinks and diggin' latrines in this fuck hole! Oh well, too late now," he said, and walked off amply amused. That night, his last on the tundra, saw Lasso forgetting all about his missed opportunities and headaches. He spent it dodging flying molten ellipses plunging in long earthward arcs, plinking off rocks and helmets, canisters and the abandoned steel of military contraption, subsumed within the dull thud of sand bags and the prostrate limbs of desperate, crouching men.

Flying out of Seattle, the plane made an unscheduled descent into Billings, Montana. The captain on board was famished and the only eating establishment near the airport (the *Zeus Diner*) was operated by a man named Apostolos, whom the locals called Apostle, and his two undernourished waitresses, Merrily, and the other girl scarcely harmonizing with that lovely name, so suggestive of her genial disposition. Vaudevillian juggling in their range of talents, the three managed to feed the entire planeload and crew T-bone steaks and fried potatoes with cold beer, which Apostle offered on his dime. The Colonel, in turn, gave the girls a forty-dollar tip, which he preferred to slip between sweaty flesh and the tops of their gartered stockings. Ten minutes in the pantry with Merrily and off they went.

The silence of the plane ride was curative for Lasso but nowhere long enough to heal the memory of his last night on the front. He thought to write to Amelia and ask questions instead of simply reporting what counted as thoughts shooting through his head, but changed his mind and closed his eyes. As a civilian, Lasso returned to his grandparent's home, Amelia not having kept her promise within five months of his leaving for Korea, falling off the pedestal with a classmate of his from Curtis, a horn player. With little serious preparation and two auditions, Lasso quickly secured a second violin chair with the Baltimore Symphony Orchestra. He was about to move his belongings below the Mason Dixon line to rehearse for his first concert, a program including the Sibelius *Sixth*, when his mother, in one of her weekly phone calls, advised him that Danäe and Andreas Dranias were in America as well and lived nearby. Lasso had not returned to Helsinki to visit his mother. Instead, he sent her an ornate Japanese tea set painted with dancing geishas serving tea to emperors and samurais, a memento of his last two years he said, his letter composed on rice paper and folded in the teapot, a veiled thank you for sending him to America at the precise moment in history that she did.

"I send you this tea set from Hokkaido," he wrote, "because there isn't a damn thing worth buying in Korea and if there was, it would stink of thawing flesh."

Lasso's mother, Niina Krohn was married with yet more children, and still lived in a suburb of Helsinki. She had learned of Danäe and Andreas' situation from Pater Alexi, who mailed a string tied bundle of Lazaro's sermons to Niina with a letter containing, among other things, a terse account of their secretive composition. He in turn obtained her address of late from Anna and Stratos Lambrou, who had gotten it from Danäe, who previously mailed Lasso notice of his entitlement to his father's land and some personal effects. Until that day, Lasso never sought to draw anything more from her memory of his father, whose image as a grown man he had never seen. Anna took it upon herself to locate one of the few photographs of Lazaros simulating a citizen of Lathra and mailed it to Niina. Lazaros wore on that occasion his usual bearded disguise, his hair tied back in a tail (difficult to see in the picture) a dark gabardine topcoat fluttering in the wind, but otherwise covering dark pants and a white shirt, and an uncharacteristic grin (as if through a mouthful of lemon), in reaction to the news of Sebastiano's dismissal as Alexi's deacon. Lasso resembled his mother in but two over-bearing genetic remissions of his father's elongated and peculiar chromosomes - her wavy fair-weather locks and wider set eyes with their androgynous iris, chestnut to brown in the depths yet blue-green on the rainbow periphery. The rest of his assemblage was all Lazaros - long, lean, brooding to inquisitive, with the same evocative smile on thin, cur-sive lips.

Even during the postmortem retelling of events, Lasso sat quietly in his seat, facing his hosts, munching on his *finiki*[93] sipping a steamy, over sweetened coffee without exhibiting emotion. He listened intently to the stories, especially of his father's alleged wondrousness, what to a wealthy man might be eccentricities but to most Lathrans remained a sign of mental ailment.

"You must visit Lathra and see where he lived so happily for so many years," Danäe advised at one point.

"Thank you, I may," he responded politely, as if asked if he wanted a glass of water.

"Lambros and Elissa, my dearest cousins, will treat you with hos-pitality like you've never known," she said proudly and with a trace of emotion. "You'll understand him better if you visit Mavrotripa." He offered no response except to shift directions in his seat and face Andreas, avoiding obvious scrutiny but evidently compelled to look at the scaring of his host's face. "Even though the door is gone, the grotto still bears the mark of him. Elissa has more photos." Danäe succeeded in dissuading him from selling the land for the time being. She explained

---

93 φινίκι- honey-dipped walnut cookies

that owning a place on Vegoritis would someday be of great value, not only because of the view but also because of the water.

"You know Thales believed that every living thing in the world has one thing in common," Andreas said. "Your father pointed this out to me. Water . . . the water is holy in Lathra. It smells a little like fish, but that's a blessing, because there are so many of them."

The only thing not self-revelatory and imparted to his hosts concerned Lasso's grandparents. At the time of Lazaro's death, Danäe had written to Alexandros and Irini Zervas, who by then were residing in a bucolic suburb of Wilmington. She had introduced herself, advising them of their son's passing and revealing that she would welcome their assistance in concluding Lazaro's affairs. She received a warm response from his mother stating that she knew who she was since her son had written of her on more than a few occasions. She assured Danäe of their trust in her ability to conclude matters as she saw fit and further advised her of the existence and address of Lasso Krohn, which at the time confirmed for Danäe that he was indeed Lazaro's son. Irini's salutation was simply "Daughter."

Irini took the death of her boy, her only child, as might be expected, like a crushing weight upon her soul and body, constricting her breathing along with certain other undiagnosed medical indications posing as a mnemonic curse, leaving her with an overbearing sadness and compunctions over having sent him away simply to avert the judgment of strangers. These dismal feelings lasted until Lasso came to live with them, which for Irini was like having her son reborn and near her again.

For Alexandros, Lazaro's death coincided with a string of bad business luck, necessitating his postponing an early retirement and continuing his entrepreneurial comings and goings, none of which succeeded in earning him much wealth, his lifelong objective and passion until then. On those days when nothing was brewing, he would take an hour or two to relieve his boredom and drive to Longwood Gardens, a few minutes north of where they had moved and near where he established a wholesale marble business. He was a regular at the botanical gardens, preferring to walk outdoors than in the grand conservatory, even in winter. He especially loved the Cedars of Atlas clustered on the south lawns and the drunken butterflies of late summer lounging on floral walks rather than fluttering nervously about anther already denuded of pollen. His strolls and meditative mourning began in earnest when Lazaros died and continued until well after Lasso arrived, which did not have the consoling affect upon him that it did for Irini. He thought his grandson to be a perturbed soul. He and Lasso rarely spoke and when they did, neither could pretend to understand the other.

On an excruciatingly blissful May morning, strolling through so manicured an Eden as men could envision, facing a stand of fragrant flora, some hairy cedars and a lone cypress, with the sound of fountains and water tumbling over rocks, with gardeners busying themselves like cherubs about the fountains and promenades, on a morning that so staggers one's senses as to create a nearly painful illuminative joy, Alexandros sat upon a secreted little bench in the deep shade and fell asleep. One of the gardeners saw him that afternoon, his eyes squinting serenely as if he were pondering a deep thought, mouth gently clamped and head inclined ever so gently to the right, his back flush against the bench. On the second day, another distracted gardener saw him in that position but noticed nothing about the scene to cause alarm. On the third, the original gardener saw him again. His carriage appeared familiar but the gardener was busy and quickly looked away. Then, later that day, he suddenly remembered Aleko, as the staff affectionately called him, being in the exact bearing two day's before.

"He retuned to the bench and noticed the squirrels ignoring him," Lasso said, "one popping up onto his shoulder and appearing much the same color as his face," he concluded with a shrug of the chin that Danäe interpreted as transitory sadness. "This was how my grandmother described my grandfather's finale - asleep in the master's grove . . . an ethereally vanishing tremolo."

"Lazaros studied Sibelius, especially the later symphonies," Danäe informed him, eventually changing the subject, sensing that Lasso was about to leave. "Play it well for him." Lasso gulped down his still-warm coffee, excused himself to use the bathroom, washed his hands as his hosts stared at each other, came out, thanked them for their hospitality and enthusiasm and left, walking in his father's ambling manner toward the bus stop on the opposite street corner. Danäe watched him, noticing his removing and shaking out a handkerchief from his inside suit pocket, raising it to some unseen position before his face. She imagined he was weeping and felt compelled to run out to him but then saw, as he turned his head, that he was blowing his nose rather clinically.

A few days later, Lasso rehearsed the Sibelius and performed it with his colleagues for the first time in his life. That night, before he went to bed, he wrote to his mother with unrestrained enthusiasm that he had heard the ostinato of his father's heart. Though he would see them again, he never returned to the Dranias home nor instigated contact with Danäe. Nor, as far as anyone knew, did he travel to the lonely rock garden of her wandering scholar, the aesthete, the recluse, the patron, the appendix, the singing swallow, the bard of Lathra, his father. He did however write to Elissa requesting another photo of his father as a grown man, since looking at photos of him in his youth was like combing his own face for answers, he told his mother in a phone call. Elissa obliged him and awaited a second letter, but he never composed one.

Not many months later, Lasso inquired into buyers for the land through an attorney in Thessaloniki. An agreement transpired, executed upon alternate copies between him and Stratos Lambrou. Stratos bought the property with extended boundaries to the east, since no one could locate the deed of registry for either adjacent parcel, or anyone's birth or marriage certificates for that matter. No one knew how, but during the fratricides some of the village records found their way to the catacombs beneath the church in a neighboring village, piles of paper stuffed into a coffin and grain sacks. The land conveyance included a half-dozen more stremata extending into a woodlot thick with a second growth of hardwoods amid the usual scrub pine, ascending to a seismic regurgitation of bald rock from the Dark Ages affectionately called *Gerondaki*.[94] Stratos bought the land on the bidding of his father, as much a gesture of sentimentality as any perception of value. As the years passed, the significance of the land became apparent, not only for its hardwoods, which Stratos chose not to harvest, even when asked to by cousin Vasili, but also precisely for the harsh and craggy features it concealed. Its drama had appeared to at least one man as pure repose, and remains among the only places facing the lake, completely devoid of men's ambitions.

———◆———

94 γεϱονδάκι - little, aged one

Remarkably, within a month of Lasso's visit to Danäe and Andreas, what all believed to be lost of Lazaro's cathedral of isolation - the great door to Mavrotripa - appeared in an exhibit in the museum Pergamon. Having weathered so heartily in its voiceless vigil over Vegoritis, the carving earned an assessment of having its speculative origins from a previous century. A few experts mistakenly attributed it to the Balkan artisan and iconographer Damian Ristovski. Apparently discovered in the walk-in safe of a destroyed munitions manufacturer, it survived with only slight damage sustained during what must have been its many transports, sporting a small bullet trail impolitely dug into its torso, en route to its lower kingdoms. Danäe noticed the door in a full-page photograph in an art magazine, lauded as a masterwork and an object of subdued nationalist pride. She read of its marvels of primitivism and composition, among the finest folk craft of old Europe. Bestowed the title *"The Entry of the Troglodytes,"* apparently derived from a note found stuck to the back, describing its function but not its location, the door was among other antiquities and artifacts donated for the exhibition, which was nearing its end of five months. The opportunity nearly passed to advise Vasili that he ought to investigate, if not attend, the exhibition. She wrote to the Pergamon immediately, but failed to receive a response to her inquiry regarding what appeared to her to be Lazaro's door and received even less reassurance when she phoned Vasili, who felt no need to wade or wallow in recognition of his work. Paid handsomely for the carving by his friend, he had since fashioned scores of carvings in relief, which adorned entrances to stately homes, banks, altars and the coffins of the Lord's servants made humble by their demise.

"Plus, if it were mine, someone with a good pair of magnifiers would have seen my initials etched with the date, on the lowest panel, within the various strands of the nymph's flowing hair. You remember her, the ecstatic one with her eyes closed." Danäe reexamined the photographs and magnified the largest photo with her glass. The nymph's eyes were indeed closed. She concluded that an illegible inscription must appear in the flow of her locks and took the glossy magazine photo to a professional photographer in Chester. As a courtesy, which happened often for Danäe, he enhanced the photo to a likeness of even greater clarity. The work, definitely the enchantment and skill of Vasilios Lambrou, bore a beta and lambda made to look like strands of hair.

"A mystery made clear," she said.

25

The high priests of science generally putter along like a backfiring engine. Every so often, they strike a lighting bolt of combustion and come up with an answer. A few decades later they endeavor, mostly in vain, to make it fit between the ears of those of us who count ourselves as common folk, to explain what otherwise defies our perception. For example, that time may not be linear after all. They tell us that we knew something like this, but somehow forgot it, or its opposite, that we knew nothing like it and they have just discovered it. Sometimes they tell us that we knew something like it, forgot it, relearned it, but still do not understand it. Then a nihilist comes along and insists that we knew nothing like it, and never will know it. Finally, a poet stands before it and suggests that we did not know the question and when hinted of it, purposely avoided it.

Around this same, unraveled, anti-linear time, Lasso Krohn blew the dust off a copy of Lazaro's *String Trio*, which he retrieved from among the memorabilia of his grandmother, Irini Arvanakis Zervas, and immediately sought out an ensemble to interpret the work. He had left the orchestra in Baltimore, dismissed nine months after his promotion to the first violin section. Amelia Everett's effect on his playing was essentially permanent but his general temperament grated prodigiously as his playing ascended to new heights. The dismissal was for missing rehearsals and arguing with a famous guest conductor over the brass contributions to the finale of the Bruckner *Eighth*, the conductor an ex-illustrious timekeeper of the Gewandhaus Orchestra of Leipzig, and, incidentally, fired from his post as well.

"You are forcing the color of the trombones onto the canvas, Herr Maestro," Lasso said politely to the survivor of Dresden, who had not yet returned to the city of his mother tongue. "The poor church organist would think someone had added the flatulence of trombones at measure eleven." The color of sunless clouds graying his expression, the Maestro stood somewhat in shock, tapping his baton against his pant leg in Brucknerian 4/4 time, making eye contact with the concertmaster, turning his back on the orchestra and then returning to face them all again, the sulfur of his disdain suffocating any humor found in the comment.

"Come and look at the score, Herr Krohn," the Maestro said calmly, for what had been the third time Lasso interjected an observation during rehearsal - his previous interruptions regarding an errant bowing and a dwindling tempo. Until that moment, the Maestro consoled himself with the idea that if the orchestra's administrators did not rid him of this impudent pest, he would never conduct in Baltimore again. Lasso's colleagues openly groaned, knowing what would come next. "You see my boy," the conductor said, "Herr Bruckner has placed a double forte beneath the trombones at measure eleven."

"Yes, Herr Maestro, but the trumpets and horns are at triple forte, aren't they?" The conductor had had enough.

"Are you a trombone player, Herr Krohn, or a violinist?" the conductor shouted. Lasso smiled sheepishly. "Then kindly leave the dynamics of the brass section to me and the gentlemen who blow for a living," the conductor said, blowing into his cupped left hand as if it were a mouthpiece, unleashing a simulated trombone blast and then walking off the stage.

Lasso moved back into his grandmother's home near Wilmington. This time she did not bother with the usual advice she gave when he appeared at her door.

"Why don't you go home and spend some time with your mother? She misses you. You can find a seat with an orchestra in Helsinki, and all those blonde beauties waiting for a dark prince." (His hair had darkened dramatically during his time across the Pacific.) By now, she knew not to ask him why he would not return to see her. Korea had ruined him for the Nordic cold. She remembered what he had said to her.

"The damn cold crystallizes your nose hairs." Next, he managed to obtain a position with the Philadelphia Chamber Music Society. No member of the Society wanted to expend time or effort on the *String Trio*, and certainly not on behalf of a violinist, albeit talented, arriving with a troublesome reputation. Unwisely, Lasso asked musicians he had never met to play his father's work just as he walked into rehearsals for a Mozart *Divertimento*, a Dvorak *Serenade* and Stravinsky's *Dumbarton Oaks Concerto*, the latter being a work none of them had ever played and agonized over like neophytes. A month later, for the sole purpose of having the troublesome *Trio* performed, he also joined the Harcourt String Quartet of Wilmington, Delaware, named after its founder,

Nadia Harcourt, the homely young cellist and only female of the group, who had practiced her retching version of fellatio upon every member of the quartet at one time or another. Recently, Nadia had so infuriated the first violinist with jealousy that he quit. Lasso filled the post and determined that while Nadia was no beauty, she was, with her requisite long legs and perpetually passion starved expression, something of an irresistible vamp, holding the cello between her legs as if it were a singing phallus.

The group worked extensively on their rendering of Lazaro's work, amidst the new jealousies plaguing the violist, who craved repeat performances with Nadia. The Harcourt Quartet transformed Lazaro's little black hole of notes from its original 92 measures of condensed madness into the etude on the flexibility of time that its composer originally conceived, music not driven by the obsession with form, but to be interpreted differently each time it is bowed. The passages crammed with quasi-serial complexity or polyphonic nonsense, depending upon one's ear and tolerance, could spread out over time at the whim of the electrons firing within each musician's otherwise starkly predictable will. Lasso was quite pleased and made a tape recording of the performance. A year later, he accidentally taped over the recording in his enthusiasm over a series of natural sounds seemingly made by running water in a local park.

Dominating Nadia first, he then took hold of the ensemble, renaming it the Ilion Quartet. Forcefully, he proposed dropping the standard Mozart and Haydn in favor of the Beethoven *Grosse Fuge* and *Quartet Number 15*, his favorites, but then after months of practice moved past them because of the despondency they provoked in him. Then he promoted the Dvorak and the Borodin quartets, but quickly dropped them as well, despite multiple performances of them, and decent earnings traveling from town to town in the Mid-Atlantic in Nadia's minibus, performances given all the way up to Sarasota, Providence and Binghamton. Next, he demanded they take time off from concerts and earn some money playing Main Line wedding receptions while they studied the Ravel, the Bartok first and second, a taxing but reflective exercise, the Shostakovich third and the two Britten quartets. The last of these they fought over violently because the second violinist, Louis Girodet, despised the music of the English. Lasso insisted, finding the

Britten mystical, homoerotically Gnostic, lyrical in the sparingly English sense, yet within a strangely modern idiom. To spite Girodet, he added a Tippett quartet as well. Finally, he suggested an American work, the Ives second, which caused them all heartburn and prompted a revolt. Nadia grew more enamored with Lasso each day and soon invited him to live with her rather than make the drive to Philadelphia. He acquiesced. Girodet and the violist finally gave up on Nadia and the Ilion disbanded.

One day, before the ensemble would reconstitute as a trio with a new member, for the express purpose of playing the Villa-Lobos *String Trio*, Lasso drove Nadia to Longwood Gardens for a stroll, to see the spot where his "grandfather had practiced being a human bird roost." Nadia had recently complained that he was embarrassed to be seen in public with her, outside of recitals of course, that he only wanted to bed her, the latter being essentially true. They chose a windy summer morning. Stratocumulus hovered like the punch lines of jokes forgotten halfway through the telling. The silver backs of leaves waved at garden strollers like the palms of so many hands. Nadia's airy, loose fitting sundress, with its delicate spray of oxeye daisies on coiling tri-leaved stems, under which she wore nearly nothing, fluttered from her pointed torso as if at any moment a cantering breeze or a mere finger flick of the strap might cause its petals to fall to the ground and expose her. Lasso caressed her shoulder blades during their walk and slipped his hand to the small of her back. Walking by a lavish bed of verbena and beyond it a cloak of purple poppy mallum, he pronounced the names aloud for her, between gentle, sensitive kisses to her nape. The colors, the sound of the names, the obelisk that was her body preoccupied him as they walked. Then he grew glum, saying nothing to her until they reached his grandfather's bench. They had marked time with labored heartbeats up the inclined walkway and sat for a moment. Mulling over his grandfather's death, Lasso told Nadia that his grandfather, "while not a pussy who chose suicide, nevertheless detested being alive." He held her hand, something he had failed to do lately.

On the hillside just beyond the entrance, when they had first arrived, Nadia had noticed the massive umbrellas of large, draping conifers and other densely foliaged specimens. She reminded him of this, wanting to change the subject, morbid and invoking the moorings of her sympathy. A delicate mist descended upon the skin, warm and glossy. They walked on, in silent cadence with his sober mood. She pulled at him and kissed him impatiently, pointing toward the hill, easily persuading him to lie beneath the trees furthest from the footpath. Protected by the canopy, on a pillow of moss, his hands gliding over her dampened skin, the occasional droplet found its way through dense needles and dripped onto her naked back. The sensation made her purr. When finally she arched her back in a surge of pleasure, a stray drop fell upon Lasso's forehead. Later, as she lay still with her eyes closed and her head upon his arm, he thought about the droplet and the lake where his father had lived. He believed in the confluence of meanings only to the extent that it was like falling in and out of sleep beneath that very same tree, cloaked, cocooned, not knowing, let alone molesting, the details of anything truly important in the whole of one's existence.

Soon after this experience, the literary pulp bugs his father had ingested as a youth, head and all, bit Lasso Krohn as well, something his mother had predicted when he was a boy. Suddenly, he began to read unremittingly, journalistic pontifications and fact-finding at first then all sorts of increasingly strenuous fiction - some good, but mostly bad, since no one he knew could tell him the difference. He read professional and technical journals, and fact patterns in legal textbooks, which led him to case law depicting in their facts an array of social mayhems and humanity's undignified worship of money, thievery and cruelty, the whole, wide swathe of its turpitude. (Facts were interesting. Legal conclusions he found to be telling of society's plagues, but quite boring). Then he happened upon a Princeton Press anthology of Paul Valéry. Enthusiasm for *Man and the Sea Shell* and *Poetry and Abstract Thought* escorted him through Mallarmé, whom he read in fits, searching for alleged faultless forms of reality, which led him through lyric sandcastles to the naiads and mermaids of Stephan George. Inch-worming his way back and forth through the mildewed musings of the Romantics, he rode the spume of modern references to Heine, whose life and career inspired in him an outline of a poetical, polemical tale of musical transmigration (social commentary carefully redacted) in the tonal manner of *Die Harzreise*. The central character was to be Gustavina Gezellea, an extravagant, green-eyed heroine, born of the first resonance of renegade seraphs, secretly strumming on the rapturous harps of heaven and discovering the orgasm of harmony. Her incarnate aesthetic descends to the world in the Eleventh Century, posing as a blithe maiden whose heart unravels with each pluck of melody and each kiss of earthly lips.

The idea brought him to a literary climax before culminating in a metaphysical dead end. Then, upon Nadia's innocent suggestion, at the mere mention of Aristotle's mental probe, he waded through a few histories of modern philosophy, stumbling upon the congenitally anti-rhetorical *des knaben wunderhorn* (his name for Heidegger), who in Nadia's reading must have been inebriated when he (the mustachioed Martin) wrote even his name on a slip of paper. *Gelassenheit* bogged Lasso down in the quicksand of conjunctions and somehow led him down a long road to Nietzsche - *The Gay Science* and then *Beyond Good and Evil* - condemning him by obligation to approximately ten pages of Hegel's *Philosophy of Right*, which he abandoned, as an edifice he could not reconstruct to scale, for Schleiermacher. Schleiermacher, the name worth repeating at least twice in the gulp of a thought or sentence, led him to an early treatise on Kierkegaard, which mired him through countless minor disciples, ingrates, imitators and commentators until he landed squarely upon Doctor Freud, as if by design. In such conversation with Freud, a medical man who envied Pandora, if you asked Lasso, he began speculating that contrary to what most of us think, the couch is quiet uncomfortable, and is supposed to be, but more importantly that *coming into being* is not just an act of extracting something from something else already here.

"It's one of two things," he explained to Nadia, emptying the bladder that he insisted was his sloshing, shell-shocked brain, "either filling something that is empty or expelling something that is full," and then he would hum a few bars of *Das himmlische Leben* from the fourth of Mahler's fourth. "The empty is precisely that, until it's filled. Expelling is something different than extracting, isn't it?" In this way, all living beings were models of the universe, he concluded, reducible to their acts of consumption and expulsion, elevating the orifice to a higher plane than consciousness.

Nadia began to worry about him but did nothing. Freud led him back to Nietzsche, the acerbic psychosis of the *Anti-Christ*, and other nihilistic syndromes. Nietzsche became a vice within the vice. The Apollonian/Dionysian dichotomy somehow (perhaps the books sat next to each other on the shelf) led him to the Ionian/Dorian/proto-Athenian trident in Thucydides and only after a brief hiatus in ancient history and the blood-mingling retiarius of cerebral combat, he unexpectedly picked up Schopenhauer and his mightily repressive will - an acute symptom of the Parmenidian absence of will. Allegedly sloppy, Schopenhauer let off a waft of the *Upanishads* and the *Gita*, whose dizzying globularity set Lasso upon the Sufis, who led him down the steep and arduous path to the Christian mystics and meta-Gnostics, of which he read the usual suspects but interestingly, avoided Origen. In the clutches of their cast-iron obscurity, the mystics led him to Matthew of Aquasparta, where he obsessed of a single thought uttered within question one of the *Ten Disputed Questions on Knowledge*: that "to understand is to suffer something and it is certain that what the soul suffers from is only from the thing understood."

This replayed for him what happened beneath the trees at Longwood, the drop of water on his forehead being the closest thing to a religious experience he had ever had. By chance, Aquasparta led him to Anselm of the dreary proofs, and coarse William's *pro istu statu* razors and then to Duns Scotus *ablatio, ablatio*, who knows if he wrote it! Scotus fed him to Roger Bacon, who, apart from his translator's corruptions, which Lasso found to be the most candid thinking he ever read, expelled him, and in this sense led him astray, as did most epistemologists. Bacon eventually pointed back through the fermentations of Ockhamites toward the curative nosh of Augustine, for reasons he did not understand. With a wink of his contrition, Augustine squeezed him into the caverns of the penitent, including Gregory of Nyssa, who abandoned him to Philoxenus of Hieraplois in his 12th and 13th *Ascetic Discourses*, where Lasso Krohn became so afflicted with "the abomination of the spiritual thorn of fornication," that he decided to stop substituting himself for Nadia's cello.

Her response was to cry inconsolably, for which he accepted, as a parting comfort to her, her clutching kisses, her tear-drenched breasts, and an abusive dismantling of his trestle. His penultimate statement to her was quoting Philoxenus: "Like the flame in stubble doth the fire of this passion lay hold upon and obtain dominion."

"What?" her response made dactyl with her heaving chest.

"I like you very much but I can't live here," he said, rising with a start, cleaning himself, dressing and closing the door behind him.

Months later, on a lost day, when the power kept shutting on and off from storm damage to the electrical lines, Lasso fell asleep at a table in a city law library, unoccupied by students because of a recent strain of influenza. He had read a fact pattern in an appellate decision with its dry depiction of the atrocities committed by a deranged man against his six-year-old stepson. The man, who could not control his irritability, burned the boy with lit cigarettes, beat him behind his legs with a broom handle, mopped the floor with his still attached hair, burned his hand on a gas oven, and, after hours of other savagery, doused the child's singed flesh by submerging him in a urine-filled toilet bowl. His mother arrived home to find her son a transgressed mutation of his former innocence, his soul extracted from between her ribs. Lasso wept.

Of course, the collectively convulsive "they" convicted the man. In his sleep, Lasso burned the case law reporter in a kitchen sink, imagining the criminal's face in the billows of gray smoke. He dreamed that he was losing sleep over the man's continued existence. The man was a savage, killing coldly, outside the scope of any orders from whatever voice of madness issued them, or perhaps he was just a testament to base stupidity. All the world's woes lay veiled in the boy's unuttered name. In his nightmare, Lasso dwelled upon the boy until he felt ill. He awoke an hour later, his face creased by the same page of facts, the marks pointed out to him by the pensive librarian, who seemed cautious in approaching him. He should have known her well, but only remembered her as Tina Bellasomething-or-other, an older woman perpetrating a hoax with refined clothing and cosmetics, exhibiting the chemically liquefying processes that make women of haggard living sag before their time. He had slept with her on two occasions while her spaniel, her true mate, watched, slobbering and then yelping at every orgasmic gurgle and moan, which made him cringe, in afterthought.

He looked out the window and went back to detesting winter, remembering the uncontrollable shivering and stinging cold and numbness that he experienced in Chosan, stepping over the frozen, bloated bodies of children in obliterated villages, people scurrying to feed themselves, like starving dogs fighting over scraps of flesh. All of the world's woes in one time and place, he thought back then. Now whenever winter arrived, he believed he would dwell on the tortured boy, forever a little boy.

None much later, Lasso noticed a father in a shopping concourse scolding, and then the mother striking their young daughter across the mouth, essentially for crying with fatigue. The slap drew a trickle of blood. She wiped the girl's mouth violently with the tail of the child's blouse, leaving a red blotch on a faded bed of pink pansies. The mother, apparently uncomfortable in the tawdry tightness of her slacks and her spectral cotton halter knotted below un-suckled pendulums, walked beside the child, haranguing her in an exaggerated, motherly cackle, pulling her ear and hair, as the father walked ahead, indifferently at first. The father had his just purchased contraband tucked under his arm, enabling the queer family dog to drag him by a long leash while simultaneously manipulating the dial on his transistor radio.

"Stay further behind! I can't hear the goddamn ball game!" he shouted.

When the girl's legs entwined with the leash, daddy turned and scowled as if his four-legged master had commanded it, forcing the girl to move back into her mother's orbit of whacks to the hairless part of the head.

"Little shit!" the mother repeated between her teeth, the father nodding his half grin of mindless accord and annoyance.

"Stinking dogs," Lasso mumbled back, taking in the facts of the scene, swallowing his spit. Someday, he thought, intervention would do, necessary to arbitrate such incidents, but not that day. At first, he stood an unnoticeable distance away, from an unobstructed vantage, and watched but then without thinking followed the couple and their child home. As they entered the house, the little girl, still cowering but not daring to whimper, received an ugly shove to the back of the head. Quickly she sat in the corner furthest from the door while Lasso ran up the steps, slipped through the swinging screen door before anyone realized he had entered the house, picked up the dog by its hindquarters, and threw it outside. Without a he word beat the father with whatever he could find, grunting like an athlete exerting brute force with every blow, waiting for the sound of cracking bones before hesitating. The baffled, previously preoccupied man fell to the floor groaning and begging for an explanation. Lasso knocked him unconscious with a glass doorstop and broke a rather large porcelain lamp across his nose, constricting his breathing at right angels to his bloodied mouth, narrowing his perception through his left eye. The woman returned with her husband's hunting rifle, the butt of the rifle tucked between her arm and breast and the weighty, drooping barrel pointing in the vicinity of Lasso's groin.

"Stop," she screamed, tugging at the rifle having its way with her, breaching her blouse. Having trouble with the safety, she re-cupped her appendage and dropped the barrel, but could not work the bolt quickly enough. Lasso reached for the rifle, dragged her by her bobbed hair and beat her between intermittent explanations.

"You will not," punch to the face, "be permitted," sight, left, "to treat," flurry to the arms and abdomen, "the girl," swat with his belt as she wriggled away, "like that." Slap on to the painful part of the overbite just after the woman begged for an explanation that was different than the one Lasso had just offered. The little girl wisely ran outside the back door of the home and caught her dog.

Realizing he was hungry, Lasso went into the kitchen, rummaged his way through the cold box, through drawers and cabinets, until he discovered enough ingredients to make himself a liverwurst and onion sandwich. He noticed a photo of the family with the dog at the center of the universe, removed the photo and threw the frame across the room.

Of course, proverbial imprisonment followed. The police found him in the kitchen, munching away, stinking of raw onions. The circumstantial bluster of his defense of another, which his grandmother paid for, proved persuasively corroborated by the little girl, whose name was Betsy Holmes. When asked why he felt it necessary to beat the couple so mercilessly he responded that it must be his Illyrian blood making him feel compelled to violence at an innocent's victimization. He spent nine months in prison and told his grandmother the experience was "interminable, like a test on the meaning of time," and yet strangely liberating - "my swim in the jailhouse womb," as he called it. During those days of ceaseless thinking, he was able to conceive of why "something like a devil might seek redemption from something like a god, well before something like a man or woman would see the need to do so." This insight explained human evolution to him. "For Lucifer, it was to earn something akin to a vacation," he wrote to his grandmother, "to avoid having to collect a soul every moment of every day, which was probably as often as pure evil had to work." The idea cast its shadow in him as the divine curse, as an endless labor, the same curse God inflicted upon men for their disobedience. Men however, found a way around their verdict and could at least enjoy a Sisyphean moment of repose and thought.

He set the idea out in this way for the benefit of his grandmother, because he was too embarrassed to tell it as he first conceived of it. The act of collecting souls was a prideful delusion, a fantasy mingled with ejaculation. The curse, the repetition of his work, was another sign of God's dominion over Lucifer. Pride in such a repetitive act, obtaining pleasure from it, was as coarse and tasteless as what evil men take pride in, what they consol each other with, how they join each other in brainless hatreds and abuses. Satan might one day feel that human subjectivity is the perfect symbol of his boredom, that he was no different then depraved killers inhabiting prisons around the world, taking pleasure in releasing the breath of life back into the atmosphere. These were the meandering thoughts Lasso practiced in prison, spurred by his reading of Teilhard de Chardin - the activation of elemental energy into a moralizing holiness. And other books lent to him by a catholic priest who enjoyed turning literate inmates, even those who could barely stomach reading the comics, into bookworms and thinkers, eventually studying strings of intellectually illicit words starving for attention, or simply helping imprisoned men forget the affliction of the tick in the tock.

Lasso learned from his grandmother that for the most part Linda and Jackson Holmes recovered from their injuries, but were deprived of their daughter and ordered to enter counseling in the art of parenting as a first step to getting her back. He also spent time in prison unintentionally frightening the other inmates with his suddenly mushrooming accent, a curious blend of Swedish and Mid-Atlantic English with a Sino-Korean impediment, and his desensitizing ideas about the nature of music, and the theater of the absurd that he insisted God had dreamt up, "all to confound, overburden and punish one of His angels." Men are collateral to the moral scheme of things. The prisoners and guards alike avoided Lasso for fear of being mentally pick-pocketed. He read to his heart's content, whistled incessantly a tune remarkably similar to the nostalgic bassoon theme of the *andante espressivo* to Prokofiev's Seventh, and was thus, warding off human contact like a petulant bowel, able to practice forgetting who and what he was.

When finally released, with significantly reduced charges, he learned that his vacated position with the chamber orchestra migrated into the talented hands of Xun Kim-So. Xun was the first Oriental player to occupy a seat with the orchestra, the son of a captured Chinese national, and a veteran of P'yongtaek who chose to marry a local woman named Eun-Mi Kim. The precocious son of a maimed nation was sent to America for an education. Capture can usher in one's lucky day, Lasso thought enviously.

Unemployed, Lasso moved in with his grandmother yet again. Irini was essentially broke from paying for his legal defense, so he began offering private violin and viola lessons in her parlor and giving her all he earned. Impoverished and unrecognized painters, unread poets and writers of fiction all went to Paris, London or Berlin for inspirational exile, but not Lasso Krohn. Centerville, a countrified upriver drive from Wilmington, was fine for him. Irini's parlor and fruit tree crammed yard was his cloud nine. Being no one of importance anywhere in the world, homelessness in someone else's home was pure self-knowledge.

Among his students, and the only one whose parents knew of Lasso's troubles with the law, was the young Gregorios Dranias. On Saturdays, Danäe, and at times Andreas, when he was not working, would drive the twenty or so mile distance to Irini's home, passing any number of schools and private teachers along the way and deliver their son into the hands of Lasso Krohn. They would greet him and then sit in the back yard or in Irini's welcoming kitchen on rainy or cold days, chatting with her, reminiscing of their encounters with Lazaros, or on those glorious sunny days, stroll in nearby parks or gardens.

After a season of lessons, Irini confided her cumulative worries in those whom she considered her son's only friends and spiritual benefactors. Lasso had taken up the rage of painting by numbers, an intentionally banal art, she said. He read to her each day in English, usually a selection from Dickens, a good translation of Flaubert or Balzac, some Hardy or Henry James, whom she found talented but tedious. At least twice a year he drove her to Brigantine, for winter days of high winds and inclement weather, to stare at the Atlantic and eat poorly at greasy spoons and at a sandwich shop with long waits. He took her to the ballet in Philadelphia, most recently a performance of *Ma Mére l'oye*, where she found the music beautiful but incompatible with the dancing, having tapped her feet to the Ray Coniff singers and dancers once too often. He took her to see the Barnes collection in Merion where she stared at a single El Greco as if it were the stylized emaciation of her son's second coming and at the changeable hues of the *Card Players*, deepening with the receding illumination of the museum windows, and dozens of other Cézannes. And at chubby, cherubic girls with baskets and blossoms, and the *Fish Vendor*, the most cunningly erotic canvas Renoir ever painted, according to Lasso, who would sit before the painting until he fell asleep, "so," as he said, "I might wake up beside her." But the impression of activity these excursions offered was false, Irini insisted, for her lonely grandson otherwise never ventured out alone or with any friends. She believed he was devoting his life to the idea of abandoning himself to a cult of minutia, to the infinite nuance of detail, to single sentences in books, to singular phrases in hour-long symphonies, to how chance arrayed his food upon his plate, and other such intricacies permitting his mind to wander free never again.

"Perhaps he's losing his will to live," she said reticently, "or perhaps I am losing my mind, for observing and concluding this of his new preoccupations." Along with reading incessantly, Lasso also made lists, she said, "lists of innumerable humdrum things," and this worried her the most. "Some things are of interest, but mostly it's just daily episodic things." He would sit up in his bed on the third floor of the house penciling his directories of calculable preferences and stare out of arched panes framing a planetarium of stars by night, or a Palladian of light by day; out unto the tops of trees and a single chimney from a neighbor's home, and the rest of his canvas, the vapors and paint of the western sky.

"Lists are not so unusual," Andreas said.

"Well, perhaps not," Irini said, "but he has a list of his lists and crazy commentaries on them, and I find that very unusual."

"I find it unusual, as well," Danäe conceded. Then, like a mother showing a prospective bride a photo of her grown son as a naked infant, in an inexcusable breach of Lasso's privacy, Irini brought them Lasso's index of his lists and finally the lists themselves, cast in a set of seven different colored notebooks, meticulously filled with his innocuous annotations. There were favorite kitchen utensils, favorites of his grandfather's old tools, favorite toothpastes, soaps, shirts and socks, insects, mammals, reptiles, fish to eat, pairs of ears, eyes, lips and legs, favorite doorways and buildings in cities he was familiar with like Philadelphia, Wilmington and Baltimore and so forth. The lists he then broke down and enumerated into sub-lists, a delineation of those things into their apparently logical parts, also planned. He exhibited a fixation with the number seven, the number at which most lists ended.

The intention was perhaps the perfect never-ending task, the emblematic tick of the Western mind, along with calculating, or mimicking an act of creation like breathing into a mud-caked figure, or defying the theorists who believed in the miracle of gathering the names of things as an act of self-conscious salvation. The more abstract lists contained commentaries that often made little sense and at times ambled back into the reasons why the items on the list ought not to be on the list. The brown and green notebooks included lists of his favorite poets and poems, playwrights and plays, *Henry the Fifth* not among them and nothing of Molière's, Strindberg or Ibsen. Novelists and novels were like composers, and works of music, his favorites on the lists crossed out and altered repeatedly, commentaries obscuring the list at times. A conspicuous exception and hiccup of indecision appeared with his favorite painters who numbered to at least forty-nine. The list was begun seven times and on each one, wildly different painters made their appearance until the last list, not having been crossed out yet, settled upon Van Gogh, Grünewald, Ghyzis, Munch, Whistler, Rembrandt and Caravaggio. Perhaps fatigue had set in. In contrast, his favorite orchestras appeared as a list of only five with two crossed out and not replaced. The Concertgebouw, being first because he liked the sound of it and since Amsterdam was on every version of his list of favorite cities along with eleven others he had never been to. The cities he chose because they had shed some attractive women that he had met and snagged on his carnal trolling, or else the cities possessed sufficient cultural amenities to function as welcoming committees for the model American tourist - for example, Dublin, for the idealized Irish pub. He had lists of his favorite dishes - French toast with syrup and crispy scrapple, among the seven; his favorite liquors, nearly anything that was not sweet, over ice; his most coveted occupations that he would never have the privilege to hold; a beekeeper, for those thousands of little holes where eggs are laid; a bookseller for the millions of ordered words; a fisherman for the countless scales; a conductor, for all those notes strung together; a strip club owner, for the legs; a baseball player and an evangelist - no reasons provided for the last two. His most preferred saying, "a stitch in time." His favorite saints, who were famous sinners first. His favorite generals grinding their brethren into submission and his accompanying note - "determined by the histories one had the endurance to read."

Danäe read every list over the course of a many visits and especially dwelled upon the list of his preferred sexual positions, which included drawings to the right of the text. The list went to eight, including a vivid depiction of number one - lying on a bed and having the woman stand to the left facing away and squatting on the horn of his saddle as if she were riding a horse, and explaining that he loved how the women who acquiesced all looked back at him over their shoulder with the same embarrassed but aroused expression. They ought not to be shorter than five foot three, he calculated, to accomplish a comfortable penetration without their feet dangling just above the floor. Like many a youthful and preoccupied man, he also made a list of his most beloved women with whom he had engaged in a pairing, using that popularly digni-fied expression over any more vulgar one, and discretely entered only their initials beside the commentary. This list of compromised females was not a simple one, suffering with its confession of regrets and the occasional attempt at humor, nearly girlish diary entries replete with descriptions, annotations and rationales. A. E., as he identified Amelia Everett's long legs and avid impatience, was on nearly every permutation of the list, entered in first place, the other six accorded their rank mostly by their immodest propensities and acquiescence. S. B. was nearly always second because, he explained, she inherited from her most brutal cuck-old of a culture the pornographic zeal to accommodate as many men at once as could be arranged without her arrest or conscription by a pimp. He noted, however, that the frenzy of sheer corruption she exhibited was all he really liked about her. R.T. was on and off the list but always had the words "black as night" next to her initials and, in the last entry, "labial domination." N. H. was also on each list for her requisite legs and the coxswain of his imagined nirvana born of a single drop of water. E. P. he listed for her perversions, like having her voluptuous breasts lath-ered to perfection and tied together with his belt and the most sensitive parts of her feminine anatomy bitten and slapped without mercy, an exploit he despised but accommodated. "I may have eventually helped her," he wrote, "had she the ability to exhibit a crumb of affection for anyone other than her ex-husband, the beneficiary of her youth, his money and spring clamps."

Immediately after this, he made a catalog of women who might be quite unhappy they did not make the prior list. For them a roll call of the full name sufficed, Belinda Monroe being the most disappointed, he surmised, since her name appeared on a few versions of the prior list but always without commentary, as if her predilections were forgettable, invisible, but noteworthy weaknesses none the less.

His favorite philosophers proved to be a failed cataloguing; the inventory crisscrossed with so many entries in so many different directions and so often that the names obliterated into a mass of letters and scrawling pen marks. Even when overtaken with a different ink, thoughtless doodling and word clusters made not a single name discernible, except perhaps Spinoza, for what other name ends in "*oza*?" His favorite languages, finished at six, but he added the caution: "none of which I speak." That list he wrote in Greek, but Greek was not on the list. His favorite famous people, who turned out to be queers, went to a list of nine. "Like the right size sinker for fairies, I suppose." Wittgenstein and Cavafy constantly were vying for the first position, then the recently translated Lorca eventually replaced Cavafy, "because the Alexandrian was convinced that the distinction was important, as if we couldn't tell from the start that he was a poet of the docks and the dark caverns of his psyche."

Andreas barely looked at the lists, whereas Danäe's curiosity obscured her better judgment until she came to the list entitled "What I Love the Most." This seemingly endless record possessed no pattern and filled the red notebook completely, spilling into the black one. Each ten pages or so had a specific piece of music associated with it, jotted down in shorthand at the bottom of the page. Thus, the list apparently began with an accompaniment of the sinewy pianissimo of harp in Stravinsky's *Orpheus* and moved on to Strauss' lavish *Also sprach Zarathustra*, the noble despair of Mozart's *Requiem* and so on. The litany of such objects of love began with "the fragrance of humidity on a summer afternoon beneath a shade tree." On and on it crawled until he reached the first entry overtly about himself, "the dexterity of my hands," which had a long space and then a musical rest after it - followed by "silence, the night after a winter snow like a face thawing into a soft pillow." The plum of wine; flowers with long, drooping stamen; long, silk-wrapped legs attached to dark-haired women, a statistical rarity; prayerful pianoforte fanfares heralding a Bruckner coda; a cool drink of water on a hot day; the scent of an infant's breath; the supple quality of the skin after a bath; the feeling of an axe splitting wood. All made the list, plus countless more.

On the list of things he found funniest, was "the decision of men to be masters of the irrelevant," along with "the frolic that must be the divine's idea of its self." The last entry in the red notebook was his list of favorite realizations, the first being "one that my father must have had: that the simple-minded impatience and Herculean effort expended in puncturing a single gushing female is an incredible waste of time. One might read or listen to music, become immersed in a painting or otherwise eavesdrop upon the heavens and attain as much ecstasy as one can endure." A bit further down, he noted, "That the ordinary idea of love as a sense of responsibility must be a replica of divine duty, otherwise why ask for it in men? In an instant, love can erase everything one suffers and make the dull ache of existence magically disappear into the sidled sleeve of eternity, which is to say that it is outside of time, a miraculous force, always already returning to where it was born." Seventh on the list was "the idea of a year without Sundays, which is like an armless swimmer, a poor mimicry of a fish." He followed this with another reference to his father. "The last generation to believe in cognate divinity, to look over their shoulder with dread, to do more than pantomime such belief, to mindlessly deny everything but humanity's future and that another's comprehension and command may lurk in the shadows of deified reason. All because we have forgotten that we wager for a living. Something Kierkegaard, the gelding (with a line through it), Tillich and Buber taught to the rocks they wrote for." Under this, he wrote in blue ink, with italicized emphasis and as an afterthought – "*this and nothing else ushers in apocalypses.*" Large space. "Some men endure life; the rest make it up as they go."

The only list with nothing on it was entitled "my favorite dates in history". Lazaro's puny *String Trio* was on the list of things he loved as well, his mother's distant voice just before it. He described both quite sentimentally, as "sounding faintly on the loose ends of a celestial filament, floating out into the stratosphere past Mars, past Jupiter, caught in the scattering rings of Saturn, which fill the emptiness of being with color. Our chiming words and notes, while never known on earth, linger and echo in the heavens as the drone of the seraph."

26

On the day before the feast of Saints Constantine and Eleni, Lambros received the news that his mother had died and immediately made plans to attend her funeral. He had visited his parents but twice in all the years of his absence, during a time when travel through the mountains was too dawdling in pace and tiresome for a large family to contemplate very often - upon the occasion of his youngest sister's wedding and the baptism of her daughter. Arrested for his passive resistance during the opening foray of the rebellion, Lambro's father, after whom they named Stratos, attempted to shield a nephew from abduction by fanatical freedom mongers, men ripping youths from their mothers' comfort and carting them off to indoctrination camps as future fodder for the fold, imprisoning them in snowy Balkan hideouts. Stratos the elder concealed the boy in a hunting blind, in the thickets above Yergola. That same day, they were discovered, betrayed by a neighbor with a grudge against the boy's father, Lambro's uncle. The nephew was hogtied and tortured. He vanished into the Yugoslavian wilds. Dragged before a quickly convened tribunal, the patriarch of the Lambrou clan was set adrift facedown in the shallow seaside, his throat slit to within a centimeter of the jugular. An old and rugged slice of rawhide, the old man survived but contracted tuberculosis, requiring a procedure to remove a lung to ensure the continued nuisance of his existence, as he was fond of reminding everyone and sporting a hideous, protruding pink and purple scar that looked as if a bloodworm had grafted itself onto his neck. From then on, minding his own business was his only occupation, notwithstanding its being contrary to his nature to remain idle, whether exchanging ideas or blows. Despite this cruel lesson for his family, his capitulation and his efforts to avoid a feud, the attempted assassination prompted years of mutual reprisals, both open and clandestine. Lambro's brothers had remained in Yergola and met their ghastly ends within a few years of each other in the various political and clannish conflagrations. His eldest brother, Mattheos, whom Lambros barely remembered and who suffered increasingly from the days of his youth with what one could only diagnose as pyromania, ended up tied to a burning mule cart sent careening through the village, the hapless animal desperately trying to escape the flames and galloping until Mattheos was all but torn to shreds. This retribution was less against his father but instead leveled at Mattheos for the many fires he relished as a young man. Stelios, Lambro's other brother, the father of the abducted nephew, surreptitiously assassinated as many rebels as he could in response, even as they lay in their beds asleep. His father discovered him tortured and shot with a single bullet behind the ear and a rag, soaked in blood and retching fluids stuffed in his mouth.

Through all of this Lambros entreated his father and mother to come and live with him in Lathra. They declined, citing the fact that their sons lay buried in Yergola, refusing to leave the graves unattended for fear that their enemies might desecrate them. They had already toppled Stelios' headstone and cracked it with heavy hammer blows. Lambros chose at that time not to return to Yergola or visit the graves. His parents had written him as much, for his own safety. Two years later, his father died quietly in his midday sleep. The defiantly self-banished son, the *scorpizmeno*[95] as his mother called Lambros, hung his head and cried as he sat on his bed, having received the news by letter. According to his children, who never saw a tear streak down their father's face, and stood outside their father's room weeping with him for the grandfather they met only once, not a single tear had actually dampened Lambro's face. His sorrow was purely auditory. Lambro's father had faded for him, like an old photo, his face forgotten. Stories in letters were all he remembered of him. From then on he openly derided the founders of his former ideological kitten (whom he neglected to stroke anyway) as mere apologists for the destruction of families and traditions. He cursed his own gullibility for having believed what he now called the

---

95 σκορπισμένο – the strewn one

insistent fairytales of desperate men. A utopian ideology might remain a noble ambition in men's minds, but had become for Lambros as heretical a conviction as any ever invented, rendering men numb and disconnected and goading them to ignore the monster lurking within their twisted ideas.

His widowed mother, the matriarch of the dead and of the living in abstention, had survived occupation, blood feuds by the dozen, drought and famine and ended her days wearily sitting on her terrace, issuing acerbic castigations to passersby and neighbors and to the birds roosting on roofs, while suffering reprimand by her daughter, Stavroula, for her judgments. Lambros received the news of his mother by phone, walked somberly to the church and lit a candle, leaving a note for Pater Alexi to chant a memorial service for her. He and Elissa embarked for Epirus that day. He asked the priest to check in on his children, whom at that point he believed could remain behind on their own.

The trip to Yergola spanned a hardy nine hours of queasy misery in his rattling, dent riddled red truck fitting three. At that last moment, Sophia and Evanthia both insisted they accompany their parents. The last of the Lambrou men to have learned to drive, Lambros consistently confused the brake for the accelerator. Adding time and discomfort to the journey, a long stretch of the road was under construction. Equipment and laborers collected at opposing ends of the worksite. Men busily scratched their collectively bargained minutia as they smoked and laughed at drivers left to clutch their way through an absurd network of barrels, passengers praying to be steered clear of open and unmarked ditches or precipitous canyons. Lambros drove through the gauntlets so painstakingly as to have finally perturbed Elissa into spastic, nerve frayed profanity. She began her diatribe with contempt for the driver and ended it with a snide reference to Lara. He had divulged to her a version of the incident at the library, in a moment of harsh reproach over her irksome habit of reminding him of his failures.

"You and your little donkey cart of a truck, painted red like the whore's lips you kissed in Thessaloniki."

"I kissed no one but you, my insecure pet."

"Well, you thought about it and that's the same thing in God's eyes, and mine."

"Then you are both tyrants," he mumbled and drove on undaunted, receiving double *moutzes* [96] from virtually every driver that passed him, while struggling to restrain his imagination from revisiting the library. It was just a daydream, he made himself believe; falling asleep over books that I did not comprehend.

On the road to Yergola, at the outskirts of a mountain village, a man lay pinned beneath his large two-wheeled wooden cart and its load of heavy stones. A group of women and children huddled about him. A few witnesses were crying out of habit, but discreetly, a good distance away, more a case of egging each other on than anything deeply felt. Two women were on their knees by the man's side speaking to him, but not in a manner that made Lambros think they knew him. The smaller children mostly scurried about on the side of the road saying nothing. Lambros was driving by slowly and saw the dire circumstance of the man from his open window. He pulled his truck over and told Elissa he would go see if he could lift the cart off him. Elissa got out of the truck with Sophia and Evanthia to stretch their legs but did not follow him immediately. Lambros grew pale with pity, for the man laid essentially cut in half just above the pelvis. Someone, likely the victim himself, had fitted a piece of sharply angled steel on the edge of the cart's flatbed to keep it from splintering further. The cart had tipped back when the man tried to adjust the load. The steel edge was sharp enough to sever flesh and bones with the weight of the load falling on him. The ornery mule sat idly munching weeds from between the rocks on the side of the road, still tightly tethered to the cart by a strand of new leather, unable to move forward because the hitch pointed to the heavens. Lambros immediately attempted to recruit the women's help to right the cart.

"Have you sent for help?" he asked as he went to pull the hitch down by himself.

"Why?" a young woman said, interrupting him. "He's as good as cut in two. Lifting the cart will make him bleed faster and he'll lose the last few minutes he has of this life."

"Let him feel the sun on his face for as long as he wants," another woman said.

"Is anyone here his kin? Are these his children?" Lambros asked.

---

96 μούτζες an open palm imprecation, sending the recipient to the devil

"No," the young woman said, "we've never seen him before. He was just passing through. Lambros removed some stones from atop the man's chest and left arm. Then he bent down near his ear and whispered to him.

"Sir, can we send for your wife and children?"

"No," the man said. "My wife and daughter died ... some time ago."

"Then I will lift this cart off, so you may see them again," Lambros said. "What do you think?"

"Thank you," the man said serenely. The women watched Lambros remove more stones, power the hitch down with his belt, using all his strength and body weight, and then secure it to the ground with a large rock within reach. The man moaned at the sight of the cart rising over him but otherwise reacted as if he could feel nothing below his reach. Lambros hurried around, took the man's shovel and another rock and wedged the cart behind the wheel, in its righted position. Elissa and the girls walked closer as he bent down beside him and held his hand.

"What do you do for a profession, sir?" Lambros asked him. The man's eyes closed slowly as he murmured, "I'm a stonemason."

"You will be a stonemason in heaven as well then, except it will not be work because the rocks and your tools will be as light as feathers." The man opened his eyes and answered with a stare, transfixed, a catheter to his soul, appearing to accept the light and air quivering in his last breath. Lambros stood up and looked down at him. "Elysium welcomes you. And your children will honor you forever," he said and walked backed to his truck.

———•———

Once in Yergola, Lambros went about his work, the dutiful son and brother. He attended to the details of his mother's funeral and memorial feast along with his sister, Varvara. He disliked his sister and had previously forsworn his youngest sibling mostly because of her obnoxious husband, for whom he had little tolerance. Her husband was Themi Kalivas, the older brother of Costa, the owner of Lambro's boyhood curio. Lambros knew from his mother's letters that his sister insisted upon the annoying practice of grumbling about her husband in private and then recounting the supportive comments made by those family members in whom she confided, without advising or admitting to Themi any of her instigating complaints. When he overreacted to unfavorable judgments by her family, she sided with her husband and denied her obvious complicity in originating the complaint. In his current state, Themi was loud and as near to obese as a Greek could be in those days, especially in the seat of his trousers. He also disliked him because he was unremittingly cheerful in the presence of his nephews, while ignoring his nieces, making him ultimately ill suited for his work as a seaman, at sea with younger men. When he was younger and quite fit, Themi settled for the narrow-hipped, flat-bosomed waif that was Lambro's sister precisely because she resembled a boy. She was a stark contrast to the other female offspring of the family, and to Themi's apparent youthful taste in the woman of his curio.

"He prefers peg boys if you ask me," Lambros concluded on the second occasion of meeting him. "Who would have known the damn satyrs were what goaded the bugger's loins, way back then?" Themi also smoked cigars with sickening regularity, never appearing in public without a smoldering stub in his mouth, a foreign habit he picked up during his time at sea in the South Atlantic. Varvara griped and boasted at once of having not kissed her husband since their wedding night. Naturally, the couple remained childless.

The morning following his arrival in Yergola, after having coffee and some store bought jam on his buttered bread, his sister's contribution to modernity, Lambros decided on a walk.

"No wonder your husband looks like a buoy," he complained to his sister, "if you feed him like this - sugared fruit and two fingers thick with butter."

"Then don't eat it, ingrate!" she snapped back, the exchange precipitating a silly, final friction between brother and sister. He left the table chewing the last slippery morsel he could stomach and strolled idly around the neighborhood of homes and businesses near the center of the village, making a clear mental note of which families lived in which houses. Most of them he recognized from his youth. He bothered no one to inquire of marriage or the obituary of old acquaintances nor whether anyone had moved away as he did. In a moment's nostalgia for his youth and mother, he was unsure of why he left Yergola in the first place. It was charming, peaceful, set before the stage of a vivid sea, churning with a woman's turbulence and gusts of heavenly inspiration. He lapsed into unambiguous regret at having abandoned both his mother and father and gradually sank into a vague chain link of guilt regarding his children, fretting over various injudicious decisions he was sure to make in the future which might affect them all and Elissa.

This mnemonic jigsaw of emotions included a fond image of a toddling Nikos, swiping at wisps of steam rising from his mother's hot soup. Even as a child, eating with the zealous inanity of a grazing goat, Nikos, unlike most other children, would, when he was no longer interested in stuffing his mouth to capacity, hurl the remnants of his meal over his shoulder, propelling half-chewed morsels from the table. This was despite repeated reprimand and spankings over the habit. In his ongoing experiment of fatherhood, Lambros overreacted once and slapped the boy's lean, minuscule thighs so heavily as to raise welts and black bruises. For two days, Nikos could not sit without discomfort, causing Lambros such mawkish remorse as to contemplate drowning himself in the lake. Now the very idea of his children's demise severed from him any sense of well being. He felt vulnerable and foolish but could not help himself. Even when rationalizing that Elissa would be there to care for them, or that any eventuality would not occur until long after worms had reduced him, the idea of their death proved unbearable and too disconcerting to ponder. During the occupation and its bloody aftermath, he rarely felt this way, living from day to day as if he knew they would all survive.

If death were the only wage, if there were not instructions for a migration of the soul to some idyllic reunion with loved ones, then of what value was a favorable judgment? If the creator conceived of life and the sepulcher as an end in itself, then he could not be the merciful fountain of being that Christ taught with such profundity, or, as Lambros rationalized, "He would be a sadist and nothing more. Only reunion with the persons I love will satisfy me, otherwise what is the point of heaven and an immortal soul. Why obey any god, or any law, let alone the drivel of men? Others must feel this way," he once confided to Lazaros or Rigos, but could not remember which. "For this reason alone God must not be observant and attentive to men's affairs."

In this frame of mind, he strolled along. Then, in the distance, approaching him from across the earthen pathway beleaguered with weeds and uncultivated dandelions was a gnarled, hobbling, black-ragged figure, sagging with age, dragged along from a short leash tied about her waist, pulled by an aimlessly sniffing beast, seemingly a scrawny black dog. Grasping her beneath her right arm was another figure, swinging a cane before him, apparently unable to make his way on his own, shuffling forward and chattering on end. As the three approached and came under his scrutiny, Lambros recognized Olga Stoyanova in the gnarled infirmity of the still living, a black cloak and headdress covering sagging shoulders, an uncharitable hump, a ravaged patina to her face, skin peeling like birch bark. A nearly blind Petros Stoyanova was on her arm, spectacled in dirty pewter-rimmed telescopic lenses, loud, odiferous, uncombed, with a crooked collar and homeless button at the top without an eyelet, completely lacking his youthful, sanitary luster. They walked by without a look or a thought to him. Olga's hands at first appeared like maces but now, up close, like two leathered tsantsas (shrunken heads) from a land of forest dwellers. Lambros stood as still as he could, hiding in the shadows of a nearby wall to the schoolhouse, staring at them, the obstinate black dog was actually a headstrong goat as they drew near and into focus. The goat brushed by him, nipping at his feet, but did nothing more. For a moment, Lambros felt as if he were still a youth, nearly motionless, the imperceptible sway of a tarred quay in a placid port, the string of his bird noose looped between the index finger and thumb, patiently hoping to snag the leg of a dove pecking at the gravel. Petros Stoyanova emerged from the dust cloud engulfing him, ethereal rays of spectral blue to violet cooling the margins of his animal aura unto his dirty, drawn-out shadow. Sniffing the air at every third step, he sensed the presence of another person and abruptly ceased his babble, turning Olga's inattention to her right. The eager little goat pulled her to a complete stop and then snapped its movement in the opposite direction.

"Evangelos! Don't pull me so hard," she said, her voice melting with tenderness. "You're going to make me fall, my son." Lambros walked away from the wall cordoning the schoolyard and watched her trundle away with her husband, the dusty apparition, the black goat's tug and pull tightening the rope about her waist.

———◆———

The funeral was uneventful and not well attended. Lambros found the local rituals strange and barbaric, or at least rousing his Anatolian sensibilities in protest. Everything offended him. The young priest's tenebrous, condemnatory attitude granted him reprieve from the nagging regret he continued to suffer for having left his mother "to these unfeeling dogs," as he later complained to Elissa and his daughters. Even the Church seemed to have evolved into a spurious shrine, a caricatured rendering of the Book of Revelations dripping with black and magenta images of a violent theocracy, icons heralding the potency of death's vacuous triumph over men. Meticulous depictions of skewered souls stripped bare and flung into the inferno of the fiend's lake and all the beastly rest that befalls the most vulgar and vicious of men. Since the days of Parthena, not only had life become a less prized cognizance, a nearly pastoral contingency, but death as well, an ignoble stint ending with worm-eaten granulation and liquidity, loveless, without penitence, without devotion. Yet, as Pater Sophocles taught him when he was a boy, as Christ miraculously lived and testified, somehow, wonderfully and incongruously, yes, even against one's better judgment, death had become the one state of nothingness that was annullable. He was intent upon remaining unmoved by the thought of village women someday exhuming and cleaning his mother's bones, as they just had his father's, on the day of his arrival. But he failed. Dwelling upon the end of the alphabet, festering in his imagination like culpability, he fell back into a quagmire of sentimentality and the kind of apprehension and apologetics he despised. He dabbed his eyes when he was alone, after the burial, but nothing appeared on his handkerchief. Tearless again. His arms stretched behind him as he lay on the smooth marble of a tomb a few meters from where the breadth of his clan lay buried in a row, the known as well as the names he would never remember. Sitting by the wharfs of memory, his heels dangling near the surface, he remembered his mother taking him to the sea for swimming lessons, how she waded in with her dress on, as deep as her waist, to keep him from sinking. He remembered her sweet smile as he lay back against her work-veined arms and kicked his legs out into the lucent sea, executing a buoyant backstroke.

27

The more pervasive the surveillance, the more heightened the scrutiny, the more a man seeks to hide what he perceives is most important about him. Like a child hiding behind saplings and believing he remains unseen, he barricades himself from the commerce and chaos of human affairs. Returning to Lathra, in a legato of moods, feeling aged and hunching into himself, his chest burning with days of suppressed emotion, which he blamed upon his sister's insistence on frying most of what she cooked, Lambros returned to his routines of leisure, taking days to speak to Elissa again. While she, a woman no longer mindful of her station, resumed her cooking, cleaning and tending to the affairs of children and beasts, Lambros resigned himself to sitting at Yianko's or fishing for much of each day. The farming was no longer his, but his son's concern. Often he would forget what day of the week it was, and at times forget to return home at midday to eat. Six months conceded into a plaintive cadence, a blur of days passing without distinction.

On one such unhurried, lazy morning, his mind played new tricks on him, leaving him afloat upon the rounded, effortless waves of memory, made sharper with the froth of invention. He grew lethargic, screening the sun with his large brimmed hat - "the rich American" he called it - dragging his fingers through the pearly cold water of Vegoritis, sipping tsipouro from a flask lodged beneath the seat of his shallow little rowboat. He began by meditating upon the dearth of fish as compared to the old days; a contrast to what Andreas portrayed half a world away and homesick. By noon, the sun and libation doused and dulled his vigilance, slipping him into a nap for so many hours that even his gristly skin reddened and chafed. His boat drifted aimlessly to the darkest waters of the lake. Entranced in the deepest sleep he enjoyed since his return from Yergola and his parents' graves, fires neither oppressing nor plaguing him, he realized, when he awoke, that his night frights had for the most part subsided with waning youth, well before he was harkened by the sight of Olga in the flesh, nearly a lifetime later. Instead, Magda Karangelos came to him in his sleep, dancing before him - the embolus of his hallucination - and then briefly the old Turk who had sold him his land appeared, wearing his fez and scolding him for wearing his whiskers long and proud, as if he were a priest, when in fact he was clean-shaven. They were a pair, Magda and the old Turk. Otherwise, his nectarous imagination led him to believe he was sailing upon the old lake or the Marmara.

On this day his romantic reverie included a vignette with Lydia and her son Samson, traveling to America, where she would take up the profession with which she survived upon returning to Cyprus, but before a cancer of the pancreas claimed Magda. Then, briefly, he drifted back to Magda and wondered if she remembered him, as she lay pale as snow in her spinster's lace, deathly still within her linen-draped skiff. Lydia had worked as a hairdresser among the locals in Cyprus, including tending to some of the more progressive Turkish women. She indeed traveled to America, at the invitation of relatives of Thalia, with high hopes, only to be cast out by her employer nearly a year after her arrival. Her English, up until her last day of employment, consisted of ten words, five of which were profanities of the wanton variety, taught to her with lascivious zeal by the covetous salon owner. She shunned the swarthy, fat-lipped Sicilian time and again, but finally, when he grew tired of her rejections and as punishment for the scratches she inflicted upon his cheek and jaw, thus forced to reveal the episode to his wife, he let her go, for her own good, he assured her. His plump cannoli of a wife, herself a beautician, detested "her skinny little ass and legs," always engorging her poor Giacomo's *cetriolo*,[97] a devout Catholic and vegetarian of which he was neither, inciting him to sin, along with the other girls in the salon.

Penniless and unable to find another position at a beauty parlor near her apartment and her son's grade school, Lydia took a position as the

---

97 cucumber

hairdresser to the dead, spending her days with the family Skuld, peculiar morticians and their embalmed wives, whom she neither understood nor could befriend for all their Lutheran compassion and Nordic dignity. Disheartened and unable to explain her profession to her son without annunciating her ignominy and loneliness, she admitted defeat and returned to Greece and the only place she believed left to her, Lathra. She wrote to Athena Kyriazis, tactfully reclaiming her brother's house, but not the cropland, by simply asking for permission to rescind the gift of the house. She no longer feared what might become the patent reproach of neighbors and a constant reminder of her disgrace, but came only to endure the cruor of their indifference. Leaving the land to Athena's husband, she could provide for her son a place to retrace steps. The men of Lathra no longer complained of a feminine touch coursing through their barbered heads (their beloved Timonakis was gone); she would pull hair and scissor away at heads as if they were plots of grain.

Lambro's dream ended suddenly. He awoke with a penetrating pang but no fire had consumed his house. With what meaning did Lydia and Magda infuse his dreams? Nothing worth finding out, he said to himself, turning to his other side and stuffing an old coat beneath his head as the boat rocked gently with the lake's shallow breathing.

———◆———

Nikos had returned from his studies in Athens for the baptism of his nephew, Stratos and Anna's son. Elissa summoned him to find his father, who wanting to escape the confusion and tension of preparations for the sacrament, took off on his usual Sunday morning routine of floating on the lake instead of nodding off through Alexi's liturgy. Lambros lay peacefully on his back in his boat, his mind drifting from one piece of unfinished business to another until it finally settled on barba Ianouli. The old man had finally died three weeks earlier after a series of firsts: a brief illness, the first in his life, and a visit to a dentist in Edessa to extract a molar, another first. The roots had exposed with age, causing him sufficient pain to demand that the dentist remove every one of his teeth, most of which were, even at his advanced age, quite healthy, and to replace them with a set of pearly dentures. Ianouli contracted an infection that swelled his gums beneath his false teeth because he refused to remove them at night, much as he refused to stop smiling to show off their sparkle. The infection, also the first in his life, bore a nefarious tumor into his gums. Some insisted that he died at the age of one hundred and eleven but looked sixty. He had survived with Lathra as his mistress and by pickling himself from the inside out with daily throttles of ouzo imported from Lesvos, which he insisted was superior to the rotgut tsipouro of endopee. Others thought his longevity to be a testament to Vegoritis and his diet of fish for his afternoon meal and yogurt devoured daily for breakfast, yogurt cultures dating back to the kefir of invading Caucasians and the kumyss fermentations of Tatars. Others said it was the greens cultivated in his tiny garden, so choked with weeds that the plot appeared like a crowded city, or Gallano's chewy bread smothered with olive oil and eggplant spread, which he insisted was like "taking my intestines for a long walk in the mountains." Alexi and Lambros went to his bedside in his final hours.

"What are you here for?" he asked them.

"To prepare you for heaven, Ianouli, what do you think barba?" Lambros said, overcome with laughter.

"Heaven is not my destination," he said sadly, "It's straight to the hot place for me. I'm sure of it." There was fear in his voice. Lambros composed himself.

"Then confess your sins and we may change that providence," Alexi said twice, shouting at him the second time because the old fellow could not hear so well.

"Confess my sins to the likes of you two?" He coughed up phlegm as he spoke.

"Not, to me," the priest said, "to God, you old fool!"

"No offense, Lambros Lambrou, I know you found your Anatolian wife in Turkey, but the only reason I would go there would be to take a shit and leave." Lambros laughed. Then he sat down and listened. Ianouli changed his mind about confessing to Alexi and let loose a stream of words, more than they ever heard him speak, as if he wanted to get them all out before death arrived to clamp his tongue.

"Alright," he said. "I admit it! I am a descendent of the Naodites, despite my small stature," he confessed without prompting, and on he went for close to an hour before giving up his breath.

"Christ and the Virgin, he talked himself to death," Alexi said when all was ended. He confessed to being a Christian, indeed, but also a Naoditi. Of secretly adhering to the rituals and habits that suited him, which he learned as a boy from his two mothers, the mother who bore him and the other mother who suckled him. Most shockingly, he confessed to fathering Jartzo. Katerina had no idea, he insisted. He took her from behind like a dog in the night and avoided being near her and his son so that neither could identify him from his smell.

"She didn't resist," he said coyly. "But I think this was because she didn't know what was happening to her. I came close to telling her before she left Lathra, but I was a coward. She was an ugly, frightful woman and I couldn't tolerate her confounded spiders." He explained that it was a custom among the Naodites to assure themselves of their virility as old men, as a wellspring of youthful survival.

"It was not a bull or mule who swelled her belly, but me. Forget Ponce de Leon," he added, "The only fountain of youth is procreation. Now she is dead, and I feel blameworthy to my immortal soul. My poor Ioanni," he cried, "my ailing son who never had his *baba* hold him."

Visibly nauseated by the whole story and the images conjured in his presence, Pater Alexi absolved him anyway, with a hasty *trisagion*,[98] just as Ianouli appeared to be embarking, almost feeling his way, into the darkness, but not before scolding him.

"There is no such thing as a Naoditi, you old goat!

"There is, Pater, there is! And I am one," Ianouli said, coming to life for a final utterance.

"Damn your lies, man. Even as Thanatos comes to collect your wrinkled carcass, you play games with God's mercy?"

"Pater!" Lambros beseeched him, surprised at the outburst. Then they fell silent. Alexi forgave the old man and told him so and after a few minutes his eyes jelled. He died like a king without an heir. The very last thing he said was, "Tell Lalas to put some lemon on it."

"Who knows what God will do with him," Alexi said.

---

98 τρισάγιον - a memorial prayer

Once word got out about his confession, the villagers forever referred to Ianouli as the mole, whose word the Naodites revered and heard. And the old rumor persisted, the mystic brutes had ushered Dimitri Baralís to his tragic end, hunting in the wilds, and, as Alexi was occasionally reminded, nearly costing the priest's life in reprisal.

———◆———

Nikos walked to a highpoint along the shore where he could see as far as Perea and observed, at a daunting distance, a speck of a dinghy. He wondered aloud, "Why the hell did the old man go all the way out there today?" Walking to the shore near Pavlides' kafenio he rang the bell at the rear of the building with a large rock until Pavlides appeared, holding his ears, warning him to stop. There was no visible animation to the boat's ant-like occupant. In a rush, he requested the use of Pavlides' lightest boat.

"I'm going to row out to awaken the senile," Nikos said.

"Barba Lambros is not senile, he's an aficionado of the fish," Pavlides said, amused, smoke crackling his voice. "He talks to them and they jump in the boat." Recently Lambros had lingered on the lake until near nightfall. When he finally came home, he described certain lunar inspired phantoms and shimmering moonbeams skimming the surface, slinking into his boat, gnawing their way into any idea he possessed. Elissa told her children that their father was losing his mind.

Nikos rowed through the aqueous tranquility for nearly half an hour before finally reaching the gently undulating boat, with nary a hand or knee or hat bobbing above the stern. As he approached, he expected to hear his father's normal soliloquies to the Almighty or to the fish, but heard nothing. Lambros should have heard the bell and the oars lapping wearily into the cool water, but apparently had not. Nikos shouted as he recovered from rowing and his breathing settled into the rollicking drift of his boat.

"Patera, what are you doing out here?" He expected Lambros to sit up with a start, to see him fiddling with his fishing lines otherwise lying inertly, unused and dry at his feet. He waited for an answer.

"Fishing," a voice grumbled having known the question was coming. He was startled at being caught sleeping. "Damn it, there's a school of mullet at my nets and you've frightened them away," Lambros growled with a simulated, misanthropic air. There were no nets in the water.

"Yes, barba before your time. You've forgotten what today is, haven't you?" Nikos said, relieved. "It's Sunday. We don't fish on Sunday." His father peered at him. "Look who is scolding me," he thought, appearing as if he did not understand, or was not listening. "It's the day of the baptism!" Nikos said. He approached his father's vessel, gently ebbing away from him, letting slip the oars of his imagination. "Christ and the Virgin, is the old man senile already?" he thought. "Are you trying to live like the hermit?" he asked. "Like the monk of Mavrotripa?" He looked across the lake to the east and saw the great empty cavern like a blot upon the sun. "You left my mother to struggle with all the preparations for the day. The baptism of your namesake! Stratos and Anna will kill you if you're late!" The waning sun baked his back and uncovered head. Nikos finally lurched forward in his boat, following his father, the oars pounding a synchronous rhythm toward the far shore, reverberating against rising cliffs, his heartbeat in time with the thrash of water, as if from beneath the surface of Vegoritis. Lambro's straining shoulders and shrouded head sidled away from him and to the right as he rowed onto the current along tiny waves. The aging idol, graying about the edges, seemed like a stranger after but a few months of absence. Then the clap of the second set of oars grew distant, the outcrop of rock between them approaching. In the past, he and Stratos marveled that their father could keep pace with them, as the three rowed home in separate slips, as if he held back the vigor to surpass them whenever he chose. Nikos rowed on without looking back. When he finally reached the shore, he turned and looked out across Vegoritis but could not see his father's boat to the east of the cliffs jutting out and framing Pavlides' cove.

An hour later, on the Sunday of the Samaritan woman, hovering above the holy font, about to be plunged into the living water, the namesake, the infant Lambros Lambrou, Ο μικροσ Λαλασ,[99] cried out, like a spring lamb led to slaughter. At eleven months the fair haired, aqueous eyed connoisseur of his mother's milk, the puerile, fleshy image

---

99 - The little Lalas

of his parents' amalgamation, oiled and lathered with the scent of paradise, the sapid air of independence banded across his greasy, hair-tufted little brow, bestowed upon him like a branding by his father and his father before him. Nikos arrived at the church a bit late, just as the child flailed and protested before his third ritualized flight above the font. He entered from a side door, unchanged, sweaty and smelling of the lake and, until that moment, felt himself to be a fortunate usher to the day's elation. He stood alone and said nothing. He had passed the tsobano in the square on his breathless march to the church and begged him to look into his father's whereabouts.

"The old man was out on the lake sleeping," he complained, ingesting the vitriol of his exasperation. "I reached the shore before him. I have no idea where he is. May a fire consume him! He's probably at home, changing and splashing cologne on his face. If he isn't, can you check and make sure he didn't get himself dragged down by the currents? Sucked into a crevice by eels, swallowed up by a beast of a fish for all I know."

"You remind me of your mother," the tsobano said, as he walked in the direction of the house, newly painted, with stone pointed for the arrival of the grandson. Elissa noted the anxious expression on her son's face when he entered the church. Vegoritis had tarried them both, but Lambros, unwilling to arrive in a disheveled state, preferred to change and dress for his grandson's grace, which he could do without bathing, since he bathed that morning and had not fished or strained himself at all. Elissa stepped to the side and revealed her husband standing between her and a marble column, closely shaven, pants pressed and the sleeves of his crisp white shirt rolled up, the bravado of grand paternity pinning his grin.

"It's too hot for a jacket," he complained to Elissa.

"Then don't wear one, my sorry Christian, as if anyone is going to be looking at you!" Aware of him, Lambros leaned forward and winked at Nikos, sagging and sweating as he was.

"A more beautiful sacrament than this does not exist," Pater Alexi boasted as Anna and Stratos strode forward to accept their white-gowned cherub from the arms of the godmother, Athena Kyriazis, her eyes awash with emotion and glistening in the candlelight. Kyriazis stood nervously by her side, the timid assistant, until the child was dried and dressed and stopped wailing. Then he warmed to the boy's antics.

During the ceremony, Kyriazis had choked back tears and mounting guilt. He could not remember the details of his Tasso's baptism. He and Athena could not bear to go to the ruins of Macarios Timonakis' home, to verify the charred remains of their son and daughter-in-law. Elissa and Yianko's widow had prepared the blackened body for burial. "My beloved son has slipped away from me," he thought, 'and I did not go to see him one last time.' Athena forbade him at the time, provoking one of the few times he possessed the courage to scold her.

"You are a man trapped in a woman's body," he had said with anguish burning his eyes, "with a woman's wiles and jealousies. A man's heart beats within you - a child's mind in your pretty head, but a man's callousness at the center." She was reduced to tears, left the room and never addressed his anger, but Kyriazis obeyed his wife.

Moved by Strato's humility and Anna's insistence that she baptize the child, Athena agonized over what emotion might evoke in her with her ceremonial role. As the day approached, an ephemeral Tasso appeared to her, from the depths of her aged yet unrelenting grief. He stood in the doorway of her bedroom and called out to her.

"*Mana, Mana,* I need you to help me with something," she heard the voice say. "Some water." She arose in the darkness, collected a glass of water and set it out for him on the table in her room. The next morning the glass was empty. Until the unexplainable had occurred, her role as godmother was purely ceremonial and assumed no meaning for its own sake. Now, Alexi hoped to obtain more than one new soul for faith's posterity. Athena had not attended liturgy since her son's death. His best efforts to console her in the name of Christ had until then been a failure. As her self-indulgence and delight in social machinations waned with her youth, the infant Lambro, and the honor bestowed in christening him, worked a veritable conversion in her, where previously no amount of proselytizing or edified inducement could have cleansed the tarnish to her heart, or whet such pure devotion.

Athena held the child for a brief moment longer before handing him back to Anna. Peering deeply into the young mother's eyes, she spoke.

"I give you your newly christened son. "Protect him from the perils of fire and water." The parents bowed their heads and kissed each of Athena's hands.

"Forever worthy," the response arose in unison. Nearly every attendant soul in Lathra exited the church, including Lydia and her well-groomed son, whom she named after her father, Samson Karangelos. Crowded beneath the deepening shade of a bountiful plane tree, the guests lingered kissing and embracing their way across a greeting line of beaming grins. The procession ended before Nikos, conscious of his appearance, leaned toward his brother, a faint siphon of emotion creasing the corners of his mouth.

"Why are you like this? Your clothes dirty," Stratos said. Nikos embraced his brother genially for the first time in his life and kissed his nephew's tiny fists. His gaze contracted a weary oarsman's ken and drifted toward Lambros.

"Half the distance from Perea," he said under his breath. "The old man beat me back here." Stratos arched his eyebrows with his modest grin. They turned together to watch Lambros smiling at something Alexi said. Stratos remembered his father's command at the gates of Parthena. He raised his yawning son to his lips and with a wavering voice, avowed his name.

Το τέλοσ

Epilogue

The notebooks of Lasso Krohn were stored in a container of olivewood, the lid adorned with brass corners and a dexterous intaglio of Christ in the Garden of Gethsemane, which must have been quite difficult to carve upon so obstinate a surface. He had emptied the box and given it to his friend and pupil Gregorios Dranias. Dranias brought it with him on his first visit to Europe and to his relatives in Perea and Edessa. He had also planned on tracking down protractedly distant relations in Hungary. Dranias agreed to accompany me, and my personal secretary, Miss Eleni Kalonis, whom he thought was pretty but an inveterate melancholic. She was familiar with the region, having lived there before moving to America.

We arrived in Budapest together and a day later, as planned, parted ways. Miss Kalonis and I flew on to Thessaloniki, and drove in a rented vehicle to Edessa, just missing the maker of the box. A day later, we drove to Perea. After cursory introductions and a day or so of rest and walking the shores of the lake, we drove on toward Lathra. On the vicinal road winding through a copiously vegetated valley and approaching what should have been her orchards, we encountered a fog of such unwarranted and extravagant thickness as to have first appeared in the mind-coring distance as the seethe of a forest fire. The roads became impassible. The vehicle sputtered from its ingestion of such foul air. We stepped outside into the moist miasma, suspended from just above the knees to the upper limits of a visible splotch of sullied sky. Every feature of the landscape was obscure. A mordacious odor and taste of ancient smelting overcame the senses. A toadstool of noxious malting stung the nostrils and coated the teeth and tongue. On our return to Pereas and our inquiry into so dramatic a climatic phenomenon, we learned from two of the locals that there is no village named Lathra and never was. They said there is no cavern named Mavrotripa. It would have been named Mavritripa anyway, had they been so inclined. And there was no rise of granite with a hole between its legs known as Parthena. The men and women whose names we recited were, according to the locals, the invented figments of a sinister mind, as all literary creation is to the extant plebiscite. In fact, they insisted the names sounded like the *morbifique* of a Frenchman who had come through the region years ago trying to find evidence of a tribe of Arians or proto-Illyrian barbarians (a confusing oxymoron to Pereans).

"The Frenchman and his gang of diggers were looking for cannibals who predated the Greeks by a thousand years," said one of the few men willing to speak with us at any length. This was Barba Photios Draconias, a sequestered, black-garbed monster of a man with a crustaceous smile, a bulbous nose and blood stained cheeks, sitting on the stoop of his house fondling his tassels and eying up passersby. He alluded to the name Lathra and proclaimed, in raucous barks as we attempted to photograph him, swinging his bastouni at us, that "the witch Vegoritis is not finished damning the recesses of her secrets."

A day later, we returned to the valley and encountered the same atmospheric conditions, only worse. The dense and murky air seemed to grow hair, irritating the throat and the lack of visibility now extended to below the ankles. We drove north to Arnissa and made similar inquiries as we had in Perea, receiving essentially the same response, but mostly unqualified yawns. We learned incidentally that Gregorios Dranias had just left the day before for Thessaloniki, having spent a day in Perea before our arrival there, and had plans to travel on to Izmir. This was puzzling since we had just left him in Hungary. Staying for the night in lovely accommodations known as the Apartments Gaby, the following morning we made one last attempt to reach Lathra. This time no mist or foul olfaction greeted us. Instead, the verdant dilation of our eyes glimpsed an earthly Eden spreading out before us - distant fields of gold granule and the orderly flora of edibles, orchards dripping with fruit - and not a single soul in the occupancy or employ of such a splendid garden. The singular road up led us to a very small plateau, but no cemetery greeted us. It was however, contiguous to a somewhat less than majestic bastion of rock that could have been Kythera. At its center was an absence, a defrayal of livelihood for but a few members of a single clique, endopee to be sure, with three small ramshackle buildings set in a cockeyed semicircle. The shacks faced nothing resembling the village square upon whose imagination this story relies. Each dwelling seemed abandoned or at least evidencing an annulment of all but the most basic signs of life - a few dry and dirty cups, a well-used table in each abode, vessels for water and grain and a pile of yellowing linens, folded neatly and set on the dingy floor of the hospice, for vagrant spirits to use. The veneer of the past had blunted into a vacuous absence, consumed by dust and the geometry of cobwebs. There was on the wall, however, a single faded photograph of a man, draping his jacket over his shoulder.

Our search for Mavrotripa and other signs of our Lathran narration proved fruitless. The water of Vegoritis presented itself with an unearthly and cerulean color near the shore and then as a sudden sapphire pool in its great depths, and indeed tasted mildly of fish. Upon our return to Thessaloniki, we were to meet up with Gregorios Dranias at the Restaurant Lendos, as previously arranged, but he never arrived, his revised plans later attested to when we met up again in America, briefly, at the home of Lasso Krohn.

Gregorios Dranias told me that he encountered a man while traveling through Turkey, a man somewhat senior to him who went by the name of Kemal Akhisar and claimed to be from Izmir. After drinking with Dranias, Akhisar revealed his alias as one Giorgios Karpathiotis, youngest son of Thanasi Karpathiotis. He spoke Greek effortlessly and explained that he lived in Macedonia for a while, until his father was murdered. Thereafter, he lived in Izmir with an older brother, under the care of a distant cousin of his father, whose surname was Akhisar, which he and his brother assumed. For reasons unidentified in the notes, the man spoke openly of his having lost two mothers, both torn from him when he was a boy. He also lamented never seeing his sisters again. For what this revelation adds to the jigsaw of lives espied by careful readers, I leave to them to discover and decree.

F. Voutsakis